Soottown

William Good   **Adam Kowal**

PUBLISHED BY APOPHENIA PRESS

Denver, Colorado

Printed in the United States of America

First Edition

"Praise" for Soottown and other works by
William Good & Adam Kowal

"Soottown had me hypnotized. Written with a blazing sense of humor and filled with complex characters that inhabit a city I truly love. I've never felt this way about a novel."
  -Jeffrey McHale, Producer/Director of You Don't Nomi

"Your a horrible human being … a no talent d bag … lack any sort of vision or true creativity complicity"
  -Daily Show Production Intern

"In short, I love it. I really dig the way … they've found various means to connect each of the stories ever so slightly whether it's the location or a character showing up in other character's stories."
  -Cody Stasiak, Freelance journalist, former contributor to GEEKmagazine and GrizzlyBomb

"You wrote a book? That's cool, but if I want to read something I'll just watch a foreign film."
  -Somebody That I Used to Know

"Potentially what the Godfather would have been if it was turned completely on its head with psychotic themes and lunacy-beyond-belief characters."
  -Anonymous Reader

"(No reply)"
  -Juan Gerardo Guadio Marquez, 10th President of the National Assembly of Venezuela (contested), former member of the socio-democratic Popular Will party, and federal deputy to the National Assembly representing the state of Vargas

"Who is your audience? Who would this appeal to? What is this point of this? … Dude, I'm about as atheist and anti-PC as possible, and even I found a lot of this highly offensive."
  -Deleted Reddit Account

Life isn't divided into genres.
It's a horrifying, romantic, tragic, comical,
science-fiction cowboy detective novel.
You know, with a bit of pornography
thrown in if you're lucky.

Alan Moore

Author's Note

While many of the names and places mentioned in these pages are real, the Detroit in this book is largely fictional:

The half-way house where police and criminals hang out together after hours, exists. Though, *The Bitter Nail* is not its name.

The statue of Robocop does exist. Good luck finding it. So does the Whale Mural, but that one is hard to miss.

The People Mover downtown pales in comparison to the grandiose Loop. However, the impetus for the latter did not entirely originate from our minds. Additionally, finding the names of the stations on a map of the city will give a pretty clear picture of the path as we imagined it.

The origin of the Nain Rouge stays close to the myth, though from there we take some liberties.

The socioeconomic descriptions of the various suburbs, both visited and mentioned, in the book are probably more accurate now than when they were originally written.

The various local artists, poets, and writers named in this book are all real, and will likely be very surprised to find themselves mentioned.

The last three minutes of *Spitting Venom* contributed greatly to discovering the end of this book.

And finally, a debt of gratitude is owed to Tom Waits, whose song *Rain Dogs* was not only lodged in a characters' head, but ours as well.

Book I

Compassion Fatigue

1
Roger

The sky was the hue of a tropical drink. A swirl of blue and pink, a twist of orange and purple.

By this age, Roger imagined he'd be on a beach somewhere sipping *that* drink, rather than four lanes deep in smog and gridlock. This had all been heart and farmland in his youth, and now even though the city wasn't quite scraping the sky yet, six, seven, eight stories at a time, it was changing his horizon. What remained of the atmosphere flitted through the glass and cranes and scaffolding. Every day, as he drove to and from work, his home became more unrecognizable.

Hanging above the Woodward Corridor and turning an hour commute into a ten minute one, The Ford/Masood Inter-Urban Loop was supposed to be the end-all solution to public transportation in the Metro area, and maybe it was for the younger generations. But for Roger, the muscley steel and glass tube was just one more scar on Detroit's vista. Besides, he preferred to drive.

Prehistorically wide and built with steel in an age when Americans didn't just talk tough, his Cadillac wasn't classic, wasn't vintage, wasn't pink, but was the only thing he recognized any longer. This city, this car, they'd both been torn down and rebuilt so many times neither was the same anymore. But while the city now belonged to others, piece by piece, the spinning odometer measuring too much time, this Cadillac of Theseus was his.

Three hundred thousand miles since his second son was born. One hundred twenty thousand since his oldest boy had gone off to Colorado. Sixty thousand since retirement. Vacations, careers, and family spun that odometer. Miles used to fly by. Anymore, time about stood still.

Fifty thousand miles since his pension ran out. Twenty thousand since his wife passed. Five thousand since he rejoined the workforce. Five hundred since the gas pedal began to rattle. Fifty miles since acknowledging this was one more thing in his life he couldn't afford to fix.

He only lived a few miles from work, and it took a month to live a day from twenty years ago. Some days, he'd roll down the windows and drive for a bit, feel the wind and the atmosphere shift, and just get a few more miles in. Some days, he'd get lost and look to the now unfamiliar horizon with worry and concern. Some days, he'd go to a park to feed the birds, stop at the Three M to refill his meds, and maybe even grab an ice cream cone and sit on top of a table as if he were waiting for someone to arrive. But most mornings Roger would drive to work, the hazy red omen of dawn fading to the friendlier righteous blue of the day without notice, the odometer ticking away another unremarkable mile.

He worked at Kingsland, an aging regional grocery chain with frontage designed to resemble a medieval castle. Today, the facade was worn and faded. Sun-bleached Old English lettering splayed across a chipped faux-stone battlement, fiberglass towers crumbled, and a drawbridge painted on the cement approach was a dim whisper from years of foot traffic.

Cars and trucks already filled the parking lot when Roger arrived, but that did not matter to him. He bypassed the parking lot and found a spot on the street a few blocks down. It was all about the miles, and at his age, even this bit of exercise helped keep him spry.

After depositing four hours' worth of quarters into the slot, Roger gathered his effects and set off down the street.

Before the city moved in, the streets had been paved in cobblestone. Along this stretch had sat his and a half-dozen other family's homes before the city built up and replaced them to give their budding community a downtown stretch. Out back, where a subdivision now sat, fields and farms had stretched for miles. Back then, in the spring, tornados ripped through the land without causing damage to anything that mattered. During the summer he had spent golden hours lying in the sunlight and the haystacks under crisp skies. One fall, their milkman switched to driving a horse-drawn cart on his route to all the children's delight. The horse's name was Red, and soon, Roger and the other children would learn to recognize that *clomp-clomp* of his hooves scraping against the cobblestone and would race into their root cellars and grab carrots and apples, and as the driver exchanged the empty milk bottles for full ones, the children would gather around Red. They would shove snacks toward his muzzle, vying for his attention and bite, hoping to be the first to come away empty-handed. On one occasion a poor girl from the smallest house on the street had nothing to offer Red but a stalk of celery, but as Red perused his offerings that day, he went for the celery first. The other children accused her of painting the stalk with peanut butter, but that wasn't true; Red loved celery. None of them knew this, except Roger. He couldn't explain why or how he knew—but, as crazy as it sounds, it was almost like he could hear Red talking. He sighed; his mother never bought celery, so he was always stuck offering carrots.

That fall was the best time of his life and Roger always intended to find a way to replicate it, to lead a simple and idyllic existence, free of worry and strife. And maybe with horses. But life and time had other plans. In his lonesome old age he found peace and comfort in that dream, and even though the cobblestones and fields had long been paved over, the memories of Red and that fall somehow never faded no matter how much else did.

When the automatic doors parted, Roger kept his chin down. Halloween decorations adorned the glass. Cats and bats and spider webs. He'd assisted the younger team members in hanging decorations last week, and normally he enjoyed admiring his handiwork. Today he avoided looking at all costs. His manager skulked about in the produce section arranging displays of monochromatic bags filled with the newest healthy snack trend, and he had no interest in speaking with that odious woman this morning. Forty years his junior, her only pleasant feature would have been her smile if it weren't so obvious that one only ever formed at the misfortune of others. She had already condemned him to suit up as a greeter; the last thing he needed was her reminding him not to punch in early. Or worse, trying to sell him on investing in her Neobiotic supplements scheme.

"Hun," she'd say. "Once you try them, they will change your world. We can never have too much crystal in our diet, am I right?"

He made it to the break room without a confrontation, put his lunch away, and unfurled his newspaper to kill the time.

His fingers smudged the newsprint and turned black. Section numbers and headlines stuck to his thumb and forefinger. He flipped through the pages. Politics and murder stuck to his eyes, depression and anger to his brain. With enough spit and time, he could smudge the news to his liking, change the world to the one he'd like to live in. Those words, printed in black-and-white, reflected the full color spectrum of the world, and changing them required nuance. Instead, he skipped the tragedies and economics, and set the sports section aside. He lingered for a moment on the fluff piece about a phantom house that appeared in random places around the metro area once a month, then vanished before any sense could be made of it, but that wasn't the type of escape he was looking for. No, instead he turned to the funnies. The comics. To those black-and-white stories told in full color, three panels or six. Calvin and Hobbes, Doonesbury, Beetle Bailey, Prince Valiant. Stories of simple contrasts that exemplified the wit, irony, courage, and compassion lacking in the real world. Before he'd gotten through the comics, it was time to punch in.

He knocked open the numberless locker at the far end of the bank and the door swung out. Inside hung a menagerie of ill kept pieces that together formed the much-maligned visage of the company mascot: a dashing medieval knight. A tin helmet, punched, shoved, and punted back into the locker, now mangled and impossible to wear. A pilled burlap brigandine. Aluminum breastplate with foil faulds. Gauntlets and cuisse spray-painted to mask the abuse.

Dressing felt absurd—a grown man donning a glorified children's Halloween costume—and he emerged from the break room mortified.

His walk to the front of the store should have been mirthless as he was further humiliated by a fanfare of japes, double-takes, and humorless laughs. Yet, instead of blushing and tucking his tail, he returned each ridicule with pithy riposte.

Roger met the chortles and snorts that came from aisle fourteen with a shake of the head as he judged them for knocking cans from the shelf. Striding past aisle nine, he wagged his finger at a tween who kicked a frozen drink cup under a broken rack.

There was something ineffable about the moment. The costume was silly, but the faux suit of armor gave his ancient gaze a scrutinizing quality.

Being a greeter had never been his retirement plan. It had been life, rather than poor financial planning, that had caused him to go into his seventies still in debt, and debt did not discriminate. He needed to make money, this was the only place that would hire him, so he might as well enjoy it.

Wind blew through Roger's tufts of wispy hair, any lingering embarrassment dissipating in the breeze. He waved at passing cars and greeted shoppers in a rudimentary attempt at verbiage that he imagined matched his outfit. This extra effort wasn't required. But once he'd begun the performance, he remembered that he enjoyed it and continued the routine.

A young mother approached from the parking lot, a toddler in her arms. "Good day, M'lady."

It was children who were most receptive to his charm, staring in wide-eyed awe at a real-life knight. He'd bow low to greet the shy toddlers behind their parents' legs. "I charge you with protecting your weary parents, are you up to the task?"

But for every shrill of delight from a child, most adults ignored his cheer, gave him a polite nod, and continued. Others didn't want to be bothered with even a simple, "Hello, there." Mostly he respected these intuited desires, saying nothing as they passed. But some people had an air of entitlement that he couldn't ignore. They would chat on their cell phones loudly, or carry terrified dogs around in their purses, or worst of all, scream at children for acting like, *God forbid*, children.

With these people Roger turned up the anachronism as much as possible.

"Good morning, my fine fellow," said Roger as one such man approached. This *Chad* wore track pants, a tank-top, and chic sunglasses. His beach body was a stark contrast to Roger's aged one. The man was taut both inside and out: skin pulled tight around muscle and bone, sunglasses hiding his thoughts as much as his eyes from observation and inspection. Roger, on the other hand, was loose: skin twisted and rung out like a washcloth, mind now dripping with intrepid frivolities of antiquity.

Chad entered the store without removing his tinted shades. This alone was enough to warrant Roger's indignation, but while some men he did not like, others he did not trust. Roger eyed the man through the store until the display of melons obscured him from sight, at which point he had no choice but to go back to greeting the incoming customers.

A short time later, while Roger was making faces at a giggly baby exiting the store, he peered beyond the mother's arm. His eyes narrowed as he caught sight of Chad again standing over a display of apples. He picked them up one at a time, pretending to inspect each shade and mix of ruby and emerald, but Roger saw his true intentions. His hands were on the fruit, but his eyes were on a nearby shopping cart where a purse had been left unattended.

Before Roger's eyes, Chad transitioned from suspect to criminal as he snatched the purse and bolted for the door.

"Stop!" yelled Roger. His voice was meek, but the echo of the cavernous store amplified it. Still, the thief did not yield. The two men made eye contact for a split second before the thief shot through the doors and navigated the congestion of pedestrians with an incredible pace.

And for a moment, Roger thought he was going to allow the man to escape as store policy dictated.

Then his foot turned, followed by his leg, and then his body.

Roger stepped off the curb and his world spun and shifted. His body fought him. His cracked feet, aching joints, and atrophied muscles sung against him. The steady acceleration burned, twisted, and cramped at Roger's insides. His armor clamored and clanked with every stride. It rode up in the most uncomfortable ways, fell loose in the least convenient places. He was no match for the thief's endurance. Nevertheless, he pressed on.

At the edge of the parking lot, the thief shoved through a line of decorative shrubbery and vanished. Roger, ten steps behind him, eleven, twelve steps and still falling farther behind, followed suit without pause. Sharp branches jabbed into his thin skin, leaving his hands, face, and neck—whatever the armor didn't cover—dotted with blood.

Beyond the leafy barrier, the adjacent street was awash in noise and activity. Cyclists spun up and down the street. Sidewalk cafes were overrun by the chortles of the after-church crowd drinking mimosas under umbrellas. Vehicles circled, searching for unoccupied parking along the curb. And, at the end of the block, a police officer was perched high above the crowd on the back of an Irish Draught whose coat caressed her frame and shimmered like silken chocolate.

Roger emerged into the ripple of commotion in time to see Chad on the ground before him, entangled with a cyclist.

"Thanks," Chad started, disoriented, as Roger gave him a hand up. Then, realizing who the hand belonged to, finished with "But, fuck off!"

He tried to shove Roger back but found the old man's grip to be heartier than it appeared.

The cyclist was moaning and swearing, but neither paid him any mind.

"Return the purse!" Roger said.

"I said," the thief brandished a knife from his belt, "fuck," he swiped at Roger, "off!"

Roger released his grip and leaped backwards. Chad took off again, but Roger grinned; he'd dodged a knife.

It was a small stunt—more instinct than feat—but enough to propel him into another pursuit.

The wake of annoyance behind the thief spread as he pushed and shoved his way through the crowd. Knife in hand, he glanced back again and again to see if he'd escaped the knight.

He hadn't.

Roger was there attempting to match him step for step. Their eyes met again, for only a moment. A distraction long enough to foil the thief's getaway yet again. In his mind, Roger asked, begged, prayed the Irish Draught step into the thief's path. And then he wished he hadn't.

Chad turned, and, moving too fast to stop, slammed into the flank of the Police Horse. The horse shuddered and cried out. It reeled up on its hind legs, bucking the officer from his saddle, knocking the thief to the ground.

The crowd gasped and scattered, and through a gap Roger could see the thief's knife protruding from her flank. No blood leaked from beneath the hilt, but still the animal whinnied and cantered. Horses were notoriously good at hiding pain, and even such a small reaction told Roger everything he needed to know.

On the pavement, the officer lay wheezing, the wind knocked from his lungs. Cell phones surrounded him: calling for help, snapping photos, rolling video. The thief had escaped down the street already, trying door handles on the parked cars, looking for one that was unlocked.

Roger placed his hands on the steed. Her tail twitched and her coat rippled. "It's okay, it's okay." He caressed her and leaned in, resting his face against her mane. He could smell the sunlight on her skin. "I need your help." He took her by the noseband, looked into her dark eyes, and met his own reflection. Not the frail, chivalrous caricature he was now. But a reflection from another time, another place, where he rode atop this majestic beast righting wrongs.

An ethereal voice echoed in Roger's mind, begging him to climb onto the waiting steed. The horse didn't protest when he planted his foot in the stirrup, but relaxed. He hoisted himself into the saddle, placed one quivering hand on the horn and twisted the other around her rein. The pair trembled, each exhilarated by the other's touch, by this instant bond between them.

"Would you like me to remove the knife?" The horse shook its head. "Alright. I understand."

When others would have spurred her side to jar her forward, Roger whispered into her ear, "Time to move now, yes? After the man." Without delay, the animal thundered away from the crowded sidewalk and carried Roger into oncoming traffic.

The crowd gasped at the sight, but the blasts of car horns swallowed the sound. Carried by kinetic stupidity, the pair dodged around minivans, swerved to avoid a fleet of motorcycles, and came to full speed along the yellow line down the center of the road. Drivers slammed on their breaks and Roger tucked his knees to avoid the smashing into side-view mirrors with either foot.

The thief was easy to spot from this vantage point.

Three blocks down the thief had found an easy target: an old car whose owner had left the window down. A Cadillac that no longer needed a key to turn over. The Cadillac's ancient engine ground to a start and bent away from the metered spot. Pushed in a way it hadn't been in years, the car sputtered and squealed like a tortured animal.

Roger prodded the steed to go faster. Eddy currents of entropy swirled around him as he drifted into the barreling path of the vehicle. It was only then that Roger's determination wavered. It wasn't the expectation of impact that fazed him, but the solemn acknowledgement that the vehicle screaming toward him carried with it the three hundred thousand miles of his past.

On a collision course with the remains of his life, he closed his eyes, ready for the impact to slam three hundred thousand miles of memories into him again, forever unfolding in an instant.

Two hundred and ninety thousand miles since his wife rode shotgun on their first date. Nervously belting his boy into the backseat the day after he was born. Disney World and Mammoth Caves.

Pictured Rocks and the Twin Towers. Flat tires and fender benders, vacations and road trips. Hundreds of thousands of miles and miles and miles and miles.

In the dark calm of his mind, the horse spoke to him. Maybe he was ready for a final rest, but she was not. Roger yanked the reins; he wouldn't condemn her to that fate. At least not without a fight.

Rather than slowing and letting the stolen Cadillac speed off, Roger strafed alongside a restaurant's patio, and yanked an unopened umbrella from the center of a table.

The glass shattered; the thin metal of the table twisted in on itself. Roger returned to face his Cadillac in dubious battle, the umbrella maneuvered into a feeble jousting position under his arm.

The yellow line was a fuse burning from both ends. The quarter mile between the Cadillac and Roger disappeared, like his life had, in the blink of an eye and before he was ready.

"I'm sorry, girl," he said, to both his Cadillac and the horse beneath him.

He braced the umbrella for impact, brushing away the bittersweet nostalgia barreling toward him. Spilled milk and lost toys. Wet bathing suits from the lake. Shed hair from long-dead pets, melty ice cream fingerprints from days gone by.

The umbrella fell from his arthritic hands.

His body failed him, and along with it his resolve to desecrate this sacred vessel.

The tip of the umbrella descended toward the yellow line. The horse, out of Roger's control, swerved away as the metal cap sparked against the concrete and rebounded. Roger winced as the Cadillac veered to avoid the errant projectile, but couldn't.

The tip of the umbrella met the windshield, shattering the safety glass. The wooden ribs spread wide, covering the windshield with fabric as the shaft finally smashed through. Gasps from the crowd were buried beneath the howl of the Cadillac's disintegrating brake pads.

When the Cadillac came to a halt, the pair cantered alongside the slain beast. The Knight reached over and ripped the umbrella from the vehicle.

Weapon in hand, the Knight looked to the street at the adoring crowd who had witnessed his exploits.

"Do not fear, the bandit has been subdued! Come, I shall shake your hands." The Knight leaped from the horse with outstretched hands. But as he approached, the gawkers backed away. "It's okay, bring your children forward! Come, little one. Come to me!"

He prepared himself for the onslaught of exaltation and applause but was instead met with silence. The crowd hung back, keeping their distance, but held their phones high to get the best shot, the best angle.

"Roger!" said a voice that rung familiar somewhere in the recess of his mind. "What—" The manager slithered through the crowd, a horrified expression on her face. "You can't chase shoplifters!"

"I stopped the thief!" The Knight shook his head at the delusional woman before him. He had done what was necessary. He had answered the call. "People! I only did what was necessary to keep a criminal from absconding with ill-gotten goods! Without my actions this man would have—" He motioned back to the wreckage, only to find the driver seat empty, the thief gone.

All around him he heard snickers, saw ear-to-ear smiles behind raised phones. But they weren't experiencing the joy and excitement of seeing justice served. Their joy was at his expense.

This revelation, it would have been devastating had it been given the opportunity to sink in. But before it could, sirens shrieked in the distance. Not seen, only heard echoing through the streets, drifting closer and closer.

The Knight had heard tales of the Sirens. Mythical creatures who lured their victims in with song, only to devour them. And today their song carried on the breeze and begged him to stay put.

For a moment, he considered it.

But when the sirens appeared, their beautiful song dissolved into an erratic droning noise meant to disorient. Their red and blue eyes flickered, reflecting the nuance of the world.

He wasn't ready for nuance, or a world where a quarter mile vanished without a thought.

Besides, the thief had escaped. He'd failed at his task.

The Knight reached down and grabbed hold of the knife's hilt, still sticking out of the horse's side. "Don't worry, we'll patch this up. He yanked the blade free and threw it to the ground. The horse didn't even react.

Without hesitation, he whispered into her ear again and set her to flight. Together they dashed through the crowd, once again veering onto that endless yellow line stretching to the horizon.

The Sirens, these creatures of nuance and order, shadowed him, screeching and calling. But the Knight did not give into their song, nor did he slow.

Yesterday a quarter mile would have only gotten him out of his neighborhood. Today, he intended to live as many lifetimes as he could, one quarter mile at a time.

He called himself a religious man, but not a faithful one. The church his family attended was less of a place to develop a personal relationship with Jesus than it was the epicenter of his community, with services there being about more than *just* God; and messages that weren't limited to those delivered on the wings of angels. It was a place for friends and family and neighbors, where the messages came from the everyman who needed help raking leaves, paying a water bill, or getting a ride to a doctor's appointment.

As Richard aged, he continued to attend the same service at the same church; he did this not out of faith, but habit. There were only three things that made a man his age find God: a bullet, love, or prison. He'd been shot in the line of duty, and that hadn't garnered a visit from the Holy Spirit. He had love, but it was a love that all but guaranteed Jesus would remain a stranger to him. And as an officer who held himself to a high standard, the only way he was likely to wind up in prison was to pull a shift at Tri-County Jail. But he'd have to really mess up to land there.

Anymore, the closest Richard had come to finding God was in the pages of a good book. Not *The* good book. It didn't even really have to be a *well-written* book. Any book that lifted him from this world and dropped him into the paradise of another; that was it for him. Because what was heaven, but the idealized escape from this reality.

Now, home from Sunday service, book in hand, he was looking to exchange the word of God for a more secular escape. An escape that would not come. The words on the page were too academic and stiff to sedate and entangle him with their serif-y hooks.

Jesuit Warrior: The Tales of Yasuke.

The cover had a stylized painting depicting a black-skinned God/Demon wielding a sword in each hand, cutting down an innumerable army of Samurai warriors. Richard had expected it to be a perfect front porch novel to dive into, a place to escape the doppler drone of emergency response vehicles circling his neighborhood. But, at fifty pages it wasn't a rollicking account of violence and action, but the study of a man at odds with his surroundings. It was David Copperfield in its aspirations, rather than Octavia Butler. There was no wit, no daring, and with its dry and trite first lines:

> *Dark as midnight, Yasuke, the first black samurai, towered over the Japanese locals and Italian Jesuits alike. Hardly the first retainer from Africa to serve as slave/warrior in Asia the agency and ambitions of those with fairer skin, but the first who the Daimyo forced to strip and wash to prove that the man's skin had not been dyed with ink to instill fear.*

Not to mention the long-winded, overwrought, and worst of all obvious observations on the historical impact of slavery, the book was a wasted opportunity. With its source material, and that cover at its disposal, a little creativity is all it would have taken to elevate the book to something far more entertaining without even having to lose its message or intent.

The book wasn't shy to point out that not much had changed in the years since the racial atrocities of feudal Japan or those on the plantations of early America, since MLK Jr. and the South African apartheid. How those with pale skin still cheered on dark warriors, only now the glorifying took place in stadiums and arenas—civil society's battlefields—rather than on the fields of war. And while the darkest were no longer made to strip and scrub down to distill any suspicion of intimidation, outside the confines of ESPN, March Madness, and Monday Night Football, an air of fear still clung to dark skin as if were a pigment itself.

He'd wanted an escape, and what the book was giving him was a mirror. Reading page after page, Richard couldn't help but see himself reflected in the samurai. He hadn't been the first black cop on the force when he joined, but he knew all too well what Yasuke had faced. Both had been dark curiosities in a pale world. They existed in a space that removed their ability to hide or blend in, size and pigment impeding any attempt to be who they were in their hearts. He couldn't speak for Yasuke, but Richard had always been a wallflower. A chair on a porch was all he needed to sit back and enjoy watching the world turn.

Instead of gluing his eyes to the page, Yasuke had only forced them to retreat, lulling Richard into an unplanned nap. After an hour of starts and stops, rereading pages and forgetting them again, he abandoned the book and headed inside to make a fresh pot of coffee.

The latest round of police sirens rose, then faded while the auto-drip did its thing. It was Devil's Night and Richard expected to hear sirens, but he'd hoped for a few hours' reprieve before the action began. Once he reported for duty, once it got dark, he wasn't likely to escape their vigilant droning, at least not if he did his duty to keep the night from succumbing to its own epithet.

As whooping and wailing faded, Richard waited for voices to emerge, the sound of the birds.

When he'd moved into this house, the garden was six over-grown scrubs and an ever-encroaching swarm of dandelions. Over three years, Richard had defeated the plague of golden-topped weeds, wrangled the shrubberies into shape, planted rows of flowers to attract pollinators and wildlife, and installed not one but three stone pedestal bird baths in front of the freshly painted railings of his porch. He'd always read that if you were the smartest person in the room, you were in the wrong room. He'd never heard the same said about having the nicest garden on the block. If truth be told, Richard enjoyed the daily compliments, and would gladly admit to living on the wrong block so long as he continued to receive them.

Riding his horse into a new village, Yasuke would receive similar attention. Throngs of children wishing to witness this peculiar addition to their world would surround him, and, if they were lucky, maybe even shyly run their fingertips over the man's black skin.

Through the open kitchen window Richard heard a lull in nature's banter. He waited for the cardinals, jays, and sparrows to resume their calls to one another, but the yard remained silent. The only thing he heard was the unmistakable clop of a horse casually moving down the sidewalk. *Clomp-clomp.* Richard sighed. As much as he'd otherwise hoped, Yasuke had wormed his way into his subconscious. Now, against his own desire, he'd have to finish the book to see what would become of the black samurai.

Clomp-clomp, Clomp-clomp, Clomp-clomp. Wait. The sound wasn't only in his mind, but in his ears too.

Clomp-clomp. Hooves coming up his driveway.

Clomp-clomp. Moving across the brick path around the garden.

Clomp-clomp. Splashing in his bird bath.

Not the playful frolic of tiny avian wings and beaks, but the sloppy mammalian splash of a thick-tongued beast lapping the basin dry.

It was a very specific scene to have appeared in his mind,

considering it was one he'd never witnessed, at least not in real life. He'd never paid any mind to horses drinking, but sound had a way of influencing perception and expectations. As powerful as the human mind is, it can be equally as fallible when there is a void present.

Richard had seen this firsthand during a mandatory sensitivity training session. The session mentor had set up an exercise to demonstrate our capability of manufacturing biases, even physical ones, when presented with incomplete sensory data. He had set up a vertical mirror and asked for a volunteer to sit perpendicular to it and place their right hand in front of the mirror in such a way that the reflection appeared to be their left hand. When Officer Gracie volunteered the class suppressed a collective laugh and scooched their chairs back. Once seated and situated properly, the mentor produced a hammer and slammed the head down where Gracie's left hand wasn't. Gracie screamed in pain, even though there had been no contact. Then Gracie smashed the mentor's face with his non-phantom fist and got them all assigned to an advanced session of sensitivity training.

The new mentor utilized the same experiment in that subsequent training on Richard, only he didn't flinch. He didn't have that good of an imagination. *Clomp-clomp, Clomp-clomp, Clomp-clomp.* That's how he knew the sound was real, even before he got a clear look through the window.

Halloween was still a day away, so when he saw the man dressed in full medieval plate armor sitting atop a horse, he picked up his phone and slid quietly out the backdoor to investigate.

Richard had assumed the armor was authentic, but as he neared the rider he realized it was all tinfoil and spray paint, and immediately placed it. It was the armor greeters at Kingsland grocery stores wore. The horse bore the crest of the Ferndale Police Department's Mounted Division. Had the old man really ridden this horse twelve miles across the city? The Knight's eyes told the tale. Richard could see from the Knight's gaze that twelve miles was just a blip in the foreground of his thousand-mile stare. The Knight was before him, but he wasn't present. Instead, he stared off into whatever imaginary reality he'd substituted in place of this one.

"Hello, there," said Richard, having snuck up on the pair. The horse whinnied and shied in surprise, but the Knight calmed him.

"Halt," said the Knight. "Explain yourself!"

"Okay. You see these bird baths he's drinking out of? They belong to me. The garden, those flowers he's stomping? Also mine. I don't own the birds that come by, but I was sure looking forward to hearing from them today."

"My good man, I apologize for the rudeness of my steed. We have only just met and so I cannot be held responsible for his manners or upbringing. I can only hope you understand that a flight from justice in the pursuit of a thief is thirsty work."

Clearly the man had suffered a break. Only the delusional, or those with nothing to lose, were ever so honest.

"I understand. And let me apologize as well. I didn't mean to startle you." He eyed the horse. "Either of you." Richard had a lifetime of practice with putting people at ease. He'd built his career, to the disdain of his superiors, on maintaining an open and kind disposition. The state of his garden had thrown him and gotten their dialogue off on a more hostile note than he'd intended. He took a breath. "Your horse is taking care of himself. How about you? You need a drink?"

Had this Knight shown up on the doorstep of any other officer, riding a horse belonging to a Police Department and touting a flight from the authorities, it was doubtful that he'd still be in one piece, and certainly not in his saddle.

"Most kind of you, most kind, indeed," the Knight said, dismounting. Graceful at first, he threw one old leg across the horse, but then his body seemed to remember its age and he toppled backward, landing between two ferns.

"Are you alright?" Richard stepped into the garden and leaned close, surprised that only the scent of his flowers greeted him and not the smell alcohol coming from the old man's pores. He'd been sure that the old man was sauced, now he didn't know what to think.

"Yes, yes," said the Knight. "At my age, falls happen. You'll understand soon enough."

"I think you've got a couple decades on me, old timer," said Richard, helping the Knight to his feet.

"We always think we have time, don't we?"

Richard checked his watch. One of them had more time than the other. He helped the Knight brush the dirt and leaves from his armor, and while he was at it, patted him down for weapons. Not that he'd expected to find any.

"You seem alright," said Richard, giving the Knight a pat on the back. He caught sight of the blood leaking from the horse. "Her, not so much."

"Truly, my friend, I am better than I have ever been. But, alas, my steed was assaulted."

"By the police?"

"No! By the thief whom I was in the midst of giving chase."

Richard studied the horse's flank. The wound wasn't from a bullet. Maybe there was some truth to the Knight's story. Maybe he could even get it out of him.

"How about that water?"

The Knight nodded, and together the pair walked up the driveway.

The horse whinnied as the Knight left her side. He motioned for her to remain calm, but she refused, and he gave in to her demands. "Alright, alright. I won't."

Richard held open the backdoor, but the Knight ignored Richard's kindness and went for the garden hose. He uncoiled the first loop from its hanger and turned the knobby handle until water arced through the air. Parched, the old man drank straight from the hose as if he were a rambunctious six-year-old.

"I would have gotten you a glass."

"I know," the Knight waved dismissively between swigs. "She told me not to go into the house. Not sure why, but she hasn't steered me wrong yet, so I listen to her."

"You sure about that?" Richard wondered what else the horse had told the old man to do, but the sirens in the distance were growing louder, closing in, and he decided not to ask anything that might spook the pair.

The Knight perked up. He'd heard the sirens too. "And with that, it is time I depart. Thank you, kind stranger, for your hospitality, and apologize to the birds for me. We did not intend to steal their bath."

"You know Halloween is tomorrow night, right?"

"Is it? To be honest, I haven't kept a calendar in years. No need, you know?"

"What's with the costume?"

"Costume?" the Knight asked. He looked down at himself, realizing that he and Richard were dressed quite differently. "Oh, this? Occupational hazard, I suppose."

"Dragons and windmills?"

"No, nothing quite so predictable. Today, thieves. Tomorrow, who knows? That's what makes the adventure worthwhile: the unknown."

"Listen," said Richard, as he caught the flickering glint of red and blue off the front window of a house down the street, "You're not wrong. I'm getting up there in years. It means a lot to see someone your age—" He didn't know how to say it. "To see someone your age so full of life. What I mean is, you've got your health. Do you have family, people who care about you? You got to, right? From what I've seen, it's when you don't got people who care about you, that's when bodies and minds start to slide. You got someone, right?"

The Knight paused next to the horse. "I have what I have. And right now what I have is a calling which I must answer." The Knight grabbed the saddle horn and raised a foot into a stirrup. His body was shaking. Richard was surprised the old man recovered so quickly from the fall from the horse; now it appeared he had not.

"You don't have to go. We can talk some more. You know, take a moment to cool down and reflect. Maybe you don't think you need that, but from what I'm seeing, it could do you some good."

"I'm trapped somewhere between Aeaea and the rocks of Scylla. Can't you hear the Sirens? I fear if I stay any longer their call will tempt me."

"Maybe you've already been tempted? Didn't Homer say the Sirens caused the sailors to go mad?"

"No. They sang beautiful songs to the crew and ate them. Madness had nothing to do with it," said the Knight, his face and armor erupting blue and red. "The sweet song of safety has already consumed too much of my life."

Richard's words had been beautiful enough to stall the Knight, to tempt him. The cruisers came from every direction, and now Richard recoiled watching the panic and betrayal fill the Knight's eyes.

The horse whinnied. It was protecting him as the police closed in from all sides. Could horses suffer from Stockholm syndrome? It circled the Knight, acting as a barrier as cruiser doors burst open and flat feet hit pavement. Tasers drawn and batons out, the officers raced forward, shouting for the Knight to get down on the ground.

One officer dove for the Knight, catching him at the knees. There was an audible snap, and the Knight yowled in pain. Someone fired their Taser as the knight fell, and his body jiggled uncontrollably. Another officer, then a third, piled on top of the lame old man.

"Hey, hey, hey! No need for that shit!" Richard put up his hand, but it was too late. The Knight was down, the officers battering him again and again to make sure he stayed put.

"Stay back, Lieutenant," one of the officers said. "We got this."

Richard stood down. He wasn't happy to see this use of force on such a harmless old man, but it was the way of things, especially when suspects were in possession of stolen police property.

Beneath that thin blue pile, the Knight cried out, "I'm not done yet! I have a calling! I'm meant for more than this!"

Paramedics arrived and administered sedatives, but soon after the equestrian team arrived with a trailer and loaded the horse, taking her to treat her wound, and the old man lost it all over again. It took an hour and another round of sedatives for the Knight to finally settle and fall silent. Strapped to the gurney, the Knight maintained eye contact with Richard as the paramedic looked him over to make sure he hadn't been harmed.

"You kidding me? LT here be tough as nails," said the officer who'd first tackled the old man. Nodding, the paramedic still gave Richard a quick once-over while the officer began to wax poetic about the hours to come. "Yeah, this is just the beginning. Crazies all hitting the streets tonight. You on tonight, right, sir? Same. Pulling a double. Hoping it'd be quiet, but shit, who'd of thought we'd be taking down a Knight, a Knight in shining armor, am I right? Maybe we'll get lucky and some dumb shit will act like a dumb shit and try to burn the city down. At least it would give us something to do. *Angel's Night*, my ass. Give me some devil to beat down and I'll call it a good day."

He prattled on, but Richard wasn't listening. His mind was on the old man in the back of the ambulance, his gaze baring down on Richard through the window. Richard wanted to go apologize, explain that he was only trying to help, that he had to report him for his own good. But that look told him all he needed to know. The old man didn't want an explanation, his eyes had found those of his betrayer.

The ambulance drove off and Richard realized he'd been wrong, he wasn't Yasuke. The old man was. A true curiosity in a pale world. Beaten, broken, and hauled away.

Richard no longer needed to finish the book to know how it would end.

Flower stems, snapped. Lawn and garden pocked with overturned rocks and uprooted patches of sod. Two birdbaths, broken.

The old man held his own longer than he should have, and as a result, the garden was the lasting victim. It was all replaceable, would all grow back—that's what Richard liked most about gardening, the forgiving nature of plants to those who put forth the effort to care for them—but the blight that his yard had become was no less heartbreaking.

Gloves and blue jeans on, unbuttoned flannel hanging loose over his tank top and paunch. As his shift drew nearer, he remained on his hands and knees replanting grass, rolling rocks back into place, filling righted basins with fresh cool water for the birds in his yard. At the moment, Richard did not give a damn about his duty.

Or at least that's what he told himself.

He stayed in the dirt until he had no choice but to stop. In twenty-seven years, he'd never been late, and that wasn't about to change because something he loved had been ruined. Ruined love was his life. Richard encountered citizens every day who'd had their lives irreparably changed, who were experiencing the worst days of their lives. He owed it to them to be there.

Staring out at the yard from the porch at the Frankenstein patchwork repairs and the scattered debris, he told himself he blamed the Knight. But he didn't. The Knight hadn't planned his layover any more than Richard had planned on hosting the old man. Richard was naturally curious, and while he'd read nothing on the psychology of the mind, his encounter this afternoon told him he needed to rectify that. The damage done to his yard was an opportunity to expand his mind. And how could he be angry at that?

Richard changed into his uniform and headed out the door. The prospect of reading and learning something new filled his head. Verging on giddy, he skipped off the porch, taking the steps two at a time. Yasuke had nothing on the old man. He only rode horses; this Knight seemed to talk to his. Off his rocker, no doubt, but that only made him all the more fascinating.

He hadn't skipped steps in decades, and at his age, maybe he should have kept it that way. He landed on the front path, rolled his ankle, and crumpled to the ground.

His bag lunch tore open and his change of clothes flew from his arm and landed splayed out on the grass like its wearer had been raptured. Pain shot through the bottom of his shoe and into his foot.

The pain put an image in his mind of blood pooling out uncontrollably. He contorted his legs, hoping to only find an errant piece of broken glass sticking out of his foot, rather than a discarded needle. But when he checked the bottom of his shoe, the rubber sole remained intact. Next to him a glint of silver lay on the concrete. A locket. He tugged at the chain and pulled it into reach.

Small and oval and plain. Richard opened it.

Inside were two old pictures. One of two boys, brothers, by the look of it, and the other an older man, the father. It took Richard only a moment to realize that the father in the photo was the Knight. Much younger, but the features remained the same.

"No shit," he smiled.

He went to stand and a jolt of heat and agony ripped up his leg. Richard cried out, lifted his pant leg, and found a dark bruise already forming at his ankle.

Damnit. He was going to be late for work.

The sun set, sinking faster and faster, the way it does once it hits the horizon. Richard sped through the city. Waves of pain shot up his leg as he depressed the gas pedal, and he was unsure if he'd be able to walk once he got to the station. He'd had to crawl to the car and pull himself in, and now every time he hit the break he willed himself not to pass out. The pain was stupid and his consciousness only hung on thanks to the mystery of how that younger man in the locket arrived at his ripe old age in one piece, only to break now.

He doubted he'd ever get a solid answer.

The locket likely belonged to the Knight's wife. That it was no longer in her possession told a story all on its own. He'd have to check the obits when he got to work.

Richard had never married. Early in his career, he realized he could never do the job of policing the streets of Detroit with a family. Not the way it needed doing, anyway. As a young beat cop, he watched the marriages of his fellow officers all go DOA. The ones that didn't end in divorce were shredded by the lifestyle inherent to the job: long hours, societal woes, and frayed nerves. And in turn, the cops passed that cost on to their spouses. Sometimes it was intentional, most of the time not. It's not an excuse, but the truth. Spouses want to be supportive, want to help. But there was no help, at least not from a spouse. It was only recently that the Masood kiosks had begun diagnosing depression and offering mood-altering prescriptions. But pills were only half the battle, and until the stigma of expressing emotions in the controlled environment of a therapist's office went away, every cop was going to keep turning to their mistress, their side piece; the women they would never bring home. And sometimes, that trollop was the city herself. Every cop had two loves, two conflicting priorities. If they missed dinner or a school concert, their family would live. If they showed up late for a shift because they wanted to see little Bobby score his first goal in soccer, the city might not.

Every man, cop or not, had to make that same choice: to syphon love and affection from one relationship to another. There was never a balance. One or the other was always left dry at some point.

Richard squeezed the locket in his hand as he turned the wheel and pulled up to the station. Any man who carried his dead wife's locket with him had made an obvious choice where his priorities lie. But why the hell did he steal the damn horse?

He parked, swung the door open, and knew before he put any weight on it that his ankle still could not support him. Richard reached down between the seat and the door and grabbed his umbrella. Crutches or a cane would have been better, but in a pinch, this would suffice.

The tip clawed against the pavement as he put all his weight on the shaft. It bowed, but didn't break, and Richard headed toward the door. He watched as, from behind the glass, two officers approached the exit: Jackson and Gracie.

The second the door opened the pair spotted Richard limping through the lot.

"God Damn, LT," said Gracie, the towering middle-aged Caucasian Cro-Magnon. "Hate to see the other guy."

"Yeah-yeah. Slipped on the front porch. Twisted my ankle."

"You sure? These cameras out here ain't working. Maybe you need some Workman's Comp PTO."

"Don't listen to him, LT," said Jackson, the introspective black kid with his sights set on earning his stripes in the department. "He may be big, but he's fucking dumb too."

"Fuck yourself." Gracie threw a playful fist at Jackson's shoulder, but the smaller man dodged it.

"Alright, get out there. This is Angel's Night, and I can't picture any more angelic looking figures than the two of you keeping the streets safe," said Richard. "Oh, Jackson, I'm reading this book. Pretty sure you'll dig it. I'll drop it by your desk when I'm done."

"Thanks. But I ain't much of a reader."

"I don't think that's true. I seen you thinkin' sometimes."

"Haven't picked up a book since high school."

"That don't mean nothin'. A reader isn't what you do, it's who you are. Try it, bet it'll come easier than you imagine."

"That's what she said," said Gracie with a deep chuckle.

"Shut the fuck up," said Jackson, smacking Gracie's arm.

"Oh, hey LT," Jackson turned back as Richard hobbled through the door. "Captain's looking for you."

"Alright. I'll call him when I get to my desk."

"No. He's here. He's looking for you."

"Shit."

"Good luck," said Gracie. It was impossible to tell if he was being sincere or sarcastic.

"Shut the fuck up." Jackson smacked Gracie again. Richard didn't have the energy to crack a smile, and the door closed behind him.

Ring-ring-ring-ring-ring.

He crossed through the bullpen, his mind on the Knight, not the night ahead of him. Tonight of all nights, to have the Captain waiting for him, he'd need a good excuse for being late. But his mind wasn't on excuses, wasn't even on his bruised foot. *Ring-ring-ring-ring-ring.* It was on the old Knight. Meanwhile, all around him, the phones continued to *Ring-ring-ring-ring-ring.* A million calls were the expectation tonight, but the relentless droll filled the room, creating an echo where there should have been none.

Ring-ring-ring-ring-ring.

"About fucking time!" Captain Belfour was waiting in Richard's office. He sat behind the Lieutenant's desk, feet up, leaning back in the chair and twiddling a pen in his fingers. So much for having a minute to get his story straight.

"Pardon me?" Richard pulled a confused look onto his face.

"Pardon you? You show up," Captain checked his watch, "twenty Goddamn minutes late, and you're looking for a pardon?"

"Can't be late Captain, City says once you get these bars, you're on duty twenty-four-seven, three hundred sixty-five days a year, sir. Just because I wasn't here doesn't mean I ever left."

Ring-ring-ring-ring-ring.

"God Damn, when did you get to be so fucking adorable? Can't be late, Dick?" He called Richard *Dick* when he felt Richard needed his hand held through a process of thought. "Dick, that is fan-fucking-tastic. I'll make sure I remember that one at Bell's retirement party next year. Tell my wife not to worry that it's two in the morning, and never mind the lipstick and pussy stink on my trousers. I got these bars, so I'm not late. Think that'll work for her?"

"If you phrase it that way, it just might, sir."

Belfour laughed. "God, you're an asshole."

The Captain was a former rifleman in the Marines. He liked to huff and puff, but all it took to gain his respect was to give it right back to him. Whether that made him a good Captain was neither here nor there.

"Am I?" Richard asked.

"No. I guess you're not. If you were, it'd make giving you hell for being late that much easier, and for showing up using a Goddamn umbrella as a cane. What the fuck? You out there singing in the rain, hurt yourself?"

Ring-ring-ring-ring-ring.

"I had a situation in my front yard earlier. You hear about that?"

"Yeah, crackhead shit in your begonias or something?"

"No, it was—"

"I don't care, Dick. Shift change was fifteen minutes ago, and I don't get a fuckin' call? Come on LT, pick up your face, or whatever you kids are saying these days." The Captain was a decade younger than Richard, and he knew it. "Need your head in the game tonight, capiche?"

Richard nodded.

Ring-ring-ring-ring-ring.

"Alright. Now, what's up with your leg?"

"Nothing. Just twisted my ankle."

Belfour pointed to the umbrella Richard was leaning on. "Is that one of those umbrellas that when you open it up, the inside is all blue skies and fluffy white clouds?"

"No, sir. It's a regular old umbrella."

"That's too bad. I want to get one of those for my daughter. Oh, well. But since neither of us has any use for that thing, why don't you deposit it right back in your car and—"

Ring-ring-ring-ring-ring.

The Captain's voice rose to a bellow, "and find out why these Goddamn phone won't stop ringing!"

Ring-ring-ring-ring-ring.

The Captain stood and stormed toward Richard. He snatched the umbrella away from him as he pushed himself out into the bullpen. "Would someone answer the Goddamn phone!" But as he looked around the room, everyone was already on their phone. There weren't enough men to cover all the calling coming in. Belfour looked to Richard, as if he'd have answers.

Richard limped past the Captain. "Dabrowski, what the hell is going on?"

"Sir, the calls are flooding in from downtown. Call center is overloaded. System is forwarding them all to us," Dabrowski replied between calls.

"The fuck is going on downtown?" Belfour barked at no one in particular.

Dabrowski answered. "Fire, sir. They're all about fires. Greektown, New Center, Hamtramck. Everywhere. There're fires everywhere."

"Does Channel 7 have a drone up yet?" asked Belfour.

"Yep. Got eyes on it now." Dabrowski held his cell up over his head. Richard tried to follow as the Captain sped over to Dabrowski's desk, but the moment he took his hand off the door frame, his ankle could not support his weight.

The Captain scurried over to Dabrowski's desk. As he reached his hand out to ask for the phone, he noticed the framed picture of a cat Dabrowski had next to his computer.

"Is that a framed picture of your fucking cat, Dabrowski?"

"It—" the rookie started.

"Get it the fuck out of here, this look like a salon to you?"

Belfour snatched the phone out of Dabrowski's hand and held it vertically in front of his face. He may have been younger than Richard, but shit like that showed his disconnect from his subordinates.

Richard held the wall and reentered his office. He pushed himself away from the wall and teetered forward toward the desk. Knees locked, he caught himself on the edge, and rounded the desk.

The blinds weren't closed, but with the lights on it was impossible to see beyond the glass.

"Lieutenant," said Belfour, coming back into the room. "You need to see this."

"I'm about to. Hit the lights."

The Captain obeyed without question and room sank into darkness. Their eyes adjusted, and soon they could see beyond their own reflections. Outside, the night sky above them was black, but the horizon smoldered.

Richard Keith never married. He didn't want to put a family through the life of a cop. A life he chose, not them. Instead, he wed the city and dedicated his life to her protection.

This wasn't a series of fires. This was a fire. One singular, uninterrupted wall of flame, with an orange glow that spanned the horizon, stretched upward, and licked at the sky. Like someone had unzipped the crust of the Earth to finally let the fires of hell finish their mutiny against heaven.

Richard Keith was married to Detroit, and Mrs. Keith was on fire.

Squatters had heat. Even hobos had fucking dumpster fires to huddle around. Four months after the fire, all the Detroit Police Department had were tendrils of frost creeping across the windshields of their squad cars and manifolds that emptied exhaust into the cab if they stayed parked in one place for too long.

Gracie trembled behind the wheel. "Fuck, it's cold."

Outside, Gracie could see icy snowflakes drift down. Inside, he could see his voice. Hot clouds hung in front of his mouth and dissipated as he spoke.

The neighborhood disappeared under the falling snow. Meteorologists at WDIV had called it a *hundred-year storm*, and said to expect upwards of forty inches over the next day and a half. The frozen baptism the city didn't need right now.

Feast to famine. Fire to ice.

Detroit needed saving, but not like this.

Driveways and porches were buried. Snow drifts taller than toddlers brushed up against each house. Boarded-up windows. Plywood doors. Lights on or off, every house a home. Abandoned, but occupied.

Hard to believe how much of this had been engulfed in flames only four months earlier.

"You want to cuddle? I can warm you up real nice," said Jackson, "Unless you're worried we're being watched?"

Gracie knew they were being watched. They were the lions in a frozen savannah and, hungry or not, the prey eyed their every move. Daylight and dark windows. Eyes peeped them from every house in every direction.

They weren't there to break up crack dens or bust low-rent prostitutes, weren't even there to gawk at the ruin porn scattered around the city. They'd come because someone erected a RoboCop statue in a vacant lot. Snow-covered now, they could only make out the bulky, robotic form. And once they'd seen it, they'd stayed put because this was as good a place as any to run out the clock. With two hours until their shift ended and a freeze on overtime, it was better to lie low than risk anything that might produce paperwork.

Two hours. In two hours the sun would be up and their shift would be over.

"Fuck off. Go back to your damn book," said Gracie. Not only was Jackson a wise-ass, and apparently immune to the cold—*brothers were supposed to hate the cold, right? Weren't they from Africa?*—but the kid had a brain, too. And he didn't use it for street lingo and handshakes. But for everything going on upstairs, Jackson lacked a profound sense of dedication. Jackson, poster child of the Detroit Police Department, physical embodiment of the rejuvenation on the horizon. He'd been cursed with terminal optimism that let him feel change happening around him at all times, even if it wasn't.

Masood was investing another billion dollars into the city to help it rise from the ashes yet again. An expensive-ass blindfold.

Gracie didn't need optimistic blindfolds to sense truth incarnate. He viewed the world through cavernous blue eyes that sunk in under his flat forehead, and his mind functioned in the vowelless grunts of a prophetic old hermit who peered out at the decaying world and preached of its doom.

All those vowels that clogged up Jackson's head let him speak well, but it was just noise. Gracie had tapped into that forgotten hunter/gatherer pedigree that made man *man*.

He smelled water and tasted danger.

Heard the spoken soul of the city crying out on the wind.

H cld s th wrtng n th wlls.

He didn't hate the city, but he knew, regardless of the amount of money Masood Pharmaceuticals poured into the rejuvenation, it was fucked.

Darwin said survival of the fittest had nothing to do with strength or intelligence. Evolution depended on the ability to adapt.

Fuck that.

He was big enough and man enough and white enough to fuck the city into whatever shape he saw fit. Gracie would unfurl his ham hocks at whatever tender sack of meat needed fucking in that moment.

He'd fuck corner kids who mouthed off. He'd fuck fellow officers who insulted his mother. Gracie fucked the culture of soapboxes that weaponized mentality.

Fuck the torch wielding alt-right. Fuck the PC libtards who clutch their pearls and lock their door when a black man walks through their neighborhood. Fuck the brothers who mug those trusting white cucks that don't. And fuck you if you don't lock your doors at night.

Most of the officers on the force avoided any inference of racial injustice. But not Gracie. With his black partner, and black and blue knuckles, he didn't give a shit about the overwhelming focus on perception the world had evolved to take on. Black. White. Red. Yellow. Brown. Gracie viewed himself as the poster child of blind justice. Black lives matter? Fuck that. All lives matter? Fuck everybody. Police lives matter, because without law and order, there was only chaos.

A sack of McDonald's breakfast burritos sat between the men.

Gracie was a dying breed.

Steam rose from the bag, the only warmth in the cruiser. Gracie shoved a burrito into his mouth whole.

He didn't even think in vowels.

Jackson gave his partner a sideways glance before looking back to his book. "Eating like that'll kill ya."

"That book ain't going to read itself, how about you let me die in peace?"

"Naw man, for real. You know all them Jews in the Nazi camps?" said Jackson, pointing to some words on the page in his book, "They was all starving and shit. Emaciated. So the Americans come in, and our fat asses, we feed the Jews up good. Let 'em gorge themselves, cause why not, they had it hard, right?"

Gracie shrugged.

"They bodies weren't ready for that sudden influx of calories, and a lot of 'em ended up dead. Called re-feeding syndrome."

Gracie reached into the brown paper smokestack with his greasy fingers. He fished out another burrito and made a show of slurping the greasy tortilla into his mouth whole again.

"We-fweed dith, bitth," Gracie said with a mouthful of burrito.

"You an ignorant motherfucker!"

The radio squelched. Dispatch called out a street address followed by the four-digit code: *9-5-3-1.*

"Ninety-five thirty-one? The fuck is that?" asked Jackson.

"Gok Garfing," said Gracie, contorting his tongue around his breakfast.

"Dog barking?! They forget we in Detroit?" Jackson picked up the CB. "Dispatch, Cruiser fifty-nine here, say again, over."

"Cruiser fifty-nine, this is Dispatch. 9 - 5 - 3 - 1."

"Com'on, dispatch, call Animal Control. We got real police work to do." Jackson dropped the CB and looked to Gracie for concurrence. Gracie nodded and reached for another burrito.

Bzzzt-bzzzt-bzzzt. Jackson's phone vibrated in his pocket.

God, the man was a fucking animal. Jackson liked the oaf, but Christ, one way or another that man was headed to an early grave. If he didn't eat himself into a heart attack, someone who wasn't familiar with his brand of bias, subterfuge, and compartmentalization was likely to end up offended and put a bullet in him.

Being a police officer wasn't easy, but being the blunt object made it all that much harder. The way an Ice Age will eat a canyon into the earth, a world of round holes will eat away at a square peg before long. But Gracie, impervious to the effects of pressure and time, was still square as ever. Neither heart disease, nor the bullets with his name on them had found the man yet, so maybe Gracie would get lucky and die of old age.

Yeah-fucking-right.

In all honesty, the department's cut-back on overtime was eating into Jackson's leisure cash, and watching Gracie square-peg his fists into some poor schmuck's round hole was cheaper than catching a movie these days. And that was reason enough to put up with his dumbass. Or so he told himself.

Bzzzt-bzzzt-bzzzt. It rang again and again.

He yanked the phone out, looked at the display. "Shit."

Calloway.

And the picture attached to the name: a blonde in a bikini on some tropical beach somewhere.

Bzzzt-bzzzt-bzzzt.

There are three types of cops.

One: The suburbanites who came down to the department seeking adventure in the lawless streets of a once great city. They were altruistic and gung-ho, confident that if they put their soul into the city, it would spring to life again like the fairies from Never-Neverland. I do believe in Detroit, I do, I do.

Two: The natives trying to protect the neighborhoods where they grew up. But all ten fingers and all ten toes couldn't plug the holes in a status quo that never stopped taking on water.

Calloway was the former. Jackson the latter.

And then there was Gracie.

Bzzzt-bzzzt-bzzzt.

"Let me see that." Gracie ripped the phone from his partner's hand. "You want me to tell her you offered to snuggle me?"

"Be my guest! She's on desk duty and pissed about it. Better she bust your balls than mine."

Gracie tossed the phone back like it was covered in spiders. Jackson snatched it from the air and answered the call. "Hey, babe. Sorry that took a minute. Me and Gracie, we was—"

"Enough, Charles." said Calloway. She was loud enough for Gracie to

hear with no effort. *"That ninety-five thirty-one, the neighbors have called every hour. Please, check it out for me."*

"Yeah, yeah. Alright. For you!"

"And quit freaking out on Dispatch. The media listens to that shit. You make it a big deal and they will too."

"Did I make a big deal?"

"Charles—"

"What?"

"You know what! You can't say calls you don't want aren't real police wo—"

Click.

He couldn't take anymore.

Bzzzt-bzzzt-bzzzt. The phone vibrated again as Jackson put it back into his pocket.

"You going to answer that, *Charles?*" asked Gracie.

Jackson may have grown up in the city, but the second he and Calloway became an item and squeezed their salaries together into a down payment for a house up in the hills, he was off and up out. Not that he didn't feel bad about it, but shit, he had a boat on a lake now. The state got rid of the residency requirements years ago. It used to be that all police had to live within city limits, and growing up, that's what made Jackson want to be a cop. Three officers lived on his street, two on his block alone. They'd water their lawns, talk to neighbors. They'd buy their kids ice cream cones and didn't beat their wives. Real members of the community. But even in their off-hours when they'd walk their dogs, or work to shingle an elderly neighbor's home, everyone still called them Officer. Calloway called him Charles at home. So did all the neighbors.

The tires spun and kicked up slush as the cruiser fishtailed away from the curb. It plowed through deep drifts of snow without slowing.

In the winter, Detroit was a snow globe tumbling to the ground. Slush and smog glued everything in place, grey and milky and thick. An ice water sky that sounded like a glass waiting to shatter. The sun, never more obviously a distant star, was frozen, like everything else in the city, until the spring.

The mayor, the city council, the budget committee, they all toed that company line: *"Snowplows cost too much money."* Taxpayer money. City Hall put their faith in God to thaw the city, sent their thoughts and prayers to its citizens, and spent those tax dollars on the municipal services they deemed necessary.

Tax dollars to haul away the waste, to keep the rats and

cockroaches at bay.

Tax dollars to repair and rebuild the fire trucks needed to keep the city from imploding into cinder again.

Tax dollars for police cruisers to patrol the streets and keep crime under control.

It was a fucking joke.

Taxpayer money lined City Hall's pockets while thieves rummaged through the burning trash in the street.

And the punchline was that while Gracie sat comfortably behind the wheel, in the passenger seat, Jackson had to straddle a rusted-out hole in the floorboards. Not a tiny hole either. They hit a pothole just right, and Jackson was likely to slip down onto the speeding pavement.

The Lieutenant expected cruisers to be spotless at the end of each rotation, so once Gracie had eaten his fill of Mickey D's, he handed the sack over and Jackson dropped it between his legs. There one second, gone the next. The trash tumbled behind them on the frozen pavement.

Ten minutes later the phone was still *Bzzzt-bzzzt-bzzzt-ing*, and Jackson ignored it as they approached the address and slid up the driveway.

Ice clung to the pavement, and the cruiser slipped as Gracie nursed the gas. They made it only halfway before it slipped, slid sideways, and bottomed out on a snowbank, blocking the sidewalk.

"I ain't no fuckin' Sherpa," said Jackson, as Gracie shifted into park. "Back up and try again!"

"Your people been here damn near four hundred years now and you still ain't used to snow? Six inches of powder ain't the Himalayas."

"My people? You ignorant asshole! You was the one shivering earlier, but you good with this, huh?"

Gracie shrugged and got out. Jackson followed, and as he slammed the door, he caught that distinct odor of death. Somewhere, they'd find a body. They could already hear the dogs. No wonder the neighbors called.

At the top of the driveway sat a garage covered in snow and broken windows. The roof had collapsed and the overhead door hung crooked in its frame. Grapevines ripped the gutters away, leaving them angled perfectly to dump gallons of rain and thaw down the drive.

A mangled chain-link fence surrounded the yard, and Gracie bounded up the driveway toward the gate. "Damn, Casper," said Jackson as he leaped through the snow, following in his partner's gigantic footprints.

"Don't lose me, now," said Gracie, blending in with the snow-covered everything.

"Listen," Jackson knelt at the garage and peered around the busted-ass door. Nothing to see. "If snow was black, man, you'd be pissin' yourself! Us brothers be sneakin' up on you on the daily."

Gracie reached for the gate, "I'd like to see you—" and slipped. Legs came out from under him and his gump-ass landed hard on the ice. He sailed down the driveway, past the cruiser, and plowed into the snow in the gutter pan. Powder clung to his stubble and his nose was gin-blossoms-red as he sat up.

Jackson keeled over, nearly going headfirst into the snow himself as he attempted to muzzle his juvenile giggles.

Gracie hoisted himself up and shuffled alongside the cruiser, holding onto the roof-rack for stability as he opened the door. "Keep it up and you can laugh your way through that tomb by yourself."

"For real, you would make me find that smelly-ass body by myself cause you clumsy as hell? That's some shit, man!"

"Karma, bitch!" yelled Gracie as he rooted around inside the cruiser.

"I'll show you karma. Wait 'til I tell the boys you keep switchin' the radio over to 96.3! Make me go in there alone and I ain't covering for yo' ass no more!"

The cruiser door flung open. Gracie climbed out, shotgun in hand.

"Shit man, I was only kidding." Jackson put his hands up and turned on his white voice. "Love me that white soul-music. Maroon 5 all the way, brah!"

Gracie climbed the driveway and slapped Jackson on the ass as he passed. "Such a fucking twink."

Gracie swung the chain-link gate open, and the pair approached the house. The dated pastel-green asbestos siding, those taut sheets of bulging plastic covering the windows. Furnace was still kicking; it would be warm inside. Only who knew what they'd find? No car in the driveway, no tire tracks through the snow. Likely be a senior citizen who couldn't get out to get groceries. Maybe her pipes froze, and she lived her last days munching on kibble with her doggies.

Best-case scenario: Cause of death would be natural.

There were too many worst-case scenarios.

They stood on the cement slab porch and Gracie hammered on the door. "Police! Here about the noise."

"And the smell," added Jackson under his breath.

No response, except for the renewed cavalcade of muffled barks and howls. Somewhere inside, those dogs clawed and crashed against some obstruction. A door. A wall. Wherever they were, they wanted out.

"Motherfuckin' Cerberus in there," said Jackson.

Gracie shrugged, not giving a shit. He pounded on the door again. "Police!"

"Let me learn you some history here. Cerberus was the hound that guarded—"

"Cerberus is mythology, not history, you dipshit."

"Ho-lee-shit, you tellin' me after all these years you ain't as dumb as you look?"

"Crazy, right?"

"I tell you, I don't know what's crazier, you banging on that door thinkin' some rotten-ass corpse gonna hear you over them pits, or we on a noise complaint for a dead man."

Gracie raised his fist to pound on the door again, but Jackson stopped him. He reached forward, wrapped his hand around the handle. He turned the knob and pushed. The door opened with no resistance.

"Scrappers beat us here," said Jackson.

Worst-Case Scenario Number One: Crackhead scrappers murder family for copper pipes. Tune into channel nothing at never o'clock for updates on the continued investigation.

The door swung open without a sound, and the house exhaled a bloated stink. Gracie and Jackson lunged back and struggled for air as the vile gasp lifted away from the house and vanished into the cold.

Shotgun in hand, Gracie took a last clean and cold breath, and crossed the threshold. Jackson stood in the doorway and fanned out the house with his hands a minute longer. He pulled his jacket over his nose and went inside.

Hot air churned from the vents, the lights burned bright, and black and white cowboys flickered on the muted TV. The peripheral details wormed into Jackson's assessment of the situation.

Worst-Case Scenario Number Two: Adult son never moved out of parents' house. Parents pass, may be buried in the root cellar, son can't bring himself to update decor. Dog's love supplants parents' love. Hitchcock estate suing for right violations.

Pictures hung on the walls, family portraits and thrift-store paintings. The family room showcased a matching set of couches and chairs intended for company that never arrived. A mid-century suburban dreamscape, a post-war ideal turned prison cell.

Jackson stepped into the kitchen and found it just as orderly and methodical. Labeled jars lined the counter. Food processor and mixer sat next to the stove. A kitchen table with a centerpiece of wilted flowers. Four chairs pushed in. Newspapers and magazines and bills stacked on the hutch. Windows lined with frilly treatments.

These touches of domestication contrasted the sodden dilapidation of the exterior. Remove the smell and the unrelenting barrage of snarls and yaps and anyone would be proud to call this house a home despite the zip code.

But something was off.

Worst-Case Scenario Number Three: Police officers stumble into 99sociopath's lair. Find killer's body alongside the bodies of a dozen kids who'd gone missing in the 90s. Movie rights up for grabs.

From every doorway and window, the house appeared well-tended. Neighbors, door-to-door salesmen, all they would see was feng shui. Everything arranged perfectly. But the house was to be viewed from outside, not toured from within. A 3-D sidewalk chalk drawing that was mind-blowing until viewed at an off angle and became twisted and malformed. And like the story of the Minotaur and the labyrinth, it wasn't until you looked back that you found trouble.

"Oh, shit!" said Jackson.

The stains on the floor looked like shadows at first. Dark, but not blood. Under the couches and tables, along the baseboards below the cabinets. *Oh, shit,* was right. Brown, but not dirt. Inside the pantry, piled behind furniture, scooped up and dumped under tables. Solid masses. Jackson kicked the trash can; another thousand pounds of shit.

"Where did all this shit come from?" asked Gracie.

"You fuckin' thick, man? From the dogs, motherfucker!"

"Yeah, no shit. But why the fuck aren't they mauling us?"

"They locked up. In the basement, from the sound of it."

"How'd dog shit get everywhere if they're locked up?"

"Man, you triflin'! Real question be: why didn't they get rid of it? Why shove it out of sight?"

A putrid slurry bubbled in the garbage disposal.

"That ain't no question." Gracie twisted the knob on the kitchen sink. No water came out. "People fucked up."

"The hell you doin'?"

"Door unlocked. Water not running. Bet this guy's been dead long enough for a couple crackheads to pick the lock and make off with the copper. Probably locked the dogs up downstairs."

"Didn't I say that shit on the front porch? Good work, Detective! I think you cracked the case."

"Fuck off. You didn't say the part about locking the dogs up."

Worst-Case Scenario Number Four: No dead body, just dog shit. Gracie gets promoted to detective. Fuck.

Gracie led the way down the cinderblock steps, shotgun raised. The cacophonous barks and howls dug into their goose-bumped flesh, going for the jugular, the heart, the soul. One step at a time. Breath hushed and controlled. The officers remained silent. And save for the dogs, so did the house.

The farther they descended, the less tangible the hounds sounded. Howls and whines and scratches morphed with wood splintering and brick chipping and tile cracking. Ugly noises. No longer excitable pups but bio-mechanical chainsaws.

Growling-ing-ing-ing-ing-ing-ing-ing-ing.
Clawing-ing-ing-ing-ing-ing-ing-ing.

Jackson pulled his sidearm as Gracie set foot on the basement floor and rounded the corner. He followed Gracie along the makeshift corridor of old boxes that filled the room the way a million layers of paint might. The cardboard held the stink and made the air thick and musty.

The main floor had been warm, but down here was rainforest-hot. Mud and cobwebs and dead insects yellowed the windows. Through the crisscrossed beams of pallid sunlight, Jackson inspected the joists overhead.

Someone had ripped open the ductwork leading away from the furnace.

Worst-Case Scenario Number Five: This recluse, this nut-bag. Whoever lived here, he invented dice or Velcro or some shit. Hid his fortune in the ductwork, and someone had gotten there before they did.

The furnace cycled on, and from the scavenged ceiling a loud *WOOOSH* of dust and dander and debris levied the air. Jackson turned as the cloud enveloped him and he caught sight of Gracie standing at a heavy-duty wooden door.

Doorknob rattled. Hinges jostled.

The dogs were on the other side.

Barking-ing-ing-ing-ing-ing-ing-ing-ing!
Yelping-ing-ing-ing-ing-ing-ing-ing-ing!

If the door was locked, their only key would be the shotgun in Gracie's mitts.

Worst-Case Scenario Number Six: They would have to kill these dogs with a blind shotgun blast through the door.

Gracie turned the handle, and the latch disengaged. Unlocked.

The discordant *yowling-ing-ing-ing* grew louder. Jackson joined his partner at the door. "You ready?" He coughed, his sidearm ready.

Gracie nodded—*CLACK-CLACK*—and racked a shell into the chamber.

Jackson kicked, and the door swung into the room, slamming into one of the dogs. For a moment, the wall of noise ceased as the stench they'd first smelled outside hit them full-force.

Holding his breath again, Gracie rushed the threshold. Shotgun raised. Finger on the trigger.

Three dogs. All chained to a thick metal bar in the back of the room with leads long enough to allow them to become tangled together. They could batter their paws against it, but without bolt cutters and opposable thumbs, the dogs weren't going anywhere.

Emaciated pit bulls, covered in mange and blood. Big skulls bobble-heading on top of dancing skeletons. Shrink-wrapped in their own skin.

For a moment Jackson saw the three dogs as one.

A single dog with three heads.

Gracie lowered the shotgun.

"The fuck you doin'?"

"Pittys get a bad rap cause of their size." Gracie wrapped a hand under one of their jaws and began baby-talking it. "But you just wanted attention, didn't you puppy? Didn't you?"

In an instant the dog's demeanor shifted from monster to moppet.

Gracie bent his head down to nuzzle his forehead against the dog's, but pulled back as he noticed the blood and gristle on the Formica under them.

"Oh, fuck me."

Worst-Case Scenario Number Eight Thousand Seven Hundred Forty-Seven: Gracie McVomited sausage burritos over his shoes.

The dogs turned their attention from Gracie to the meal he'd produced. It was chow time, and they crawled and rolled over one another to get some. They lapped up the bile soup, chomped on the pork croutons. Pale and pungent reds and yellows splattered as their paws painted shit and piss and slobber across the floor, their slick and sloppy tongues lapping at rotten aspic.

Gracie lurched out of the room.

Worst-Case Scenario Number Eight Thousand, Seven Hundred Forty-Eight: Under paws and sausage burrito lay a man, legs spread apart, hands behind his head. Only his hands weren't there, nor most of his head. A twisted rawhide of ear and neck lay on the floor. Teeth and fingers caught in the floor drain. Intestines scribbled and knotted between the dogs' chains. They'd eaten whatever treat he'd had between his legs.

Jackson heaved, and the dogs' attention darted up, waiting for their next meal. But when nothing came, they went back to Gracie's offering. He ducked out of the room, stumbling back to the stairs where Gracie stood talking with Dispatch.

"Dispatch, we've entered the house." Gracie was calm and composed, even as bile still clung to his stubble. "Advised the owner to get the dogs under control. Over."

Calm and composed was code for: *this doesn't belong over the radio.* Jackson pulled out his cell and dialed Calloway. It rang only once.

"You motherfucker! You ever hang up on me again and we are done! My mother told me—"

"Babe, babe. I'm sorry for that. But listen." Jackson didn't yell, he just apologized.

He never apologized, and that phrase snapped her back into cop-mode. *"Charles, everything alright?"*

"Gracie just called in to Dispatch."

"Yeah, I heard. Sound like everything's good. Waste of time, right?"

"We need a detective out here. And Animal Control."

"Detective? Animal Control? What's going on?"

"Babe."

"Yeah?"

"Need the fucking coroner, too."

"On a noise complaint? The hell did you catch?"

Murder police weren't coming. Calloway called back and said their description of the scene was enough to rule out homicide.

Animal Control wasn't coming either. Turns out whatever ingrate they hired to run transport didn't get the memo that texting and driving didn't mix. Two days earlier they'd smashed into the median on the Lodge. Caused a six-mile back-up. Four dogs got out. Shut down the freeway for hours.

Coroner was on his way though, so they had that going for them, which was nice. But he wouldn't set foot in the house until the dogs were out.

Another six inches of snow had fallen while they searched the rest of the house. Covered the cruiser, the street. Everything was silent and white. Jackson used one hand to shovel mounds of powder off the windshield. In the other, he held his cell away from his ear as Captain Belfour chewed him out.

"*You son-of-a-bitch! Overtime over a noise complaint? Gimme a break, Jackson!*"

The frigid air tugged at Jackson's lungs. But the air was fresh, and he'd take just about any reaming in exchange for that. He sniffled and spat, the putrid salinity of the house still sloshing around in his sinuses.

"*Are you getting sick, you son-of-a-bitch? You logging hours now, just to duck out early next week?*"

"No, sir."

"*Good. You request any time off in the next month, be Goddamn sure I'll see that when you come back, you're on drunk tank duty up at Tri-County.*"

"They call it a Sobering Center now, sir. Not the drunk tank."

"*I'm going to tell you to shut the fuck up and pretend I didn't hear that. You made an impression on me on Devil's Night, and that doesn't happen a lot. I like you, Jackson, you and Gracie both. Good fucking police. Let's not change that, sound good?*"

"Yes, Sir."

"*Well, alright then. Any problems with the dogs?*"

"Other than risking our pretty faces wrangling the man-eaters out?

No, no problems."

"Good. You want me to tell Calloway you called Gracie pretty, or does she already know about you two?"

"She already knows."

"I bet she does."

"Sir."

"Alright, well get this shit done before the neighbors call the news." The Captain punctuated his directive by hanging up the phone.

Jackson tucked his cell away, returned to the house, and took a seat on the slab outside the door. The frozen concrete greeted his ass like an old friend. He'd seen worse fates come to people who'd deserved it less, and, more often than not, he'd seen real shit bags get off scot-free.

The evidence said that Mr. Body had been training his dogs to fight. Kept them separate for a long time, starvin' 'em mean. Or at least trying to. When it wasn't in their nature to turn bad on their own, he put them together, hoping they'd turn on one another, and he'd get one good money-making monster.

Instead, they'd turned on him. The most fitting a punishment for a crime he'd seen in a long time.

"Comin' up behind you!"

Jackson leaped to his feet and shielded himself behind the screen door as Gracie led the dogs out. The thick chains clinked and rattled together as Gracie's enormous hands fought to keep the dogs under control. They were strong and wild, but not violent. Weren't even barking anymore, just panting as they sniffed at their surroundings.

"Careful, man," said Jackson as one dog turned to sniff Gracie's boot.

"Oh, they're fine."

"They ate a man. Don't tell me they fine!"

"Asshole had a heart attack or something. Look at these guys. It ain't in their nature."

Gracie had a point.

The dogs chomped at the falling snowflakes and pounced into the deep drifts, staining the fresh powder red, leaving gruesome little snow angles in their wake. Their nature was that of puppies, not killers. "Captain sending a van for these guys?"

Jackson chuckled. "No. Says we should load 'em up ourselves."

Gracie held the dogs, getting sentimental for a moment. "I miss the Lieutenant."

"Same," said Jackson. Belfour had transferred Lieutenant Keith up to the 11th precinct at the first of the year. The Captain put on a show about how it was for the Lieutenant's health. Everyone knew that wasn't true. It was that umbrella he limped in with on Devil's Night. Captain didn't like weakness. Could have been worse for the Lieutenant, could have ended up at Tri-County the way Belfour had threatened Jackson.

Didn't matter. Either way, they were still stuck dealing with Belfour's bullshit.

Tires squealed. Brakes shrieked. The officers shifted their attention from the dogs in time to see a big white van come around the corner.

Traveling too fast for conditions, the driver spun the wheel and pumped the breaks. The van stayed upright, even if it looked for a moment like it may tip.

The vehicle slid past the cruiser and crunched into the snowdrift blocking the neighbor's driveway.

Both Jackson and Gracie winced at the crack of the plastic grill. Snow compressed into a whale song under all that weight.

For a moment, the reverse lights flickered on and the engine revved, but rather than try and fix the shitty parking job, the van lurched into park and the passenger door opened. An ancient black man climbed out, looked at the snowbank, and shook his head. He had chalky dry skin, a scraggly beard, and moved like an old stop-motion skeleton, full of fits and spasms as he made his way through the powder. "Someone says you boys got a body."

"You the coroner?" asked Jackson.

Jackson shuffled through the snow to greet the man. As they shook hands, he glanced at the van's driver—green hair, pierced face, *My Little Pony* hoodie—a white-knuckled kid out of his element.

"Dogs out?" asked the coroner.

Jackson motioned toward the cruiser where Gracie babied the dogs into the backseat, carefully drying their paws with a rag to ensure they wouldn't slip on the hard-plastic surface.

The coroner gave Jackson an incredulous look, but before he could verbalize his thoughts, the van's engine sputtered to a stop.

"The hell you stop it for? Keep it running! I'm on blood thinners, boy!"

The driver rolled down the window and shouted, "Trying to save gas."

"To hell with gas. City pays for gas!" A second later the van groaned back to life, and the coroner proceeded toward the house.

Jackson fell into step with the old man. He wanted to offer him a hand over the ice, but thought better. At that age, doing this job on this cold-ass day, the coroner was the hardest man here. "Tough finding good help through the city, huh?"

"The city? Ha! That's my grandson. City don't give me no driver. But the snow messes with my cataracts."

"*Three M* ain't got nothing for that?"

"Mayhaps they do. I ain't trusting no machine to diagnose me. Likely tuh diagnose the wrong balls, say my eyes are fine, but it's my testicles that I need to get taken care of. No, I don't trust them things."

Gracie lifted the last of the pups into the cruiser and slammed the door.

The coroner wasted no time. "Come on, son!"

The coroner's grandson hopped out of the van and dallied toward the house. His eyes wandered as he kicked at ice pebbles apathetically. They shared some physical attributes—crooked nose and sharp eyes—but that's where the family resemblance ended. Jackson had seen enough youths like this one to feel bad for the coroner. It wasn't like the kid had a future, look at him. And coming from the lineage of a man who'd worked his way up to a respectable station in the hierarchy of the medical examiner's office, that shit pissed him off all the more.

As the pair passed, Jackson *accidently* shoulder checked the punk.

He slipped on the ice, but caught himself; green hair flopped into his face, and he stared at Jackson through the strands. He wanted to make a move, Jackson could feel it. Jackson silently wished he would.

Knock his ass out.

"Watch yourself, boy," said his coroner as he pulled the boy from the stalemate. "Icy all the way up to the door. If you go down, I go down, and I can't afford another hip."

Jackson waited until they had both gone into the house, then joined Gracie in the cruiser. He pictured the kid going down those stairs, puking up a little dose of reality all over his *Pony*-shit hoodie.

The coroner's van had dug large ruts through the snow, which made exiting the neighborhood easier than it otherwise would have been. But the snow-filled side streets were only half of the city's road-related problems. Once the cruiser made it out of the hood, it had to contend with that war-zone Michigan calls roads.

Potholes. Deep as landmines, random as grenade blasts. Gracie was convinced City Hall got kickbacks from the insurance companies.

They passed under The Loop, sped down Woodward toward

Animal Control. The car shook as they rumbled over patches of potholes. A grinding crunch and a rusty scrape, Jackson lifted his feet from the floor as the snow and ice and road flooded into the cruiser through the hole and under the seat. The Loop was supposed to bring enough tax revenue to fix the roads, but Jackson would believe that when he saw it. And when were they going to set aside money to fix their damn cruisers?

The dogs slid back and forth in the backseat, their nails tip-tapping on the plastic bench as they struggled to stay upright. They smeared the Plexiglas divider in drool and paw prints.

"Hope these guys end up alright," said Gracie.

"Alright? What the fuck you mean *alright*?"

"You know, their forever-homes and shit."

"They ate a man, and what? You want to see them get adopted. Want Little Timmy to wake up Christmas morning and find his new puppy under the tree?"

Gracie shrugged.

"Tell you what's gonna happen. Little Timmy's gonna get a dog, but mysteriously, he ain't gonna be able to find his cat no more. His little sister neither."

"Just saying, that guy had it coming. They don't have to get adopted, but that ain't got to be put down neither."

"How many options you think these dogs got? Adoption or the fucking needle. That's it. These dog's getting what's coming to 'em," said Jackson. "It's that simple."

It was never that simple.

An hour ago he'd have been able to draw a through-line linking his work to the renaissance of the city. If planting an unregistered handgun got an abusive father out of a house, it used to be that that was on the up-and-up, because somewhere some deadbeat was getting off on a technicality. Put enough dirt on the scales and eventually a balance is struck. That was the system. That was the lens through which Jackson's optimism had been formed. Detroit was getting better because those who cared did what was necessary to make it so.

Hell, take Devil's Night. He and Gracie had apprehended the bitch that started the fire. Made sure that shit didn't go unpunished. Ran her friends down too, but they were faster than she was.

Everything had been five-by-five until those double-edged, emaciated sacks of karma landed in the backseat. Just because their owner got what was coming to him at the paws of his own attempted creations, didn't mean they wasn't going to get it in return for what they done. Now Jackson was spiraling because he could see the dirt for what it was.

Gracie said the city was fucked, but Jackson refused to accept that regardless of what he saw around him. Couldn't deny it either, though. To find hope in the ridiculous, Jackson's tolerance slid to reconcile the two perspectives. Little by little, that dirt on the scales of justice had realigned his ideals, and the radical had become the norm.

The snow was coming down hard. Gracie swerved to avoid a deep pothole, and the dogs yelped as they slammed into the door.

Jackson turned, "Oh, shit!" The dog vomited.

The cruiser hit another pothole and swerved. Back tires hopped and swung out. Gracie corrected it before they fish-tailed into oncoming traffic, but he over-corrected and sent the dogs cascading back across the car.

The other two joined in. Vomit. Vomit.

It was the basement all over again. Chunks and colors. Blood and smells. The mess sloshed and smeared along the seat and floor.

"Fuck!" said Gracie. He cracked the windows to air out the vehicle. He hit the brake, and the cruiser drifted along the ice.

"The fuck you doing?"

"Slowing down, man! Don't want 'em to get hurt."

"Naw. We getting these guys outta here. Gun it."

Animal Control was an unpainted cinderblock building with steel bars over every window and door. They called it an animal shelter, but it still looked every bit like a pound.

The cruiser hopped the curb as it turned into the drive, and past the barbed-wire fence that secured the lot. Around back, a group of women wearing scrubs waited for them. Two of the women smoked cigarettes and looked pleasant enough. One of them, Jackson recognized from the after-hours place he went to following his shift some nights. But the third looked like she forgot how to smile years ago; had a stare that said she'd seen some shit.

Jackson wasn't in the mood for her.

The cruiser had barely come to a stop when Jackson threw open his door, climbed out, and rapped his fist against the rear window. "Get these fuckin' dogs out of my car before I shoot 'em!"

"Are you serious?" said the unpleasant one. She walked up to the car, leash in hand, hand on hip.

"Fuck, yes! These shits puked all over my backseat!"

"The way you were driving, I'm not surprised."

"Listen lady, I don't got the time, nor the patience for your—"

"No, you listen, Officer." She cut him off without raising her voice. "We get people in here every day saying they're going to shoot their animals if we don't take them in. People toss kittens over the fence or shove them into unlocked cars. We got kennels filling up, a waitlist that never ends, and twice as many animals as we got runs. Not to mention, we're running low on food. Last thing I want to hear is police spewing the same bullshit as the fucking trash on the street. You're supposed to be the good guys, right? Act like it."

The other techs stubbed out their cigarettes and came forward with leashes. Jackson opened the backdoor. The dogs climbed out without issue and followed the techs into the building.

The woman glanced into the backseat, then at Jackson. "Good luck getting rid of that stench."

"Tell me about it."

"You didn't happen to grab their food, did you? Every bit helps."

"Ain't no food there. Man was starving 'em."

She looked again at the mess in the backseat. "They ate something. That's more than bile you got back there."

Gracie peered through the Plexiglas and Jackson ducked his head into the open door while Smiles turned and led the third dog inside.

A slick pink slurry dripped and drizzled off every surface. Meaty chunks of half-digested man peppered the backseat. Fingertips and an eyeball. Bone chips and muscle mass.

Jackson threw his hands in the air. "Fuck this. I resign." He unclipped his badge and tossed it to Gracie, still sitting in the driver's seat. "You deal with it!"

"Fuck off. If I wanted to clean human remains out of a back seat, I would have become an evidence tech." Gracie chucked the badge back.

Jackson caught it in midair. "That's right you fuckin' would!" He pulled out his cellphone and dialed.

"Who you calling?" asked Gracie. Jackson held up a finger as he paced in front of the squad car with a shit-eating grin on his face.

"Hey Captain, dogs are at Animal Control," said Jackson. "No problems. Here's the thing, there're pieces of him all over the backseat. Dogs threw him up. Thinking we should get evidence down here to look at the cruiser and—"

Jackson pulled the phone away from his head until he heard the Captain go quiet.

"Alright, sir," said Jackson when he returned the phone to his ear. "Yes, sir. Sorry, Captain." He hung up the phone.

"What did he say?" asked Gracie.

"The fuck you think he said? Have it cleaned by the end of shift."

"Well, best get to it." Gracie banged the side of the cruiser. Fucker didn't give a shit about shit.

"Naw, fuck that. This is some bullshit. We're burnin' this bitch! Straight up fucking arson." Jackson paced the lot, kicking rocks and ice pebbles at the frozen fence.

Police don't even look out for their own. Man, this city be fucked.

It used to be that once a year, Detroit would burn. That one cold night in late October when all them wanna-be arsonists would get their fifteen minutes and abandoned homes and factories would be set ablaze. And for a while, the extra patrols made a difference, and with the media's help Devil's Night became known as Angel's Night. Then last year one fifteen-year-old girl trumped everybody, burning the whole Goddamn city herself.

There's not a cop or firefighter or civil servant who wished to see another Devil's Night like that again, but the fact that it happened only proved the fire had never gone away.

The flames hadn't been in the news, but the embers were there. They'd quietly crawled over to City Hall, filed the papers, got their permits, signed all the legal documents, and then they burned freely.

Only, instead of giant flames spreading wildly across the city, instead of being a spectacle, the flames became the norm. Detroit was a furnace, a kiln with cracked exteriors and burnt-out buildings as it's finished product. No one cared about the kiln if the potter's work was mesmerizing. Terracotta Packard Plant. Porcelain Michigan Central Station. All those smashed stoneware homes.

The idea that the city even wanted to be saved was a joke.

Justified or absolutely fucking not, it's no surprise someone picked up that torch and burned it all down.

Too bad she threw away her life making a point that would fall on deaf ears.

City didn't give a shit about her. Didn't give a shit about anybody.

After the fire in 1805 that destroyed most of Detroit, the city adopted the motto *"We hope for better days: It shall rise from its ashes."* Thanks to Masood, maybe that hope was finally here. But Detroit's past was so steeped in fire that Jackson thought his mantra was more appropriate. Because where most saw a phoenix, in truth there was only the smoldering ember waiting to erupt again and again and again. Detroit's future was ash. Easier to burn a problem than clean it up. *Straight up fucking arson.*

Gracie tapped the horn. "You done?"

Jackson kicked one last rock. It hit the fence hard and made a reverberating laser gun sound that gave him enough satisfaction to round the cruiser and climb in.

But fuck it. Someone had to save the fucking place, right?

"Worried that if we wait much longer, Dude might claim squatters' rights back there. Don't want his ghost haunting us, do we?"

And it sure as shit wasn't going to be Gracie.

"You're a fucking idiot."

He was a fucking idiot.

Six self-service bays sat empty and unused. Empty, except for the snow. In the summer months, this self-serve quarter carwash would teem with life. Forties and splifs. Working-class Joes keeping their livelihood from rusting away and minstrel-like hooligans booming their bass and rattling their hoopties to an early grave. In the dead of winter, this watering hole was devoid of prey.

Gracie plowed into the first bay. Snow cascaded up the windshield as the squad car lodged itself in the drift. He repeated this half a dozen times. Rammed the front of the car into the snowbank, packed it tight and shoved it far enough out of the bay for them to work.

Instead of shutting down the system for the winter, the owner allowed the lines to remain open and drip, drip, drip until the floor was ice. The men climbed out. Gracie inched across the space with a fist full of change.

"Careful there, Pete Rose," said Jackson.

Gracie flicked him the bird and pecked a few quarters out of the assortment.

Six hours ago, their shift was supposed to be over two hours ago. Now the sun was up and they still had paperwork waiting for them when they got back to the precinct.

He deposited them into the control counsel and the bay filled with steam. The lines hadn't frozen, but enough ice had built up to create pressure at every joint and coupling. A pitiful stream of water limped out of the tip of the pressure wand, but as the system thawed, the stream built into a blade.

Jackson opened the back doors on either side of the squad car and took the wand from Gracie. He squeezed the trigger, and the hose recoiled against him.

The water swept across the black plastic, creating a mist of soapy water and particled viscera. Flesh and blood washed away. Bile and bone cleansed in the hazy light. Chunks of man lobbed into the snow, splattered against the chipped wall.

Amongst the gore there was something else. A flap of black leather.

A wallet. Stomach acid and bile still sandwiched between the folds from the time it had spent inside a dog's stomach.

Gracie skirted around the hot stream and snatched it from the snow. He shook off the sinew and snow, peeled it open. Credit card, library card, driver's license.

All expired.

Darwin said survival of the fittest had nothing to do with strength or intelligence. Evolution depended on the ability to adapt.

Jamal Taylor was too busy living in the past to adapt.

Squatters had heat. Bums had dumpster fires.

Expelled by his dogs. Blasted to mist. Plastered to the wall. Newly appointed winter watchman of the quarter carwash east of the Jeffries, Jamal Taylor now had a macabre mural to commemorate him.

Even in death, Gracie recognized a kindred spirit. Recgnzd th ft f th cty. It was all temporary. Spring would come and the thaw would wash Jamal down the drain, vowels and all.

Grc shvrd.

On the first day of summer, shortly after 11:30 PM, the DeForests walked into the 11th Precinct hand-in-hand. They were trembling, eyes red with tears, as they asked to make a statement. Randy DeForest was wearing a royal blue blazer with a matching narrow tie, and a Tuscany-yellow Henley with matching trousers the day he reported his son missing. His wife, Moonjava, was wearing a rainbow-sleeved boho goth hippy festival jacket. She said she had no son.

The Desk Sergeant on duty tried to explain to the couple that, unless the circumstances were dire, there was a waiting period to file missing person's reports. Mrs. DeForest was already pounding that zero hard enough to short-circuit the automated system, trying to get connected to a live operator before the officer even finished speaking. "This isn't a missing person's report. We're here to report a hate crime!"

"I got this one, Hollings," said Gracie. He'd been up there waiting for his food to be delivered, bullshitting with the Sergeant, when the couple had come in. "Buzz me when my food shows up."

He escorted them to a backroom where he handed Mr. DeForest a standard complaint form.

"Please explain in detail the crime that took place. Where, when, how it happened. I'm going to ask you both a few questions as well." Before Mr. DeForest put pen to paper, his wife snatched the pad away from him and began to write.

Gracie rolled his eyes, but kept his mouth shut. Whatever family drama they had going on, he did not want to be in the middle of it.

"What is your birthdate, Mr. DeForest?" Gracie asked.

"Yes. It's April 2nd, nineteen sixty-eight."

"And your wife's?"

"Seriously?" Moonjava said. She lifted the pen and stared at Gracie.

"Is there a problem?" asked Gracie.

"What do you think? There are only three birthdates a parent can name their child Moonjava without disrupting that child's astrological energies or negatively affecting their future earning potential. And two of those are exclusively for redheads. Do I look like a redhead?" She brushed her hand through her chestnut hair to make her point.

"She was born on January 13th, nineteen seventy-one."

They'd been there for all of five minutes and Gracie was already sick of their shit. Reading body language was second nature, and he'd become accustomed to both perps and witnesses being deceitful and dishonest when comparing what they say to how they act. But that was part of the game. Dodge responsibility. Place blame.

But these two were too smug and arrogant to lie. Too righteous to deceive.

While Moonjava scribbled across the pad, Randy sat with his hands folded on the table and his legs crossed so high above the knee that Gracie had to adjust his own sack to relieve the discomfort. Randy smiled while his wife wrote. A smile like a wink. A smile that said how proud he was to have a wife who'd step on his balls and call it foreplay.

"I'm sure your son will be fine, Mr. Deforest."

"We don't have a son," said Moonjava without looking up.

"Oh, I'm sorry. Hollings must have written it down wrong. I'm sure your daughter will be fine."

"Oh, well, you see—" said Randy.

Moonjava cut him off, "Don't, Randy. Our child is missing, and this ignoramus is imbuing his cisgender identification bullshit on the situation." She turned to Gracie. "How are their pronouns important or any of your business? My child is missing. Find them."

"I understand you're upset, and forgive my ignorance here, but you said *them?* How many children are missing?"

"I am not a terrible mother!"

"Ma'am, I didn't—"

"My name is Moonjava! And I am dynamic, restless, independent, and outspoken. Don't *Ma'am* me!"

Gracie looked to Randy, said, "I apologize. I'm sure that your son—that *they* don't think you are a bad mother."

Randy reached across the table and placed his hand on Gracie's folded fingers, "See, now you're getting it." Gracie pulled his hands away a little too quickly and Moonjava let out a *PFFT* and rolled her eyes.

Gracie ignored Moonjava. "Now I'm getting *what?*" he said to Randy.

"*They*," said Randy. "Our child's preferred pronouns are they/them. Until tonight they've been non-binary."

"Until tonight?"

"Don't waste your breath," Moonjava interjected without looking up from her statement.

"Tonight's sweet sixteen extravaganza served two purposes. It was both a birthday and a gender reveal party."

"Like they do for babies?"

"No, no, no." Randy chuckled and reached for Gracie's hand again, but he was out of reach, so Randy feigned a stretch to cover the awkwardness. "The idea of cutting into a blue or pink cake is a construct of our heteronormative society. Tonight's festivities were more of a pansexual polycurious Rumspringa."

"Right. Okay. Let's get the simple stuff out of the way. What's your child's name?"

PFFT!

"What is it now, Ma'a—" Gracie caught himself. He was getting good at this bullshit. "Did I say something wrong, Moonjava?"

"Oh, so you know my name is Moonjava, and you know his is Randy. Exactly how many names do you think we had to choose from that harmonized with our family and their due date?"

"I couldn't even guess."

"I'm done. Randy, you deal with this obdurate thug."

Randy smiled at his wife and turned to Gracie. "Our child's name is Friendo."

"Friendo?"

"Yep."

"Friendo DeForest?"

"Is there a fucking problem with my child's name? Is it funny to you?" asked Moonjava.

"No. Just making sure I got it right," said Gracie. He turned to Randy. "Okay, so try to stay calm. Typically, kids like yours get mad and need time to cool off. Nine times out of ten they come back within a day."

"Kids like ours? What the fuck does that mean? White kids? Privileged kids? We are not privileged, you asshole. Randy spent five years in prison. I had to raise Friendo on my own!"

"What were you in prison for?"

"You don't have to answer that!" Moonjava grabbed her husband's hand.

"Are you his lawyer?"

"What, never seen a lawyer without a penis?"

"There's no need for hostility," said Gracie.

"Hostility? I'm ninety pounds soaking wet. You give elephants inferiority complexes. Not to mention how fucking white you are! Your existence is pure hostility."

"Moonjava, love, I think we can all identify as Caucasian here," said Randy.

"Yeah, but Officer Squarejaw makes it feel ugly." Moonjava slammed the pen down and shoved the pad of peel-away complaint forms across the table.

"Your child is missing, let's try to stay calm. You said it was a hate crime. Can you elaborate on that?"

"If you don't understand by now, what use is an explanation?"

"I'm only trying to help. Where do you think he could have gone?"

"He?"

"Ma'am, please…"

"Ma'am?!"

"God damn it! Will one of you give me a straight fucking answer?"

"Straight!?" Moonjava slammed her hand onto the table.

"Oh, for Christ's sake!"

Randy raised his hand. "They might be at their girlfriend's house?"

Moonjava kicked Randy's leg under the table. *PFFT!* She turned away.

"Name?" asked Gracie.

"Samantha Thomas," said Randy, as Moonjava backhanded his shoulder.

"Thank you." Gracie stood. "Got an address?"

Randy rattled it off as Moonjava continued to slap him.

Gracie ripped Moonjava's statement off the top of the pad and tossed the blank pages to Randy. "Now give me your statement."

"I already gave you our statement!" said Moonjava.

"You gave me yours. I'm asking for his."

PFFT! She looked away.

"Sit tight. Gonna step out and read this. Be back in a bit," said Gracie as he stood and made for the door.

Unbeknown to her, Gracie subtly gave her the finger as he walked out of the room.

He looked back in at the couple. Randy held his arm across the form, shielding his statement from Moonjava as if he were taking a math test. She pulled at his arm, trying to get either the pad or the pen away from her husband.

The last thing he had time for was marital bickering. He had to get a squad car over to the girlfriend's house to either confirm or rule out the kids' presence. It was a formality. Eleven times out of ten, a runaway at that age is with a significant other.

Gracie's shoes squawked across the linoleum floor. His stomach growled, echoing down the hall. The most difficult thing to adapt to being stationed this close to the suburbs was the silence. Inner-city stations echoed with bombast and clamor at regular enough intervals that the only way to escape the drudgery was to take a squad car out on patrol. Depending on which side of the various snaking socio-economic divides they served and protected, stations took on unique tones and registers. In the suburbs, the noise came and left with the sun.

During the day, foot traffic was so high it sounded like a perpetual game of basketball being played up and down the hall, but by third shift the station was peaceful. It became an echo chamber of foley sound effects: chainsaw pencil sharpeners, bank-alarm telephone calls, the 3:10 percolating puffs of the automatic-drip steam-train.

He stopped at the coffee pot to make both himself and the Lieutenant a fresh cup. It was a bargaining chip, something to sweeten the deal and keep the Lieutenant from making Gracie go check on the kid himself. The address they'd given him was on the border of Ferndale and Detroit. If it were up to Gracie, he'd pass the buck off to FPD. Knowing the LT though, if the report was filed here, he'd make Gracie look into it.

But maybe, just maybe, he could change his mind.

He didn't want to go scavenger hunting for some horny teen, he just wanted to eat his food.

While the coffee percolated, Gracie looked over the statement the kid's mom had made.

City of Detroit – 11th Precinct
Witness/Victim Voluntary Statement Form

I am no man's property!	*Moonjava*	*n/a*
Last Name	**First Name**	**Middle**
███████████	*Detroit*	*MI*
Address	**City**	**State**

Statement

    For years Randy and I wanted a child. Someone who could fight for equality and against oppression well into the future. But when I found out I was with child a terrifying thought struck us. What if our child had a penis? What if our child was white?! It crushed us. The very tool of oppression, the bulwark of oppression in our world. The white male.

    It took a decade and four pregnancies, but we finally figured out how to make it work. Randy reminded me that our child would be just that. Our child! How they was raised was our choice, not theirs, not the worlds. We decided then and there that we would not contribute to nor participate in a heteronormative world. If we had to raise a white penis, so be it. We had friends who taught their children different names for the colors of the rainbow in order to free them from the dominant social constructs and norms. And if the colors of the rainbow could be fluid, so too could our child. If we birthed a white penis, we agreed to raise them to be gender neutral.

    But a plan cannot stave off depression. The day we learned I was pregnant with a male was devastating. And it only got worse as he grew inside me. Just the experience of a white man inside me was nauseating. For months I felt him dominating my uterus with his thoughts... with his taste for controlling women... with his greed... with his need to abandon his family for younger women. To the point that when I woke every morning, I would literally vomit. It made itself right at home too. It knew exactly how it was making me feel. They had violated the very essence of my womanhood, my most sacred space, and every ache and pain was caused on purpose to show me who was really in charge.

Barely bigger than a lima bean and already practicing to live a life of unearned privilege on the backs of others, already the essence of oppression.

The white male.

We prayed to mother earth for a dark-skinned child. Or at least a woman.

After seven months mother nature finally heeded our prayers and liberated my uterus from the oppressor. But the pale skin... the penis... they were more than I could bare. I could get used to one or the other, but together... there was no way. So I pleaded with Randy to fix it. To fix our plight. And so Randy was arrested and spent five years in jail for attempting to swap Friendo out for an African-American baby at the hospital.

Our friends assumed that Randy was in Ethiopia completing his Hamar Cow Jumping ceremony because that was what we told people he was doing.

Those years apart were hard for me. But with Randy gone, I grew to find true companionship with Friendo. And they became the child I never had.

It was hard, raising Friendo without Randy, but the one thing that got me through was knowing that when they turned sixteen, our family would be able to atone to the Earth for thrusting another privileged white penis into her bosom.

Today is Friendo's sixteenth birthday, and earlier this evening Randy and I enacted our plan that was two decades in the making, thus absolving our sin of raising a white child with an elongated flap of skin between their legs.

It was a momentous day for our family as Friendo took the stage and proudly declared their chosen gender and sexual identity.

Then that bitch ruined everything.

The Lieutenant's door was ajar. Gracie knocked once and let himself in without waiting for an answer.

"Hey, boss," said Gracie as he stepped into the office. Lieutenant Keith held his desk phone to his ear and cordially answered whatever questions were being asked of him. Gracie set the second cup of coffee on the desk before retreating to the threshold to lean against the doorframe and listen in.

"Yes, sir," The Lieutenant said, reaching for his coffee. "No, sir, I'm not aware of any such file. Yes, I am aware of the arrests and the changes, but beyond that I don't know anything more than you. Well, alright then. I'm sorry I couldn't be of more help."

He hung up the phone and Gracie opened his mouth before the Lieutenant could.

"City hall?"

"Yeah. About the fires. They're getting calls from Masood Pharmaceuticals. The name Kate Hill mean anything to you?"

Gracie shook his head.

"No? Well, as it turns out, Masood is thinking of fully funding the Torres legal defense. Ms. Hill called the press office at city hall to vet the legitimacy of a rumor that the body cam footage from that night proves her innocence."

"Fucking bullshit!" Gracie pushed himself away from the doorframe, stepped in, and closed the door behind him. "Seriously, fuck Masood. First, they campaigned to have the fireworks cancelled for sensitivity to the victims of the fire, and now this. It's all fucking social justice, cancel culture bullshit. Jackson and I didn't do nothing wrong."

"Well, then you ain't got nothing to worry about, do you?"

"Hate this shit."

"I know you do." Lieutenant Keith sipped his coffee. "What, no cream?"

"Thought you liked your coffee the way you like your cock."

Lieutenant Keith gave him half a smile. "Why don't you take a seat?"

"I'd love to, but I got *Trough* getting delivered any minute, plus the missing kid's parents are still down in room three. Don't want to leave them alone too long. I was coming down because from the sound of it, the kid is likely in Ferndale. You good if we transfer this up to them?"

"I said, pop a squat, Officer. Let's talk."

"They're a pair of rascals. I ought to get back, we'll be lucky if they ain't lodged a complaint already."

"And you're lucky they didn't catch you giving them the bird. Sit."

Gracie took a deep breath and fell into the chair opposite the Lieutenant.

"It's the middle of the night and a pair of peacocks come in," said the Lieutenant. "You think I'm not pulling up the closed-circuit feed?"

"Shit, LT, if you were listening, you heard 'em."

"I did. Heard you, too. And right until your little Tweety Bird popped up, you were the poster-child of poise and grace."

"I'm tryin'."

"You are. Just need to be mindful of your feelings becoming actions. Emotions don't exist outside the body. But they can manifest in unhealthy ways."

"Sometimes unhealthy was the only way to get respect in—"

"And see, there's your problem. We're only in Detroit cause they say we are. For all intents and purposes, we're in the suburbs, Paul. You find it funny we both ended up here? I do. They transferred me cause they said I was too soft for the city. And you because they said you was too hard. And now here we are, trying to reconcile that. But what I need from you is poise and grace. Something you're capable of, right?"

"Yes, sir."

"Good. Cause let me tell you, shit goes wrong up here, it's my ass too. They likely to transfer me to Tri-County. And ain't no one want that shit detail, do they?"

"No, sir," said Gracie as he slunk into the chair.

"No one is asking you to be an automaton, Paul."

"Good," said Gracie. "Cause I got no fucking clue what that is."

"You know why I saved your ass? Why I brought you up here regardless of the shit you pulled? Affirmative action."

"Hate to break it to you, LT, but I'm white."

"That don't mean shit. I don't see diversity and skin color being mutually exclusive. You have a viewpoint that most of the officers here don't have. But that doesn't make you wrong. It makes us strong."

"And what viewpoint is that?"

"Up here, they are stuck on this treadmill of victimhood. Good schools, running water, and nice homes. Yet, here they are, inventing struggles. Keepin' up with the Joneses of their own misery. And you don't recognize their problems as *real*, cause you seen *real problems*."

"Goddamn right."

"Now, knowing that. I need you to understand that people can't help who they are without empathy. We are all products of our environment, and we can only achieve growth through shared knowledge. You can be a teacher as much as you are a student, but you need to be more aware of how you present yourself. Are you familiar with Poe's Law?"

Before Gracie could answer, the door swung open and Hollings stepped in. "Sorry to bother you."

"What is it, Sergeant?" asked the Lieutenant.

"That couple in room three. The wife had to use the bathroom, and before Baker could stop her, she walked into the men's room and dropped trou. She's trying to use the urinal. Making a mess everywhere."

"God Damnit. See?" Gracie gave the Lieutenant a look, then turned back to the Sergeant. "Alright, I'll fucking put her in her place."

"Nope," said the Lieutenant, "Why don't you head over to the girlfriend's house? I'll handle them."

"The fuck? I can do my fucking job."

"That's right, you can. And right now, that job is to head out to the girlfriend's house."

"Fine. Imma transfer it up to Ferndale. Ain't going on a bullshit welfare check for a teenager."

"Oh, yes you are. You're seeing this one through. There are teaching moments and there are learning ones. This is a learning one, and I expect you to come away with a—"

Gracie stood and kicked the chair, sent it skidding across the office. "That's her statement on the desk. Good luck with that one."

"Paul—" But Gracie was heading out the door. "Don't you walk away from me."

Gracie stopped but didn't turn. Lieutenant Keith stood and rounded the desk. He slid up next to Gracie and whispered, "I'm giving you a chance to cool down and reflect. Maybe you don't think you need that, and you are welcome to that opinion. Whatever the case, go for a drive, talk to the kid, cool down, and reflect. And I expect you to come back with a new perspective on the problems and woes of those you cannot relate to. Dismissed."

Reflections. Fck rflctns. Gracie liked the Lieutenant. Fck th Ltnnt.

The parking garage was as cavernous and silent as the station above, until Gracie hopped into the squad car and turned the key. The engine roared and thanks to the rusted-to-shit muffler, an extra-sensitive car alarm on the other side of the lot came alive. The whooping siren filled the garage and Gracie chuckled as he typed the girlfriend's address into the onboard computer.

Before he pulled out of the parking space, his phone vibrated, and he pulled it from his pocket.

Your Uber Eats Has Arrived
Time to meet Jesus.
Your order from TROUGH is here.
Tell them your PIN is 1806 to confirm the delivery.

Fuck it. If duty had its way, he'd eat when he was dead. He ignored the text and shifted the squad car into reverse.

He drove up the ramp, leaving the alarm for someone else. Fuck that car. He glanced up to the night sky. The Ferndale skyline had changed so much in such a short time. For one, it had a skyline. Fuck the skyline.

Six and seven and eight stories of glass and steel shot up from the grass and sidewalks and narrows streets of this once tiny enclave. Eleven towers in total. The roadways downtown were still lined with the turn-of-the-century brick-and-mortar storefronts, some of which still housed decades-long family-owned businesses (*Satori Junk*, a resale shop; *Natural Food Patch*, an organic grocery) but most were places that didn't reflect the same longevity of clientele (*Noir Moon*, a trendy record store; *Trough*, the hip eatery Gracie finally ordered from, and had to leave behind). On foot, and even by car, the suburb remained the tree-lined, lifestyle-friendly hamlet it always purported itself to be, but behind this front, the future was on the rise. This trend of building up instead of out began in neighboring communities, who saw their residential areas encroach on the money-making downtown areas and adapted to stay relevant to the younger generations with more disposable income. The citizens of Ferndale fought against this literal skyward thrust for years, but financial interests became too great to ignore, leading the city to follow suit with the adjacent, and thriving, nearby cities.

Every square mile of real estate had been packed tight with chicken-and-egg combinations of microbreweries and condos, fusion restaurants and lofts. It was impossible to tell which came first: the commerce or the consumers. Impossible to tell where all the snow from a long winter would be plowed and piled now that they had transformed every parking lot in the city into a rising structure to house the local tourists who came to drink.

At midnight, hipsters and hep cats clotted downtown as they roamed from pub to pub for another two hours before scattering at last call. Gracie liked to camp out at the Nine Mile and Woodward intersection and watch the taillights drunkenly flow from that epicenter. At two in the morning, every morning, he watched the city bleed.

Ferndale, a city built on community, was now thriving by capitalizing on that as if it were a commodity. All those towers. All that housing they created. It wasn't enough. Bidding wars filled the high-end apartments and loft spaces, but too many housing crises kept the youth from buying long-term, and the homes for sale in the old neighborhoods remained on the market.

A dozen blue lights hung over the old neighborhood. One, the moon peering through the trees. The others, the moons reflection off the towers.

The squad car careened through the side streets toward the Thomas residence. Someone needed to fire the fucking city planner. The way new Ferndale mixed with the old, there were so many streets that the GPS claimed went through, but when Gracie turned down them, they came to a dead end. And the ones that didn't end turned and wound themselves back through another neighborhood full of more dead ends that prevented him from getting back onto the path that the GPS had originally laid out for him to follow. Gracie accidently happened upon the street he was looking for after circling and backtracking for too fucking long. A few blocks down he'd heard that there was another one of those stone statues that had been popping up.

Someone said this one was M. L. Liebler, whoever the hell that was. Either way, this statue made it nearly two dozen of these monuments that had gone up around metro Detroit in the last seven months, and Gracie didn't give a shit about any of them (except for maybe Robocop, but that was more out of boredom than genuine patronage). This hadn't stopped the area's hipster population from making pilgrimages to each and every one before they were scheduled for removal due to their illegal installation. If there was any random shit he actually cared about seeing, it was that stupid phantom house that the boys downtown had been going on about. Gracie had called bullshit on the thing, but officers he trusted and believed said they'd seen it too.

The neighborhood was soft and quiet. Big stone porches strewn with lawn furniture and grills. Chinese lanterns and tie-dyed mandala tapestries strung up along fences and pergolas. Wind chimes and potted succulents in macramé hangers. Trees and rocks and shaggy lawns. Without the Big Brother of a HOA, landscapes both manicured and gone-to-seed could flourish devoid of reward or repercussion.

He'd kept his eye out for it, but Gracie arrived without ever seeing the statue. The Thomas residence was sandwiched between a small four-unit apartment building and a home whose yard was overgrown enough that it was probably time for the city to intervene.

He parked the squad car and stepped out, then climbed the front steps and peered through the window. The flickering glow of a television screen could be seen through the closed curtains, but aside from that, he couldn't make out any voices, any movement.

"Police." Gracie rapped on the door.

Figures shuddered through the neon glow, shapeless masses springing up and drifting toward the door.

"Um, hello?" said a female voice within the house.

"Ms. Thomas, Ferndale Police. Can I ask you a few questions?"

"Um, okay."

"Could you open the door, Ma'am?" Gracie braced himself, having uttered the M-word. But no barrage came.

The deadbolt slid. The handle jiggled. The door swung open.

Behind it stood two figures wrapped together under a floral patchwork quilt. The girl was pretty and blonde, wearing PJ pants and an oversized t-shirt. She didn't seem like damage-bait, didn't have the air of a self-described healer either. Her quilt-mate, a boy who wore blue jeans and a Nine Inch Nails t-shirt, was obviously the not-quite-as-unfortunate-looking-as-he-should-have-been spawn of Randy and

Moonjava.

"Samantha Thomas?" Gracie asked.

"Yeah. What's this about?"

"And, Friendo DeForest?" He turned to the boy.

"Um, yeah." The couple exchanged a surprised glance.

"Happy birthday," said Gracie.

"Oh no." Friendo took a step back. "You aren't a stripper, are you?" Gracie looked down at himself. It was the first time he'd even been mistaken for a stripper. "My parents went a little overboard this year. Let me tell you, I'm underage, so please don't show me anything to corrupt my impressionable mind."

"Do I look like a stripper?"

Friendo tilted his head and shrugged. "You look like a stripper my dad would hire, yeah."

"I could see that," Gracie said.

"You know my dad?"

Gracie shrugged. "Your parents came into the station tonight and reported you missing."

Friendo rolled his eyes. "Aren't you supposed to wait seventy-two hours or something before you come looking for me?"

"Your mother made it sound like your disappearance was a hate crime."

"A hate crime," Samantha laughed. "Holy shit! She is fucking crazy!"

"That may be, but in the current atmosphere we need to take all such claims under advisement."

"There wasn't any hate crime," said Friendo. "God, this whole thing is a never-ending fucking joke."

"Can we talk inside?" Gracie gestured past the kids. "Are your parents home?"

"No, um, they're at the movies. But sure, come in." Samantha and Friendo stepped aside.

The room was small, filled by a mud-brown sectional and its matching ottoman. Some banal Adam Sandler comedy from the 90s played on the seventy-inch screen that hung on the far wall, and on the ottoman sat a flat serving tray, its contents covered by a sheet of leopard-print muslin.

Gracie took a seat on the long side of the sectional, in front of the covered serving tray. Under the sheet he made out the shapes of beer cans and an ashtray. All he smelled was cigarettes, but he imagined there was a joint propped on the edge for later.

Gracie laid his hand on the edge of the tray and pushed it aside. The muslin slowly slid from the tray as he watched the color drain from their faces. But he pulled his hand away before anything incriminating was revealed. A couple cans of beer wasn't a big deal. Even a joint. He was fucking with them because when you try to hide shit under a semi-transparent cloth that form-fits to whatever is under it, you're creating your own problems.

In Detroit, he would have already heard that *them beers* were *someone else's*, and that *they stepped out*, and *no, we don't know when they gonna be back.*

"Why don't you come have a seat?" Gracie gestured to the couch.

In unison, and still under the quilt, the pair sat on the short arm of the couch. Moments ago they looked so cozy. Now, Samantha and Friendo stared at the illicit leopard-print bulge with eyes full of guilt. Yet, like their parents, were too entitled to lie about it or make up an excuse.

"So, sixteenth birthday today. What happen, parents don't like little Miss Thang here and didn't invite her to the party, so you run away?"

"What?" Friendo retracted, looking almost offended.

"I don't know? Help me out. Parents report you missing, say there was a hate crime, and I find you here with your girlfriend."

"She's not my girlfriend. We just kissed."

"Listen, the entire party was a shit show," said Samantha. "I've known Friendo since first grade, and this is who Randy and Moonjava are. They use Friendo to push their socio-political agenda."

"Please, Sam, it is totally not that big of a fucking deal. You make them sound like Nazis. At worst, they are postmodern rednecks parading around in proverbial Technicolor capirotes."

"Enough with the vocabulary gymnastics. Can you tell me why you ran away?"

"I didn't run away. Dad freaked out about his place in the world. See, his brand of midlife crisis would always hinge on what I said and did tonight. Then mom passed out, or pretended to. Who can tell the difference anymore, right? So, I said my piece. After that, I came here."

"What did you say?"

"Okay, so this going to sound like an apology video on YouTube, but it just has to. I'm not sorry, but I'm straight."

Gracie waited for an elaboration, but none came. He realized he'd missed something when he saw the incredulity glued to Samantha's face.

"I mean, isn't that fucked up?" said Samantha. "They go to the police for that?"

"Hold on, let me get this straight." Gracie connected the dots in his head: Birthday party. Gender reveal. Disappointment. The kids were waiting for him to catch up, but he was lost. "Nope, I don't get it."

"Don't get what?" asked Friendo.

"You're straight." Gracie hesitated.

"I came out as straight."

"So, when you kissed Samantha, all hell broke loose? What, did your parents want you to come out as gay?"

"God, no! They would have been just as pissed about that. It's all just so fucking binary."

"And I'm lost again. Is this a transgender thing?"

"My god. You really are straight, through and through, aren't you?" said Samantha.

"This isn't about me. Help me understand where the hate crime story originated."

"I told you. I came out as straight and they're pissed about it."

"Straight, gay, trans, bi? I don't get it? What do they want from you?"

"Thank you!" Samantha said.

"Anything else on the spectrum. Perioriented, demisexual, gynosexual, androsexual. There are dozens of genders and sexual orientations to choose from, they wanted me to come out as something that challenged the status quo. So, I did. I challenged their status quo."

"And it was totally fucking worth it. You should have seen Moonjava hit the ground when we kissed."

"Bitch, you had your eyes open?"

"Sorry, not sorry. I had to."

Gracie reached forward and pulled back the leopard-print covering. Friendo and Samantha's celebratory giggles ceased, and they froze as he exposed the evidence of their evening. Gracie ignored the minor drug paraphernalia and grabbed one of the unopened beers from the tray. He cracked the top and guzzled the swill down in one go.

"Your mom," Gracie crunched the can and set it back where he got it, "back at the station she called me Cis. What is that?"

"Basically, it's the opposite of transgender. You can be Cis and not straight."

"That's it? Your mom used it like it's a fucking insult."

"Well," Friendo shrugged. "If the shoe fits."

"The fuck? We're both straight, here. Why is it an insult for me?"

"Oh, I'm not straight. I'm gay. I came out as straight to make my parents mad."

"Kid, I don't got time for this. Fuck with your parents all you want, but don't fuck with the police, and definitely don't fuck with me."

"Why not? This whole thing is a never-ending joke. Why stop now?"

"Just be straight with me. You're gay?"

"Yes, Officer."

"And her?"

"Oh, I'm not gay," giggled Samantha, and Gracie just now noticed how stoned they were.

Gracie put his hands to his face. He wanted to scream.

"Look at him," laughed Friendo. "He is so the kind of dude who would think it was gay to suck a woman's dick."

"What?" asked Gracie, trying to reconnect the circuits in his brain that Friendo just fried.

"Oh, please. You and your strict genital preference, you just love to tell all the boys down at the station how straight you are, then when it comes time to suck a girls dick you get all gay on her. So fucking Cis."

"Very Cis," said Samantha.

He shook his head and got to his feet. "Y'all create your own fucking problems."

"Oh, look at him," mocked Friendo. "You know they say the most sensitive part of the penis is the man attached to it."

Gracie ignored that comment as he inched his way around the ottoman and made for the door.

Outside, the cool night air was bullshit and everyone breathing it in at that moment could get fucked. The door swung open and Gracie stopped on the porch long enough to choke in a lungful.

Friendo came out after him. "You think I create my own problems? Fuck you. My parents are the problem. This fucking city and people like you are the problem. I didn't choose to be who I am. I am who I am! God, I can't wait to get out of this city and its faux-progressive façade."

"Have a good night, Mr. DeForest." Gracie stepped off the porch. "You've had a rough evening, Imma look the other way on the MIP tonight for both you and Ms. Thomas."

"Like anyone cares about fucking pot anymore! Get fucked, Porky!"

As Gracie stepped off the porch, exhibiting that poise and grace the LT had asked of him, headlights fell across the front lawn. A little Prius veered toward the house, hopped the curb in front of his squad car, and came to a stop. Both the driver and passenger doors swung open in unison, and out climbed Randy and Moonjava.

Randy bolted past Gracie and leaped up the porch steps. He wrapped his arms around Friendo. "I've got them! I've got them!"

Moonjava followed Randy across the yard, but stopped in front of Gracie. "Why the hell aren't they in cuffs yet?" She shoved Gracie. He didn't budge.

"You come to the station to report a missing person, then it turns into a hate crime, and now you want an arrest? Listen, I've had enough. Go home!"

"Go home? I've had just about enough of you." Moonjava side-stepped away from Gracie. "If you won't arrest my child for the crime of hate they committed against the world by declaring their straightness, then I have nothing else to say to you. Randy! Bring them down to the car."

On the porch, Friendo shoved his father away. "Dad, will you stop? This is ridiculous." Randy stumbled back, tripping over a wicker end table and crashed onto a matching padded bench.

"Assault! Assault!" Randy cried as he writhed into a fetal position and softly lowered himself to the cement porch floor.

"There! See! Now you have another reason." Moonjava pointed toward the porch.

Gracie slid her aside and continued toward the squad car.

"Everything alright?"

The call came from the shadow of the apartment building next door. A man stepped into the night light: late 30s, African American. He held a tiny cooing baby, snug in a pink sleep-sack, in his arms.

Gracie stopped. "Everything's fine. Why don't you head back inside?"

"All due respect, Officer, I was asking the neighbors."

"No, everything is not alright!" said Moonjava. "This *police officer* has been harassing our family all night! Now, he even witnessed an assault on my husband, and he still won't act on our behalf. I'm sure a strong black brother like yourself can understand." She began to chant: "No justice for minorities in Ferndale! No justice for minorities in Ferndale!"

"Brother? Lady, who are you?" The neighbor looked past Moonjava to Samantha, who was on the porch next to Friendo. "Sam, you good?"

"I'm okay, Chris. Thanks." She shrugged and put her hand to her mouth as she shook her head.

"Why don't you head back inside, Sam? Wait for your parents to get home," said the neighbor.

"Thank you, sir. You should head back inside as well, take care of that baby," said Gracie.

"Naw, we're good here. Standing on my property, and all."

Gracie turned from the neighbor as whooping and hollering echoed against the trees and parked cars and sleeping houses in the distance. The first wave of downtown drunks leaving the bars and heading home.

"Randy, get up! There are fifty-two genders, is this really the one you want to identify as right now? If the police won't act, we will." As Randy got to his feet, Moonjava turned her attention to Friendo. "I'm sorry, but we are going to have to place you under citizen's arrest."

"Mom! Enough. There is no such thing. Go away."

Moonjava looked to Gracie. "Is that true? That's not true. I can arrest someone as a citizen, right?"

"Oh, so now you want my advice?" asked Gracie. "Enough of this bullshit!" In the distance, the drunken laughter, which had grown closer, fell silent. "Let's everybody go back inside or get back into your vehicle. Time to call it a night."

"I'm calling the cops," said the neighbor.

"The cops are already here!" The neighbor glared at Gracie as he pulled out his cell phone. "Fine, call the police. Mrs. DeForest, you and your husband need to leave."

"This is private property. You can't ask us to leave unless the homeowner requests it." Randy put his hands on his hips and cocked his head at a jaunty angle.

"Shut up, Randy! Did he just *Missus* me, again?"

"Oh, shit!" The drunken slur bellowed from the sidewalk. "Mama's pissed!"

Gracie turned. On the sidewalk, in front of the overgrown yard, stood three dudes whose facial hair looked like progress pictures: One was clean shaven, one had a twisted-up mustache, and the last had a full bushy beard. They all had their phones out, capturing the moment for mobile posterity.

"Oh, man. You are so fucked," said the one with the beard.

Moonjava fed into their calls. "This ignorant Cis has infringed enough on me tonight."

"That's some bullshit, man. Leave her alone," said the one with the mustache.

"You three, keep fucking walking!" Gracie ordered the drunks, but they didn't listen. He turned to Moonjava. "Mrs. DeForest, please get in your car and go home!"

"I'd like to report an incident involving a police officer," said the neighbor into his phone.

Moonjava shoved her finger into Gracie's chest. "I told you that my name is Moonjava, and still you insist on delegitimizing me as a person. It's time we take back our city! Citizen's arrest!"

Moonjava grabbed Gracie's wrist with both hands. She twisted her arms, trying to maneuver Gracie's behind his back, but he didn't budge.

Poise and grace. Poise and grace. Poise and grace.

"This is so going on YouTube," called the bearded one again.

Poise and grace. Poise and grace.

They surrounded Gracie. The Millennials with their cameras behind him. Moonjava in his face and twisting his wrists, Randy with the high ground on the porch.

Poise and grace.

And Friendo.

Friendo was on his phone. Thumbs busy. Texting or gaming or tweeting, he was a twenty-first century social media fucktard. Implicit in the destruction around him, but disinterested in the precise moment the rest of the world went to hell.

The neighbor was gone, disappeared back into the apartment building as dispatch would have instructed. Poor, confused and stoned Samantha was gone too. Her door closed. The lights inside turned off.

Those with something to lose hunkered down. Those with something to gain held their ground.

The Lieutenant put it in Gracie's head that it was class issues or race matters that made him resent the suburbs. That it was hard to feel empathy for affluenza related crimes when he'd seen real plagues. Things like babies freezing to death in squatted homes and young mothers selling their bodies to feed their families.

It wasn't a lack of empathy that caused the resentment, but the lack of roots. The lack of community. Marginalized places, like Detroit, were made to endure substandard infrastructure—failing schools, undrinkable water, streets buried in snow—while those on the outside asked why their residents didn't just move, why they didn't just better themselves. Be it by choice or by circumstance, endurance let roots grow deep. And roots let a place become part of who someone is.

Sam cared about her home.

The neighbor cared about his community.

Friendo didn't give a shit that his parents were causing this scene in an otherwise quiet neighborhood.

The hipsters, they'd be gone in a year or two or ten. Transients who would never contribute to the city or community in any meaningful way but with their pocketbooks. They marginalized the neighborhood for views and karma and the approval of faceless millions online.

Moonjava and Randy had commoditized a community that was based on self-realization rather than municipal borders. Identity became currency, and judgment a credit card. They exploited the LGBTQ+ culture for their own superiority, with no interest in propagating compassion and understanding.

Capitalists of enlightenment, they didn't give a damn about Ferndale. They bought out real estate, pricing out the potential of third- and fourth-generation families, co-opting the brand and communities for their own gain.

It was too bad Gracie didn't think in vowels.

"Let go of my arm, Ma'am." Gracie twisted free of her grip and stepped back.

"Don't call me a fucking woman!" She stepped back into his face. "Do you have any idea the struggle we go through because of people like you? Never witnessed actual pain or suffering, never experienced a moment of discrimination unless you were the one doling it out. I don't identify as Ma'am! How dare you assume my pronouns are *she/her*, you Cis piece of shit!"

Moonjava shoved him again, but he'd moved enough. They called him Cis, but he knew he wasn't. He was just a straight white man who believed in community.

Thr prnn wsn't sh.

Moonjava cocked her neck back and snapped it forward, letting loose a glob of spit that smacked Gracie square in the nose.

"I used to wonder if chromosomes were a social construct invented to keep the white man in power. A tool of the oppressor. But after meeting you, officer, I am a believer because it's clear that you have never met an extra chromosome that you didn't like. So, you listen to me now, I am Moonjava of Ferndale and I—"

Poise and grace?

Ps nd grc ths.

Gracie balled his fist and broke Moonjava's face.

The video received a million views the week it was uploaded on YouTube.

Book II

The Yannis Institute

rattled through the vintage horn speakers. The vinyl spun on a 1974 Hi-Fi Magnavox Imperial. An oak monster with ornate cabinet pulls and a hidden turntable underneath the slide top. They were a formative pair, the stereo and Waits, each having taken their own toll on Chris's life.

Chris had tweaked his back pivoting the beast through the doorway, Adrian smashed a toe positioning it against the wall, Stella broke a nail wiping the cobwebs from the horn, and Erica, who escaped all but unscathed, stopped laughing when the claw foot gouged a deep track in hardwood and the corner took a chunk out of the drywall in the stairwell.

And that was just moving it into their apartment.

Once in place, the stationary piece went on to do further damage.

Friends stubbed their toes on the player whenever they visited. The sliding top decapitated unsuspecting wine glasses. And a short in the AM/FM wiring sometimes interrupted their themed party music with dead radio static that wouldn't go away until their guests left. Not to mention the noise complaints from the neighbor—though this did get Chris some good album suggestions from the high schooler who lived in the house next door.

Despised and lauded in equal measure, the record player not only provided a centerpiece for their home, but it gave context to his and Erica's life. It was the first piece of furniture they had picked out together, and even when it stopped working, he'd be damned before he got rid of it. Besides, with all the damage it caused coming in, he wasn't likely to have any friends willing to risk moving it out.

Without understanding what he might find inside, Chris pulled the cabinet away from the wall. With hammer and screwdriver in hand, he squeezed into the gap, and pried at the jagged nails that held this flimsy protective covering in place. A dozen nails later, Chris stared at the indecipherable innards: wires and transistors layered in a quarter inch of dust and dirt and dander.

A large square manual lay on the floor of the cabinet. He dredged his fingers through the dust and lifted the shape, revealing the pristine original condition of the wood below. He'd hoped the manual might offer a place to start with the necessary repairs, but as he brushed off the cover he found not the booklet, but an album.

Erica wanted the player so they could host martini parties and classy soirees with era appropriate music. Chris didn't collect vinyl yet, but he wanted to. He'd always loved music, and his curated playlists on Spotify weren't enough to prove it any longer. So, while Erica picked up Harry Belafonte, Benny Goodman, and Serge Gainsborough albums (along with a few Riot Grrrl classics that reminded her of her young and less-than-vulnerable teenage years), Chris got the Nirvana and Tribe Called Quest and Violent Femmes and Public Enemy albums he'd grown up on.

The first album that played through the cabinet once Chris had fixed it was the one found buried in its dusty heart. *Rain Dogs* by *Tom Waits*. Waits had the voice of a decorative bullhorn, and it was unlike any other music Chris had heard before, despite his self-professed musicophile status. When the needle dropped, the percussive assault both choked up and roused Chris: a startling experience that, thanks to the hisses and pops of the neglected vinyl, turned him from a casual fan into a collector.

Each of his records had a story. There were hundreds, maybe even thousands of them. There was more than music pressed into those grooves; memories and moments of life were ingrained into every album he owned. Pint glasses stolen from hep breweries, plants left behind by fired managers, and bullshit trinkets from who-the-fuck-cares. Every moment had a track, a song. Lines and lyrics sparked sprawling tales of the life he and Erica had built together. And while they may have been broke for the majority of it, they were never broken.

Now that Erica was pregnant, she was looking to fix what was baroque. Replace their carefree hodgepodge—which had become a treacherous and extravagant minefield—with a home that was both respectable and restrained. Big box rather than thrift store or garage sale. She wanted everything to be trackless. Music wasn't as important to her as it was to Chris, and she was ready to make new memories, rather than associate everything with the baggage they used to call adventure.

The driftwood sailor that sat next to the printer, the coatrack made of baby doll arms, the gasmask thumb-tacked to the wall over the dinner table, and the miniature statue of the Archangel Gabriel that they had both found so hilarious. She wished them all gone. These quirky conversation starters had become, at best, reminders of the life she wanted to leave behind, or at worst, choking hazards.

The baby was still six months away, but Erica was nesting.

Fresh coats of paint, oriental rugs laid over the dingy old carpet. All that baggage put on the curb or shoved into boxes in the backs of closets. Bassinette next to the couch instead of their globe with the hidden mini bar. Diapers and wipes where his video games used to be.

It was hard to be angry folding baby clothes, tiny, delicate, glorified doll apparel. Be easier to get mad at a kitten mewing to be held. But Chris managed. He tucked in the little arms with the fervor of an assassin snapping a neck to avoid detection, tossed each onesie into the basket as if dunking on an opponent in NBA 2K2X on the PlayStation. Only that made Erica his opposition, and she had to refold every one of Chris's missed free throws.

"If you don't want to do this, you don't have to."

"Who said I don't want to do this?"

"Your effort." She gave him a snide look.

"I'm fine. Didn't sleep well last night."

"Then go to bed. And, I'm not trying to be that woman, cause this isn't a competition, but neither did I. I know carrying your baby doesn't imbue me with magical privilege, but I am existing in this bubble of borrowed time. My body isn't mine right now. And the stress that I deal with, she does too—"

While Erica schooled him in this new facet of his pre-fatherly responsibility, Chris watched her fold their baby's clothes on their glass-top coffee table. Meticulous and perfect, and one more way he couldn't keep up with her. She was smart and dedicated and loved him. Chris worried the next thing to go would be the coffee table. It was all steel and glass and unique. A glass top with a functioning reproduction of a Belgium train station clock face below. They had gotten the table on an impromptu road-trip to Frankenmuth. It had been their fifth date, and after browsing Bronner's CHRISTmas Wonderland, eating their fill of Zehnder's roasted chicken, wiener schnitzel, and burnt-butter spätzle, they finished their day at a secondhand shop where they spotted the table and agreed they had to have it.

They had sex for the first time that night. A compact disc copy of Tricky's *Pre-millennium Tension* played on the big beefy stereo that all the kids their age had growing up, and which they'd held onto because its sleek lines and matte black looked sick, but was shit at reproducing any decent sound quality. Not that they were listening to the music, anyway.

Every day the apartment became less and less theirs, ownership given up to that mass of cells growing in Erica's belly. Maybe if she were showing, it wouldn't have been such an adjustment. But new aversions popped up all the time: food and sex and sharp objects, and at three months every instance of irritability seemed directed at Chris.

"Oh God! What's that smell?" The queen of multi-bitching found something else that rubbed her the wrong way, and it was easier to attempt a blind fix than to ask for clarification. Because more often than not, there was no clarification.

Chris stood and walked to the window. A cool mid-day breeze brought in the patter from the street below—young professionals, city natives, and bar-hoppers parked in the subdivisions to avoid parking fees downtown—and with the sounds came smells of cigarettes and restaurants and passing vehicles.

He slid the window closed, cutting off the sounds and scents that had brought them to this apartment in the first place. Anymore, Ferndale was changing. New high-rise construction projects and increasingly gentrified neighborhoods. But when they had moved in, of all the neighboring communities, this was the place to be in the Metro area. Royal Oak had begun to believe its own hype a decade ago and was festering in that echo. Ann Arbor was fun, but full of intellectuals—both earned and self-described—and Chris had no time for elitist bullshit. Detroit had been teasing a renaissance for years, and only now, thanks to Masood, was that even beginning to come to pass.

No, it was Ferndale that fit the couple's lifestyle of hip breweries, unique ethnic eateries, and rustic boutique shops. But beyond all those aesthetic attractions, Ferndale lived up to being the welcoming and inclusive city it promised to be, and was the only place where the landlord didn't glare or smirk or leer or comment at his tattoos or her lithe Irish dreads, at his deep black hand interwoven with her pale white fingers.

"What are you doing?"

"Closing the window? You said something smelled bad."

"In here. Something smells bad in here. Open it back up, please?" she said as unkindly as possible.

He slid the window back open, accidently jamming it into the sill loudly. All he could smell was waxy residue coming from the stumps of the tiny green candles she'd been burning earlier and the copious amounts of basil leaves she'd tucked into her purse.

"Seriously, where is that coming from?"

"All I smell is basil."

"Stop. That's not it. You can't smell that?" A nauseated frown appeared on her lips as she scanned the room. "It's that."

Erica pointed across the room at the turntable.

"The fucking record player?"

"Don't swear at me."

"I'm not swearing at you. I don't want to get rid of everything."

"We're not getting rid of everything."

"It sure as hell feels like it."

"Why are you in such a shitty mood?"

"I'm not. And don't swear at me!"

"You're throwing the clothes, snapping at me. How am I supposed to talk to you?"

"I'm not—" He took a deep breath, "I'm not doing either of those things."

"Whatever. Never mind."

"No. Not never mind. I don't want to get rid of the record player!"

"I didn't say we should!"

"You pointed right at it!"

"I pointed at the skull!"

Chris looked at the skull. "You want to get rid of the skull?"

"It could fall on the baby. And besides, we're not going to be burning incense once she's here. Smoke is bad for the baby."

"No shit."

"I said don't swear at me."

"Sorry."

"Whatever."

Erica went back to folding the baby clothes while Chris contemplated taking the bait again.

Whatever.

Neither of them wanted to fight, but the reality of having a baby was scarier than either wanted to admit. Even to each other. Their friends who already had babies talked like the change was instant. One second the baby was an idea, the next it was there and everyone had to step up. They didn't talk about the nine months of hospice leading up to the arrival. The slow and terminal case your freedom suffered as responsibility spread to every facet of life.

While Erica stopped having her period, and felt her breasts swell as the embryo settled in her womb—and would eventually feel her pelvis separate and pop with each step she took—Chris had nothing physical to tell him that life had flipped to the B side.

He could smell the skull now, the Shiva and Osiris, Litha and Mabon. Nag Champa, Egyptian Musk, Patchouli, and however many other scents that had collected on a hollow ceramic skull over the course of their relationship. None of it was offensive to him. The skull sat, covered in an antique dusting of burnt incense, on a decorative tray on top of Chris' Magnavox. Erica's spirituality and connection to the natural world was nothing Chris ever felt—no matter how hard he tried to for her. But he liked the smell of her worship and spells, and enjoyed relaxing in the earthy aromas together. It was a subtle and small reminder of easier-going times.

"Can't we hold on to it until the baby comes? See how you feel then? We can put it out of the baby's reach?"

"This isn't about how I'll feel later, it's about how I feel now!"

"Well, it never bothered you before!"

"I was never pregnant before!"

"No?" Chris regretted the word as soon as it passed his lips.

They hadn't spoken of it in over a year, and that tiny word was cruel and loaded in a way he hadn't intended.

Erica dropped the pink onesie she'd half folded. It landed in a tented heap. She got to her feet and crossed the room.

Their apartment was small, and it took deliberation to cross the room as slowly as she had. Standing in front of the turntable, she snatched the skull from its alter. She gagged nauseously as the incense dust coated her hands and sleeves. Chris half-expected to have to dodge the skull if Erica decided to chuck it at him.

But she didn't.

She marched back across the room, past Chris, and turned toward their bedroom. She passed the bookcase next to their door and slammed the skull down on the top shelf.

"Out of baby's reach." Her voice was flat and stern, and she coughed and gagged as the dust sifted down onto her. Without another word, she disappeared into the bedroom and slammed the door behind her.

The tremor rattled the shelf, and the skull tumbled off the edge. It landed on the floor with a bounce-less, concussive *thunk*.

She'd made her point. The skull had to go.

Chris rose and scooped up the skull, grabbed his jacket from the baby-arm coat rack—which would surely be their next fight, but one thing at a time—and opened the apartment door.

"I'll be back later!" Chris yelled and *tried* not to slam the door as he left.

Nate tried to hide his disappointment. He'd ordered the sliced artisanal brioche loaf appetizer with the pureed nut spread and grape relish reduction, and what showed up was a peanut butter and jelly sandwich. When the server asked if everything looked good, he was uncomfortable saying that it did. But it was better than the awkwardness of being honest.

Comfort zones were Nate's forte. And in the last hour, he'd stepped out of his more times than he'd ever care to again. So sure, everything looked great. All the other artists he knew loved this shit: hip eateries, outsider art. Anything dark, challenging, off-putting, or strange. Nate was an artist too, but he hated this shit, and *Trough* was the absolute epitome of all that he was averse to.

After suffering through the reservation line, where he watched dozens of people pose for selfies with the mangled patio table out front, and being led through the profoundly barren space of the restaurant itself—which the *Metro Times* described as a "scathing indictment of the faux-upcycled whimsy so many other establishments try to shove down their patron's throats" and served dishes "created exclusively by trans people of color"—the evening was teetering on the event horizon of bedlam.

Nate liked comfort, both in his surroundings and his art. Not motel art. Not motel comfort. He didn't want to shock people, nor drown them in trite nostalgia or kitsch mediums. He didn't paint beachside vistas at sunset, or impressionistic crowds of people walking the streets of Paris. His art was, as described by a buyer, "high-class, low-thought, and impulsive. Obvious and infuriating, because anyone could have done it." It was a quick sketch of the Detroit Riverfront that he'd done on his iPad as an NFT.

Non-fungible tokens (NFTs) were the current trend in the world of modern art. Unlike other digital images, NFTs were verifiable assets. Unique and incapable of being forged or copied in any true, worthwhile sense. From digital trading cards to a spacious and totally virtual four-thousand square-foot house, the use of NFTs to monetize that which previously would have been logistically impossible due to the fluid nature of digital data was exploding. To jump on the bandwagon, and as a joke, he'd set the buy it now option at $500,000.

It sold in two hours.

The sale provided a much-needed ego boost after a near decade of his wife, Kate—the Chief Community Relations Officer for Masood Pharmaceuticals—being the sole wage-earner, but at the same time he hated it. He'd created nothing out of something. He'd physically sketched the breathtaking Detroit skyline and created a piece of blockchain art that the right power outage and server crash could wipe from existence. And the fact that it sold for half a million dollars only added more fuel to society's fire to display affluence.

"You alright, babe?" Kate reached across the table and squeezed his hand.

"Yeah." He smiled, but gazed past his wife. Men and women dressed to the nines surrounded them, while the staff looked like they came from a Rock n' Roll BBQ. Piercings, dyed hair, leather, spikes, and chains.

"I know this place is a bit wild for you, but I've heard amazing things. Trip Advisor, Metro Times. Even the trolls on Yelp are raving."

"Yeah." He picked up half of the PB & J sandwich. "It looks impressive."

It looked like a PB & J sandwich.

"Right? Plus, I wanted to get you out of the studio, to be amongst the people again." Kate took the other triangle. They tapped the halves together and dug in.

It's not that it was bad, but like everything else in life, it didn't live up to the hype. And it was a peanut butter and jelly sandwich, so it's not like there was much hype to live up to. Not like girlfriends or cars or home ownership, those had hype. Staying up late, being an early bird, lot of hype there, too. Rebooted movie franchises and revived television shows, holy shit, the hype!

But perusing this menu, being forced to choose between the night's specials of Nutella Lasagna and American Falafel (with red sauce!), adulting really wasn't living up to its hype either.

Raised under his parents' roof—the moral Fuehrer's that they were—Nate had longed to move out, be an adult, to do what he wanted when he wanted. Under his parents' roof the only thing that ever lived up to the hype was the same thing that was tantamount to slapping his mother across the face: sex. Premarital sex. His father had made grandiose statements attesting to his continued virginity, and that Nate's mother herself had never been naked a day in her life. And, having been taught of the immaculate conception of Jesus in Sunday school, it wasn't until Nate was sixteen that he realized he wasn't the second coming of Christ, immaculately conceived by God's chosen parental beings.

When Nate hit puberty, the birds-and-bees speech he was given detailed how erections disrespected his parents, grandparents, and future wife, and touching your erection disrespected Ronald Reagan and God.

His family values were taught in a tongue-in-cheek manner, but were nonetheless enforced tooth and nail. Both of his older brothers had been caught in various stages of undress with girls, and Nate had learned to improvise thanks to their mistakes. Not that premarital sex was even in the cards for Nate in his teenage years (shy around girls as he had been) but there was always the next best thing.

And thus, Nate became the MacGyver (the original, not the reboot) of masturbation.

He would pull the basement railing from the wall, crack a tile on the bathroom floor, remove the doorknob from the pantry, and then "lose" all of his father's screw drivers. He'd find coupons and sales going on at craft stores across town, let his mother's car run in the driveway so she'd have to stop for gas while she was out. He used his unconventional problem-solving skills and extensive knowledge of the TV guide to plan his weekend around his father's trips to the hardware store, his mother's scrapbook outings, and re-runs of Baywatch to assure that he would not be disturbed, and that his secret shame wouldn't lead him to meet the same fate his brothers had. The house would be still and quiet, and in his room he'd build a pleasure palace of pillows and blankets. And for five, ten, fifteen minutes, he'd melt away to his own private Pleasure Town, population: Nate.

Well, Nate and C.J. Parker.

When he and Kate got together, she thought his rituals and the way he set the mood were romantic, thought they were for her. In reality, he'd become so accustomed to his own grip of reality that it was the only way he could hope to perform in any intimate fashion. By the time they were playing for keeps in the baby-making department, neither of them even noticed how formal their sex had become. Because even with tracking ovulation, wearing specific underwear to optimize sperm count, and being cognizant of both the depth and angle in which their moment ended, sex still lived up to the hype, and he was confident in his abilities to perform and deliver.

"So, I'm sure you've noticed that I've been a little quiet since I got back from Ohio," said Kate as she finished her appetizer, "But I have some news."

Kate had been talking about coming here since they moved to Ferndale, kept saying that they would have to *go eat at Trough for a special occasion.* Now that they were here, Nate was fairly certain she was going to tell him she was pregnant.

"What did you buy?" he asked, toying with her, not wanting to ruin her surprise.

"You think that the only reason I take you out is because I bought something?"

"Well, when you planned an eighteen-day trip to Disney, this is pretty much how you told me."

Kate crossed her arms and smirked. "I didn't buy anything."

"I know you didn't buy anything."

"You know? What are you giving me shit for?"

"Because." He was about to do what he promised himself he wouldn't. "I didn't want to ruin your surprise. We've been trying for so long now, and like you said, you've been a little distant." Nate reached across the table and took Kate's hands. "Plus, not that I was snooping, but I found the tests in the bathroom trash."

"Oh—"

"No, it's great! At first I was a little sad that you didn't tell me right away, but when you said we were going out for a fancy dinner, I understood. Seriously, Kate, you are going to be the best mom!"

"No, um, I mean, thank you. But," she hesitated longer than Nate liked, "I'm not pregnant."

"What? What about the tests?"

"I don't know. They were all negative. Maybe you had them upside-down?"

"I'm not an idiot!"

"I didn't say you were."

"Why are we here? You said you had news. You aren't leaving me because we can't get pregnant, are you?"

"Will you shut up?! I'm not leaving you. I made us an appointment at a fertility clinic."

"Come again?" Nate grabbed his beer and took a swig, half of which dribbled down his chin and dotted his pressed button-down.

"Don't freak out. The consultation is still a few months away. It is the absolute most exclusive fertility clinic. And your sale, it almost entirely covers the process from inception to birth."

"Almost covers?! Kate, that was—how much was—holy shit." Nate started hyperventilating.

"Calm down, calm down. If you want me to cancel I will, but The Yannis Institute is on the bleeding edge of genetic research. I know it's a lot of money, but," again with the long pause, "you do want a baby, right?"

And there it was. He did. He did want a baby. At this rate, it was only going to cost him his first born. "No, no. I do. Don't cancel. So, what, we go in, consult the doctor, give blood samples, and we're on our way?" Nate gulped down his beer and nodded. And nodded and nodded and nodded. "Alright, I can do that."

"Yep. Exactly that. Except, instead of blood, they'll need a semen sample."

Nate opened his mouth, but he could only fill the gaping silence with another swig of beer. As if Pam Anderson and Carmen Electra and Nicole Eggert screamed out in his head and were suddenly silenced. He didn't live with mom and dad anymore, but even still he planned his day around the extra time needed to build and dismantle his pleasure palace to ensure Kate never discovered his shame.

"Nate, relax."

"So, you're saying that I'm going to have to—*do that*—there?"

"It's a professional clinic. It's what they do. Please, don't make this weird."

"Can't I just bring a sample from home?"

"Ew! God, no! I said don't make this weird!"

"Kate, I have a hard enough time doing that when you're home. I'm not sure if I can perform in a building full of strangers."

"You do it when I'm home?"

Nate hesitated. "I have—"

"Seriously? Why didn't you come and get me? Maybe I would have been in the mood."

He did. She wasn't. He shrugged, smiled, "You in the mood now?"

"No! And from now until the appointment, you need to keep your junk under control. I want an accurate sample. We're going on a strict regimen. This is about procreation, not recreation."

"Do I get a last meal before we go on lockdown?"

"Your Nutella Lasagna is on the way."

"That's not what I meant."

"I know what you meant, but I'm serious. I want a good sperm count from you. That means none of your forts, or whatever. Think of your mother or Ronald Reagan or whatever you need to do to keep it in your pants until it's time."

"Forts?" She knows! "What forts?" How the fuck does she know?

"Forts, whatever. Don't make me say it. Just don't." Kate glanced aside. "Let's table this, here comes the food."

A young woman of color, with purple hair and a pierced lip, marched across the restaurant, holding a serving tray over the heads of the other seated patrons. Steam rose from one half of the tray while mist drizzled down from the other.

"The Nutella Lasagna and the Balto-Slavic Mucho Nacho?" asked the server.

"Um," Kate replied.

The server lowered the tray, and with uncanny precision and balance, presented their meals. She set a steaming pile of crusty bread triangles, piled high with wild mushrooms, millet, barley, and oats, and smothered in a borscht and birch-tree-syrup cheese sauce in front of Kate. Nate's meal took a little more maneuvering, as the server fished a thick mitten out of her back pocket. The Nutella Lasagna was served on a slab of dry ice and garnished with an unpeeled banana.

"Be careful," the server warned Nate. "That plate is cold."

"I can see that." He looked down at his entrée and back up to the server. "I'm sorry, I have a question about the menu, please."

"I'm sorry, but the men I please are none of your business."

Kate snorted a laugh and covered her mouth as Nate turned red.

"No, no, no. No, no. No." Nate tried to be eloquent enough to fumble over his words, but instead just repeated the same one over and over again until he finally took a deep breath. Said, "I mean, I thought I ordered an entrée. This looks like a dessert."

"Our meals aren't tied to that flap of meat in your mouth that you call a palate. When the divine whispers inspiration into Chef Alejandro from the great beyond they consider not what the masses want, but rather what nourishment their souls need. Would you like me to take it back and let the Chef know that you do not care for the cuisine of the transgender community?"

"That's fine, I was just—"

"Eric!" She turned and shouted back toward the kitchen.

"Babe, you're making a scene." Kate hid her face behind her hand.

"Table thirteen doesn't want the Nutella Lasagna!"

"No, no, no. That's not what I'm saying—"

"So, you're happy?"

"Yeah, I just—"

The waitress turned to Kate before Nate had even fully conceded. "You?"

Kate nodded.

"Good." She trotted away as Nate peaked sheepishly at the nearby tables whose patrons had snuck glances during the waitress's tirade. But the scene was over, and they'd returned to their meals as if nothing had happened.

"Babe, that was super embarrassing."

"You think that was embarrassing?" He glanced around to make sure no one was listening. "You're asking me to masturbate in public with some nurse on the other side of the door knowing exactly what I'm doing."

"Stop being dramatic. You'll go in, look at some porn, wham, bam, finish in a cup."

"How can you be so nonchalant about this? You don't even like porn."

"This is a means to an end, not a routine."

"You want to know how this is going to end?" Nate grabbed the half-frozen banana from his plate and downed the last of the beer. He slid the mug over and death-gripped his banana provocatively to demonstrate its lack of flexibility. "See? It doesn't bend like that. There's no way I'll even be able to get a sample into the cup, let alone—" His enthusiastic squeeze broke the banana in half. Pureed fruit squeezed through his fingers. The ooze drip-dropped and landed in the mug.

Kate smiled at his fortuitous aim. "Never doubted you."

"That was a fluke! Please, Kate. Don't make me do this."

"Do I have to be the man in this relationship? You get to masturbate into a cup. You want to know what I have to go through?" Kate opened her purse and grabbed her phone. She unlocked it, tapped her bookmarks. "Okay, this is from his website: *Doctor Yannis will perform a general physical exam, a breast exam, and a comprehensive pelvic exam that will determine the size, shape, and position of your reproductive organs*—"

"Whoa-whoa. The doctor has to stick stuff inside you?"

"Did you not take Sex-Ed? Holy shit, did aunt-mom and uncle-dad home school you?"

It wasn't that he didn't know what a pelvic exam was, it was more that he had willfully pled ignorant to the jury of his hormones. He liked how women curved in all the right places, and it was way easier to imagine that they did so for his enjoyment, rather than for the greater biological good of the species.

"I don't enjoy thinking about it, okay?"

"Neither do I. But again, it's a means to an end. And like you said, I'm going to make a great mom. And you, you'll surprise us all and make a really great dad."

"Hey!" He fished the broken banana out of the mug and tossed it at Kate.

"Or at least our child will have an older sibling to look up to," she said as she plucked the banana chunk up off her lap and tossed it onto the table.

After they finished their meals, Nate excused himself from the table. The night hadn't gone as expected, and while he wasn't excited at the prospect of the goings-on that would take place at the clinic, the idea of being a father after all this trying was exciting.

On the way to the restroom, Nate paused for a moment to look out the front window of the restaurant. The line still felt days long, and he couldn't imagine that all those people waiting would be seated before closing time. But they didn't mind. In fact, the longer he looked, the more he realized that most of the people loitering out front weren't in line at all. They were gawkers and hipsters and influencers, all buying into the bullshit of the broken table out front as if it were a pointed and influential piece of art, not the remnants of the car accident that had happened that morning. The way they flocked to it, it was what? Inspiring? He hated to admit that, but—but there they were: high-class, low-effort, impulsive. Making something out of nothing. It was such a basic and intrinsic element of human nature. The way generations survived back when we were all living in caves. It's strange, the way inspiration manifests.

He and Kate needed a clinic to create such nimble symmetry.

Despite the validation of worth the sale of his last piece provided, it also left him profoundly unsatisfied in a way that he could not pinpoint until now. Regardless of the cashflow he'd been able to create with his NFT sale, he longed to see, if not interact with, some random patchwork of people standing in front of something he created. Whether it was to praise or deride it, it didn't matter. At least not in theory. In practice, Nate wasn't sure he could take a thoughtful and harsh critique of any of his work. Though making a stupid amount of money did help him care a little bit less about that.

Whatever was happening around that broken patio table had an energy, a truth that was unique to the physical world. It was tangible and visceral in a way could never be recreated virtually. And he wanted a piece of it. Whatever he created next needed to be free of affluence and commoditization. Something the world would to be able to touch as much as it would touch the world.

The Bitter Nail was a smoky place full of drunkards and musicians and connoisseurs of complex microbrews. It looked like a hole-in-the-wall diner. Booths lined the walls, and a lone window let in light from the street. A long counter stretched the length of the room and an old Armenian woman, the owner's mother, stood where the counter met the wall smoking cigarettes and barking orders. The staff was warm, tables always clean, and local hooligan artwork hung for sale on the walls. In the summer they would hoist the side wall open, creating a steel canopy over the sidewalk, and the loud music would pour out into the streets, imbuing patrons with permission to match the jukebox's volume. Now that fall had arrived, the patrons kept a more moderate volume, one that matched the equally seasonally-depressed jukebox.

But it was all a façade. Behind the counter there was a short and dark brick hallway that gave way to the joint's real appeal. A backroom, an unofficial bar with no windows and club lighting and gloomy corners. The place was a halfway-house where the city's off-duty municipal service men could blow off steam alongside locals and late-night EDM-heads looking to keep the party going. There was no door, no one to stop anyone from going into the back. Admission was granted purely by knowing where to go. The state ordinance was no alcohol sales after two. *The Bitter Nail* served until dawn, sometimes later. It was a demilitarized zone where, so long as nothing truly fucked up went down, everyone there let a lot slide without condemnation or arrest. Where, come morning, it was not uncommon to see cop and criminal alike walk out side-by-side shielding their eyes from the sun and part ways, off to punch the clock of adversity once again.

Chris and Erica had remained comfortably drunk there from paycheck to paycheck for the better part, and parts, of their relationship. Now Chris shared a narrow booth with Stella. They'd met when they worked at *Trough* together and had become fast friends. Which was easy to do there, considering the executive chef's pretentious bullshit.

"Better slow down there, cowboy, daddy issues work both ways."

Stella, with her short black hair and bangs that cut across her face like the wing of a raven, sipped her estery Raspberry Ale.

"Been a long day." He rolled the triple IPA around his mouth.

"Sounds like it! So, you saw the accident? Was the guy really dressed like a knight?"

"I swear! Craziest shit I've seen in a long time. Dude galloped down the center of the road, and wham! Launched that umbrella through the car window."

Stella smiled, amused by the mental image. "What were you even doing out that early?"

"Erica ordered carry-out from *Trough* again. Was picking it up for her."

"At least their brunch isn't bullshit. More than I can say for the rest of the menu."

"I was, like, right there when the dude ripped the umbrella from the table."

"And did you see everybody out there tonight, taking pictures of that table like Tyree Guyton put it there?"

Chris shook his head, took another sip of his IPA. Stella turned her attention to the dusty skull in the middle of the table.

"So, she really wants you to get rid of that thing?"

"The smell bothers her, I guess."

"What's her deal with scents? I remember, like a year ago, she was over at my place and she got super nauseous about like, the way a plant smelled or something."

Chris swallowed hard. He caught their server's eye, raised two fingers for another round, and changed the subject. "Where's everyone else tonight? Figured I'd run into more than just you. Maybe Christine, or Gwen and Rick, even Eric's crazy ass."

"Well, Eric's working down the street. Rick and Gwen are fighting. Again. So, who knows with them? And Christine, I don't know where she is, I'm not her mom." Stella finished her beer. "You got a problem with just seeing me?"

"No. Not at all. Was looking to blow off some steam and Rick is a good, obnoxious blunt object to catch it."

"Tell me how you really feel?"

"Sorry. Erica's got me in a mood."

"And that's why I stay single."

"Smart girl. You already done with, what's his name?"

"Who, Javi? Maybe not done with him, but he's working up north until it snows. And it's not like we were going anywhere. We hardly made it out of the apartment."

The server came up behind Chris and set their drinks down. He slapped Chris on the back. "Hey, heard the news. Congrats, brother. This round's on the house."

"No. You don't have to do that."

"It's no problem. My kid is almost six. Great age, man. Being a parent is incredible. Enjoy it!" He slapped Chris on the back again, gave a quick nod and a sincere smile before wandering off to another table.

Stella smiled sarcastically and matched the server's cadence, "I hear six is a great age."

Her acerbic tone in the face of the server's earnestness didn't sit right with Chris, and he faked a smile to keep the evening light. In another life Stella would have been his type, regardless of the fact that she had been only three when he graduated high school. But now, his outlook on life had bittered, and he'd lost his taste for that sweet ego boost malicious cruelty provided. Her cruel sarcasm only cemented the age difference even more.

Chris had come out to appease Erica and get rid of the skull, maybe recapture a little youthful vulnerability while he was at it. But beer after beer and he still couldn't get drunk, couldn't even catch a buzz. He was old and resilient. It wasn't only his body that felt old and nostalgic, but the moment as well. Sitting with Stella, Chris felt like it was Erica across from him. Not the Erica of now, but the Erica of then, of when they first met. Back when they would sit and stare at each other, knowing full well that they would end the night in bed together.

PJ Harvey's sonic wall of reverb pouring from the jukebox was all that kept Chris and Stella apart. Under the table, their legs intertwined. The booths were small, but this was something else.

The server brought another round and, as the echoing esoterics of *To Bring You My Love* swelled, Chris pressed his knee against the inside of her thigh. Stella sipped her beer, leaned in close. "You familiar with the Latin phrase: *Amor Fati*?"

"Naw. I don't think so?"

"It means: Hey, wanna go back to my place?"

That didn't sound right to him, but at the same time it kind of did. Sound right. And wrong. And nice. Chris had no desire to abandon Erica and the baby, but he'd be lying if the idea of settling in for a life with Stella didn't give him pause. Maybe even more than pause. For a split second he saw that life with her. A glimpse of some other timeline where right now he reached across this table and kissed her and they paid their tab and left together. A long silence followed by the bed. A long silence followed by a life where personality wasn't something to be purged, but embraced.

Stella blushed. Chris slid his hand across the table and opened his mouth, but before he could voice his intrigue, a voice coming from across the room interrupted their moment. "Ho-lee shit!"

Chris and Stella pulled their legs apart and turned. A thin man in a black coat, his hair pulled up into a bun, drunkenly swaggered toward them.

"Hey, Rick." Stella waved.

Rick fell into the booth next to Stella, put an arm around her. "You hear Gwen and I broke up? I invested all our savings into Rocket stocks. She thinks it's stupid. I think she's impatient."

"Yeah. She told me."

"Seriously, these hedge funds are trying to short-sale this shit. All we got to do is hold that shit. You want to talk about redistributing wealth? Just wait. Wall Street is gonna be in fucking panic-mode by this time next year."

"I don't know anything about the stock market."

"I would ask if I could go home with you tonight and explain it to you, but I'm so fucked up I don't know if I could even manage to make a puddle in my own belly button."

Chris rolled his eyes in disgust as a second shadow fell across the table. He'd expected it to be the server there to get Rick a drink, but when he turned he found a tall and olive-skinned stranger, with hair and beard that could have belonged to a lapsed Hasidic Jew, standing there.

"Can I help you?" Stella asked.

"This is Yannis." Rick held a hand out to introduce the man. "You may know him from the internet."

Rick was dressed from head to toe in black, but Yannis's ensemble more than made up for that drab attire. To the untrained eye, his outfit was more fey than couture. Every piece of clothing he wore was a different, solid shade. Each shoe, each sock. Pant, shirt, jacket, tie, hat. A mismatched rainbow mafia. But Yannis carried himself vainly. He understood which colors suited him, but rather than impress, he dressed to disrupt.

Chris held out a hand. "Good to meet you."

"Time is an artificial construct. Chances are we've met before, it just hasn't happened yet. Whether this meeting is good, or our first, is entirely up for debate." Yannis shook Chris's hand.

"Right," said Chris. "You want to sit, or is that going to disrupt the laws of the universe?"

Yannis hesitated for a moment. "Too early to tell."

Chris shook his head and slid over, letting Yannis take a seat.

Rick looked across the table at Chris. "I know you, right?"

"No, I'm not sure we've met before." They had. They worked together at *Trough* too. The aloof bullshit was Rick's thing, and Chris knew how to feed it back to him.

"Shut the fuck up, man. We used to work together. Chris, isn't it? Glad to be out of the service industry, am I right?"

"Wouldn't know, man. I'm still cooking."

"My condolences. But buck up, chap. Careers are proof that we're living in a simulation. Dead-end jobs preserve our future."

Stella finished her beer and turned to Rick. "Wait. You're not at Hockeytown anymore?"

"No, not for more than a year. I'm a professional asshole now."

Chris could raise a glass to that. "Cheers," he said to himself, and took a sip.

"Shut the fuck up." Stella shoved Rick. "What the hell does that mean?"

"I'm a physical manifestation of Yelp. A human message board. A rouser of rabbles. The official title I've given myself is Avant Garde Philistine, but that's only a fancy way of saying asshole. People, businesses, whoever, they hire me to spread messages, influence feelings, create movements. Speaking of that, have you two been to *Trough* yet?"

"We used to work there. That's how we know each other," said Chris.

"Right! So you already know the secret. Cool. If people only knew, right? Man, only reason that place is popular is because they hired me. You know that? Sometimes I organize unions, sometimes I pass out tiki torches, sometimes I'm the ninety-nine percent. If the money is right, call my name. I'll be your sledgehammer."

"So, you're more of a dick than an asshole?"

"Tomato, tomato." He didn't say the words differently.

Chris turned to Yannis. "And you're good associating with this guy."

"Good with it? Shit, bro, I hired him. I'm up to my elbows in work. It never hurts to have a cheerleader getting the crowd excited about some of it."

"What do you do?"

"I'm an alchemist."

"Oh, for Christ's sake. Buckle up, Stella, we're sharing our table with an asshole and an alchemist. Shit, society is worried about Gen Y yeeting into traffic, while every other generation is turning the world into their own personal vaudeville act. But don't worry, these two got us covered. So, did you figure out how to turn lead into gold yet?"

"Not lead, but vinyl. I own Noir Moon. By far my most profitable venture. And let me tell you brother, you don't dress like this if you're poor." He popped his teal collar with his orange and magenta gloves, fished a business card out of his pocket and handed it over.

"No shit? I been meaning to check you out." Chris looked at the card. "This says Indo-Uranium Sauna Sessions, Lysergic Perception Detoxification, and Defenestration?"

"Oh, sorry. Wrong card." Yannis went back to his pocket. He shuffled through dozens of cards and finally handed the *Noir Moon* one to Chris. "You buying or selling?"

But Chris couldn't bring himself to look at the card. "Um." He watched Rick drunkenly nuzzle his head under Stella's arm and rest it against her breast. "Not sure yet." He hated Rick even more now.

"You better not be selling." Stella bumped her leg against Chris's under the table.

"Not planning to. Least not yet."

"I'll be pissed if she makes you sell."

"Ooh," said Yannis. "Am I missing some drama here?"

"My girlfriend's pregnant, and honestly, we're pretty broke. Been purging to make ends meet."

"His collection is amazing. Should be like, sent to a museum or an archive or something. Tell him, Rick." Stella jabbed her elbow into Rick.

He jolted awake, said, "Soon, there's only gonna be seven planets left, because I'm gonna destroy Uranus."

"Don't be a jackass, tell your friend about Chris's record collection."

"Chris is broke? What's new?" Rick reached for his wallet. "Don't worry, I got this." He slapped his credit card onto the table.

"You're a useless drunk." Stella picked up the card, about to ignore him, but the name on it caught her attention. "This says Richard Nistarim. Did they spell your last name wrong?"

"No, I did. Wanted to see if they'd catch it when I applied."

"Right, anyway," said Yannis. "I'm intrigued. I hope for your sake that you don't have to sell, but if you do—" He pulled a business card from his pocket.

"Yeah, man. Thanks. You already gave me a card."

"I gave you one for the record store. This is for the baby. I'm a fertility specialist. If you need a doctor or midwife to deliver your baby, please think of me. Also, come 4th of July, think of me for your firework needs. I'm selling the big ones this year. Can lift a car right off the ground!"

"I'll keep that in mind," Chris said, rolling his eyes. But he was only half paying attention to Yannis at this point. Rick's laser-like focus on Stella was distracting. He was in love with Erica, but in the back of his mind, Stella had always been a maybe.

"Hey," Rick said, and Chris felt him kick Stella under the table. "That's my fifth card with the wrong name on it."

"What?" she asked.

"I'm vanishing into a sea of noise."

"No, you're just drunk."

"I am. But that's my body." Rick sat up and leaned in toward her. "My identity is decidedly less attributablbelblellele. Attributableble—Attributable." Rick finally slurred.

"What does that even mean?" asked Chris.

"Attributablelele means—"

"No, jackass, the names on the cards."

"My card there, with the wrong name, it's mine, but only legally. I have other cards through that same bank, all with different names. Stupid names too, like Terry R. Wrist, and Pierre Delecto. Or with misprinted or transposed social security numbers or addresses. It all used to be done by computers, but ever since the AI Protection Act was passed, a certain percentage of human jobs needed to be retained for every position. The occasional human error allows things to slip through the cracks. And I'm persisthan—perthast."

"Persistent," Chris helped him out. "Don't hurt yourself."

Rick gave Chris a thumbs-up, flipped open his wallet, and handed another card to Stella. "Here. Take it. Buy some stuff. Pretend it's a gift card. Pretend you won a contest and here's your prize."

"Rick?" She held her hand out but didn't take the card.

"It's not perfect. Received thirty rejections for each one of my successes, but I kept at it for a while."

Chris shook his head. This guy's bullshit was off the charts.

"Seriously, take it." He offered the card to Stella again. "There's five hundred dollars on there. Take a trip. Max it out. I've given away all the other cards, and by this time next week I'll have spent money in all corners of the world." He smacked Yannis. "Right?"

"What's that?" asked Yannis, giving Rick a moment of attention.

"Using that card I gave you, where did you go again?"

"The Danakil Depression in Ethiopia. Scary place. Exciting."

"And all on my dime!" Rick knocked his fist on the table.

"And all on your dime." Yannis raised his drink.

"But, if it's all in your name, won't you have to pay it back?" asked Stella.

"Maybe," said Rick. "But I can't be in all of these places at once. Someone somewhere fucked up, and unless I notice and report the fraud, the bank's not going to notice most random transactions until it's too late."

"What's the point?" Chris asked, unable to hide his annoyance. "I mean, at best you fuck your credit. And at worst you get a bunch of entry-level people, maybe even some cashiers fired, because you want to prove that you can be David to Goliath."

"Sure, you know, there's that. But in my line of work—"

"You mean being a professional asshole?"

"I do." Rick nonchalantly took a drink. Chris felt like he did it just to annoy him. "In my line of work, existing off the grid has its benefits. And if we're really going to be honest, unless you go full train-hopping, rubber tramp, living-in-the-woods-off-of-twigs-and-berries-Grizzly-Adams, there ain't no way to disappear no more. Not unless you create so much signal, all they see is noise."

"Fucking genius!" Yannis raised his glass again. Chris had nothing to say, but he did begrudgingly raise his glass as well.

"That's amazing!" said Stella, and Chris's heart broke a little. "Can we all do that? Fucking quit life and go live!"

"And there's the can of worms." Rick leaned back. "Me doing this, it's easy to slip under the radar. If more people got in on the scam, it goes to reason that the banks would catch on."

Stella deflated. Chris felt doubly bad about this. He didn't enjoy seeing Stella become disenchanted, but neither did he like being so protective over a woman that wasn't his pregnant girlfriend.

"Unless," Rick said, "Unless everybody did it."

"Right." Chris laughed. "Good luck getting Ma and Pa Republican to purposely shove their shit into the garbage disposal so a bunch of us lowlifes can, as Stella put it, quit life and go live. They don't give a shit about us."

"Nah, they don't need to *give* a shit. They've already *given* their shit. Stella, you ever have a Hotmail account?"

"Is that like a porn site?"

"You're really dating yourself there, Rick," said Chris.

Rick ignored Chris. "No, the other spelling of male. Owned by Yahoo, it was Gmail before Gmail. Doesn't matter, what *does* matter is that it was the site everyone used for their email back in the day. Back before anyone was really concerned with cyber security. And in 2016, Yahoo learned they were hacked by the Russians, and that five hundred million user accounts were compromised."

"Holy shit." Stella smiled. "That's crazy!"

"No, fuck that. That ain't shit," said Rick. "At the same time they discovered that hack, they discovered another one that had happened before. One they never noticed. One that had exposed three billion people's personal information to the public. Social security numbers, bank information, school transcripts, security questions, password history. Basically, anyone who has ever used the internet, everything that they had ever put onto their social media, any information they have ever entered onto a website to order something, every keystroke in every search bar. It is all out there. Somewhere. And someone has it."

"Someone?" asked Chris. "I thought you said it was the Russians?"

"That was the small hack. The big one, the three billion, no one has any clue who did that. So, you see, Ma and Pa Whatever don't need to agree or consent to anything. Whoever has all that info, all they need to do is time it right, and everything will come screeching to a fucking halt. And then yeah, then we go off, quit life, and live!"

"That's fucking hot," said Stella. She was looking into Rick's eyes now.

Chris had no reason to hit him and was contemplating whether that mattered when Rick spoke again.

"So, um, just remember, if you, ah, get a gift card in the mail saying that you've won some contest or sweepstakes that you don't remember ever entering—spend that shit. Live it up, cause before long, shit ain't never going to be the same."

"And we'll have you to thank for that?"

"Chris, I'd never expect you to thank me for anything."

"Cheers." Chris lifted his empty glass.

"Cheers," said Stella

"So," said Rick, grabbing Stella's hand, "I'm heading down to a Devil's Night costume party. Wanna come?"

Stella wavered for a moment. She turned from Rick to Chris. When she didn't meet his eye, Chris knew what her answer was going to be.

"Sure! Yeah."

"Excellent!" Rick stood and helped Stella to her feet. "Let's go."

As the two stepped away from the table, Stella grabbed the skull and said, "I'll call you later, okay?"

Chris watched them leave and contemplated ordering another round.

"Well," Yannis said, patting Chris on the back. "That ain't going to end well for any of us." It was unclear if Yannis meant Rick's credit card scam, or the pair of them leaving together.

Kate caught Nate looking back at the mangled patio table one last time as they left the restaurant. When he'd come back from the restroom, he informed her he'd finally found inspiration. When he said it was the broken table out front, she didn't get it.

"Look at the way everyone gathers around. They all want a piece of it. It means something to them."

"Isn't that the table from the old man with the horse? They want a piece of what?"

"I don't know, but I don't think it's about the table. We're all stuck in this consumerism driven society, and along comes this guy who's like: Nope, to hell with that, I'm going to be a knight."

"I think the news said he was delusional, babe."

"That's beside the point. He broke free."

"I think everyone thinks what he did was silly. He got his literal fifteen minutes. By tomorrow everyone will move on when something bigger happens."

"Absolutely. Agree one hundred percent. But maybe they shouldn't. It's so easy to get lost in the tragedy; what if everyone needs to be reminded of that feeling that at any moment, that any of them could decide to be a knight?"

"I don't get it. If everyone went around riding horses, the world would turn to chaos."

"Yeah. I'm not sure I get it yet either. But there is something there. Gotta chase it, whatever it is."

"I'm happy for you." Kate stared at him, still deciding if she really was. "Hey, I want to stop at *Three M* really quick. Need to pick up some prenatal vitamins. That fine?"

Nate shrugged, and she could tell he'd disappeared back into his head. It was only vitamins, but she wanted to see excitement from him about her potential pregnancy. Instead, she was sharing him, again, with his art. His *métier*, he'd call it when he was at his most pretentious.

"Hey," she laughed, after they'd walked a few blocks. "Can I tell you something?"

"What?"

"You know those nachos I ordered?"

"Yeah?"

"I didn't order those—"

"What? Why didn't you say anything?"

"After the way she yelled at you?!"

"Kate!"

"What? She really laid into you there! I didn't want to be next!"

Nate's mouth stood agape as they basked in dim blue light.

"Hold that thought, be right back." Kate stepped away and entered the door under the three neon M's on the side of the building. She enjoyed coming for prescriptions this time of night. There was never any wait. And only needing the prenatal vitamins, the questionnaire was short and sweet.

The waiting room was empty, and the dozen kiosks around the room all stood vacant.

"Hello, KATE," said the kiosk as she approached.

She and Nate were hardly star-crossed lovers from different sides of the tracks, but if it weren't for her, his focus and dedication on his passion projects would have petered out into an obscure pipedream long ago. That's who Nate was. A pipedream kind of man. His heart was in the right place, but he focused on bettering the world around him so often, that he never bettered himself. Financially or otherwise.

He'd gotten fired from his last job—an electronics salesman—because he humiliated the owner. They had gotten in the first batch of 100-inch flat screens, and the owner was coming in to see how they looked. As the team got the store ready for his arrival, they realized the remote control for the floor model was missing. No problem. It had Bluetooth, so Nate programed his phone to control the TV. Only he hadn't noticed that someone had already attached the retractable-remote-tether to the top of the TV. The owner, who had a penchant for blowing everything out of proportion, was predictably pissed and already rattling on about how this perfectly good TV was unsellable with its remote missing, when Nate stopped him.

"Actually," Nate had stepped in to resolve the problem. "That's not for the remote control. That's the pull start."

"Excuse me?" said the owner in disbelief.

"Yeah, all these new TVs operate via Bluetooth remote. Problem is, the units are so big that they need a good priming before you hit the power button."

"No, they don't," said the owner. It was less of a statement and more a call for demonstration.

"Sure, they do. Watch."

Nate had told this story so many times.

He put his foot up on the coffee table under the TV, grabbed the tether, and gave it a good yank. And another, when, silently, the TV blinked on.

The owner lost his shit, saying, "I'm going to lose so much money on these Goddamn things!" And, "No one wants to pull-start their fucking TVs."

After an hour, Nate came clean.

They fired him on the spot.

Kate made more than enough money to support them long-term, and that stunt showed her that maybe Nate needed a breather. He'd talked about trying art, so she got him what he needed and let the phase run its course.

A decade later, here they were.

Which was fine. She wanted to see him live up to his potential. And that meant being a father.

She wanted to press the fertility issue farther, but held her tongue and enjoyed the atmosphere of the surrounding city. Record stores and restaurants and gift shops lined the road. It was all so pristine—cracks in the sidewalk weeded, planter boxes full of lush seasonal greenery, garbage cans emptied and odor-free—so perfect.

The sun was nearly set and still the streets teemed with life. It was the exact downtown experience Kate had expected in the move. A decade ago, Detroit was the destination-of-choice. Maybe to some, it still was. Maybe Nate would have fit in down there, but she wouldn't have.

Working at Masood, she would have been labeled as part of that not-so-exclusive group of young professionals flooding into the city at the behest of the global conglomerate. Over-paid, over-educated, but under-cultured masses who didn't actually care about the city.

Seeing the city on the rise in the news was always fantastic. Being part of the organization responsible for The Loop, Three M's, and returning commerce to the city in a meaningful way was exciting. But there's a difference between appreciating the hard work and effort that goes into an endeavor and caring about the end results, and wanting to build your personal life around that.

Detroit wasn't her scene, and there was no way for her to pretend that it was.

When the Ferndale Towers were announced, Kate suggested they look into reserving a unit. Ferndale was the perfect medium for them. The city had always been a haven for artists and outsiders—Nate fancied himself as both, though he'd deny calling himself either—and was now too becoming home to those with means, as well as ideas.

Their three-bedroom unit on the top floor of Building Four gave them what they each desired. The open floor-plan loft space came pre-furnished in the latest trends, they had access to a shared rooftop patio and community garden, Nate had the second (and smallest) bedroom to use as he saw fit for his studio space, and Kate turned the last bedroom into her library and study. Eventually, when she got pregnant, there would have to be a conversation concerning which one of them would give up their space to make room for the baby. The prospect was far enough away that she was sure Nate hadn't even given it any thought, while she was already building her argument in favor of keeping the library intact, as it was a shared and more universal space, over his studio.

Nate held the door for her when they arrived at their building and let her cross the threshold of the elevator first.

Once in their apartment, Nate kissed her forehead and disappeared into his studio, while Kate made her way into the bathroom. She peed and wiped, using the last of the toilet paper. And when she dropped the empty roll into the trash, she saw her discarded ovulation tests from a few days earlier.

She wanted a baby. She hadn't always; in fact, for a long time she and Nate had both been set on remaining childless and free. But one day, some maternal drive or instinct kicked in, and that all changed. As far as she could tell, too, she wanted one for the right reasons. Her career defined her, her husband gave her love. Their prospective child would not be brought into this world to fill a void, would not be a drunken mistake that she was eventually unable to live without. Their child was going to be as ineffable as her sudden urge to have one was. She wanted a baby.

Without changing her clothes, without any of the precursor work and mood setting that Nate usually required, Kate barged into the studio and kissed Nate on the back of his neck.

His studio wasn't the eyesore so many other artists' studios were. He was a hoarder through and through, but an organized one. His collected tile and brushes and wire and paint all had a place. Hood ornaments and Velcro straps and scraps of sheet metal were all sorted. Dried flowers and powdered chalk, buttons and switches, were all organized into neat drawers.

She bit his ear. The hair on his neck bristled up. It jabbed into her soft cheek painfully. She liked it. Another kiss, and another. Whether she was ovulating or not, it didn't matter. There was some deeper issue within one or both of them that kept them from conceiving. It was so unfair that so many ill-prepared people could conceive by accident, and yet, two steady, well-to-do people couldn't throw caution to the wind and make the same mistake. Only, it wasn't a mistake. Special underwear and optimum sperm count, ovulation tests and effective angles of penetration. They weren't looking to make a mistake; they were looking to make a baby.

Wet, their mouths met. Her fingers on his chest and moving down. His hands already greedily in her pants.

Bzzzt-bzzzt-bzzzt. His phone vibrated on the drafting table.

"Ignore it."

"Ignore what?"

"Your phone," she said.

"I don't hear anything," he said, pretending not to hear the phone.

Bzzzt-bzzzt-bzzzt.

Then her phone began to ring.

"Ignore it," Nate said.

She did, and unzipped his jeans. She could ignore the phone for thirty minutes.

Bzzzt-bzzzt-bzzzt. His phone again.

Bzzzt-bzzzt-bzzzt. Hers too.

What if it was work?

Bzzzt-bzzzt-bzzzt.

Bzzzt-bzzzt-bzzzt.

What the hell was going on?

Nate kissed her, and she reached for his phone.

"What are you doing?" he asked.

"It's probably some stupid weather warning. I'm turning it off so we don't have to hear it."

Kate picked up Nate's phone and stared at the Emergency Alert. This wasn't a weather alert; it was an evacuation notice.

Erica didn't know how long she sat in the bedroom after he left, but she could no longer see the incense dust from the skull swirling in the stale apartment air when she came out. Chris wasn't home yet. That was alright. He still needed to go out for drinks with friends to cool down after a fight or a long day. Hell, until Erica found out she was pregnant, whenever she had a shitty day at work or at school, she'd have done the same.

Now, when she had a bad day, she turned to the universe. She turned to the book.

After letting go of whatever intrinsic negative force resided within her, Erica imagined a comforting and calming light surrounding her. She'd let her hair down, take a deep breath and turn inwards. Once she'd heard Chris leave earlier, she let her fury go. Legs crossed, she sat on the bed, massaging her arms and body and face with her fingertips. Slow, swirling motions, like clouds. Careful, at first, to ensure that her hands flowed toward her heart. Positivity in. Soon, though, the movements became thoughtless and intuitive. That's when she saw the sigil.

It was never perfectly clear. Vaguely circular, with two appendages rising out of it. Horns, maybe, or twisted roots that branched off. And at the tip of each, five tiny fingers radiated out. She called it her *Claire de Lune*. Her moonlight.

The book—that's what she called it, but it was more of a manuscript. And even then, it looked like someone tried to write the recipe for an atomic bomb on a series of cocktail napkins. Complex calculations sandwiched between grocery lists and quotes from movies. The book was not bound, but a bunch of stained and bent pages, bundled together with rubber bands. It had been left behind at the bar a few weeks earlier, where it stayed until Erica was sure that no one was coming back for it.

She took it home and began to just glance at casually. After a week she found herself flipping back through the pages, which lead to her dedicating time to reading the teachings within. When she was younger, the idea of witchcraft and the spiritualism of nature seemed so silly despite her attraction to them. As she grew up, she assumed those inclinations would fade as so many youthful eccentricities did. The opposite happened. As she grew older, she felt more and more at peace with the frequencies of the natural world, found herself drawn to the woods and water and the moon, their clean energy giving her perspective on the clutter that had encumbered her life and heart and home.

It was after the procedure that Erica came to embrace the call, become the change she wanted. She declared herself a student of magick, and no longer was she going to accept the energies of others to drive her being. She was going to be the energy that shaped her world.

Then she got pregnant again, and the true potential of the universe became apparent.

After emerging from both her state of calm and the bedroom, the first thing she noticed was that the skull was gone. And she was sad, because she had willed it gone.

The book had taught her to affect the world with her will. It said that the journey would be difficult and slow, but that was by design. In order to perform real magick, all one had to do was declare themselves a magick user to the universe. But it was only the most stalwart who both declared this and believed it. And that was all it took. A little bit of gatekeeping kept the majority of wanna-bes and half-assers at bay. And the instructions in the book were just difficult enough to follow and live up to that it became obvious to Erica why it had been left behind at the bar.

The sadness associated with the skull being gone was only her hormones, though, the way they snip-snapped between love and hate unpredictably. She'd asked the universe to take the skull, and it had. Like cottonwood or ragweed, whatever dander lingered on the surface of the skull, her body rejected violently. Not through sneezing fits or trouble breathing, but smell. Chris had looked at her as if she were mad when she said it. A burning stick of incense had been a staple of their lives together as much as was the thick aroma from the French Press every morning. Now, it was revolting.

One summer when she was a little girl, something went bad in the refrigerator. For days, whenever she or her parents opened the door, they'd been bombarded with the scent of decay. Each of them would hold the door open with their rear ends and shuffle through the produce or the cheese drawers. Shoving aside Tupperware containers full of leftovers, inspecting each for mold or rot, and finding none. But the smell disappeared, aired out by the compressor fan clicking on from the door being held open. Then the door would shut, and all the produce and Tupperware left where it had been found. Only to have the smell return, spoiling the appetite of whoever opened the fridge next.

It was a lowdown, sweet smell that, when inhaled, sunk into the lungs and had to be coughed out. It was her father who'd finally had enough. Erica had come into the kitchen to find him on his hands and knees, a bucket of hot suds on the floor, kitchen sink overflowing with the contents of the fridge. He had a wire scrub and was scouring every surface. Spires of soap bubbles erupted from every surface, and as the compressor clicked on and off, the appliance looked as if it were breathing. The crystalline, soapy stalactites flittering out and hanging still over the course of the hour or more that her dad worked.

Finally, he closed the fridge, and with a triumphant gait, he slammed the door shut and threw away everything that he'd piled in the sink. It didn't matter if it was good or bad, new or old. It all went. And once the overflowing kitchen trash had been emptied into the garbage bin outside, her father went back to the fridge, opened the door, took a deep, deep breath, and heaved. He didn't vomit, if only because anger overpowered the urge.

The smell was back. Or it had never left.

"Is the fridge dead?" little six-year-old Erica asked. "It smells dead." Even at her age, she'd spied in on enough TV shows and movies to see how the detectives acted around a newly discovered dead body. And the smell made her want to act the same way.

"No, honey. Refrigerators don't die like that," he started, but the sentence trailed off. Without a word, her father closed the door, pressed his body against the unit, giving it a giant bear-hug. He pulled. It took a moment for the fridge to come unstuck from the spot on the floor in which it had sat for forever, but once it did, it slid freely.

Erica saw it first. The brown puddle and yellow streak leading away from it. Her father rounded the fridge and froze.

"Go." He shoved her back, maybe a bit too hard. "Go away."

"But I—"

"You, nothing. You listen to me when I say something. Go!"

She listened. He watched her back out of the kitchen and disappear around the corner.

When she heard the fridge move again, she returned, confident that her father would be too busy to notice her. She was right. But too, upon learning where that brown puddle originated, she wished she would have listened to her father.

Her hamster, Princess Toadstool, had disappeared from its cage months ago. She'd made up stories about its misadventures in the wild, the friends it had made along the way, the plots of the invading ant armada that it had foiled, the castle it had built in the attic amongst the clouds of insulation.

But there it was. Dehydrated and long dead. Its body crushed and smeared, and now, in the summer heat, finally decomposing.

It was a memory, a smell that she had blocked out and forgotten until that cool breeze had hit the skull, and that dead-pet musk hit her.

Erica stood in the doorway and rubbed her belly. Princess Toadstool had been the first thing she'd cared about and loved, aside from her parents. Now she had Chris, and soon she'd have their baby. And the smell of that skull put the image in her head of the two of them being dead and smeared across the ground.

With the skull gone, she could focus again. Before Chris returned, she finished folding the baby clothes, picked up the mess of video games that spilled out onto the carpet from the cabinet below the TV, and replaced and alphabetized the stack of records that Chris had been listening to earlier. Filing away *Built to Spill* and *Tom Waits,* she came across his *L7, Bikini Kill,* and *Sleater-Kinney* vinyl's. For a long moment, she contemplated throwing one of them on and disappearing into nostalgia the way Chris did some days. But she didn't. Nostalgia didn't have the same hold on her that it did on Chris. Not just music, but their apartment was filled with near two decades of acquired junk. And most of what they still had on display: the gasmask, the baby-arm coat rack, even the framed photos of friends and family dressed up all fancy from when she was going through her dual Steampunk/amateur photography phase, no longer held any importance to her.

Nate's sleep suffered in the months leading up to the visit at the fertility clinic. Night after night, he'd wake from a recurring dream of one faux pas after another: finishing too quickly, or too slowly, entering the lobby with his fly down and still aroused, not producing a large enough sample, or terrifyingly, producing way, way too much. In his dreams he couldn't remember if he was circumcised or not (something he was unsure of until he'd accidently seen another boy in the gym shower room). Covered in cold sweats and erections, Nate would lie in bed until dawn, trying to recall if any of the nurses were prettier than Kate, and if so, was that dream-cheating?

But on the morning of their visit, Nate was well rested, either because he'd given up on Kate agreeing to give the old-fashioned way one more try, or because no matter how badly he wanted to keep it from happening, he knew this day was going to come, and when it did, regardless of his hang-ups and habits, he was going to have to as well—in a cup.

In the waiting room, Nate was both relieved and disturbed to see that they weren't alone. A dozen other husband and wife teams sat, squeezed together as they perused release forms and medical documents. They were all there for the same reason. All there to do the same thing Nate was there to do. And if he knew why they were there, then they knew why he was there. And if all he could think about now was the erection he'd have to produce, that meant the other men were thinking the same thing. All these straight men crowded into a room together, thinking about erections. It didn't help him relax at all.

"Oh my God, did you see this?" Kate tuned her phone toward Nate. Someone on her Facebook feed had posted a photo of Camila Torres, the fifteen-year-old who'd started the Devil's Night fires last year. She was being led out of Tri-County detention center, wearing an orange jumpsuit and a bulletproof vest. "It's so sad, isn't it?"

Nate nodded. Sad, yes. And terrifying. Not because of what she did, but because of who she was. She was nobody. She was just somebody's daughter, somebody's sister. Fifteen years ago, she was just a baby that her parents had wanted. And now there she was, making them proud. Maybe she was a mistake, maybe not. Either way, she was raised and cared for enough to make it to fifteen. She was likely conceived the traditional way, but despite that, nature took its course and look how she turned out.

And how did that bode for them? They wanted a baby so badly they were willing to make it happen even as nature continually denied them.

This was too much. He needed his comfort zone. Bringing a baby into the world was all Kate wanted, was all they both wanted. But right now, this world was constricting around his mind, coiling into his lungs until every breath was short and shallow. He tried to eavesdrop on the conversation happening next to him, but that only made things worse.

"Ti tns'I, gnizama yttrep st'i?" said the woman.

"Tihsllub dellac evah dluow I erofeb em deksa evah dluow uoy fi. Si ti," the man replied.

What the hell was happening?

"Oh," Kate slapped him. "I didn't tell you about this earlier because it was coming from Trip, but—"

"Who is Trip again? I know you've mentioned his name, but you work with a lot of people."

"He's the COO's son. Kind of a weirdo, you know, every material wish granted, every emotional need ignored type of trust-fund kid. Anyway, originally, we heard this from him, so we ignored it. But I got the call from legal, and I guess there is some validity to it."

"To what?"

"There is body-cam footage of the night Camila Torres was arrested. Masood is thinking of covering her legal fees. I guess the footage is pretty damning. For the police, not the girl. I tracked down the Lieutenant who was in charge on the night of her arrest and spoke with him, and—"

"Kate and Nate Hill?" said a young nurse holding open the door to the back. She was pretty. Dangerously pretty. Pretty enough to snap Nate out of his spiral. Not like a femme fatal sexy/gorgeous/body-like-a-switchblade pretty, but not the inbred brick-chewer type that Nate wouldn't have thought twice about embarrassing himself in front of either. From one spiral to the next. It was all so shallow, yes. But a lifetime of learned behavior wasn't likely to vanish under this type of stress, so he ran with it and hoped Kate wouldn't notice.

"That's us." Kate looked to Nate. "I'll finish telling you about the work stuff on the way home."

"This way, please."

Kate pulled Nate to his feet, and they followed the nurse through the door.

"So, this is your first visit to our office?"

"It is. But we've heard great things," said Kate.

The hall was short, with three doors on either side. The nurse led them to the last door on the left and knocked.

"Yes?" said a booming, but friendly, voice from the other side of the door.

The nurse cracked the door. "The Hills are here."

"Great! Send them in."

The nurse pushed the door open and motioned for Nate and Kate to enter.

"Hello, I'm Doctor Yannis. Welcome." The olive-skinned man behind the desk held his hand out as Nate and Kate approached. The doctor had a timeless quality about him. He could have been twenty-five years old or fifty. Nate guessed he had to be closer to middle age, as he had the liberated stature of a man who no longer worried about his personal appearance.

The office, as expected, was more of a study than a man-cave. Cream walls with wood accents, bookshelves full of both books and knickknacks from a lifetime of travels, framed degrees filling the wall behind a sprawling desk, and in the corner, under a large heat lamp, a glass enclosure filled with volcanic rocks.

"Come on, babe," Kate said as she sat, patting the seat next to her.

Nate turned his focus from his surroundings back to Kate and took a seat.

"Thank you so much for seeing us today."

"Oh, it's my pleasure," said Yannis. "But let's get down to it. Without testing, it is impossible to identify where the fertility issues lie. Our first step here will be to run some preliminary tests and make sure there aren't any underlying health issues preventing pregnancy."

Nate's knee bobbed like a Geiger counter until Kate slapped her hand down to stop it. "Sorry, he's a little nervous about this whole thing."

"That is understandable. It's not every day we attempt the Seahorse Maneuver and transplant eggs from wife to husband and impregnate him with his own semen, but as we discussed on the phone, I am open to trying anything."

"Huh?!" Nate's eyes went wide.

"Um, no," said Kate. "We're here for the normal fertility consultation."

"Are you sure?" The doctor looked down to the calendar on his desk. His finger moved across the page. "Oh, you're right. I'm sorry. I had you confused with my next appointment. Happens a lot! They're both named Jerry. One with a *Y*, the other with an *I*. Great couple. Typical gender non-conformists, though. He used to be a she, she used to be a he. They wanted to try on each other's skins, so to speak, so the plumbing is still hooked up one way, they just changed the fixtures. Anyway, it was your names that got me confused. Nate and Kate. Jerry and Jerri. But Nate, don't worry about a thing. Once we identify where the kinks are, we'll iron everything out and I'll get her preggers in no time." Yannis leaned back in his chair. "And that's all I got. I like to schedule the testing a few weeks out, give the men some time to adjust to the idea of it all. So, what do you say, should we get you two lovebirds scheduled?"

Nate was uncomfortable with so much of what Doctor Yannis said, but mostly his emphasis on the *I'll* part of getting Kate pregnant.

"Yes," said Kate, definitively.

"Um—" Nate hesitated.

Yannis held up his hand. "Kate, why don't you head down to scheduling. Two doors down on the right. Your hubs and I are gonna have us a little man-on-man time. I'm known for being able to talk men into anything, so don't worry, he's onboard, he just doesn't realize it yet."

"Great!" said Kate.

"Um, babe, can *we* talk—" said Nate. But before he could finish, Kate was up and out the door.

"Talk to the doctor," she called back as the door closed.

It clicked shut, and Nate was alone with Yannis.

"You're an artist, right? I think your wife mentioned that in the application. What are you working on now?"

"Yeah," Nate was taken aback by the sudden shift to normalcy now that they were alone. "Actually, I'm working on a series right now. They're kind of my reaction to the Devil's Night fire. The way random people, places, and events turn into zeitgeist moments."

"That's beautiful, man. Truly it is. And who are you making this for?"

"Oh, um, I haven't quite—"

"I'll tell you who," Yannis cut him off. "The children! Whitney Houston said, *I believe the children are our future.* Are you going to disagree with her and disgrace the memory of the only artist to chart seven consecutive number one Billboard Hot 100 hits?" Yannis slid his chair back, pulled open a desk drawer. "I didn't think so. Without a future there is no art, without children there is no future, and without me there are no children. I am the future, I am art, I am children." He retrieved a bottle of scotch and two glasses from the drawer and slammed them down onto the desktop. "Let's take care of those nerves."

"I'm not sure a drink will help."

"My experience says otherwise." Yannis popped the cork, poured two fingers into each glass, and slid one across the desk. "I like you." And as if the credibility of the degrees on the wall weren't already suspect, "Tell you what, I get that you're nervous about letting loose in one of the designated rooms. How about I let you take care of yourself in here? At least you'll know that only one other person has ever crossed that finish line behind these doors."

"What? God, no! I don't want to do it at all. And especially not in here!"

"I knew I liked you!" Yannis downed his shot. "The last guy, I told him the same thing, and if you head over to one of those lady-boner websites, sure enough, you'll recognize this office in dozens of those videos. It's not much, but any supplemental income in this economy, am I right?"

Nate looked up to the corner of the room, and sure enough, there was a webcam pointed right at the desk. "Are you even a doctor?"

"Absolutely! I recognize I come on a little strong, but it's only because I care. I am a sperm expert. Did you know you program your sperm the moment before ejaculation? If you're scared, so are they. In your moment of bliss, they are being deployed into foreign soil. Now, do you want them to hunker down and hide, or do you want them to conquer the uterus? With my help, you can turn your sperm into a Mongolian horde"

"I find it hard to believe that that's how sperm work." Nate got to his feet. "Listen, thanks for everything, but I really don't think this is for us."

"I understand. Let me try one more thing. Okay?"

"No. Thanks."

"Okay. Have fun telling your wife that you don't want to have a baby."

Nate gritted his teeth. "Fine. What?"

"Good. Now, sit down and stare into my eyes."

Nate sat again. He half-heartedly looked across the desk.

Yannis looked back. His eyes were a deep, dark brown. It was hard not to admit that they were beautiful eyes.

"Now," Yannis said. "Picture me masturbating."

"Fuck this." Nate shoved his chair back and stood. "I love my wife, but baby or not, I'm not putting up with this B.S."

As Nate's hand reached the doorhandle, Yannis came around the desk.

"Stop," he said. "This works. Look at me."

The men again made eye contact, though their intentions differed greatly.

"I'm masturbating. Do I move my wrist, my entire arm? Are my Kegels good and strong? Does the carpet match the drapes? I don't know, this is your fantasy. Spoiler alert, there is no carpet, all hardwood down there!"

"Come on, man—" Nate looked away.

"You see that? You know me now. I know you. You want to see your wife with a belly full of baby, and deep down, you know I can get her pregnant."

"That's what I'm afraid of."

"And you should be! Because if I wasn't one-hundred percent certain, I would never be this bold. Now, do you want me to get your wife pregnant? Or do you want her to schedule you an appointment to fill up a Goddamn cup and see if you can too?"

The weeks between the consultation and this specimen visit seemed to pass faster than the three minutes he'd been waiting here. At least they weren't made to wait in the lobby up front. After checking in, a nurse greeted Kate and took her to an exam room. Nate, meanwhile, sat and waited in the hallway. He wanted to text Kate, to express, yet again, how uncomfortable this made him. But when he remembered what her examination was comprised of, the last thing he wanted to do was stress her out any further.

"Mr. Hill?" said a voice with the sugary rasp of a sitcom grandmother. Nate looked up, and sure enough, a round elderly nurse approached him. "You're a touch early. I'm surprised you didn't pass the last fellow in the hall. If you're in a rush, I can skip cleaning the room and you can go right in."

"No, no. Please, take as much, if not more time than the state requires by law."

"Oh, you. It doesn't take long at all. Just need to give her a good pat-down with a sanitation napkin. Be back in a jiff. Then I'll show you around the place. Sound good, sweetheart?"

It didn't. It didn't at all.

His skin was pale and his stomach churned as he watched the nurse vanish into the room with a spray bottle and a roll of paper towels.

Without skipping a beat, Nate swiped his phone open. He tapped away with his thumbs.

Nate: *I can't do this.*

He waited, foot tapping.

Kate: *Man up!*

Nate: *I'm trying!*

Kate: *I've seen pictures of your ex.*

Kate: *If you could finish for her, a cup should be no problem.*

She wasn't helping. He closed the chat and clicked on Reddit to distract himself.

The top item in his feed was, no surprise, Camila Torres:

Torres lawyers FOIA Police Bodycam footage from Devil's Night.

He tapped the headline, but before the article could load, the old nurse peeked around the corner at Nate.

"Alright. She's ready for you."

Nate thumbed his phone closed. He stood, hiding his urge to run, and followed her in.

The room itself was small. Clinical, sterile, nothing special at all. It was drenched in taupe, a neutral color for a room meant to illicit extremes. A lamp, large screen TV, recliner, healthy selection of pornographic videos and magazines. All it needed was beer mirrors and sports pennants to be the man cave Nate had always imagined.

"Have a seat." The nurse motioned to the chair.

"I'm good."

She shrugged. "Okay. Well, I can see that you're itching to get going, but I have a few items to go over."

Nate nodded.

"How long since you last ejaculated?"

"Um—uh—" Nate blushed. "Five days."

She checked a box. "Any nocturnal emissions?"

"No!"

Check. "Method of collection for today's sample?"

"Excuse me? Is there more than one option?"

"Mr. Hill, we are a state-of-the-art facility, and offer a variety of options for our clientele. Of course you are welcome to stick with the old standby," she motioned toward the wash station, where dozens of single-use bottles of mineral oil were stacked, "but we can provide a prostate massage, artificial vagina, penile vibratory stimulation, and," she opened a cabinet above the wash station to reveal a medieval-looking probe that gave off a magnetic hum, "electroejaculation. What do you say? No fuss, no muss. Done in a jiff."

"Jesus! No!" Nate backed away from the cabinet and fell into the recliner. "Gonna go with the old standby."

"Suit yourself." She closed the cabinet and turned her attention to the library of stimulants. "Over here you'll see that we have some literature for your perusal. Although I hesitate to call *The Feltching Quarterly* literature." She ran down her checklist. "Oh, I don't know if you brought your own lubrication, but please refrain from using it. It could taint the collection."

"Nope. Did not bring my own."

"Great. Well, if there is anything you need, don't be afraid to ask. I'll be right outside." The nurse stepped out of the door, but stopped. "Almost forgot." She pulled a small plastic specimen cup from her scrub pocket. "Here's your cup. When you're done, I need you to fold down the adhesive tab and put your initials on top."

The door clicked shut. Nate was alone. A lump formed in his throat and he had to ball his fists to keep from crying or throwing up.

He took two deep breaths and spun the recliner to make his selection. Without daring to make contact with any of the material before it was absolutely necessary, he gazed across the video titles—*Die Teekanne Arschloch, Filling Her Freudian Void, Kako Da Služi Ljudima, Black Cock Down, Pasolini's Salò, Les Cousins Dangereux, Did Nazi that Cumming*—and tried his luck with the magazines.

With two fingers on an arm that he fashioned in his mind to be a ten-foot pole, he grabbed the worn spine of a single magazine and pulled it free. Like an arcade claw-machine game, he rotated back around and released the magazine. It landed on the floor between his legs and fell open to an article. Nate flipped the pages with the sole of his shoe, looking for tits or bush or anything that would help move the lump from his throat to his pants.

After two or three big swipes, he found what he was looking for.

Big fake tits.

He undid his belt, his zipper, and worried his business awkwardly.

They looked nothing like Kate's. It had been so long since he fantasized about anyone but his wife that he was taken aback for a split second. They were unnatural. Not inhuman, but not warm and comforting either. When he was younger, all it took was a tan-line and a nip-slip to send him over the edge, but anymore, staring at the two hypnotically misaligned nipples, his orgasms were not the result of external stimulation, but internal connection.

Sure, he needed his Pleasure Palace to let his guard down, but beyond that, all other sexual energy stemmed from Kate.

He kicked the magazine away.

He didn't need it.

Nate closed his eyes. Tribal drumming filled his mind, waves rolling and crashing in the California sun. The piano came in as the surf washed across the sand and a wind-sailor shot across the horizon.

Nate ran down the beach in his red swim trunks, and Jimi

Jamison's Baywatch theme song lyrics sang from his lungs: *"Some people... something something something"* He never really paid much attention to the lyrics.

"Hey, babe." And there was Kate running next to him, dressed in her Baywatch red one-piece. "Let's have a baby."

She slipped the straps off her shoulders and revealed her—

"Hi, Nate," said a familiar voice to his left. He turned from Kate. Pam Anderson ran alongside him in a red two-piece. "Are you ready?" she asked.

And Nate belted out, *"I'll be ready! Whenever you need!"*

"Hey!" Kate smacked him. "How are you going to get me pregnant if you're thinking about her?!"

"What? No, no, no. I'm not thinking about her. This is just where she works." Nate reached for Kate, but she pulled away.

"Don't worry about her," said Pam.

"Oh, okay," said Nate, and the two of them fell to the sand as the tide washed over them. "This'll work."

A shadow fell across the sand.

"Actually," said a man's voice. Nate turned to find David Hasselhoff standing over them. Well, at least his body. From the neck up, the man had the face and voice of Doctor Yannis. "It's a scientific fact that you program your sperm to impregnate the woman you're thinking about when you ejaculate. If you're not thinking about your wife, there is a zero-percent chance this will work." Yannis looked to Kate, took her hand. "I would only think about you."

"I know you would. He's not even taking this seriously."

"No! I am. I am! I swear."

"How could you be if you're still there with her?" asked Yannis. He stood behind Kate, massaging her shoulders and kissing her neck.

"Hey!"

"Hey, nothing," said Kate. "This is your dream. You think I'm enjoying this?"

"Sure looks like it!"

"That says more about you than it does about me."

Yannis interjected, "I'm enjoying myself, in case anyone is curious."

"We're not!" said Nate and Kate in unison.

Nate pushed Pam away and stood. He was no longer wearing his bathing suit, but was too full of rage to be embarrassed by his exposure.

The sand glistened in the sun, and with every step, Nate became more of a threat. His muscles bulged and his height increased. By the time he stood in front of Kate and Yannis, he was seven and a half feet tall and carrying a glistening samurai sword.

"You don't have the stones," said Yannis. A split-second later Nate loosed his sword, and the blade severed the doctor's head, sending it flying dead-eyed into a saltwater grave.

"I can't believe you fought for me," said Kate.

"Believe it, babe," said Nate. "Now get ready."

Kate smiled. She held a cup up over her head.

Nate laughed as behind him, a lifeguard station exploded, and shrapnel tore through his body. The French call an orgasm *le petite mort*. The little death. And as Nate's herculean visage was blown to bits on that pristine Pacific Beach, so too was his cup filled in real life.

Chest heavy and back sweaty, his fingers cramped and stiff.

He set the cup on the armrest and reached for the lid.

Knock-knock! The door handle jiggled.

Panic.

P a n i c.

P a n i c!

Nate spun the chair.

The cup toppled over to the floor. Its contents poured forth from the lidless opening.

"Everything okay in there? I thought I heard a scream," asked the nurse through the door.

"Um, yeah. Give me a minute."

"Okay. Your time *is* almost up."

"What? You never said there was a time limit?!"

"No? Oops. Must have slipped my mind. You have five more minutes, or we'll have to reschedule."

"Alright." Fuck. "Thanks." Fuck. Fuck.

He couldn't do this again. No way. Nate had five minutes to turn his middle-aged refractory period into a viable sample.

He pulled out his phone and texted Kate.

Nate: *Hey*

Kate: *You done already?*

Nate: *Um… Yes and no.*

Kate: *What does that mean?*

Nate: *Dropped the cup. Sample gone.*

Kate: *WTF!*

Kate: *Make another one!*

Nate: *Talk?*

Nothing.

It went through, but she hadn't read it. She hadn't read it. Shit.

He texted her again: *Talk?*

Again: *Kate?*

Again: *Talk? Hello??!*

Bzzzt-bzzzt-bzzzt.

His phone vibrated in his hand. He tapped *talk*.

"He*l*—"

"*My legs are in stirrups at the moment. How do you expect me to help?*"

"I don't know. I can't, you know, go again right away." Nate looked down at the sleepy little nothing curled up on his lap. "It needs a recharge, you know?"

"*What are you saying?*"

"You remember when they flew you down to Orlando for training?"

"*Yeah, but what does that have to do with—we can't, babe. Not here.*"

"It's the only way, babe." The clock on the wall ticked. "I need you to talk me off."

"*No! I am not doing that right—*"

Knock-knock. Nate's eyes shot to the door. It hadn't been five minutes yet, had it? But no, the knock wasn't from his end, but hers.

"*Hello, Mrs. Hill. Sorry to keep you waiting.*" Nate could hear Doctor Yannis's voice over the phone.

"*It's no problem. Just browsing Amazon. Should I take my ear buds out?*"

Her voice. It stirred something.

"Babe, it's working. Just keep talking. Talk about anything. I just need your voice," Nate said into the phone. It was working. It was really working.

"*No, no need. Do whatever you need to do to relax,*" said Doctor Yannis.

"Keep talking," said Nate over the phone.

"*Have you ever wondered how some items on Amazon end up with such high sales rankings?*" asked Kate. And there it was. The tingle was back. Nate moved his wrist, his elbow, and she continued. "*I heard companies pay hundreds of dollars for fake reviews. And you know, it would make sense, cause how do reusable dryer balls end up as best sellers, right?*" She rambled on about a podcast she'd listened to that explained the fallibility of Amazon's product review vetting process.

And there it was. Dryer balls to podcasts to skyrockets.

Nate was in the Pleasure Palace of his mind.

He collapsed back into the recliner, cup gripped in his hand. Before he even caught his breath, he screwed the lid on the cup and secured the tab.

Knock-knock.

"Mr. Hill, that's time. I'm sorry, but if you haven't—"

"I've got it right here. On my way out."

Fifteen minutes later Kate and Nate sat in the doctor's office again, waiting for Doctor Yannis to join them. Their fingers intertwined.

Kate glanced over at Nate and smiled.

"What?" asked Nate.

Kate shrugged. "Just proud of you."

"Hey, couldn't have done it without you." Nate leaned over and kissed her on the cheek.

"I can't believe it was dryer balls that did it."

"I'm as surprised as you." He squeezed her hand.

Click. The door swung open and Yannis strolled in. "Alright, lovebirds, you are all set for now. We got everything we need from you. As soon as we get the results back, we'll be in touch and we can figure out our next steps. Sound good?"

The pair left the clinic hand-in-hand and looked up at the Broderick Tower across the street. For a time, it was the second tallest building in the city of Detroit, but it became iconic because of a massive humpback whale mural painted on its façade. Much of the mural was destroyed in the fire.

Across the street, directly below the charred remains of the mural, stood another sculpture. This newest one was, as had been the trend, larger than the rest. It was a three-dimensional recreation of the lost mural: a small pod of whales swimming below the surface of the ocean, with one member breaking through the waves and into the world above.

Kate squeezed his hand as they walked to the Ren Cen Station of the Ford/Masood Inter-Urban Loop. "I like that one."

"I did it for you. Wasn't easy."

"I know."

Once the Westerly arm of The Loop opened, it would be a quicker walk to the Millennium Village Station, and then transfer at the Ren Cen to the Northerly arm, but after all the fire damage at Ferdinand Station, that was still a few months away.

It was only a mile walk to the station, and the afternoon breeze helped Nate to relax after the day's ordeal. They'd ridden The Loop down here, but between the hum-drum design of Magic Bag Station in Ferndale and the looming knowledge of the appointment, Nate hadn't paid attention to the opulent size and meticulous detail of the station as they'd made their way to the clinic. But now, with his head cleared twice over, his pace slowed and he removed his sunglasses to take it all in.

The entrance to the Ren Cen Station was the pièce de résistance of the entire Loop system. Constructed to resemble the grill of a classic muscle car—one which Nate would never be able to name—it was nonetheless an impressive architectural addition to the already impressive riverfront. Great glass tubes, one heading north, the other west, protruded from the station. They stood at least thirty feet above the ground and gave him the feeling they were entering a theme park more than a mode of public transportation.

Inside, he'd expected to find long lines and massive crowds of suburbanites with their families and day bags and strollers and little doggies on leashes clashing with the corporate players running frantically from one meeting to the next. Instead, he found a careful order that matched the sleek glisten of the aqua quartz glass subway tiles and chrome accenting every surface. It felt like an aquarium. Benches and maps lined the walls and the couple stepped to the left to file through the turnstile and joined the queue for entry into the Loop itself.

"It's actually pretty impressive. I'll give 'em that," said Nate

"Right?" Kate took The Loop to work every day, and it no longer held the awe for her the way it did Nate. "The first few weeks I couldn't stop staring. It's just amazing. And to be part of the company that put it all together, you know?"

The line wound along the walls of the room, leading them to one of two circles on the floor. Each circle was at least fifteen feet in diameter, and, like the wheel train of a clock, it slowly guided the movements of the entire operation. Ten-seat pods that looked like clear gel caps slid out of a shaft near the roof, and with the help of wheels and pinions, wound down around tall arbors anchored to the floor and ceiling.

Kate and Nate stepped onto the great wheel and were guided toward one of the waiting gel caps.

"Destination?" said the young man in his squarely-creased green uniform.

"Magic Bag," Kate replied.

The young man nodded and led them and three others toward a pod that had a faint yellow glow to it. The pods were color-coded to the destination station.

The five riders stepped across the near invisible threshold and into the pod. They took their seats, and as the pod spun away along the track Nate could see another pod now in the position where theirs had been, and behind that another, and another. The Loop was a clock. Perfectly tuned and in time, each piece performing perfectly and precisely at every given moment. The pod didn't even jostle as it was whisked off the ground toward another shaft in the wall—this one on the opposite side of the room—that lead into The Loop itself.

"Here we go," said Kate.

The pod spun upwards and entered the shaft. For a moment, they plunged into darkness as the pod transitioned from the commuter atrium into the sealed environment of The Loop.

Nate had heard that some people could feel a magnetic pull in the fillings of their teeth during this shift, but he did not.

He squeezed Kate's hand and as they emerged from the darkness and found themselves thirty feet above Woodward, traveling four hundred miles per hour. At that speed, Nate expected all but the horizon to be a blur, but it wasn't. For the entirety of the five-minute trip, Nate stared out across the city from a vantage point that, until now, would have been impossible. And while Kate undoubtedly reveled in the prospect of her looming pregnancy, Nate gazed out, looking for a location to erect his next monolith.

Even though Steven, the VP of Digital Marketing at Masood Pharmaceuticals, liked Melody's red hair, he told her that she had resting bitch-face even when she smiled. She saw it as more of a resting what-the-fuck-did-I-do-with-my-life-face, but to each his own. He also called her a whore after she slept with him but wasn't interested in another date. The sex wasn't bad, he was just way too high maintenance for her.

They had met at her job interview for Masood and hit it off enough to meet for drinks that weekend. He'd promised reservations at *Trough*, but when he picked her up, he had to admit that his inside-track bailed on him. Instead, they walked through the Masood mid-town botanical labyrinth and gardens.

"I'm in marketing now, but coming from finance, I get called into the office of the COO himself." He flirted with her by talking about how great he was at his job, which was whatever, but whatever. "He's all losing his shit now because I guess Masood has thirteen billion invested in Sempere Capital, and they know I got the connects at Phoolan Developers." Steven said all this like she knew what he was talking about. "And BAM! Like that! Next day, Phoolan Dev is shutting that shit down. No more buy-ins, only sales. Gonna save us a couple billion at least."

"Sweet," Melody said. "Do I have to know what any of that means?"

"Naw, girl. You gonna be working with Katie Hill, right? She's all community outreach and shit."

#DodgedABulletThere #NowIfOnlyHeWouldShutUp

"Hey," she said when he segued from his stock portfolio to his collection of matching shoes and luggage. "Want to go back to your place?"

Next day at work he tracked down Melody's cubical and asked if she wanted to Netflix and chill later. She declined, and that's when he called her a whore, and a liar. Now he's posting on Facebook that he's dating an executive assistant. He called Melody a whore and didn't even have the decency to unfriend her on Facebook.

#MarketingGenius #WhatsHisName #FuckThatGuy #Literally #fml

At five thousand friends and twenty thousand followers, her social media was filled with dozens of these encounters. Every job interview led to another handful of friends and followers. Fellow applicants and secretaries, VPs and executives. CEOs, corporations, parent companies, imprints, off-shoots, MLMs. Saying *"Hello"* used to be a nicety; now, it was an invitation to follow, join, connect, and network. Strangers don't talk about the weather anymore, because there's an app for that, and some friend of a friend of a friend just launched a better one.

Melody was hired as the IT liaison between the corporation and whatever philanthropic groups and organizations Masood was looking to turn into their next tax write-off. This meant it was her job to vet every individual involved with the charity to ensure that there would be nothing that was going to come back to bite the hand that was about to feed it. She spammed emails, cloned Facebook profiles, sent friend requests and PMs, engaged in Discord groups and Slack conversations to gain backdoor access into the personal lives of those Masood was going to help.

Masood Cares? Yeah, right. Masood cares, *#AboutItself*

Today she was violating Adrian Banks and Sebastian Cooper, the two spearheading the #FreeCamilaTorres petition. They were clean, boring. Both had day jobs making under $40k. Adrian drove Uber in the evenings to make ends meet. Sebastian sold Marvel and DC art on Etsy and drove his grandfather to work. None of which was interesting nor admirable, yet their feeds were full of passenger stories, new art for sale, and updates on Grandpa's health struggles.

And as clean as these two were, they were just the right wagon for Masood to hitch itself to. It hadn't come out yet, and even within the hallowed walls of their downtown headquarters it still hadn't been mentioned, but sooner than later Masood's financial connections to a handful of hedge funds would come out, and these two and their grassroots movement gave Masood the right kind of social currency to beat whatever rap the woke mafia wanted to throw at them.

#IFeelSick

Social media used to be a way to stay in touch; now, it was a never-ending audition for the fifteen minutes of fame promised to us. And if you couldn't get famous, you could at least get rich trying.

It was all a performance. Facebook, Instagram, Tinder. They were all just private, sometimes platonic, episodes of *The Bachelor* and/or *The Bachelorette* which turned any attempt to make an actual connection into nothing more than life imitating art. If you can call reality TV art.

#SorryNotSorry #GivingUpOnDating

Intense and eye level, the glow from the monitor cast the room in a sheen of consuming aquatic wreckage. The haze of a hundred fathoms. Flickering blue dust and dander. Not the smell of chlorine or brine, but drowning nonetheless in Doritos dust and the carbonated spray of Mountain Dew. Melody hadn't always been a slob, but she was working from home and when in Rome, it was easy to emulate your coworkers.

Trenches of wrinkled shirts and pants and hoodies and bras, a coral reef of calcified pizza boxes and cans of Redbull. Shadowy tentacles crept from each piecemealed hunk of garbage, stretching away from the glowing monitor Melody stared at. She'd been *sick* (read: disgusted) for the past week, and her boss gave her permission to work from home until she was feeling better (i.e. until Jeff from accounting got the hint and stopped dropping by her desk and asking her to lunch again).

She'd met Jeff at the company game night and friended him when she saw that he was an Elvis fan. He sent her a DM, asked if she wanted to meet for a drink to talk over company expectations. When they met at *The Bitter Nail,* he'd already ordered her a drink.

"What's this?" she took a sip.

"A Susan Collins." He winked.

A Tom Collins is made of gin, sparkling water, lemon juice, and sugar.

Jeff meant to say Tom Collins.

#JeffIsAnIdiot

A Susan Collins is the same thing, only with roofies.

#JeffIsAFuckingCreep

Melody feigned cramps and talked about it being a heavy flow day until he got up and left. He paid the bill, but must have also marked his calendar, because five to eight days later he was back hounding her, wanting to pick up where they'd left off.

#Wink #Wink #Eew

She hadn't been back to work since, and because she couldn't prove he'd tampered with the drink, going to HR would have been moot. He called and texted regularly. At first she ignored them, but once he called her out for working from home, once he called her a liar, she blocked his number.

Now her days were split between YouTube and Instagram stalking. All on the clock. All on her own schedule. She was getting paid to watch viral videos, retweet clever posts, and judge Facebook Live Feeds.

Really, it was all so lonely. And while Jeff from accounting, and Steven, the Marketing VP, and damn near every other guy who'd social media-ed their way into her life over the past decade had all failed to live up to anything she'd even want to call an acquaintance, she hadn't given up on the other forty-nine percent of the population yet.

She blamed Henry for this.

Melody followed him on Twitter and Instagram because his cat was cute, but at some point, his meme game, *Game of Thrones* theorizing, and taste in music got the best of her, and she struck up a conversation.

The way Bill Gates and Steve Jobs and Elon Musk and Charles Manson all inspired blind faith amongst creative types, geniuses, psychopaths, and artists, Akbar Masood, the founder of Masood Pharmaceuticals, did the same. Even her friends outside of work wouldn't shut up about the man; they'd gone wild when she got a job working in the same building as he did. They wanted her to ask about his inspiration for the Three M Kiosks. They tagged Melody in a post about the amazing work Masood's crews were doing cleaning up the city in the hopes that Akbar would like the post. They even floated non-profit ideas past Melody to gauge whether any of them might stick and catch his interest.

Henry wasn't a Masood acolyte. He didn't give a shit about The Loop, the ocean floor mapping, or the looming cryptocurrency launch. He was karma neutral, a political void who only ever wanted to bullshit and unwind at the end of a long day of doing whatever he did. They hadn't talked about their jobs yet.

For going on a year now, their conversations had been a much-anticipated night-cap. He was there to congratulate her successes, and no matter how badly her day had gone, he was an ear to commiserate with. She hadn't put him in the friend-zone because he wasn't a friend. For all she knew, she was part of some covert Turing test and she was really carrying on a platonic relationship with some advanced AI that was testing her loyalty to Masood.

#JudgmentDay #Skynet #MasoodIsWatching

That was until he asked her out.

She found the DM waiting for her the day she'd left work *sick* and hadn't responded.

When she finally did, she lied: "Sick. Talk in a few days."

Since then, she'd buried herself in work, dodged his messages, and fell down into an ever-deepening YouTube rabbit hole. A thousand videos from one to the next to the next to the next to the next, watching Penn & Teller and Key & Peele and road rage videos and police dash cam captures and Reddit content being pilfered and monetized. All without a single click. It was a constant stream running in the background. Something to keep her mind from wandering to Henry and his unintended betrayal of expectations.

It wasn't his fault. In fact, if she was being honest with herself, she wanted nothing more than to type: *Yes yes yes yes yes.*

But she'd been burned before.

They were perfect for each other. As long as they never met.

As soon as she clocked out, she'd traded her Redbull for beer. Depression wasn't only the gift that kept on giving, it was also the friend she made along the way.

#ItsTheJourneyNotTheDestination #TaylorSwift #MileyCyrus #BeerMe #BeerMeStrength

At three in the morning, she'd killed the half-case of beer that had been in her fridge and as she let YouTube roll, debated cracking open one of the fancy six-packs she had in her pantry.

An olive-skinned man with wild eyes appeared on screen.

You can skip this ad in 5… 4… 3…

He wore an ugly-ass suit, soaring through the sky as he spoke. "Through radical rigorous research and re-polishing reports relinquished to the refuse heap, The Yannis Institute is perfectly pleased to present you with Social Lube!"

2… 1… Skip Ad.

She didn't.

Melody chuckled to herself. The places the internet took her on random were both surprising and not at all in equal measure.

#Hello #BellsTwoHeartedAle #WhereHaveYouBeenAllMyLife

"Hello, I'm Doctor Yannis, and Social Lube is the language of the next millennium." As Yannis spoke, he feigned walking, and the background scrolled aside. The cloudy sky was replaced by a candid angle from a hidden camera in a restaurant. The echo and din of the room resounded behind him. "Every video, every picture, every post online is filtered through the lens of a moment. Social media has taught us all how to solicit approval and congratulations while sitting on a throne of unpaid bills, self-esteem issues, and raging inferiority complexes. As a result, we now bring that hashtag-unfiltered-life into the real world."

Beer dribbled down her chin as she leaned in toward the monitor. Whatever algorithms her ISP was using to track her, they had her number. And she was cool with that. Beer and YouTube were way cheaper than therapy.

"Social Lube is a Rosetta Stone designed to unfilter and de-hashtag life," Yannis continued. "Be it a high-stakes meeting with foreign investors, a classroom presentation in front of hundreds of students, or an intimate first date with a potential love interest, with Social Lube, all of your fears and insecurities will be a thing of the past."

She finished one beer. Opened another. Working for Masood, vetting every well-intentioned beggar had turned Melody into a curmudgeon. Dating had made her bitter. Sure, she was drunk, but maybe *Social Lube* was what she'd been looking for. Maybe this could change her life.

"Now before you say, *this could change my life; this is what I've been looking for*," said Doctor Yannis, "stay tuned and pay attention. Over the next thirty minutes, I will show you how Social Lube has been used in practical situations, and explain not only the immediate results, but the long-term implications as well."

#HurryUp #WhyIsTheRoomSpinning

"Behind me you will see the last date between Vanya and her beau Eric. After dating for three months, Vanya came to me with her concerns about the relationship and agreed to use Social Lube to surmount them." He paused, looked directly into the camera.

Directly at Melody.

"The following footage has not been edited or altered in any way."

The doctor faded away, and the volume in the restaurant increased.

Vanya and Eric sat opposite each other at an unremarkable table. He was handsome and blonde, and all smiles as he fidgeted in an ill-fitting polo shirt and jeans. She was dressed like a hipster librarian: Slayer t-shirt under a cardigan, long skirt with a wallet-chain belt, and pink glasses.

"So, how are you doing? You okay?" asked Vanya.

"Alright. Long hours, school is killing me. Needed a break, you know? Glad to get to see you finally."

"Yeah, so I was thinking we should talk about some—"

"Did you see that article in Scientific American about life on Mars?" asked Eric.

The screen froze.

#StupidInternet

Melody clicked her mouse. Click. Click. Click.

#370ClicksShouldMakeADifference #Right

Yannis's voice reverberated over the frozen image of the couple. "It is obvious that this relationship was in its final throes, but what isn't immediately clear is the reason why. Now, let's re-watch that same scene with Social Lube applied to it."

The scene rewound dramatically.

#VHSInstagramFilter

It played again.

"So, how are you doing? You okay?" asked Vanya.

"Alright. Long hours, school is killing me. Needed a break, you know? Glad to get to see you finally."

The moment screeched to a halt, and then played backward.

"Yllanif uoy ees ot teg ot dalg. Wonk uoy, kaerb a deaden. Em gnillik si loohcs, sruoh gnol. Thgirla."

And it played backward again and again and again.

…Yllanif uOy ees ot teg ot dalg. wonk Uoy, kaREb…

Y…O…U…R…E…

The words and inflections and tones pitched up or down.

… woNk uOy, kaerb a deaTen …

N…O…T…

The cadence changed. New words emerged. A message. A statement.

… EM Pnillik si lOohRs, sTuoh gNol. Thgirla…

EM…P…O…R…T…N…T…

"You're. Not. Important."

#HolyShit #PretentiousGolfClap

The restaurant faded away, and the doctor walked onto the screen again. "Without Social Lube the lovely Vanya may have been subjected to who-knows how many more days, weeks, months, or even years with this man who exhibits zero interest in who she is as a person. Her hopes, dreams, and aspirations. And that's just it, isn't it? We can't trust our own judgment anymore, because people aren't being truthful about who they are because they don't trust their own judgment anymore. We're stuck, all of us, in this loop. Some of us more than others, but that's another story. What I'm trying to say is I believe you. I believe in you. You're an intelligent person. Now, be honest with yourself. Are you faced with a potentially life-changing opportunity, but have become so jaded beyond recognition that rather than act, you simply lie in bed and watch YouTube all day?"

At the bottom of the video, an 800-number began to scroll, followed by a list of cities in which the service was available. Los Angeles. Denver. Chicago. St. Louis. Orlando. Boston. Detroit.

"Do you only see faults and disappointments in your interactions? And are you worried that some of this may only be in your head? If so, call. The line is open twenty-four hours a day, seven days a week."

Maybe it was the beer, or maybe it was because she was lonely, but this pièce de résistance really landed: *Maybe it was in her head.* Sure, some amount of paranoia was healthy, but this was Henry she was taking about. Henry. Harmless and perfect Henry, who'd been there for her so many times. And what if he was the one?

On the screen, Doctor Yannis was moving onto his next example, but the phone was already in Melody's hand. She dialed the number and instantly sobered up. Was this stupid? A scam?

#CouldVomitRightNow

She closed YouTube, content that, yeah, tomorrow she was going to judge herself pretty harshly if she called this number.

But behind it was the chat with Henry that she'd been avoiding.

Henry: *How you feeling?*

Henry: *You okay?*

Henry: *Back to work yet?*

Henry: *Talk?*

Henry: *Need anything?*

It was spelled out a dozen ways. He cared for her. She was too jaded and aware to risk that maybe she cared for him too.

Henry: *Hey, want to get dinner some time?*

She typed.

Melody: *Hey, sorry. Been out of it.*

Melody: *Yes.*

Melody: *I'd love to get dinner.*

The doctor's 800-number stared up at her from the screen. Mocking her, daring her to call.

#BetterSafeThanSorry #ImNotJudgingYoureJudging

She hit the little green circle on her phone, and after three rings, a man's voice sleepily answered, "Hello?"

The Ford/Masood Inter-Urban Loop stretched through the city over her head. Less than nine months earlier, all that was around her now had been engulfed in flames. Despite her indifference toward working for Masood Pharma, it was impossible to deny what they were doing for Detroit. The city was going green, both in appearance and functionality. Parks were popping up everywhere, public transportation was affordable and on an income-based sliding-scale. The long-standing stigma of Detroit as the Ruin Porn capitol of the country was finally fading. The winter had been rough, but when spring came, Masood went at the infrastructure with all its might, and the results of that were more apparent than ever.

Melody made it to the address in time for her appointment, but standing in front of the fertility clinic's glass doors, she felt like she must have written something down wrong. She'd woken up hungry and hungover, and whatever address she'd chicken-scratched down on the inside of a greasy, old pizza box was next to impossible to read.

#IDontDrinkTooMuchYouDrinkTooMuch #YouDrinkTooMuch

When she stepped inside, she found herself painfully out of place. The couples in the waiting room all glanced up from their phones and forms to stare at her.

"Can I help you?" asked the receptionist as she slid the glass window open. "Hello? Ma'am?"

"Um, yeah. I think I'm in the wrong place again."

"People think they're in the wrong place a lot when they end up here. Usually they're not."

Melody looked at the receptionist again.

She threw up in her mouth a little bit.

#TwilightZone

It was Vanya. From the internet. Vanya from the *Social Lube* video. Vanya still wore her pink glasses, but she had scrubs on instead of her hipster attire. But it was her alright.

#JustBecauseYoureParanoid #DontMeanTheyreNotAfterYou

"Um, I have an eleven o'clock with Doctor Yannis?"

"Eleven?" Vanya looked down at her computer. "You?"

"I guess? That's what I was told on the phone." Or was it one o'clock? Shit! She needed to quit drinking. But until she got around to that, she'd just stick to her story. Melody pulled out her phone and pretended to be the type of person who entered important dates into her calendar. "Yep. It says eleven o'clock right here."

"Alright. This way." She buzzed open the door next to the window.

Melody found herself in another hallway with three doors on either side. Vanya led her to the last door on the left and knocked.

"Here you go."

"Sorry, I gotta ask. You're the girl from the internet, right? Is he for real, or is this all bullshit?"

Vanya gave Melody an equivocal smile.

#Bitch

She opened the door and stepped inside. "Your eleven o'clock is here."

"Send him in," said the doctor. Melody entered and Vanya closed the door behind her.

Sturdy wooden bookshelves lined the walls. Books, trophies, and knickknacks filled the shelves. Degrees and photos from around the world hung behind a massive desk. The doctor scratched notes into a manila folder as she approached.

When he finally looked up, he tilted his head. "Well, aren't you a surprise?"

He'd exchanged the reckless clashing patterns and prints he'd worn in the YouTube video for a rather drab lab coat. White and crisp and professional. She was as surprised as he was.

"Excuse me? Is something wrong?"

"No. Not at all. Just judging by our conversation, I was expecting you to be taller, and well, if I'm being frank, a man."

#HolyShit #DoISoundLikeAManWhenImDrunk

"What? No!"

"It's okay. I don't judge. This is a safe space. If your pronouns are he/him and there's the soul of a six-five, two hundred fifty pound man inside you oozing to be released, more power to you, my dude."

"Man, I'm not gonna lie. You're confusing the hell out of me."

The doctor slid the manila envelope he'd been scrawling in toward her. "This should clear things up."

She hesitated but stepped forward. As she sat down, she picked up the manila folder, and Yannis rose from his chair.

"Inside you will find a detailed rundown of the subject at hand." Yannis inched his way out from behind his desk. "Speaks seventeen languages. Has the ears and eyes of a predator—"

#Amused #Bewildered #WhoTheFuckIsThisGuy #WTFIsGoingOn

He circled the room. Melody tried to follow him, looking back and forth over each shoulder, but he vanished into a blind spot and she gave up. She stared out his window at the half-melted whale mural on the building across the street.

"Our subject partakes in the freegan lifestyle regularly. Has dozens of credit cards with slight variants to the name and social security numbers on file. Meaning that he has effectively erased himself from the financial grid. An able-bodied mountaineer, a prize-winning angler, bowls a two-seventy, frequents the opera, despises carbonated water, has no known allergies."

"What the hell is this?" She read the hand-written dossier in her hands.

#Okay #WhoDoesntDrinkSparklingWater #PeasantWaterIsGross

"Listen, I think there's been a—"

"This is no mistake. Everything I've said is true." Melody scanned the desk, only half-listening anymore. There was a cute statue of a monkey reading a book, a bottle of regular old peasant water, and yeah, a bowling trophy. "His skills are many. His weaknesses few. When you're ready, turn the page to see a photo of your target, Mr. Gracie."

#WhoTheFuckIsMrGracie

Melody flipped the page and found a professional headshot of Doctor Yannis staring back at her.

"Is this you?"

"It is. That's the man I want you to kill."

#HolUp

"The man you want me to what?"

Melody turned in time to see Yannis looming over her, a baseball bat clutched in his hands. The moment they made eye contact he brought the bat down onto her head.

#HeMissed #FuckThis

Melody threw herself to the ground as the bat bashed into the chair. The backrest buckled; the bat cracked.

"What the fuck are you doing?!" screamed Melody. She kicked the chair back toward Yannis, crawled around the desk, and reached up, blindly sweeping her arms across the desk. Her fingers found the brass bowling trophy and she held it, ready to gouge or bash with it.

"Oh," Yannis smiled, "you're good! I had reservations about hiring a woman to kill me, but I can see I made the right choice."

"Good? Okay, yeah. I'm calling the police, you Goddamn psychopath." Melody fished her cell phone out of her pocket. "Is this what you do? Lure unsuspecting women in here with that Social Lube bullshit and then beat them to death with a bat? You're a sick fucker, you know that?"

"Social Lube?" Yannis lowered his bat. "How the hell do you know about Social Lube?"

"The Goddamn internet! How do you think? You're going to fucking jail, buddy!"

"Well, yeah, but, is that why you're here? For Social Lube?"

Melody fumbled with her phone, trying to dial and keep an eye on Yannis at the same time. Meanwhile, Yannis had pulled out his own phone and was tapping away.

"Shit," said Yannis. "I see what happened."

"Do you, now? Make sure you remember it so you can tell the judge."

"Vanya double booked me. Your name's not Gracie, is it? No, you're Melody!"

#DingDingDing

"No shit, Sherlock!"

"Man, why didn't you say so?" Yannis leaned the bat against the nearby bookshelf and wiped his brow. "Wow, I was really about to provoke the wrong response from the wrong person, wasn't I? But honestly, you need some help. A man tells you to do something, and regardless of all the threatening vibes I was putting off, you still did what I said? Girl, you damaged."

Melody kept on the defense. Trophy clutched tightly, she strafed away from Yannis as he sauntered back toward his desk. "You tried to cave my head in with a baseball bat, and you're telling me I have a problem?"

"A misunderstanding, I assure you. You're here for Social Lube. It was my other eleven o'clock who I was hiring to kill me."

"Give me the bat and I'll be that eleven o'clock too. Fuck, what is wrong with you?"

"Now-now, let's not open a can of worms that we can't close. There is plenty wrong with me. In this case, sometimes research requires getting one's hands dirty. Sometimes the only way to gather raw, untainted data is to make yourself the hors d'oeuvres. Humanity can only be understood by studying all its facets. Including its end."

"Yeah, okay. I'm going to go now. See you in court."

"I understand. See you then."

Melody backed to the door and grabbed the handle.

"No. Actually, I can't understand why you're leaving. You came all this way. And I did try to kill you. The least I can do is offer you Social Lube free of charge."

"Go fuck yourself."

"Fuck me yourself, coward."

Melody stopped, smirked. She turned, "Are you serious? Buddy, I'm gonna own your ass."

"And yet, you still won't be happy. So many trust issues. So damaged. Is that what you want? Money? All this? Or do you want to feel like you again?"

"You don't know me."

"But I'm starting to. I can already hear it in your voice. You want to believe. This conversation, we're saying things to each other, but is what we're saying all that we're saying? Turn me on, dead man! Paul's dead, Melody."

"Who the fuck is Paul?"

"McCartney! Are there any other dead Paul's significant to this conversation?"

"Are there any Paul's at all who are significant to this conversation?"

"Only the one. And I know what you're thinking but don't want to say out loud: I have lost my mind."

"Pretty sure I made that thought infinitely clear."

"You did, but what you didn't say was that you're disappointed. Disappointed that I'm insane, and can't actually help you the way you wanted me to. Disappointed that I ruined your one chance to emerge from your cocoon of self-loathing by trying to kill you."

#WellNoButActuallyYes

Melody opened her mouth to say otherwise, but couldn't.

"See? Can we start over, put the attempted murder behind us, and let me help you? I mean, you're already onboard. This is a formality."

"Hot take asshole, I'm not onboard with shit."

"You can lie to me all you want. Only hurts when you lie to yourself."

#TheMoreYouKnow #AfterSchoolSpecial

"Dur, thanks, Dad," Melody mocked. "My lawyer will be in touch."

"No, they won't, but okay."

"Will you stop with that shit? I'm not a fucking liar."

"It's okay if you are. Lying can be nice. It spares feelings, but it hinders connections. And genuine connections need honesty. All we need to do is tell the truth and humanity could soar!"

"Dude, this ain't a TED Talk. Who are you performing for?"

"This isn't a performance. This is who I am. And, believe it or not, Social Lube is not bullshit. But to develop it, I had to let go of my inhibitions and accept who I was as a person. John Lennon tried to tell us, but we weren't ready. He told the truth and he was killed when he tried to warn us that Paul was dead."

"Paul McCartney isn't dead."

#HeresAnotherClueForYou

"Isn't he? Listen, Paul's dead, John's dead, George is dead. Three down, one to go. I'd be surprised if when the final battle for the soul of our planet happens, it isn't between Ringo and whatever lizard is parading around in Paul-skin. The Beatles were divine. You ever think about where the human race comes from? In the blip of time that we have been on this planet, look how fast we've destroyed it. You think we originated here? I spent some time in Ethiopia, and you know what I found there? Martian metals. What if I told you that man is from Mars, and after we fucked up that planet, our escape pod crash landed here and caused the extinction of the dinosaurs? Well, most of them. The smart ones went underground, and boy, do they want their planet back. What would you say to that?"

"Um, I'd ask, is Social Lube available for recreational use? Cause it sounds like a hell of a party drug."

"And that's not even the best part. That escape pod from Mars, guess what it was called? The Atlantis!"

"So, you've full-on drank the Kool-Aid, haven't you?"

#Jonestown #HeavensGate #Creedish

"Social Lube isn't the Kool-Aid, it's the sponge that soaks it up." Yannis took a step closer to Melody. "We want to connect, so we form thoughts. And these thoughts become language. And that language moves from our brains to our mouths to each other. It's all organized in such a way that two communications are expressed at once. Language is bi-level. Forward and reverse. It's why parables and fables, the Bible, all the stories that move us, are all full of subtext. Because subtext is programed into our DNA. Until now, we haven't been able to access it in its rawest form."

"And you figured this out how?"

"Eh, you know. I was up late one night drinking cocaine and doing lines of antifreeze and it came to me." Yannis smiled. "No, I translated sub-vocalized sound patterns. They're just words, and like anything else, once you get past all the small-talk, gibberish, and bullshit, what people are actually saying is pretty clear."

"Gotta say, last night, I was pretty drunk. And I can see how all this blew my mind. But sober, I don't know if it was the attempted murder or your dapper lab coat there, but I'm not feeling it."

#Truth #Unfiltered

Yannis held up a finger, telling her to wait. He reached into his coat pocket and retrieved a small audio recorder. The red *record* light illuminated. "Listen, I didn't ask you to come here. And I'm sure as hell not judging you for being skeptical. But you're here, and if you have questions or fears, or if life simply has too many unknowns for you at the moment, why not seize the day? Our lives and lies and actions ripple out. We're all connected, whether or not we realize it. Once those connections are apparent, what then? It's like stringing a guitar. Do we leave the strings loose and incapable of making a chord, or do we tighten and tune them?"

"It's a nice thought, but the world is a little too broken for that."

"Broken chords can sing a little, right?"

"Alright, enough of that crap." Melody thought of Henry. "Not gonna happen. I'm just not that into this."

"You're not a liar by trade, Melody, but that hasn't stopped you from convincing yourself otherwise. You can say you're not into this all you want." Yannis clicked stop on the recorder. "Or, I can play this recording of you backwards to tell you if that's true or not."

In any branch of the service, when you leave or retire, you don't stop identifying as a member of that branch. It's not former Army, not ex-Army. You're a solider no longer on active duty. The orders may be over, but the duty lives on in the heart. The same shit wasn't true for Gracie. He was ex-Police through and through. He followed orders, gave respect when it was earned, and got shit-canned for it. The video on YouTube painted quite a picture, and no matter the nuance Gracie used to spin the situation, perception was king. And they fucked him. The department spun Gracie's ousting as *Blight Removal* with the press. Now, months later, he took the only job he could find that didn't pay shit: fire clean-up. Removing blight from the city.

The irony was not lost on him.

Nearly a year after Devil's Night and there were still huge sections of the city where soot and ash lay untouched. Areas which the city had long abandoned before the fire, narcotic tissue they allowed to fester until whenever they got around to cleaning up the mess. H cld s th wrtng n th wlls; the city wasn't done suffering, not by a long shot. Those who could afford to leave had done so already. Leaving behind those who couldn't.

The crew was in Gold Coast this morning, but no one called it that anymore.

Fucking bullshit.

Neighborhood names used to elicit fucking pride. It was a city so vast it required a thousand of them. Gold Coast, Poletown, Cass Corridor, Bricktown, New Center, Millennial Park, Midtown, Brush Park, Woodbridge. Used to mean something to say that you were from Detroit. Born and raised, or simply lived there now, it didn't matter. The city adopted all who wanted to claim it as home. Before the fire, thanks to Masood and The Loop, the boundaries of the city stretched from Lake St. Clair to fucking Ann Arbor. Gracie didn't live in the city, didn't grow up here. But, fuck if he didn't still call it home, care about it like the little brother only he was allowed to pick on, and whose bullshit only he could call.

That's exactly what he'd told his lawyers, too, when they asked about his arrest of Camila Torres and her friends.

"The second I realized it was them that started the fire, I got angry. I snapped. No one fucking does that shit to my city."

And since The Loop was finished and opened to the public, the new nicknames for the neighborhoods had only gotten worse. Seemed like half the state was riding The Loop in to have lunch in the city before fucking off back home before dark. It was the suburbs all over again. No fucking community. And these fucks were renaming his city.

Gold Coast was now *Fire's End*. Bricktown was *Ashville*. Detroit was just *Soottown*.

Fuck that bullshit, and fuck Masood for letting it happen.

Fingers crossed he wouldn't have to be on that teat much longer.

They'd arrived before dawn. The streetlights still stood, though they no longer functioned. Burst orbital husks on long metal stalks, burnt black. As the city continued to rebuild they would be replaced, but Gold Coast was at the end of a long, and potentially never-ending, list. The high-beams on their trucks barely cut through the fog. Pin pricks on twilight streets. Tunnel vision.

Everything was a fucking metaphor if you let it be.

The big-rigs and dump trucks would be there at noon to begin the teardown and haul away, leaving Gracie and his two cohorts just hours to canvas the area for copper, and for bodies. Any bodies needed to be gone before the rest of the crew arrived.

Block by block, house by house, it was grueling work, ripping pipe and wire from walls. All the while, keeping vigilant for any sign of the dead. Gracie doubted that either Aleksei or Chris had ever seen a body, knew that when they inevitably stumbled upon one that he'd have for sure seen worse.

Gracie turned his brain off and performed his copper vivisections in peace. But every now and again he'd catch Chris glance his way. Chris was new, this was his first shift with Aleksei and himself. He reminded Gracie of Jackson, and not just because he was black. He was one of those dude's whose mind hadn't quite mastered the art of shutting off.

"Need something?" asked Gracie. "Wire caught or something?"

"Naw," said Chris. "Look familiar to me. Can't place you though."

"Well," Gracie never volunteered that he'd been a cop. "Been around the city for a while doing various municipal duties before I crossed over into the private sector. Probably seen me around."

"Yeah, I don't know."

Gracie shrugged and went back to twisting the cutter around the pipe in the wall.

"You like this work?" Chris asked.

Shit. He was a fucking talker.

"It's fine. Not my long-term path, but it's means to an end. A foot in the door."

"Yeah? What you looking at? They really move grunts like us up to anything decent?"

"Depends." Gracie picked up a sledge. "You got a brain, sure. If all you got is muscle, security division has open positions every once in a while."

"So which you got?"

Gracie said nothing as he brought the hammer up over his head and back down through the doorframe next to the pipe, splintering it with one hit.

As the sun rose, beams of light cut through the clouds of dust that lingered behind their work, and it became more obvious that these ruined places used to support life, foster love and creativity. These were people's homes. Now that was all gone.

"Gracie, motherfuck. Get ass here," Aleksei called from another room in his thick Russian accent.

Gracie and Chris dropped their shit and found the big man.

Aleksei stood in a kitchen, the sky burning bright and blue overhead. The ceiling and roof nothing more than a burnt frame to hold the clouds and the sun and the birds. A living portrait of the natural world played out for thousands of feet above their heads.

"I find under sink. Look." The Russian handed a sheet of paper to Gracie.

A single piece of handwritten sheet music. The Four Tops - Reach Out (I'll Be There). The initials LD scribbled in the upper right-hand corner.

"Holy shit," said Chris.

But Aleksei wasn't listening. He'd already begun to sing in a way which made it obvious he had never read sheet music in his life, nor, somehow, ever heard the song.

"What? Is this famous song?"

"You serious, man?" asked Chris.

"I never hear of these Four Tops. What is Four Tops?"

"Come on, brother! That's blasphemy!" Chris waved away Aleksei's ignorance.

"That's nothing," said Gracie. "Check out the shit I found." He produced a normal copper penny. Held it in his hand. "You smell that?"

Chris and Aleksei shook their heads. "No? What is it?"

"It's a scent," Gracie laughed, pointing to the cent in his hand. He dropped another penny next to that one. "You see the fruit?"

Again, Chris and Aleksei looked at the pair of pennies and shrugged.

"It's a pear."

"Man," said Chris, "Done with this shit. Getting back to work."

"No, one more, one more," said Gracie, hardly containing himself. He dropped a third penny into his hand. "You see the pussy?"

"No," said Aleksei. Chris stared blankly at him.

"Not for three cents you don't!" Gracie laughed and tossed the coins over his shoulder.

As Chris walked away unamused, Aleksei made a face and called out to him, "Hey, new guy. Who is Stella?"

This was a thing that Aleksei did. He would randomly call out a name, and a minute later that person would call on someone's cell phone. When there was a group of them around it turned into a game, especially when the name he called out was one of the crew's girlfriends or wives. When that happened, it turned into a tense, but jovial, waiting game to see if Neil's girl was stepping out on him with Tom. This was never the case, but it didn't stop the clean-up site from turning into a middle school classroom for sixty seconds.

Aleksei had pulled this shit a few weeks ago when The Yannis Institute called to set up today's appointment. The boys wouldn't let the shit go and Gracie came out and said that he'd gotten into wetwork and that they were hiring him to murder somebody. They all took it as a joke, but it got them to drop it, so Gracie didn't push the issue.

"The fuck," said Chris when his phone rang a minute later, and it was Stella. "How the hell you do that?"

"KGB implant antenna in brain. Let me see future," he replied.

The explanation always changed from one fantastical and ridiculous bullshit story to the next. But the *how* didn't matter. It was just funny as shit.

"So?" Aleksei pried, "Are you going to tell me who this Stella lady is?"

"Just a friend, man. Just a friend." Chris walked away from them.

"Just a friend?" asked Gracie.

"Yeah. Just a friend. Used to work together. I got this side hustle DJing, was at her place last night. Her boyfriend was throwing some stupid-ass party."

"DJ? Is this, uh, how you say, euphemism?"

"What? What the hell are you talking about?"

"You bang this Stella lady, yes? You bang her last night?"

"No. I didn't bang her. Got a baby girl at home, man. Ain't finna step out like that."

"If you say so," Aleksei said with a laugh. Gracie giggled.

"Hey, Stella," Chris gave them both the finger and stepped out of the room.

"What you think of new kid?" Aleksei took the sheet music back from Gracie, folded it up and tucked it into his pocket.

"He's fine, you know. A bit of a talker, but can talk and work at the same time and probably an IQ higher than the room temperature, so I don't give a fuck." Gracie pulled out his cell and checked the time. It was already ten AM. "Shit. Hey, Aleksei, I got that appointment at eleven downtown. I gotta duck out. Already gonna be late."

Aleksei nodded and the two parted ways with a simple bro-shake of hand slaps and fist bumps. As Gracie walked away, Aleksei shouted, "Have fun with the murder!"

Fucker still thought it was a joke.

At ten after eleven, Gracie walked through the front door of the address they had given him and stood in the waiting room of a fertility clinic.

Shit.

He stepped back outside and looked at the address again. How the hell had he written it down wrong?

"Lost?"

Gracie looked down from the fertility clinic door to find a little red-headed girl standing in front of him. "What?"

"You look lost," she said.

"Yeah, no. I don't know. I didn't think I was, but apparently I wrote down the address wrong."

"Yannis Institute?"

"Um, yeah." Gracie stepped back from the girl like she was a witch. "How did you know that?"

"I did the same thing fifteen minutes ago. This is the place. I don't know if the fertility clinic is a front, or what."

"For real?"

"Yeah. Place is weird, man."

"Yeah?"

"Oh, yeah."

"Well, thanks. Was supposed to be here at eleven, but couldn't find the place."

"Oh. You're the eleven o'clock?" she asked.

"Yeah, why?"

"Good luck," she stepped around Gracie and patted him on the arm. Gracie watched her go. A moment later she turned back to him. "Watch your head in there, dude."

"What?"

"You'll see." And she kept walking.

Whatever the fuck that meant? But, if she was any indication, this place was going to be weird.

"Hey, Stella," Chris said as he flicked off his coworkers and walked away.

"Hey! I didn't know if you were going to answer. Last night you said you had to work."

"Nah, it's cool. I'm here now, but it's a slow day."

"Cool, cool. Listen, thanks for spinning last night. Did you see I set that skull out on the table?"

"Heard. I did! Good seeing the old girl." Chris smiled, thinking back to the night he gave her the skull. "Was nothing at all."

"I know. I was just—" He swore he could hear her smiling on her end, too. *"It was nice to see you. I feel like, like I never see you."*

"Trinie keeps me busy. I'm sure Rick keeps you busy, too."

"I wish. He's always working. Even when he's home."

"Thought he was a professional asshole or some bullshit, the hell does he do at home?"

"Stocks. Do you know who Phoolan Developers are?"

"You talking about that App? For investing shit or whatever? They're fucking with the hedge funds, right? Don't tell me Rick's in on that shit too."

"Oh yeah, big time! He's at it for hours, too. It's fucking stupid. I miss going out to the bar. Like we used to."

"Fuckin' A." Chris tried to remember the last time he was at the bar, but came up blank.

"So, I know you're at work, but there is a reason I called."

"You needed an excuse to call me?"

She ignored the quip. *"You forgot a crate of records here. I didn't know if you wanted to swing by after work and pick them up?"*

"Shit," Chris pulled the phone away from his ear and paced back and forth. He retraced his steps at the party: the setup, the work, the pack-up. Sure enough, there it was, that one crate that he pushed aside after midnight. He had no recollection of repacking it into his car. "Thank you so much, Stella. I don't know what I would've done."

"You looked tired. When I saw the crate this morning, I figured you hadn't

even noticed it was gone."

"I didn't. Just glad it was at your place and not at some place that's just gonna keep my shit."

Chris was already walking back toward the site when Stella laughed. His stomach twisted at the sound. He and Erica were both too tired to laugh with each other anymore. Trinie was too young to laugh. Stella, though, her laughter was the finger of Jesus reviving a Lazarus.

"Okay," she said, *"I know you got to work. See you later?"*

"Yeah. I'll swing by. Thanks."

He hung up the phone and slipped his gloves back on.

"Oh my! Yes," said Aleksei, his back against a half-fallen wall, posed as a sexy pin-up, "You bang her now, yeah?"

"Shut the fuck up, man. We got all the copper?"

"Yes. This house is done."

"Okay, let's get going." Chris slipped his gloves back on and climbed through the broken foundation, very aware that he did not have an answer to Aleksei's assertion.

"Hey, Aleksei. Gracie? What he do before this shit? He looks so damn familiar. Can't place it."

Aleksei shrugged. "Never asked."

They had stripped three blocks clean of wire and copper before the big rig crew showed up, and hadn't come across any bodies, either. This was a big deal from what Chris understood. Usually they found at least one every shift.

Aleksei was ecstatic about this, and high-fived him as they clocked out.

"See you tomorrow, friend. Tell Stella I say, hello."

"Fuck yourself, Aleksei. Have a good one."

The two waved, and as Aleksei walked back to his truck, he began to sing again, *"For I am a rain droog too!"*

"Hey! The fuck, Aleksei? Why you singing that song?"

"Why? I don't know. Maybe it get stuck in my head from you singing it all day!"

"The fuck you talkin' about? I ain't been singing shit!"

"Oh, my friend, I agree! Your voice, it is terrible, I have been suffering all day."

"Man, I ain't been singing!"

"Singing? Mumbling? Whatever. It has tune that get stuck in my head. *I am a rain droog too!* Is catchy, no?"

Chris shook his head without saying another word. He got into his car and slammed the door shut. He didn't know what shit Aleksei was playing at now, but he didn't want any part of it.

Pulling off the lot, Chris avoided Aleksei's gaze by tapping out a quick, one-handed text.

Chris: *On my way. See you soon.*

A few minutes later he sped westward in the shadow of The Loop and got her reply.

Stella: *Okay. I'll meet you downstairs. Parking can be crazy.*

But when Chris got to The Park Avenue Hotel, he found a spot right out front, beside the terrace covered in dead vines.

"Hey," she said as Chris stepped out of the car. "You got lucky."

"At least one of us did. Rick has you guys living in a hotel?"

"Right?" she laughed, "No, it's actually apartments. Used to be a hotel way back in the day. We're renovating a unit on the seventh floor. It's crazy. But here, I brought your crate down."

Sitting behind her was a milk crate full of albums.

"Thanks. So what you gettin' up to?"

"Oh, you know, I'm sure I'll find some kind of trouble. You?"

"Looking to give myself a reprieve for a few before getting home. Just work, baby, sleep. A man ain't got no time to think in there."

"Yeah," she said, exasperated. "Was going to see if you wanted to come up, but I guess a contractor is coming over. They asked if there were any open spots up front to save it for them."

"You need me to move?"

Her face cringed an apology.

"No, it's good."

"I mean, you can still come up. It's just that there's going to be a bunch of guys around."

"No, I better get back to Erica and Trinie. Thanks for the LPs back." Chris bent and picked up the crate.

"No problem." Stella stepped forward and wrapped her arms around him. "See you later."

The hug lasted a long time, and Chris, awkwardly, could not reciprocate, his arms occupied with the crate of records. Finally, her finger sunk into his arms, and on her toes, she planted a soft kiss on his cheek. Without another word, she turned and disappeared back into the Park Ave.

Chris looked up at the building, trying to count windows up to see the seventh floor, but this close to the building it was easy to get lost in the cloudless blue vertigo sailing overhead.

It didn't matter. He'd never be able to give Erica and Trinie a place like this. The rent here, even before renovation, would be astronomical. And he was counting coppers just to eat, just to afford to put gas in the car. Hell, just to afford the damn car itself.

Like the job, Chris had gotten this old Omni when Erica started to show. Until her belly started to grow it was easy to act as if the current status quo would continue to suffice. That they could both keep taking the bus to and from work and the grocery store and doctor's appointments. But there came a point where the firmness of Erica's belly could no longer be ignored and he wanted to do right by her, and by Trinie. So, they splurged.

It was a piece of shit, this hatchback. Five hundred bucks out the door, and every morning was a coin flip whether the thing would turn over on the first, second, or third time he wrenched the key.

He buckled the crate of records into the backseat, climbed up front, and turned the key once, twice. After the third turn, the vehicle still didn't turn over.

"Motherfucker!" Chris didn't baby the car either. Piece of shit didn't deserve it. Fickle motherfucker. He tried it again. A faint whine, a few clicks.

Bzzzt-bzzzt-bzzzt. His phone vibrated out of nowhere. Where was Aleksei to give him a heads up?

Bzzzt-bzzzt-bzzzt.

He looked at his phone. It was Erica. Fuck. How the hell was he going to explain why he was all the way out here? At Stella's apartment.

The crate of records was both a reason and an excuse. It was true he was there to collect his property, but, against his better judgment, he made the effort to cross town so that he could see Stella.

Bzzzt-bzzzt-bzzzt.

And Erica would see through that difference in a heartbeat.

"Hello?" he grumbled as he tried the car again. Still nothing.

"Okay, hi," said Erica in response to his tone. *"What's wrong?"*

"Nothing. Been a long day."

"You going to be in a bad mood when you get home?"

Chris took a deep breath before not answering.

"Are you still there?"

"Yep? What's up?"

"Nothing. You leaving soon?"

"Yeah, just got in the car."

"Cool. Can you stop for me? I ordered food from Trough. Did you know they

do carry-out now?"

"I didn't realize. What did you get?"

"The Sultan."

"What the hell is The Sultan?"

"It's a Greek-style sushi burrito."

"Awesome. What did you order for me?"

"Oh, I didn't think you'd want anything. You always say we should save money. You usually never get anything when I order out. Sorry."

"Okay—"

"We can split the burrito if you want."

"Nah, I'm good. I'm gonna go, though. Listen to some music. See you when I get home."

"Alright. Love you."

But Chris already hung up.

Bzzzt-bzzzt-bzzzt.

His phone vibrated again. Christ, Erica. He just needed a Goddamn minute of peace. He pulled it out and looked at it. Not a call, an alert:

Missing Person
Missing: Roger Green, White Male
76 years old, 139 lbs. Last seen in vicinity
of Red Run Retirement Village. Danger to self.
Contact Police if spotted.

Didn't have time for that shit, either.

He tried the key again and again.

"Fuck!"

"Car trouble?" came a voice from outside. "Sounds like your battery's dead."

A middle-aged white dude in a cardigan stood near the hood of the car, holding hands with another man.

"Naw, I'm good, man." Fuck! How much did a battery cost? How the fuck do you even take a battery out of a car?

"It's no trouble. Pop the hood. I can help."

"Said I'm good, man! The fuck?"

"Come on, Chester," said the boyfriend, urging him to keep crossing the street before things escalated. Fucking white people. Black man has a bad day and suddenly they get scared.

The first dude, Chester or whatever, he smacked the hood of the car. And as he did, the digits on the radio blipped on for a split second.

"Have a better day," said Chester, and he continued on with his boyfriend into the pub across the street.

Chris held in the urge to tell the dude to go fuck himself, but with his luck, this moment of shit would turn into a world of hurt, and he'd become a statistic or stereotype. No. Saying anything, he'd end up fucking himself.

He turned the key again, and the car sputtered to life.

"Fuck yeah, motherfucker. You piece of shit! I knew you could do it. Ha Ha! Fuck you!"

He had three things on his mind as he gave both middle fingers to the dashboard, shifted into drive, and sped away.

One, he crossed his fingers the car would start again after he got Erica's food. Two, he hoped the card wouldn't get declined when he went to pay. Three, he fucking prayed that after this they'd still be able to pay their bills. And if not, that at least the Greek Sushi Bullshit would be worth it.

She always imagined herself as a cat person, the old spinster standard: moving from her parents' house to a dorm to a stated-platonic-but-assumed-lesbian relationship. Only with cats rather than a person.

At first it would be a little kitten, small and clumsy and adorable. It would curl up and fall asleep in her shoe, and Melody would have to be careful not to crush it. She'd feed it, and snuggle it, and forget to scoop its litter box often enough that she'd end up with pinkeye because of all the fecal matter that got stuck to its paws. She'd feel bad and get it a friend. And she'd get another and another. Somewhere down the line, they'd start having kittens. Eventually the toxic fumes from the unscooped boxes would overcome her, or she'd choke on dinner, alone, still watching YouTube. When the cats had eaten all they could find around the apartment, they'd move onto her. And when someone found her skeleton, mummified in hairballs and feces, they'd shake their head and go, "Yep, she was a cat lady."

#CatMom # CatLife #Meow #TheWalkingDead #Help

Henry had a cat, Mr. Pistols, which he did everything with. And Mr. Pistols wasn't a kitten. He was a full-blown hulking tomcat. Henry's social media was an autobiography of their misadventures. From bar-crawls to mountain climbing to road trips, from South America to Australia to Africa. Mr. Pistols had lived more in his brief life than Melody had in all of hers.

If Melody knew the first thing about Photoshop, she would have already right-clicked each image and inserted herself into Henry's life. Henry, Melody, and Mr. Pistols camping on the beach. Henry, Melody, and Mr. Pistols going for a midnight stroll. Henry, Melody, and Mr. Pistols having a candlelight dinner.

Instead, she had to imagine it. Had to dream about their life together.

This is the type of behavior her college self would have slapped her for.

#OveriesBeforeBroveries
Bzzzt-bzzzt-bzzzt.

She closed Henry's Instagram and answered the phone.

"Hello?"

"Melody," said Yannis on the line. *"I'm outside. Did you message Henry about the venue change?"*

"Yeah, I did." She switched the phone to her other ear and stood. "Not sure he totally believed me. How the hell did you get reservations at *Trough?*"

"I'm double parked, why don't you come down, I'll explain it to you on the way."

Melody hung up and grabbed her biggest purse. Yannis had instructed her to wear something nice, but also something that would have easy access to be wired-up in. And to bring a bigger purse, not one of those little clutch things. She needed to carry the transmitter with her.

Outside, the rusty old Econovan didn't stand out in her neighborhood, but neither did it blend in. While it would be difficult to find a vehicle on the block that didn't have rust spots and chipped paint, locating another vehicle that so unapologetically ran on fossil fuel would be.

Neighbors peaked out windows and joggers gawked. Even the birds and squirrels that usually sat in the trees outside her building seemed offended before making themselves scarce.

Yannis sat in the driver's seat and waved as Melody approached the van. At first it looked like he was wearing a turban, but as she got closer, she realized it was bandages.

When she opened the passenger door, she saw the extent of the damage.

Black eye and bandaged skull. Dried blood on his collar, the sleeve of his blazer torn and hanging by threads.

"What the fuck happened to you?"

"My other eleven o'clock may have been late, but boy did he deliver. It's all good though, I'm here for you now. Hop in, let's get you wired up."

"Um, yeah. Hold the line, Toto. Before I get into your creepy kidnapper van, how the hell did you get reservations at *Trough?* There's like, a hella waitlist."

Yannis smiled. "I own it."

"You own a restaurant too?"

"No, I own *Trough.* But *Trough* is not a restaurant, it's a social experiment."

"The fuck you mean it's not a restaurant? That line has been out the door, people raving about the food online for over a year now."

"And it's got a Michelin Star, and been called the secret sauce in the revitalization of Detroit, and people are dropping thousands and thousands of dollars on frozen meals we pick up at the Kingsland the night before. Employees are all friends of friends of friends having a good time and getting paid. Chef Alejandro used to be my mechanic. Even sold me this beaut'." Yannis slapped the van.

"That's fucked up."

"Imagine some shithead college kid built a website and told everyone that it was about connecting with each other, but really it wasn't, was it? Both that platform and my restaurant thrive on its user's obsession with bragging rights and/or virtue signaling. Only difference, *Trough* isn't exploiting anybody beyond their own egotistical musings."

#Facebook #Instagram #Twitter #TikTok #Tumblr

"Dude." Melody didn't know what to say. "Like, do people know you own it?"

"No. I stay out of the spotlight as much as I can. I detest attention," said the man with *#ThreeMillionsViewsOnYoutube*. "But none of that matters, I'm here for you, now." Yannis checked his watch. "We've got a little less than an hour before your boy shows up. You want to get hung up on irrelevant semantics, or do you want to hop into my van and see if you two are in this love together?"

The drive between Melody's apartment and *Trough* was short. But in that time, all Melody could think of were those dupes ranting and raving about *Trough*. The diatribes and tirades that knocked the handful of reviews online that weren't glowing. She watched Yannis as the lights from the city flickered on his face. It was easy to imagine him loving every bit of his life, his work. There was a manic calmness to the man which made him both comforting to be around, and difficult to talk to, and it was a relief when the neon *Trough* sign came into view.

"Hey," said Melody. "Can I ask you something? You own this place, right? So, last year, that old man, the knight who busted up the table out front while riding the horse. Was that you? I mean, not the old man, but was that like a publicity stunt or something?"

"No," Yannis smiled without looking up from the wires he was coiling around his hand, "That was not me. That was a lynch pin event. Nothing even I could do to stop or change that, not that I'd want to, you know?"

"What's a lynch pin event?"

"We can circle back to that. We're here now, let's focus on the date!"

He pulled the van into the back parking lot and backed it up to the rear wall of the record store next to the restaurant. She did most of the handsy work herself—threading the various small gauge wires down her shirt and clipping them to her bra straps and waistband—while Yannis went over the broader details of the evening.

"Fly casual. Speak like you normally would. No need to project or enunciate." Yannis picked up a small black box from the makeshift workbench at the back of the van. The box had a small, curly antenna and a blue LED on it, but otherwise it was smooth and seamless. "I'll be right in here on the wireless. You talk, this little guy transmits it all back here, and Social Lube will do its magic."

Yannis motioned to the array of CPUs, monitors, and soundboards that filled one entire wall of the van.

The stupid rock in her stomach was throbbing. It was dumb to get nervous, for *her* to get nervous. She wasn't the type to fawn over dudes or let things like emotions or feelings get the best of her. But here she was, parading around like a half-cyborg, embroiled in this science fiction bullshit, hoping to find out if a boy really likes her, or just wants to do her.

"So, you'll be in here the whole time?"

"I'm not going anywhere. He'll speak, I'll run his audio through Social Lube here, and good or bad, I'll give you the lowdown on what's up."

Melody nodded. This was happening. No turning back now.
#NeedADrink #LivinLifeLikeItsDice #SnakeEyes #BottomsUp

Once inside *Trough*, Melody ordered two Black Engine Oil Ales and pressed her finger to her ear, "This thing working?" They'd gotten there early enough to order a few rounds and test out the equipment before Henry arrived.

"We got you. Take your finger out of your ear. Relax." Yannis's voice came through the near invisible earpiece.

"Relax. Right." With wires fastened between her breasts, a suspicious black box loitering in her purse, and a self-described mad scientist's voice in her ear, the last thing she could do was relax.

Yannis assured her that nothing on the menu would cause her any harm. The entrees were designed to exist some place between total nonsense and absolute chaos, and named to highlight and extrapolate the nature of pretension. American Falafel with red sauce. Balto-Slavic Mucho Nacho. Korean PB & J. Ramen Noodle Sliders. Deconstructed Ethiopian Gummy Bears. Greek Linguini Sushi. Deep-fried Soft-shell Crab Choco-tacos. Maple Bacon Tikka Masala.

After ordering her third beer, she glanced back toward the door and saw the hostess escorting a familiar face toward her table. She sat up straight and adjusted her shirt. She smiled and tried not to feel like the *Manic Pixie Dream Girl* in whatever narrative was going on in Henry's head.

"Hi, Henry."

His smile beamed back at her. "Melody. Hi. Wow. It's great to finally meet in person."

#Swoon #BasicBitch

He pulled out his chair but didn't sit. Instead, he swung around the table and opened his arms to instigate a hug.

"Oh? We're hugging? Okay." Melody had grabbed his hand to shake, and now their arms were caught between their chests.

From the earpiece: "First impression coming in. Hold tight."

Henry pulled away and tilted his head. "Excuse me?"

"What?" Melody played dumb.

"Did you say something?"

#OhShit #PlayItCool

From the earpiece: "Better looking in person." Yannis interjected, "You're killing it, girl."

"No. I didn't say anything. But it is cool to meet in real life. It's stupid, I know, but like online, we're like friends or whatever. Out here, I don't know? Feels like crossing a line but like in a good way."

"Oh, you mean because physically we're total strangers, but in truth we probably know each other better than our real friends and family do."

"Totally."

"Cool, cool. At least I'm not alone."

"Not at all!" He was still standing beside her at the table. "You want to sit?"

"Oh, right?" He rounded the table and sat. "I guess maybe I'm a little nervous."

From the earpiece: "Man, this girl can talk." Then Yannis said, "Slow your roll, girl. Let him get a word in."

#ShutUp #ItsMeNotYou

Melody took a breath; this boy had her feeling some type of way.

"Sorry, I know I can talk. Want to get a drink?"

"Thought you'd never ask."

Ten thousand years ago, Gracie would have been king of this fucking city. The fucks in their hovels would bow when he walked and shit their pants when he fought. His brand of masculinity would have been revered. He'd grunt and fuck and fart, and they'd feed him grapes until his piss turned to wine. Jesus would have nothing on him. Go far enough back, and Gracie would have been worshipped as the son of God.

The world wasn't built for strong men anymore. Hard times weren't overcome with fists, but with brains. And with knuckles bruised, ear busted, and left eye bloodshot, Gracie hadn't expected the bat. That bitch had told him to watch his head. Maybe she could have been a little fucking clearer, because it was a fucking cosmic joke that the little shit had gotten the jump on him, but he wouldn't be a punchline again.

After Yannis fled the office, Gracie ransacked the place for clues and made a phone call to the one person in the department he suspected might help him.

"Holy shit," said Jackson over the phone. "How the hell are you? You still coming to Bell's retirement party?"

"That's the plan. But shit, brother, landed on my feet. Working security and personal protection for Masood Pharma."

"For real? What's that pay?"

"Better than we were making, that's for fucking sure."

"They hiring?"

Gracie laughed and moved on to his inquiry. "You think you can help me out with some background on a guy?"

"Hol-up, I'm serious, man. Belfour busted my ass over to Tri-County. Got three months of lock up duty over shit that you pulled."

"Shit that I pulled? What the fuck you talking about?"

"Fucking Camila Torres. You ain't got the subpoena yet? Her lawyers pulled our fucking body cams from that night."

"So?"

"So? So you know what you fucking did, man!"

"They fucking resisted. Shit, you ran two of 'em down. They ain't got shit on us."

"Don't fucking matter. You see the way the world is, man? Everyone on eggshells but you."

"Hey, I got fucking fired."

"Yeah, and since that's all they can do to you, they taking the rest out on me."

"That's fucking bullshit."

"Fuckin' A, it is."

"Shit, Charles, I'm sorry, man." And he legitimately was. "If there's anything I can do, let me know."

"Yeah. Masood hiring?"

"Ain't heard anything, but I can look into it."

"You do that. Cause from what I seen, three months turns into six turns into a year real quick here. And I ain't looking to make a career babysitting drunks."

"I hear you." Gracie pondered if it was a good idea or not to ask Jackson for that favor. "So hey, think you can help me out with that background search?"

"Fuck man, you got a one-track mind, don't you?"

Jackson informed him that nearly every detail from Yannis's manila folder was a fabrication. He had no passport, no formal defense or tactical training, couldn't speak multiple languages or even drive a stick shift. In the moment Gracie thanked Jackson for the info and went on with the job, but stewing on Jackson's line-by-line rebuttal of the info in the manila folder put him back in the *police mindset* and got him asking: *why?* What fucking record is going to track someone's capability of driving a stick shift? Was this counterintelligence? Did Yannis plant misinformation to purposely confound any investigation on him? Or was Gracie not the first cop Yannis had hired to kill him? He could see Bell taking on the gig to pad his retirement, only to fail miserably and put together a bullshit file so that the whole fucking department failed together.

After the conversation about the only thing Gracie was sure of was that Yannis was both wealthy and fucking intelligent. Oh, but hard times were coming. The world didn't have room for another smart man.

By sunset, Gracie had tracked Yannis to a parking lot behind the main strip in the Downtown district of the suburbs. It was sandwiched between the mom-and-pop storefronts and the skyscraping towers. As the sun continued to dip down, the high-rises cast a giant shadow over everything, like a hand ready to swat the city flat. The Doctor had been stupid and used his credit card to pay for six hours in the lot. It was almost insulting that Yannis had put so little effort into learning about the man he'd hired to kill him. Gracie had skills and connections that made him more of a threat than most contract killers. And while it gave him an advantage in this instance, it also gave him a cancerous notion concerning his reputation out in the world. And if Jackson was right, if there was shit coming down from that bullshit on Devil's Night—

Fuck.

He hadn't been subpoenaed. Were they building a case against him?

God damnit. This was the shit. Legit paths were shutting down for him, and it was looking like either he pulled this off and made a name for himself, or he didn't, and ended up in Tri-County with Jackson. Only on the other side of the bars.

Yannis's van was easy enough to spot. No one paid him any mind as he skulked between the parked cars. He was neither young nor pretty, so any stray glances that landed on him quickly drifted onto something, anything, more pleasing. That was fine with Gracie. The lot was always too dark for any of the CCTV cameras to capture any usable identification, and the fewer people who even remembered seeing him the better.

Gracie approached the van and peered through the window. A bank of computer monitors and other old school equipment lined the wall. And lounging in front of them: the doctor. Maybe he was rusty, but his instincts still served him well when he listened. He swept around the passenger door and grabbed the handle of the open door. Inside, Yannis was distracted. This could all be over in half a second. He had a garrote in his back pocket, a knife on his hip, and a 9mm in his glove box if shit really went sideways. But he didn't want to use any of those. He had his fists, and it had been a long time since he'd been able to really let loose with them.

This had to go perfectly, so he waited and watched.

From the speakers in the van, Gracie heard voices.

Over the speakers: "I guess we should probably order," said a man's voice. Familiar, but he couldn't place it.

The reel-to-reel tape slammed to a stop every time the man stopped speaking. *Snap!* It rewound and stopped. *Hiss!* Back and forth. *Thunk-thunk-thunk!*

On the computer monitor, a series of words appeared: *Having. Great. Time.*

All in seconds.

Yannis repeated the readout into the mic on his headset, "Having a great time."

Over the speakers: "Oh, something tells me it takes most people a bit of time to decide," said the woman's voice. "Have you looked at the menu?"

"This is good, right? I mean, they've really got it, right?" Yannis nodded to himself as he leaned back in his chair and watched his machine work. "Love," he said to no one in particular, though he covered the headset's microphone as if he were engaging in a private conversation.

Over the speakers: "What do you think the Deconstructed Ethiopian Gummy Bears are?"

Snap! Hiss! Thunk-thunk-thunk!

Readout: *What. Is. This. Place.*

Gracie watched in utter confusion as the voices on the other end of this setup continued what sounded like a date, while the computer here did its thing.

Snap! Hiss! Thunk-thunk-thunk!

Readout: *Like. Taking. It. Slow.*

Snap! Hiss! Thunk-thunk-thunk!

Readout: *Hope. Likes. Cats.*

Snap! Hiss! Thunk-thunk-thunk!

The woman's voice came through the speakers: "So, what do you do for a good time, you know, besides staying up late talking to me?"

Snap! Hiss! Thunk-thunk-thunk!

Gracie was mesmerized. But he had shit to do.

Snap! Hiss! Thunk-thunk-thunk!

Trinie Claire Anderson had been born eight pounds, seven ounces, and twenty-two inches long, and had come into the world in the usual way.

Labor was quick, and Chris held back tears as his daughter was laid skin-to-skin onto Erica's chest. She didn't cry, and only opened her eyes for a second, as if to make sure she was okay with whom she'd been born to. She cooed, and smiled, and closed her eyes, content and safe with the world that had been thrust upon her. Without trying, the three of them inhaled as one. Erica, Trinie, and Chris. Inhaling and exhaling. The three of them were one in the way that he and Erica previously were.

It was then that Chris finally cried.

In the weeks prior to Trinie's birth, Chris and Erica made regular dry runs to the hospital. They grabbed overnight bags and pillows and blankets and car seat, and made the eighteen minute drive. On one chilly evening, Chris had draped his coat over Erica, and when she tucked her hands into the pockets to warm them, she found three business cards.

"Who's Yannis?"

"What?" Chris turned the wheel. The previous six months had passed like six years, and that word—that he would soon remember to be a name—was as strange to him now as the man it belonged to was when they'd met.

"Yannis? You've got a bunch of business cards."

Chris laughed, recalling that night, and retold most of the details of the encounter. Though he left out any mention of Stella from the tale.

When Erica went into labor, they did not contact Yannis to assist with the delivery. But his wasn't a name that Erica forgot, nor did she let his occupation go. From time to time, she'd mention Yannis and bring up the idea of selling his records. Never any pressure, but more to fund the mutiny against poverty they'd dreamt of.

He'd never been able to bring himself to sell.

While Trinie slept in the nursery and Erica slept in her hospital bed, Chris went home to shower and change, and bring back everything they had forgotten in their midnight exodus to the labor and delivery triage.

After his shower, he put pen to paper and figured out all the math that he should have worked out months ago. Salaries and diapers and formula (Erica had decided early on that she would not be breastfeeding, and despite the shame the OB/GYN nurses tried to make her feel, Chris supported her decision without question) and daycare and rent and food and transportation.

Leaving the hospital, Chris sped, eager to get home and back to hold his daughter again.

On the return trip, he never cracked the speed limit.

He was in no rush to look Erica in the eye, to hold Trinie's tiny, tiny hand, and tell them both that they could not afford to support, raise, and care for a child.

After rent and car insurance and utilities, they were left with fifty dollars per week for groceries and gas and diapers and clothes. Which put them over the limit for any type of assistance from DHS. Chris's initial instinct was to drop his hours. Shave one hour off each week and reap the rewards. This was only a short-term solution, though. Eventually, Erica would need to go back to work—no matter how you cut it, netting fifty dollars per week after bills was no way to survive, let alone sustain, and if Chris wasn't working at least twenty hours per week, they would not qualify for daycare assistance.

And even then, daycare would still be half their income. Rent would be their other half.

And with summer utilities going up one and half times during peak hours to *"give you more control over your bill,"* their margin of error didn't much matter anymore. Making dinner, warming a bottle, or watching TV between 2PM and 7PM became just three more luxuries they couldn't afford.

They had saved for months. Saved as much as they could. And for a little while they had a cushion that would support and sustain them. One way or another, they were trapped between the choice of both working, and only being able to afford daycare and rent, or of them staying home with Trinie and only being able to scrape by because they qualified for assistance.

And eventually something would happen. A bus would run late and one of them would have to take an Uber to work, or to drop Trinie off at daycare. Or one of them would get sick and have to miss work, or Trinie would get sick, and they would have to pick her up from school and miss work again. Formula alone was going to cost two hundred dollars per month. Little by little, or all at once, one way or the other, that extra money would be all used up before they could even get by.

He'd heard talk that what people needed was a hand-up, not a handout. But what's the difference, really? Is it that people who fall on hard times ask for a hand-up, but people who are systemically there only ask for handouts?

And then there was boredom. And depression. Without disposable income, the American Dream becomes a disciplinary exercise. Planning out life under the poverty line turned into a utilitarian adventure, where survival alone becomes the priority. But once the body is taken care of, the mind shifts to fulfill its own musings. Entertainment. Movies and music and books and television and the internet. Because none of that is accounted for in figuring out a cost of living. Because those are considered luxuries. Because God-forbid someone barely scraping by dare to need a temporary escape from their reality, or wish for something beyond what they can see with their own eyes.

The luxury of dreams.

Available only to those who can afford it.

The sky above opened up on the way home from *Trough*. A million little rain droplets hit his car all at once. This cacophony was muted though, as Chris swiped to his *Driving In The Rain* playlist on Spotify and hit shuffle. *Rain Dogs* by *Tom Waits* played.

Nothing had changed. In the months since Trinie was born, they were no better off than they were before. He refused to say they were worse, but—

Chris was spiraling. For months now, time had seemed to slow down when he'd wanted it to fly by, or speed up when he'd needed it to come to a crawl. He was stuck in a loop. Even the music hadn't changed. What's it called when you do the same things every day and hope that it will be different? Oh yeah, being normal. He was a snake, stuck inside a broken clock, eating its own tail. And some days, when the right song came up on his playlist, he could slip down some rabbit-hole fantasy and find himself in a different world, with a different life. Fitter in some of these times. Happier in others. But in every one of these timelines, Trinie was no longer in his life.

And that's what snapped him back every time.

"Hey," Erica said as Chris walked in with the carryout bag. She and Trinie lay on the rug doing some tummy time. "Really coming down out there, huh?"

"Yeah," Chris said and handed her the bag.

At a month old, Trinie smiled. At first Erica took the smiles as random little ticks and spasms that the doctors had told her about. "Don't make too much out of them," they'd say. "Babies all develop at their own pace." But it was difficult not to be overwhelmed, not to make a big deal about it. This baby, this life that Erica had carried for nine months, now conveyed the same love which Erica had shown her. These weren't ticks and spasms, these were love and smiles.

And Chris was missing all of it.

In the past six months she and Chris had experienced a hell of baby clothes, centipedal tails of blue diaper-genie sausage casings stuffed to the point of bursting, pale vomit, dark rashes, and the way a watched pot never boils a baby never sleeps. Even at only days and weeks old, the newborn picked up on her parents' moods. Chris and Erica had been lost and found, stressed and at ease. With her arrival, life both came into focus and doubled down on its unknowability, and it was only through exhaustion that either of them ever recuperated. If the definition of insanity was doing the same thing over and over again and expecting different results, parenthood was a self-diagnosing prophecy.

Broken clocks and dogs and weather. Shipwrecks and whispers, being swallowed by the night. All these phrases or lyrics which Chris repeated under his breath without even noticing. He was a skipping record. The needle finding a scratch and skipping back. Sometimes he would get farther into the song, but she'd hear the chorus again and know that the skip had happened. It wasn't a perfect analogy, but she could think of no other way to picture what was happening. A broken record was something she could fix. The same didn't go for some debilitating and degenerative mental illness taking hold of the man she loved.

"Chris, look." Erica said as Trinie's eyes beamed at him, her lips curling up into a wet grin.

Chris looked over to his daughter and smiled back. He tickled her chin and sung those damn lyrics to her like they were a nursery rhyme.

She wanted to be upset with Chris for vanishing off into whatever world he was stuck in, but she was no better. Some couples vanish into their cell phones and reality shows after a long day. Not Erica and Chris. They ignored each other via magick and music. So much time spent with her head in the rites, trying to find a way out of their current life. The one difference: she didn't look dead inside.

Trinie had Chris's eyes for sure. It was uncanny looking into them, seeing how busy they were at one age, and then looking into Chris's and finding a dead, matte finish in another.

"What are you and Daddy going to do when Mommy eats her lunch? Are you going to read? Are you going to play?" Erica tickled Trinie's belly, and the baby cooed.

Chris smiled, but said nothing. She couldn't take this much longer.

She stood and walked into the kitchen with her lunch in hand.

In the bottom drawer of the pantry, she kept her supplies and her book of spells.

And as she ate, she worked.

Something was wrong with their relationship, and money and peace and calm, those were just band aids. Until now, she'd been treating symptoms of the rot. It was time to pull out the corruption by the root.

It had worked once before, two weeks before Trinie was born. She could make it work again.

The asshole had come up, slammed his palm down on the bar, and demanded "Another PBR, momma!"

"Be right there," said Erica over her shoulder. On busy nights she liked to give eye contact whenever someone called for a drink behind her back. It was the impatient ones who were most likely to bitch and moan if they had to wait longer than they'd like for a drink, and making eye contact doused the complaints before they even started. At least most of the time. Tonight, she was having trouble enough keeping her gaze forward, let alone spinning her neck around to make the dude feel heard.

Her belly had made it difficult to turn around behind the bar. For the last few weeks, she'd had to make her rounds one direction at a time, moving all the way to either end of the bar—taking orders along the way—and working her way back down the other way once she stepped out and turned around.

"Oi! You hear me?"

Her feet ached, her back felt like it was going to go out at any moment, her breasts were so full that they hurt to touch, and she wasn't in the mood to deal with this dude's bullshit.

"Said, I'll be right there. Gotta turn around."

"Yeah, maybe you shouldn't be working if you can't do your job. Gonna be a rough life if the kid's already getting in the way and it ain't even out of you yet."

Erica kicked open the cooler with her foot. She bent as far as she could and found two cans of PBR right up front, so she didn't have to drop to her knees. Can in hand, she made her way out the end of the bar and turned to slide back down and deliver it to the asshole. He wore an ironic mustache, and in one of those moments that pops into your brain before bed, she stared at it for way too long, imagining shaving it off his face while he bitched and squealed.

"You going to give it to me, or do I have to take it?" he asked.

"Oh, sorry." She set the can down on a coaster in front of the man. "Just getting distracted."

"Maybe it's time to call it a day, no? Let someone more able-bodied handle the bar."

"That would be fantastic. Unfortunately, babies like to eat. They like places to live. And unless this able-bodied replacement wants to donate that paycheck to those causes, I'm going to stick it out as long as I can." Erica smiled at him. "Three bucks."

He dangled a twenty-dollar bill in front of her and looked to the register at the far end of the bar.

"You don't have a five? Hell, even three singles? I'll consider no tip from you a tip in and of itself."

"Nope." The asshole shook his head.

Erica snatched the bill from his fingers, and scooched back down the bar, remembering those times when doing so wasn't such a chore. She dropped change from the asshole's twenty-dollar bill on the bar in front of him, not waiting for, nor expecting, any sort of tip, but before she could slip away he rose from the stool, reached across the bar and placed a palm on her belly. Erica tried to step away from his hand, but there was nowhere to go quick enough.

The baby kicked at his fingers. "Yeah, maybe she wants a new daddy. I tell you what, you were my lady, I wouldn't be letting you work this far into it. I'd let you put your feet up on my shoulders and watch the tube while I took care of you." He smiled. "Bet you taste like cotton candy."

"That's fucking disgusting." She pulled his hand off her belly and shoved him back.

"Doesn't have to be," he laughed.

"You need anything else?"

"No, not right now. I'm good."

Before she could tell him to fuck off, she caught a glance of the wet stain on his coaster and was suddenly tongue-tied.

"Um, I," she said, scooting down the bar away from the asshole. "I'll be right back."

She grabbed her purse from under the bar, and popped out the end.

"What you got in there?" He stared at her purse, bulging out and full. She ignored him and waddled past the bar stools. "Where you going?"

"I'd rather not say."

"Can I watch?" he laughed again.

She rounded the bar, pushed her way through the swinging kitchen doors.

It couldn't be. It fucking couldn't be. She closed her eyes and saw it again. The coaster, the wet stain in the shape of her sigil. The Claire de Lune mark. The circle with the horns of moonlight emanating from it. It had never appeared to her outside of her mind.

It was a sign. She had to get to work.

This late, the kitchen was closed. The two line cooks and the manager had gone home; the place was hers to shut down in a few hours. She didn't mind working alone. But Chris did. Until he got his second job, he used to hang out there to make sure she wasn't dealing with anything she shouldn't have to. It was a sweet gesture, but as much as Chris talked, he was never one to jump into action. Take this asshole tonight. If Chris were here, even if he'd overheard this shit he was saying, he wasn't the type of man to step up to the asshole and start something. Instead, he would have followed Erica into the kitchen now and interrogated her in a whispered tone to make sure she was alright.

Erica was more proactive, but she couldn't be gone long. She had to move fast. The *Rite of Banishment* had been dedicated to memory months ago. The prefect spell for a bartender to know. She'd fantasized about using it many times. Tonight, it was no longer going to be a fantasy.

From the spice shelf next to the steamer, she pulled down salt and cinnamon, but couldn't find any lavender. She found vinegar tucked under the brunch prep area and stole an empty and sanitized kombucha bottle from the manager's office.

On an order slip, she wrote: Asshole at the bar. She half-filled the bottle with vinegar, and got to work filling the jar with the required herbs while she recited the memorized words:

Find happiness, where we cannot see
Find your peace but not from me
Far away, far away, be thy free
Take your life, I banish thee

The book says that the lavender and cinnamon offer certain protections to both the diviner and the intended. As the slurry of salt and cinnamon and vinegar reached the brim, Erica had a split second of hesitation in her foregoing of the lavender. Without the lavender, there was no way to know if this performance of the rite was legit or not, but she wasn't turning back now.

Erica dropped the order slip into the jar and sealed it with the lid. She snuck out the back door, and under a nearby hedge, she dug a shallow grave where she dropped the jar and buried it. On top of the grave, she drew her sigil.

Returning to the bar, Erica locked the back door, swept off any of the mess she'd left behind, and pushed back through the kitchen doors into the bar area.

She held her eyes closed for that split second the door blocked her view of the seat where the asshole was, or, maybe, had been.

Erica wanted him gone. And when she opened her eyes, he was.

Stool empty, cash on the bar. She smiled.

Outside, tires squealed and plastic cracked. Two hollow thuds shockwaved into her: meat being slapped, and then that meat slapping the concrete.

The patrons of the bar flooded into the street, and Erica followed. She didn't want to, didn't need to. She already knew what she was going to see.

There was no crowd to push through. As soon as the gawkers saw the asshole's skull cracked open and leaking down the street, they turned away, now sober and sick. She was the only one who noticed the pattern the leaked blood had begun to form on the pavement.

Erica turned away and vomited. She'd seen enough cop shows to know that detectives always think that murderers return to the scene, and she didn't want to be called a murderer, regardless of how it looked. Because this was her fault. As she held the door open for the returning patrons, she caught a whiff of lavender on the breeze and understood the makeup of the rite. The cinnamon had been for her protection. The lavender, for his.

She'd just killed a man. It had been unintentional, but his blood was on her hands either way, and in the weeks following the murder she'd sworn off magick and spells. Though, they hadn't done the same for her.

She'd catch sight of the sigil everywhere. In graffiti, in smoke, in flocking birds in the sky. And every time she did, the guilt of that night washed over her, only receding when she whispered a spell of clarity to herself in her mind. Slowly, those whispers escaped her mind and then gained volume until, now, whenever she saw her Claire de Lune, she stopped what she was doing and practiced whatever magick was called for to resolve whatever was on her mind at the moment. She was on a path, and as long as she stayed on it, answered the questions the universe asked of her, she'd get her answers. She never forgot the accident, but instead found solace in his sacrifice. His death had given her a face to remind her of the science behind the magick: that energy never dissipates or disappears, that whatever is taken from the universe has to be returned.

Tonight, when Chris had come in and plopped down on the couch and stretched, she'd seen her sigil in his body. His head, with his arms raised up towards the ceiling.

Erica didn't flip the pages in order or even one at a time. She jumped back and forth in chunks like a game of hot and cold, feeling her way closer or farther away from the correct rite to free Chris from whatever was holding him in his stasis. Magnetic energy pulled and repelled until, after a dozen or more flips, she landed on the intended page. The Rite of Release.

She gathered the lemon balm, rosemary, and mint. The gotu kola and eyebright herb. For good measure, she'd include lavender for Chris's protection, but when she reached for the cinnamon, the little plastic dollar store container was empty.

Her heart sank and her ears went deaf. Chris was lost. He was off somewhere in his own head, stuck on some loop, repeating those lyrics. He needed this. He needed it now, but if she went forward, it would be without offering herself any protection. She'd be tempting fate, inviting the universe to meet her challenge.

But Chris was worth it. Trinie needed a father, and if she could give that to her, the risk was worth it. Besides, she wasn't an asshole. The universe had sought out that man from the bar after being singled out by her spell because he'd been a drain on society. Erica was nothing of the sort. She helped people, volunteered when she could, donated whenever they could afford it. She always tried to be the bright spot in others' dim days.

This was going to work.

She was going to be fine.

She closed her eyes and focused. She massaged her arms and body and face with her fingertips. Slow, swirling motions. Thoughtless and intuitive, her hands flowed toward her heart. Vacating all negative intentions until her mind cleared and focused, and a comforting and calming light surrounded her.

One by one, Erica added the herbs into a mason jar and repeated an incantation in her head.

The atmosphere in the room shifted as Erica read the words aloud. Her ears popped, the lights flickered, moisture beaded on the faucet and sink.

She kept Chris in her thoughts as she stirred the ingredients. He needed to come back, the Chris she loved. Right now, he was a shell, a husk. All stress and anger, none of the light and love and laughs that he'd been before. Whatever ate away at him needed to go. It needed to go now.

In one fluid movement, Erica dropped the lavender into the jar, grabbed the lid, and spun it tight. While she waited, she finished her lunch. When it was ready, she opened the window and released the ingredients to the wind. They fell, and they spun and swirled, carried off to do what she'd asked of them.

Henry had settled on the Government Shutdown Soup, and Melody on the Cornucopia El Esperanto Salad. She'd tried to talk him out of the soup—Yannis had warned her to stay away from the soups, especially the Government Shutdown, which was unserved leftovers piped through a garbage disposal and reheated—and into the Spiced Potatoes and Rooster's Feet Platter. But he insisted.

#GuessWhosNotGettingAnyTonight

"Oh," Henry said. "Most nights it's just me and Mr. Pistols running around with a laser pointer. Although last week he got out. I was terrified."

"He got out? Oh my God, why didn't you tell me before?" Melody realized the answer before he gave it and blushed.

"Well, you were kind of dodging my messages, so—"

From the earpiece: *"Hope you feel guilty."*

"—I'm not trying to make you feel guilty. Just saying."

From the earpiece: *"Yes, I am."*

"I know." Melody hung her head. "I get weird, okay? Sometimes I avoid things I want, because, I don't know. I'm afraid of being let down. Maybe? I don't know. It's a flaw. A big one. And if I'm being honest, I'm not doing anything about it. So, if that's the deal breaker, I don't know what to tell you." She shrugged.

"No. I get it. After I sent you the message, I even cringed a bit. Like I knew we hadn't, like, talked romantically or anything, but I don't know, guess I was trying to be honest about my feelings for once."

From the earpiece: "He likes your honesty." Yannis continued, "And holy shit, he's telling the truth too. You got a veritable Boy Scout in front of you, girl."

#LooksLikeSexIsBackOnTheMenuBoys

"I'm glad." Melody smiled. "So is Mr. Pistols alright now?"

"Yes, and no."

"Oh, no."

"He wasn't hurt or anything, but when I found him, he had pus running down his face. It was coming from his eye. I thought he got into a fight and his eyeball ruptured."

#Gross #IJustThrewUpInMyMouth

"Oh, my god. Was it? Did you have to rename him Sir Didymus?"

#Oops #TooSoon

Henry laughed. "Thankfully no, although they live by the same code of ethics. No. Took him to the vet. Turns out he had a herpes flare up. It can happen when they get put in stressful situations."

#ThatEscalatedQuickly #DidNotSeeThatComing

From the earpiece: "Having a really good time."

"Sorry to interrupt." Their server arrived at the table with their appetizer. "Here's your artisanal brioche loaf." She set the dish down and backed away.

Henry and Melody both looked from the plated square of bread to each other.

"Is it just me, or is that a peanut butter and jelly sandwich?" asked Melody.

"It's not just you," Henry replied. "How do you like it cut, straight or diagonal?"

Henry picked up his knife and reached for the sandwich.

Before she could respond, Yannis's voice silenced her.

From the earpiece: "Fuck you, you son-of-a-bitch!"

The woman's voice resounded over the speakers: "Is it just me, or is that a peanut butter and jelly sandwich?"

Gracie ripped the door open and shoved his fists inside. He grabbed the chair Yannis was in, and together the pair fell backward to the asphalt parking lot floor.

"I'm going to fucking destroy you," said Gracie. His arms were wrapped around the chair in a bear hug now, his hands clamoring for Yannis's neck.

Over the speakers: "How do you like it cut, straight or diagonal?"

Yannis threw his head backward into Gracie's nose. Stars and tears and coppery blood. A split second of white, followed by hazy black, and Yannis was out of the chair and fleeing through the lot. He turned back and shouted, "Fuck you, you son-of-a-bitch!"

Gracie was up and after Yannis in half a second. Ears rung and eyes blurred, but the parking lot was an open field, and so long as Yannis kept moving forward, he wouldn't lose him. Rather than follow his weaving path through the lot, Gracie flanked to the left. He wasn't as fast or agile as Yannis, but unobstructed, he could outmaneuver him with ease.

One car after the next, he zipped forward, closing in on Yannis. In one fluid motion, Gracie scooped up a fist-sized stone from the curb and launched it.

The stone whizzed through the air and caught Yannis square in the shoulder, knocking him to the ground between two vehicles.

Gracie pulled out his knife and stomped over to the crash site.

"I was a rowdy kid when I was young," said Gracie. "Fucking broke a kid's nose in third grade when he lifted my Game Boy from my backpack. Now my knuckles don't even bleed when I break faces. You ready?"

Yannis leaped up. "I'm gonna gouge your eyes out and shit into your fucking skull."

He threw the stone back at Gracie. It missed, clattering into the side panel of a nearby car.

"Um, excuse me?" She had gone white.

"I said, let me cut the sandwich. You know, since it's like a date. You know what, never mind, you can do it."

"No, no. By all means, please."

From the earpiece: *A thunk. A crash. A moan.*

"I wasn't like, making a comment about feminism or anything. I totally see men and women as equals."

From the earpiece: "I'm gonna gouge your eyes out and shit into your fucking skull."

The subtext had taken her aback so much, not because of the content.

#VulgarAsShit

And not because she had been wrong about Henry.

#UnderstatementOfTheYear

But because she'd been right. In that week that she'd dodged his messages after he'd asked her out, somewhere deep down inside her, she'd had an aching feeling that for all the nonchalant musings and sweet words of support Henry had showered her with, he was still just a guy.

#GuysLiterallyOnlyWantOneThing #AndItsFuckingDisgusting

And the one thing Henry wants is even worse than that.

#HelterSkelter #ShouldHaveSwipedLeft

Her keen sense of cynicism and disenfranchisement with society had guided her in identifying Henry as a skeeze, yet her decency as a human kept her from identifying him as the abhorrent creature he was at heart. Which, she figured, was as close as she could get to identifying a single, unifying characteristic of her generation.

Melody dropped her knife and sat back. Henry cut the sandwich in half and served her. But as he slid the half off onto her plate, the knife slipped from his hand, clanged against the plate, and bounced to a landing in front of Melody.

"Oops, sorry. Could you hand that to me?"

She hesitated. She'd prided herself on making smarter decisions than the women in horror movies. But this was kind of a grey area. She reached for the knife—

From the earpiece: "Don't touch that fucking knife!"

She froze.

"Oh? Are you okay?" Henry asked.

Melody scratched her ear, waiting for another interpretation from Yannis. All she heard was a faint coughing. Or was it choking? She couldn't tell.

"Sure. I'm fine." She pushed the knife across the table with her finger.

#WhyIsntThereSarcasmPunctuation

He tilted his head as he picked up the knife. "Are you sure? I feel like something happened that I don't understand."

From the earpiece: "I can see your soul!"

"You're perfectly aware of what's going on here, Henry. I think the confusion you're experiencing is your own."

"Um, yeah. That's what I'm saying. We seemed to be having a good time. Maybe we even shared a real moment here or there. I mean, Christ, this is a fifteen-dollar peanut butter and jelly sandwich. And all of a sudden—"

From the earpiece: "You think I'm going to flinch when your blood drains into the moonlight?"

#Sociopath #Psychopath

The restaurant hadn't gone quiet, but it may as well have. Melody apologized for acting weird, blaming it on cramps and the beer being stronger than she imagined.

"Sorry," Melody said. "Just, ah, cramps. The beer didn't sit right with the sandwich."

"Oh my god," said Henry. "Same! I was afraid it was only me."

From the earpiece: "How does it feel to know that you ate your last meal tonight?"

"People try too hard to appear to be a certain way. If they would let their guard down, be themselves, even for a moment," Henry slurped up his Government Shutdown soup. "It's really nice that you're so honest, so trusting. You know?"

From the earpiece: "Yeah! How do you like that? Huh? Huh? That darkness closing in around you? Is God calling to you yet?"

"Fuck this." Melody shoved her chair back and stood up.

"Melody," Henry said. "Are you alright?"

"Um, yeah. I will be. Cramps," she lied. "I've got to use the bathroom. Be right back."

Past judgmental stares, Melody clomped through the dining room. Either Henry was a psychopath, and she was dodging a bullet and an early grave by ghosting him now, or Yannis, in his pursuit of understanding the human condition, was fucking with her.

Melody rounded the corner into the back hallway. As soon as she was out of Henry's sight, she bolted out the back door.

The night air was cool and crisp, and Melody hadn't realized she'd been half holding her breath until it hit her lungs. Thumping bass and drunken laughter echoed between the buildings and parked cars. Steam poured from manhole covers and headlights blinded Melody for a split second as a car screeched around the lot.

She dodged between the parked cars and under the harsh and stagnant streetlights above, her shadow stretching out in front of her. When she got to the van, she found the door open and Yannis gone.

"The fuck?" She turned, eyes sweeping the area for the doctor.

She found him pinned up against the building, face red and arms twisted as he pulled the garrote tighter and tighter around a gigantic man's neck.

She recognized him. He was Yannis's other eleven o'clock. He recognized her too, and as he struggled against Yannis he said, "Wtch yr hd? Gv m fckng brk—"

"Oh, fuck."

Melody wanted to look away, but she couldn't take her eyes off Eleven O'clock's quivering lips.

His limbs shivered. He exhaled one last time, and his eyes closed. There was no blood, but the wires were sunk so deep into the man's neck they couldn't be seen.

Yannis let go. He and Eleven O'clock collapsed away from each other.

"What the fuck," said Melody.

"Oh, wow. That was a close one." Yannis wiped his brow. "Pretty sure he broke my leg. But don't worry, I'm okay."

"I don't give a shit if you're okay. Did you fucking kill him?"

Yannis checked the big man's pulse. "Nah. He's still there." His eyes brightened as he realized that it was Melody he'd been speaking to. "Oh, hey! Sorry I got distracted there. How did the date go?"

"Distracted?!"

#Fucking #Understatement

"Yeah, man. Remember that thing I said about putting myself in the hot seat? Turns out I'm quite the survivor. If you ever find yourself playing The Most Dangerous Game, remember to—"

"Shut up! You had me thinking that this guy I actually like wanted to kill me, or worse!"

"To be fair, I never promised that Social Lube would—"

"Shh!" Melody stood. "Just, shh!" Henry was back in the restaurant waiting for her, at least she hoped he was. All this bullshit, all her bullshit. If she were him, she would have bailed so long ago. But fuck, Henry really was a good guy. "I'm done here."

She turned and headed back to the restaurant.

"Um, Melody," Yannis called. "Can we get our equipment back?"

Without turning around, Melody reached into her cleavage and ripped handfuls of wires free. She reached into her pants and unspooled five, ten, twenty feet of wire from her person. It was a twisted ball of yarn that grew bigger and bigger until she dropped it on the ground and didn't look back.

"What about the transmitter in your purse?"

Melody raised her hand and gave him the finger. "I'll fucking mail it to you."

Back in *Trough*, she strolled up to her table, but didn't sit.

"You okay?" Henry asked with a concerned smile.

#OneInAMillion

"Yeah. I am now. You want to get out of here, stop at *Telway* for some real food, and head back to my place?"

"Now? What about the tab?"

"It's taken care of. Wanna go?" Melody held out her hand.

#NoMoreBullShit #NoMoreLies #NoMoreHashtags

"Absolutely." Henry stood.

#Confused #Horny

He took her hand, and they walked out of the restaurant together.

Shit. If this relationship goes anywhere, he was going to have to steal his neighbor's cat.

So far, it had gone better than he'd ever imagined. When he first met Melody, he hadn't expected their conversations to lead to anything more that the casual online flirting that he'd perfected when he was a teenager. Reddit without the sarcasm. 4chan without the angst. Tinder without the physical contact. Movies and memes and longings to travel across the country to meet, where truth didn't matter, only the ability to connect.

With Melody he'd finally been honest, and now he was in her bed. He wasn't a virgin, but never had he made love in such a way before.

Deep and sensual and stupid.

Now his mind was racing as he tried to reconcile the one actual lie he'd told her, the only lie that he'd built all the other truths on top of: Mr. Pistols.

Mr. Pistols wasn't his cat, but his neighbors, and on his days off, Henry was an amateur photographer. He'd spend hours snapping photos of that cat playing around his apartment complex and Photoshopping them together on adventures and excursions.

Now Henry couldn't sleep.

Melody was soundly snoring beside him. Content, relaxed, pure.

And he was a liar.

It was three AM and he fished his phone from the pocket of his jeans next to the bed, but it was dead. But he needed his fix, and carefully reached across Melody and grabbed her phone from the nightstand and plugged his AirBuds in.

He swiped the screen—no password set. Stupid, but it worked to his advantage at the moment. His face lit up as he found solace and comfort the only way he knew how.

YouTube.

Russian road rage videos, Joe Rogan's lizard conspiracy clips, r/EntitledParents, sovereign citizens getting owned, audits on police interactions.

Their search results were identical, and as the mess of red hair clumped next to him tossed and turned, Henry fell even more in love.

As the video loaded, one of those B.S. self-improvement ads played. Only this one was strange. The man talking looked manic and disheveled, and as he was about to skip it, the man spoke directly to Henry himself. It was stupid. He wasn't really speaking to him, but then again, he said, "Did you become a master at Photoshop by inserting yourself into others' photos so your life looks more interesting? Have you slept with someone on the first date and now you're worried that they're going to catch you in a lie? Do you feel as if you have no discernible inner life, and your only purpose is to teach broodingly soulful young men and women how to embrace life and its infinite mysteries? If so, call me. Maybe you need some Social Lube!"

The next morning, Chris awoke more well-rested than he had been in months. Trinie had slept through the night, which meant Erica had slept through the night, which meant he had slept through the night. It felt almost like paralysis, his sleep. Where the warmth in his toes slowly crept up his legs until his entire body was a furnace. He lay there and let the stress burn away from his mind and body until he awoke with a calcified snail-trail of drool creeping away from his lips.

He brewed his coffee and the aesthetics of sleep wore off his face, a vague recollection of a dream bringing itself to light. He hadn't dreamed in months. Now, the hazy remnants of the pain and hardship and confusion of the last year or more were being allocated and sorted in his mind. He drank his coffee, and rather than focus on all that had plagued their life and relationship, his mind honed onto a single solution that took root in his consciousness and became gospel by the time his cup of coffee was gone.

Today would be the day the music died.

Vinyl had defined Chris as a person. It gave him adulation and esteem, a frame of reference to friendship and art and life. The music pressed into that vinyl informed his opinions and decisions, gave voice to his politics and beliefs.

Today, Chris was going to sell his record collection.

If he felt anything as he carried those crates down to the car, it was relief. Not only for the money they so desperately needed, but for the defragmenting of his mind. The way memories are made to fade and morph into heightened ideals, rather than accurate depictions, this no longer happened for Chris. It was as if he had infinite depth perception, where nothing ever went out of focus, and the closer he looked and zoomed in and inspected, the more imperceptible the world became. This began a few months before Trinie was born. It was almost as if something prevented that from occurring in his mind. It started, he realized now, when that song became stuck in his head.

He lugged crate after crate down to the car, careful not to wake Erica or the baby, and as he placed the crates in the backseat, he allowed his hand to linger on them the way it would on Erica's pregnant belly. His hand surfed over the ribbed spines in the hope that he would feel the memories he'd attached to all those albums, that he could conjure a legit reason not to part with them. But now, touching them like this, he found that all those memories were in him, not being held in perpetuity in those spiraling grooves of sound.

He stared at Noir Moon for a moment before stepping out of the car.

Located next to *Trough*, Chris knew the place well from his tenure as a server at the restaurant. Back when he worked there, he'd go out for smoke breaks and look up at the empty building, imagine some sort of Bohemian lifestyle for him and Erica there. They could rent the building, live upstairs, and run a retail space down below. Maybe a metaphysical shop for Erica, or even a record store for himself.

That never came to pass. But here it was. Chris had always imagined moving his record collection into this building; now it was about to happen.

There were too many records to bring in at once, so he had cherry-picked the most notable pieces from his collection that morning and loaded them all into a single crate. The ones with alternate artwork or colored vinyl, the live recordings and first pressings. If Yannis took all these, then he'd bring in the rest, but he wanted to show off the rarer pieces first, the valuable ones.

Morning joggers and dog-walkers veered out of Chris's way as he carried the heavy crate from his car up to the recessed doorway. He fumbled with the door handle, and for a moment he thought that he'd read the hours wrong and the store hadn't opened yet. But with a little extra push, the door gave and Chris entered.

The room was something between a monastery and a mausoleum. It took a minute for his eyes to adjust to the dusty light, to see the deep bins full of albums materialize from shadows and stretch along each wall. Layers of decades-old vintage concert posters plastered the brick walls.

He glimmered at all the records he'd never own as his eyes fell on long sought-after LPs, strange EPs, and forgotten classics.

But they had been filed into utter chaos. There was no alphabetization, no commonality in era or genre. Only hodgepodge rows of soundtracks, R & B, children's sing-alongs, folksy spoken-word releases, and hair-metal interspersed with each other. Stranger still, while the organization was random, it didn't feel haphazard. It felt designed to keep the individual wares obfuscated and lost. Hidden in plain sight to stay put rather than be sold.

It didn't feel like a shop. It felt like a depository.

And then there was the music. Chris would recognize Kurt Cobain's agonizing howls anywhere. Growing up, when all his friends were obsessed with the East Coast/West Coast rap wars waging, Chris would hide out in his room and tune in to hear those fucking power chords. It wasn't like Biggie and Tupac hadn't done anything for him, he'd just grown up listening to Run-DMC and LL Cool J, Otis Redding and Nina Simone. Nirvana had just been the first thing he'd heard that had jarred his knowledge of the language of music. He'd witnessed a similar event transpire at summer camp, when all those suburban kids experienced Wu-Tang for the first time after years of road trips and weddings set to classic rock soundtracks. He knew every lyric that Cobain ever wrote, every song he ever recorded and sung. But he didn't know this.

At first it sounded like a track from the *Unplugged* album, as raw as it was. But where was the audience? Maybe this was an unreleased earlier soundcheck recording? The song played on, and somehow, Chris sung along. He was shook. As intuitively as he knew the lyrics, it came to him that he had never heard this song before.

But that wasn't true either. He knew the song and the lyrics. But they weren't Cobain's.

"Can I help you?"

Chris turned. Yannis emerged from some unseen corner. His face was bruised and swollen, and he wore bandages around his head and right arm. But through whatever injuries he'd sustained, he smiled in recognition of Chris. "Hey! Rick's friend, right? With the baby on the way?"

"Uh, hey." The song and lyrics had displaced his thought process, and it took him a moment to emerge. "Yeah, that's me. Baby's here now, but yeah."

"She's here? Congratulations. Has it been that long?"

"Has it? I don't know, man. Feel like I've run into you since then," said Chris.

"Don't think so. Unless you're remembering something I'm not. Or maybe vice versa."

"You said *she*. How did you know we had a girl?"

Yannis shrugged. "I see you brought me some records?"

"Yeah, it's, hey," he went lightheaded, "what the hell happened to you?"

"Research project went sideways. Doesn't matter. What made you decide to part with these after all this time?"

"Just time, you know?"

"I do, I do. Come on, let's go take a look. It has been a while. Let's see if you have anything I can still use." He held his arms out for the crate. "Better let me take that."

Chris fell into step behind Yannis.

"Hey, what are we listening to here, sounds like Cobain, but I know it's not."

"Oh, but it is," said Yannis. "Follow me, I'll explain."

As he followed Yannis toward the counter, his feet sunk into the green shag carpet like it was moist earth, and the sun, hanging high above, beat down and baked Chris in his uniform.

The grass was soft and plush from the rain the night before, as Chris wandered between campsites. He floated between tents and canopies, past campfires and picnic tables. He ignored the snickers and laughs from the other scouts. The catcalls about the uniform. His Scout Master made the troop wear their dress uniform for the entire Jamboree. Other leaders allowed their boys to change into Class-B t-shirts and shorts. But not theirs. Most of the time the required uniform, and the ensuing chuckles and gestures it got from other troops, bothered Chris so much that he stuck around his site for most of the weekend. But that morning a song clung to the breeze, and he followed its moan. And when he found its source, he stood dumbfounded before a group of older boys gathered around a boom box.

"What—" Chris was shy, had to step far out of his comfort zone to speak to anybody, let alone a group of older boys. "What are you listening to?"

"It's Nirvana, man. The singer just killed himself."

Chris spent the rest of the afternoon poring through the Nirvana discography with the older boys. When twilight fell across the camp, he finally placed the lyrics coming through the speakers. They weren't Cobain's, but Jason Molina's. It was *Ring the Bell* by Songs: Ohia.

He was listening to Kurt Cobain cover a song written almost a decade after his death.

Chris asked the boys how this was possible, but only found Yannis flipping through his LPs.

One by one, Yannis pulled out the albums, gave them a once over, and placed each back into the crate. Passing over *Spurm Wail* by Tommy Melody (his solo debut after leaving The Bloodyshow) was understandable, but when he set aside the original pressing of *Time & Place* by Lee Moses, Chris realized something was off. Yannis was not interested in everything in the crate; he was only interested in that one lonely album. With everything he had in there, how was that possible?

"Hey. You saw *Death Mix Live,* Afrika Bambaataa in there, right?"

Yannis nodded, kept on flipping. He pulled out *The Man in a Blue Turban with a Face* by Man Man and set it with Lee Moses. Chris didn't understand. It was a great album, but far from a collector's item.

"Come on man, you see I've got the turquoise Led Zeppelin self-titled LP?" Yannis held up a hand, urging Chris to chill. But he couldn't. "You see *The Wall?* Translucent orange vinyl, man."

This was bullshit.

He'd curated this crate of rare and special editions to entice this so-called collector, and all his efforts were being refuted without comment by this charlatan. Yannis had called himself an alchemist when they'd first met, and this encounter was more than proving that to be true.

To keep himself from punching the man, Chris kept tapped his foot, sung along under his breath and paced in front of the counter.

It wasn't supposed to take this long. Into the car, a quick drive down the road. That was it. Instead, the windows were down, and he was chain-smoking cigarettes, the phone call from his mother repeating in his head: "Your father collapsed at work."

The last thing his mother needed was another dead body, but he was speeding, weaving in and out of traffic. He was drumming on the steering wheel to a song he'd never heard. Whatever girl he'd been out with the night before had left the CD in his car. She'd spent half the night raving about how Jason Molina changed her life. And now Molina was changing Chris's life, singing how he *can't get there fast enough.*

He pressed the gas, now making green lights where he explicitly remembered being stopped at red. He couldn't get there fast enough. When he got to the hospital, the paramedics had said that his father had regained consciousness.

They held hands and said goodbye.

His throat closed up, and the tears came. He couldn't breathe.

This didn't happen.

He wasn't even there. This was a record store, not a car.

"Tissue?"

"What? No." His fingers curled into his palms, wrapped around an invisible steering wheel. "What the fuck—sorry, I don't know, baby is fucking wiping me out I guess. Anyway. So, which records don't you want?"

"To be honest, most of them. But I'll take these two." He held up the Lee Moses and Man Man records.

"Seriously? You know a lot of the albums in there are extremely rare. They'd go for thousands of dollars on auction sites!"

"I'd suggest you try to sell them online."

"You said when I was ready to sell to bring my shit in. Here I am!"

"That was almost a year ago, man. Research don't wait for the willing."

"The fuck does that mean?"

"It means you've mistaken me for a collector or a reseller, when I am neither of those things."

"What the hell you want records for then?"

"Clinical studies."

"Clinical studies. Okay. So what'll you give me for the two?"

"Thousand each."

"Fuck you! Are you serious? A thousand each? Are you fucking with me?"

"I'm not. These two albums are new to me."

"The Lee Moses one is a first printing too."

"Oh, I don't care about that. I've just never seen it before. Do we have a deal?"

"Fuck yeah, brother!" Chris stuck his hand out to shake, but Yannis didn't budge.

"Can I ask you something?" said Yannis. "Is it money you're looking for, or happiness?"

"Come on now, don't start none of that hippy bullshit. I got bills to pay, man. And last I checked, DTE don't take hugs and smiles as payment."

"No, that's not what I mean. How long have you been here?"

"What do you mean? I don't know nothing about none of that existential bullshit?"

"No, I mean, how long have you been here, in the store?"

"I don't know? Fifteen minutes?"

"Two hours."

"Shut the fuck up. No, I haven't."

Yannis nodded. "Check your phone."

Chris pulled his phone out, and sure enough. Aside from the four missed calls from Erica, two hours had passed.

"What the fuck?"

"You know why dictators ban music first? Because music can change things. You've been here for two hours, but not just here. In that time you've gone, I don't know, somewhere else, twice."

His stomach dropped. The sweat under his arms went cold. Chris went to the door and flung it open. The dull morning sky that had been there fifteen minutes earlier was now replaced by near-noon light.

"The fuck you doing here?" Chris stared back toward Yannis.

"Very little, actually. It's what *here* is doing to you that interests me. I spent some time in China a few years ago, lived in the Upper Yuneng Village in the Meili Snow Mountains. It's the village where I first learned how to rewrite Akashic Records. When I was younger, I'd have called the village ancient. Now I understand it's not so old, but all the same, the generational and communal roots there are deep. And much like the Native Americans here, and the aboriginal tribes in Australia, and the countless other indigenous peoples around the world, they too had a tradition of music that was passed down, memorized, and repeated in order to access the records."

Chris reached across the counter, but Yannis leaped back out of reach. "How the hell have I been here for two hours?"

"I don't want to be presumptuous, but when I asked you if you wanted money or happiness, it's only because I saw the way you and Stella looked at each other at the bar that night."

"We didn't look at each other like anything." But even Chris couldn't tell if that was true or not.

"Have you noticed celestial radio is dying? There are fewer radio stations on the dial. It got me questioning whether the dead spots on the dial were a natural phenomenon, or something more nefarious."

"I don't care!"

"I think it may be a bit of both, but here, in this building, I get no reception. It's not always like that, but at regular intervals, three days per week for three hours or so in the morning, all radio signal dies here. No radio, no phones, no interference. Just silence. It feels, I don't know, like a gateway opens up. You know how hard it is staring at yourself in the mirror for ten minutes without looking away? Imagine having three hours with unfiltered access to your soul. Anyway, I'd experienced this in a few other places around the world, but they have been in such remote locations that they are useless in studying the effects on people. So, when I found this place, I had to buy it."

"Fuck this." Chris grabbed his crate from the counter, but as he reached for the two records Yannis had pulled out, Yannis pulled them to his chest.

"You want to know how you've been here for two hours?"

"Yes!"

"What you've been listening to, the music. You know how people mash-up songs with similar beats-per-minute? What I'm doing here is kind of the same thing, only bigger. I use the records to create a true map of the musical genome of our species. It's gold from lead. You were triggered by Kurt Cobain and Jason Molina, but that song comprises dozens of other artists. It's been created to trigger everyone differently. Like that dress online, is it blue or yellow? Or, more aptly, that *Green Needle/Brainstorm* audio illusion. You hear what you want, where you program your mind to go."

"And how does it trigger you?"

Yannis pulled his hair back to reveal earplugs. "I can hear the music, but it's muted enough to have no effect."

"You son-of-a-bitch."

"I know, I am. But I have to remain impartial. In the middle of a major market like Detroit, finding a dead zone is an X on a treasure map. Why do you think it's songs that are passed down? Because music is a beacon that attaches us to our past. And here, without all the noise and distraction that we don't even notice anymore, music can still function as it was intended to when it first came to be."

"And how's that?"

"Exactly! You tell me. Where did you go? You were gone for two hours. What happened? Revelation? Realization? Did anything change? Did you change anything?"

The day his father died, he'd hit every red light on the way to the hospital. It was a truth that he'd tortured himself with for years. But now, that torment was fading, replaced by green lights. Replaced by his father's last words that he'd never heard, but were now ingrained in his memory like a keystone supporting everything that came after.

"I heard my dad's last words."

"Good! Now that's just a start. Those are just words. Think bigger."

"How did you know what I heard in the song?"

"Chris, this isn't our first iteration together. Now listen, what else do you hear? Come on, Chris. Really listen. Cause I'm going to tell you something now that you are not going to want to hear, but you have to. Stella, she cannot go home with Rick. We have to change this. I tried a few times with a few other people to stop the Devil's Night fire, but I couldn't do it. The variables behind it were too systemic and widespread. But what's coming next month, that we can change. And it's real easy. We need to keep Rick and Stella from getting together."

"What? What's happening next month?"

"I really shouldn't say. The Akashic Records aren't something to play lightly with."

"What the fuck are the Akashic Records?"

"They are everything, Chris. Who we are, who we were, who we'll be. They are the exception that proves the rule of free will," Yannis ran his fingers through his hair and paced nervously, "But I can't say any more. Can't take the chance of this moment changing things."

"Well, fuck it, if you're not willing to say more, I guess I'm willing to take that chance for both of us. See you around." Chris picked up the records Yannis had set aside and began loading them back into the crate.

"No, no, no. Fine. Next month Stella is going to break up with Rick. And in the depths of that anguish, he's going to go on a bender, and every scheme he's got swirling in that head of his, he's going to let loose without any concern for how they turn out. Now, Chris, I know you love Erica, but for the greater good, are you willing to give that up? Would you trade being there when Trinie was born if it meant you could save the world? It would be a good life, brother. A happy one. All you got to do now is hear the right song, and you can walk out that door before Rick and I ever see you. So listen, Chris. Who do you hear?"

He could hear every song he'd ever listened to. It was a tesseract of sound moving through his mind, a timeline of his life told through music. And there, next to PJ Harvey, was Stella. A sonic wall of reverb poured from the jukebox. Music was all that kept Chris and Stella apart. Under the table, their legs intertwined. The booths were small, but this was something else.

The server brought another round and, as the echoing esoterics of *To Bring You My Love* swelled, Chris pressed his knee against the inside of her thigh. Stella sipped her beer, leaned in close. "You familiar with the Latin phrase: *Amor Fati?*"

"Naw. I don't think so?"

"It means: Hey, wanna go back to my place?"

And for a second, he saw it again, the glimpse into that other place. Choice manifested into a realized existence.

In a moment, Rick would arrive, and all he had to do was say yes, and he and Stella could be together, never seen by him.

Chris huddled against the doorway of his memory. As Stella took his hand and that single word formed on his lips, in his mouth, on his tongue, another song emerged from the turbulence. Low at first, barely a whisper. But moments or hours later it was all he could hear. He could go back and change anything he wanted. He could find his happiness.

The needle dropped, the record spun, and the sound of Tom Waits' voice crooned and croaked and

Book III

WWJPTSD

Twisted metal and shattered glass. What was once a glass-top patio table was now a shimmering astrolabe surrounded by yellow caution tape. Legs and supports bent into an abstract sextant incapable of reading any stars or navigating any seas. Little diamonds of tempered glass shimmered across the pavement, glimmering in the sodium-vapor streetlights. A dozen tables stretched between the sidewalk and the restaurant. Eleven of them were in pristine condition. Umbrellas tucked down, chairs pushed in. But the broken table, that piece had a deliberate glow to it. A glow which attracted the attention of the hipsters and foodies waiting in line for *Trough*.

As hip as *Trough* was, this is the type of shit Camila imagined they would keep on display so that their name would stay trending on social media. When the hype around the food dimmed, they'd need the glow of something new and shiny to keep the right type of tastemakers walking through the doors.

She sat on the curb next to the table and had to lean back to keep from having her face show up on dozens of Instagram and Facebook feeds while she waited for her Uber. From the front door all the way to the street, the men and women in line twisted themselves into pretzels to get their smartphones into whatever artistic angle they needed to turn the table into the next outdoor art/political protest project in Detroit.

But this wasn't the Heidelberg Project, wasn't even Hamtramck Disneyland, and they were certainly not in Detroit.

It was a Goddamn broken table in the middle of the suburbs. The result of some traffic thing that had happened that morning. She followed a lot of people on Instagram, and it was all they were posting about. But she'd barely even looked at the photos past the first one; they were all so identical. And if she had to read one sophomoric diatribe about the table being a messianic representation of outrage over the new redlining of the city, she was going to something something.

She didn't know what, but she'd show them what messianic

outrage over redlining really looked like. Because it sure as shit was not a broken table.

That it happened in front of *Trough* was a Goddamn joke too. A coincidence that allowed hipsters to make two pilgrimages for the price of one.

Whatever. This wasn't her city. Not really.

"Hey, you Camila?"

She looked up to find an Accord idling beside her. A round-faced young man sat behind the wheel.

He had a smile that said the world hadn't jaded him yet, and a haircut his mother probably still paid for. "Adrian?" she called back.

He nodded.

Camila hoisted herself to her feet, and for the few steps it took to reach the car, she felt like a celebrity or a criminal. Caught in the crossfire of flash photography and internet infamy.

The Accord pulled away from the crowd, merged into traffic, and motored out of downtown. Camila was relieved to be escaping the manufactured bliss of suburban life. Even if it was just for the night.

"So, Springwells, huh?" The driver smiled at her through the rearview mirror. "Most of the kids I've been carting down have been heading to New Center or Millennium Village."

Camila nodded as the car merged onto I-75 south. She wasn't in the mood for small talk. Camila had told her parents she was heading to a coffee shop to study with some friends for her physics mid-term, and she couldn't shake the feeling that they would find out she wasn't still there. "You can call me Age," said the driver.

"Got it."

"You got family down there? Springwells can get pretty crazy on Devil's Night. Just sayin'."

Maybe he wasn't trying to *White Knight* her, but, in her experience, whenever a Caucasian man was *just sayin'* to a pretty, young, dark-skinned girl, he was either a *nice guy,* or just plain ignorant.

"Friends. Kind of a party thing."

"Nice. Yeah, my friends are all having a party tonight too. A costume party."

"Yeah?"

"Yeah. We all kind of do the cosplay thing. You know, dress up as characters from Star Wars, Borderlands, Marvel, and whatever."

"You know Halloween's not until tomorrow?"

"It's not a Halloween thing, it's an us thing."

Camila shrugged. "I could see you passing for Luigi."

"My boyfriend tells me the same thing every Comic-Con. I say I got Luigi's height, but Mario's body."

"Well, Comic-Con is the place to go if you want to see what your favorite characters would look like if they let themselves go."

"Fucking perfect!" Age laughed. "You a gamer?"

"Not really. I like Nintendo, but don't play much." And then, unwittingly finding herself part of their conversation anyway, she asked, "Why are you driving instead of living it up with them?"

"If you direct your attention to the photo array on the back of my seat," Age said, with a well-rehearsed Vanna White wave of the hand. "I want to work for Masood. After seeing how the kiosks worked out, and with the new arm of The Loop opening soon, they feel like an exciting place to be. But I can't afford school yet, so here I am."

Laminated maps and photos covered the backs of both the driver and passenger seats. A signed and personalized Akbar Masood headshot, an artist's rendition of the route for the new Ford Inter-Urban Loop, and publicity photos of the state-of-the-art station and trollies that will, within the next few months, connect Detroit to Ann Arbor via a sub-hyperloop. Once operational, The Loop would quadruple the workforce in Detroit. It was supposed to be up and running a year ago, but like Amazon in Tennessee or Foxconn in Wisconsin, citizens protested, and plans were delayed. But in the end Masood won out because instead of tax breaks or subsidies, Masood only asked for time and space, and provided with both, they delivered on the promise of jobs and revenue and innovation. Even Camila's father worked for Masood.

Camila studied the map. The Loop had two arms. The first stretched north to McLaren Oakland Hospital in Pontiac from Renaissance Center in Detroit along the Woodward corridor. Between the two primary stations sat hub stations, stops along the way where other trollies from outlying neighborhoods could connect to the main loop: Cranbrook, Poppleton, Beaumont, Magic Bag, State Fair, Planet Ant, DIA, Ren Cen. The second arm, connecting Ren Cen to University of Michigan Medical Center in Ann Arbor was still under construction, but Age's map listed the hubs along that arm as well: Health Center, Prospect, Denton, Wayne, Gulley, McMillian, Altar, Schaffer, Wyoming, Ferdinand, Millennium, Ren Cen.

"You saving?" asked Camila.

"Slowly," Age said, and smiled.

He was nice enough, but listening to a white man take his struggle in stride like this was un-fucking-bearable. Even without the leg-up of a father who worked for Masood, this man had so many privileges that Camila could never dream of. She was looking at colleges right now too, and the only advantage any of the applications offered her was to compare her struggles to those of every other woman and person of color by checking the right boxes.

"Let's say you weren't driving tonight, who would you have dressed up as?"

"It was a couple's costume. So, since its Devil's Night and we're in Detroit, I put together a pretty sweet Nain Rouge costume."

"The Nine what?"

"Not *Nine*, the number. It's French: The Nain Rouge. Shit, you don't know what that is?"

"What, should I?"

"Bash told me it was common knowledge here. I'm not from Detroit, so he made me study up on it. He was kind of obsessed. Now I am too. But shit, now I'm worried that everyone is going to think I'm doing some bad *Chilling Adventures of Sabrina* cosplay."

"So what is it? The Nine whatever."

"You want me to get into it? I'm kind of obsessed. I can talk your ear off."

The hell, you say.

Camila shrugged. What else were they going to talk about for the next twenty minutes?

As they drove along the concrete scar that was I-75, the new Detroit skyline came into view. Years earlier, Masood Pharmaceuticals swooped in and began to buy up abandoned and deteriorating properties, and either through teardowns or refurbishments, set Detroit on its path of rejuvenation. With its crowning jewels being the state-of-the-art hotel and convention center where Cobo Hall once stood, the massive tech campus was sandwiched between Little Caesars Arena and Eastern Market, stretching from The Fisher Freeway all the way to Mack Ave, and, of course, The Loop. Once complete, Detroit's riverfront skyline will rival Chicago's. Thanks to the foundation laid by Masood, other corporations came swarming to this city whose greatness was once thought to exist only in the past. And in the face of all that had changed, Age told Camila the history of Detroit, and of the creature known as the Nain Rouge.

He told it like they were sitting around a campfire:

"The Red Dwarf of Detroit. Red flesh and puckish horns. Blazing eyes and rotten teeth." Or at least he tried. He kept interrupting himself. "Maybe I'm a little tall, but the costume I put together lights up and smokes, really looks like I'm on fire."

"I'm sure there's a joke in there about being flaming," Camila joked.

"Please! Bash won't shut up about it! Every time I tried the costume on, he'd say *'everyone knows you're gay, you don't need to prove it.'* So annoying! Anyway, the costume is awesome, but the legend goes that the appearance of the Nain Rouge foretells disaster. You know how Detroit's motto is something about rising from the ashes? Well that's because of Antoine de la Mothe Cadillac, the founder of the city. He was the first person to see the dwarf.

"He wrote in his diary about an encounter he had with a gypsy who advised him to appease the man in red or lose everything his family held dear. Cadillac, not one to heed superstitious bunkum, ignored the warning. A few weeks later, as he walked along the river, he encountered what he described as a red baboon. Cadillac hit the creature with his cane and it ran off into the woods. After that, he wrote that he heard an aberrant laughter echoing through the city every night since. Then in 1805 the creature showed up again, and a fire burned six hundred homes to the ground."

"So, what was it? The red baboon?"

"You ever see a red baboon before?"

"No. But are you saying you believe in this thing?"

"I'm just telling you the story," said Age. "And there's more to it. The sightings kept happening. In 1863, when white citizens of Detroit burned the city's black quarter to the ground. 1897, the Detroit Opera House exploded. 1915, a cart hauling embers tipped over on the Belle Isle Bridge and caught fire. In both 1943 and 1967, during riots, the city burned again. And, of course, it's seen every year on Devil's Night."

"You've rehearsed this, haven't you?" asked Camila.

"Is it that obvious?" Age laughed. "Okay, where was I?"

Outside the car windows, spotlights swept across the sky and lit skyscrapers dotted the horizon. Peaceful. Cool. Silent. Age continued his diatribe, but Camila had already stopped listening.

Detroit loomed on the horizon, and with it came memories of Camila's old life. She had been gearing up to see her old friends for weeks, and now that the time was here, she was feeling a middling sense of nostalgia. Life seemed to comprise of three parts of equal length: Before high school, high school, and after high school. Maybe they weren't truly equal, but surely they were in the way time passed during each.

Camila had emerged into adolescence with an insatiable urge to live. Even if that life was a constant flutter of delicate wings towards a flame. And now she was stuck in the middle of the middle. Only fifteen, but ripe for upheaval. Still young, but old enough to have gained a perspective on the transition from the first part of her life to the current one.

Three years earlier her friends Paola and Renata—twelve going on eighteen at the time—had been torpedoed into puberty with chests that brought boys begging, and a penchant for mistaking their own limited worldly experiences as the end-all of everything. In school, they spoke and acted with an effortless confidence that Camila envied. But school was where their self-assurance ended. They could manipulate their peers, yet in private, they lacked any drive to delve inward. It had been Camila who propelled them to push the boundaries of their adolescence. Their last summer together was spent spelunking through the abandoned mansions north of their post-war-bungalow neighborhood.

These weathered, grand estates had wraparound porches and majestic staircases, deep in-ground pools and carriage houses with cobble stone drives. The manors were not only a sight to behold, but served as fuel for imagining the type of people who could both frivolously occupy and then vacate such homes.

Inside, they found decades of mildew and mold blossoming on every surface, filling the air with spores that looked like stardust in the bolts of sunlight coming through the cracked walls and ceilings.

While Paola and Renata crept softly over the rotten floorboards,

Camila bounded past them, bolting up the stairs and sliding down the curved banisters. Floorboards creaked and walls shuttered under her vibration. With every step, she prayed to slip and crash through the floor or pummel through a dry-rotted wall. She was twelve going on five and wanted to prove that she was as indestructible as she thought she was.

Or, at the very least, bankrupt her parents with medical bills so maybe they wouldn't have to move away. Back then, she did not know that her parents had no choice.

Camila's parents said that they would be in their new home by Thanksgiving, so when fall arrived Camila and her friends rallied in Clark Park with toilet paper, bars of soap, and cartons of eggs; they were going to give their friendship a proper sendoff.

But as they gathered around the picnic table, their young eyes witnessed the night take a sinister turn. Black plumes rose against the orange and purple sunset, and the wail of first responders' vehicles sounded like the notes opera singers would hit to shatter glass. The Detroit skyline leaked into the clouds, lifted by the glow of a small handful of fires.

"Oh my God," said Paola, and she pointed to the sky north of the park.

The darkened sky disguised most of the smoke, but the red flicker on the horizon detailed enough. There was a fire in their own neighborhood. "That's up where all those old mansions are," said Renata.

They watched the smoke rise in silence. Somewhere, the grand staircases turned to ash, the pools filled with cinder and twisted nails, and the brittle floor fell through with no prompting from their weight. The last defining moment of their friendship carried off in the breeze, and with toilet paper and eggs and soap in hand, their childhood went with it.

"Shit," said Age, breaking Camila from her reminiscing. "You got your ID on you? They got a checkpoint up here."

Camila looked out the front window, surprised to find that they were no longer on the freeway. Blue and red flashing lights lined the road, and a line of cars moved forward through a makeshift barrier constructed between two of the gigantic cement pillars which supported The Loop. Most vehicles were waved through, but a few had been directed to a secondary inspection point where armed men surrounded the vehicle.

She hadn't seen the structure up close. On the news, for sure, but it was always hard to tell the scope and size of something as abstract and unique as The Loop from a TV screen.

It was intimidating beyond words. Otherworldly in design, but bulky and massive in a way that fit Detroit's muscle car history. The flashing lights from the checkpoint created a film of light pollution that kept Camila from getting a clear glimpse at the tube itself that hung above her. It was supposed to be a glass tube, but scaffolding and tarps obscured whatever work was being done inside.

Fifty yards wide, fifty miles long. Like the freeway they had taken to get here, this mass transit marvel was another scar on an already abused city. Eventually, the city would rebuild around the tube and its stations, but the infrastructure needed to develop The Loop displaced thousands of families and hundreds of businesses and left only a shadow and bare soil below. Salted earth from one horizon to the other.

An officer wearing a tactical vest and holding an assault rifle motioned them forward. The Accord inched up until it was entombed under the cement Loop and surrounded by a bevy of loitering officers. Only two or three officers approached the cars crossing the checkpoint. The others were only there for show, to intimidate in the unlikely case of an actual issue arising.

Age had already rolled down his window when the Security Officer asked for ID and shined a flashlight into his eyes.

"Here you go." The officer took his license, but didn't even glance at it.

"Where you headed?"

"I'm an Uber driver. Taking my passenger to her destination."

The beam of light traced back to the rear window. The officer bent over and found Camila sitting in the far corner of the vehicle. He smiled.

"Roll down your back window, sir." Age complied.

"Evening," said the officer to Camila. "Got ID on you?"

"I do. Something wrong?"

"I don't know. You do something wrong?"

"No."

"Don't need the attitude, I'm here to keep the neighborhood safe. What you heading into the city for? How much cash you got on you?"

"You think I'm going to Detroit to what, buy drugs?"

"You said it, not me." The officer smiled.

"I'm going home."

"And where's home? Let me see *your* ID."

Camila caught Age's eyes in the rearview mirror. There was a silent plea to cooperate; neither of them had done anything wrong, and some battles weren't worth fighting.

It was an easy stance for a white man to have.

Bullshit.

She wanted to say, "Can I see your ID?" Instead, she answered his question.

"Ferdinand Street," she half-lied. It's where she lived before they moved to the suburbs.

The officer motioned with two fingers to see the ID. Camila rolled her eyes and opened her purse.

When her father was offered the job at Masood, the raise in pay was so significant that they took their first-ever family vacation. To Columbia. It was a fun trip, except that between the sun and swimming and relaxation, her father was relentless in reminding Camila and her brother that this is where their family had come from. Camila and her brother were both born in the US, but her parents immigrated. Her father thought it was important for them to understand how far they had come. To leave the US, they had all needed enhanced IDs. Since the move, they had all gotten new ones with their new address on them. Camila had held onto that old ID though, and she fiercely protected it, as it had become one of her most cherished possessions.

Her parents figured it was a sweet tribute to her father's words on their trip: a reminder of how far they had come. But really, she kept it because their old address was on it: she wanted to remember where *she* had come from.

Camila pulled the ID from her purse and handed it over to the officer. He looked it over and chuckled. "The fuck you doin' up in the burbs?"

"Shopping with friends."

"And where are they?"

"I had to be home before them."

"And if I look in your bag there, am I going to find any items without receipts?"

"Yeah, you are. Cause I didn't buy anything!"

The officer looked at the ID again, turned the flashlight back to Age. "You know you're not supposed to be driving anyone underage without an adult, right?"

Age whipped his head toward the backseat. "You're not eighteen?" Then back to the officer, "I swear, the app didn't say she was a minor."

"You really going to give us shit cause I called an Uber to get home? I'm not buying drugs, I didn't shoplift. Not trying to get drunk." Maybe that last one wasn't true. "I'm just trying to get home."

The officer tucked his tongue into his lip and rapped the edge of her ID on the roof of the car. He glanced away and shut his flashlight off and handed the ID back to Camila.

"Now listen, Camila of Ferdinand Street, I don't want to see your face again tonight. I don't want to hear your name or see this ID come up in a report tomorrow morning. You get me? You get home and you stay there. There's enough fucking riff-raff on the street, don't need one more wanna-be hoodlum getting caught up in it. You hear?"

Age answered, "Yes, sir. I'll drop her home and that's that."

The officer banged the roof of the car with his hand, a signal that he was done with them, and walked away. Without waiting to be second guessed, Age shifted his car into drive.

It was no accident that the checkpoint was set up where it was. Right under The Loop. The inadvertent physical manifestation of the poverty line. Through the rear window, Camila watched the checkpoint, awash in the red glow of the Accord's taillights, shrink away and fade into the night as they sunk farther below that redline.

"Man," said Age. "What an asshole!"

"Whatever. I'm used to it." She was glad that the ride was nearly over. She could tell Age wanted to say something about her being underage, but he was too much of a Social Justice Warrior to harass her about it, especially after that encounter with the officer.

"Seriously, I bet in your neighborhood shouting ICE in a crowded room gets the same reaction as shouting fire." A smile pursed his lips for a split second, but just as quickly, guilt flattened his wit. "No offense. He was an asshole, though."

"Nah, he wasn't. You have to give a shit to be an asshole. They get off on fucking with brown people. If he cared about keeping the neighborhoods safe and not harassing people who look like me, he would have questioned the address on my ID."

"Why is that?"

"Because he would have known it doesn't exist anymore."

Five minutes later they arrived at the address and Camila stepped out of the car.

The Uber drove off, leaving Camila to her own devices. She didn't watch it leave, too focused on the house before her, on willing herself to step toward it.

Paint flaked from the ramshackle old bungalow and the overgrown lawn was littered with trash. Music boomed from the house, rattling the glass, and a dozen teenagers milled around on the porch in a blue cloud of smoke.

The parties at Camila's new school had been an immense disappointment. Before the move, Camila had seen her fair share of high school parties on her block. Parents gone, booze flowing, music blaring. She, Paola, and Renata had even tried to crash a few of them by hopping neighbor's fences and sneaking in through backdoors. And while they often gained entry, it didn't take long for them to be shown the door. But as they were being escorted out, Camila committed snapshots of the parties to memory: couples making out, drinking games, clouds of illicit smoke. Dancing, swearing, fighting.

Upon matriculating to high school herself, Camila was more than ready to face a real high school party. But once invited to one, the experience proved to be lacking. They were small gatherings in basements, with pizza and pop and helicopter-parents upstairs listening through the ductwork to ensure that the games of spin the bottle and truth or dare remained PG. And even then, most of the kids were glued to their phones, taking selfies and posting about how fucking dope the party was, and how lame you were if you weren't there.

She was ready for an actual party.

Camila didn't immediately recognize any of the people on the porch, and they eyed her as she walked up the cracked cement pathway. She avoided direct eye contact with them, even as memories formed in her mind and she saw familiar faces emerge behind the changes of puberty. Boys and girls who, three years ago, were pudgy children still playing with Barbies and Legos, were now, with cigarettes and beers in hand, playing at being men and women. This was the party she had been looking for.

"Chica!" called a familiar voice as the front door swung open. It was Paola, and as swiftly as it had come on, Camila's trepidation vanished.

"Paola!" Her friend had changed little from Camila's last memory of her. Maybe she was taller and wore more makeup, but she had been one of the first in their class to find a curse word that fit each of the parts of speech, and her vulgarity held fast.

The two hugged on the steps as if too much and no time at all had passed.

"Rich bitch slummin' it tonight, huh?" Paola laughed.

"Shut the fuck up."

"I just playin'. How's life up in the fucking hills?"

"I'm hardly in the hills."

"Shit, bitch. Look around you. Three blocks north is the hills compared to this street." They separated, and Paola took Camila's hand. "Come on, let's go find Renata."

Camila followed Paola, hoping, expecting, waiting to find the den of debauchery that her mind and the music told her was waiting for her inside. Sadly, the music was a ruse. For a moment, she thought to blame her mind for misremembering the parties she'd crashed. But those images were burned into place. And none of them contained cell phones.

Again, modern convenience had robbed her of the expectations of her youth.

The music was loud, the room chock-full of teenagers and not a parent in sight, yet the prevalent attribute of the room was silence. There was no din of conversation to fill the space while the beat was gearing up to drop, only muted smatterings of laughter as small groups stared at tiny cellphone screens.

Snapchat, group-text auto-correct flubs, YouTube videos.

Someone handed Camila a beer as Paola led her through the room. Whatever liquid courage it was supposed to have offered her, she didn't need it. She'd been to this party before.

One song ended, and before the silence built to an unbearable level waiting for the next to begin, Renata's laughter cut through the crowd. It was a shriek, a contagious cry that begged everyone who heard it to question why they were taking their lives so seriously.

"Hey, Re! Look who showed up."

Camila and Paola came up behind Renata, who, alongside three older boys—two of whom Camila recognized from the old neighborhood: Gael and Mateo, but the third was a stranger—stared at yet another cellphone screen.

"Oh my God! Hi!" Renata said. She craned her neck back, half-hugging Camila, while keeping her eyes attached to the screen. "Have you seen this guy? He's stupid insane!"

Out of politeness, not interest, Camila leaned over her old friend's shoulder. On the tiny screen was a cheap and fast infomercial—the kind that usually promises some sort of get rich quick scheme, with a douchey host showing off his elaborate Los Angeles home and plethora of fancy sports cars—only this guy wasn't trying to use his surroundings to sell anything. He was badly chroma-keyed into a background of soaring clouds. Wild-eyed, and wearing a mismatched suit, the olive-skinned man sermonized, "And now, through radical rigorous research, and re-polishing reports relinquished to the refuse heap, The Yannis Institute is perfectly pleased to present you with Social Lube!"

All around Camila, they laughed. She didn't get the appeal, but she let Renata's laughter infect her anyway. It was easier to fake a laugh than be left out of an inside joke. "That's ridiculous," chortled Camila.

"I know, right? Keep watching. This guy is a dumbass," said Renata. Unlike Paola, Renata had changed significantly. Her raven black hair was now infused with blonde streaks, and besides no longer wearing glasses, she also could no longer maintain eye contact or carry on a conversation.

"How have you been?" Camila tried. "Whose house is this?" and "What's school like now?"

In response, all she got was a passive, "Huh?"; "I don't know"; and "What?" between outbursts of laughter.

Renata was consumed with clip after clip of this infomercial guy. Paola flirted with the boy holding the phone. And as Camila was feeling that maybe coming here was a mistake, a dark and lean boy turned his attention toward her.

"Who are you?" he asked. His deep voice and facial hair made her rethink calling him a boy.

"Who am I?" Camila made a dubious face. "Who are you?"

"Chill, girl, just extending an olive leaf."

"Olive branch. The expression is olive branch."

"Cool," he looked back to the phone. "Forget I said anything."

Cool. Camila cracked her beer and took a sip. She looked around the room and imagined that this is what her high school reunion was going to feel like, and decided that she wasn't going to go.

"Listen." She put her hand on the boy's elbow and said, "I'm Camila," as an apology.

"Cool." He didn't look up. Not at first. Then his eyes moved up, and as he smiled his head tilted toward her. "Cassius."

"I used to go to school down here, but my parents moved."

"I moved here this year."

"So, it's your first Devil's Night, huh?"

"It's crazy, you know, back where I come from, we called the day before Halloween the day before Halloween."

"Detroit hustles harder."

"Yeah? What do you know? You don't live here anymore."

"And just when I thought I was starting to like you."

"Bet I can win you back."

"How's that?"

"You ever see anyone breathe fire?"

"Like at a circus? Are you a clown?"

"Goddamn right he's a fucking clown!" Paola chimed in, "Don't listen to his lies!"

"Oh, I wasn't," Camila said to Paola, flashing a flirtatious smile at Cassius. "So, what are we gonna do tonight?"

"Bitch, we doin' it! This is a party, bottoms up!" Paola flipped her beer up and guzzled it down.

"For real? Come on, Paola, don't you remember those parties we used to crash down the block? Dancing and drinking and—"

"Making out!" Paola shoved Camila. She stumbled back and fell into Cassius. His arms caught her like a vice.

As warm as he was, she thought maybe he could breathe fire.

"You okay?" he asked and helped her back up.

She nodded, but didn't look at him, afraid he'd catch her blushing. "I'm serious. Everyone's on their fucking phones."

"Sorry, Mom," Paola laughed. "We're young and dumb, wasting our lives and frying our brains! I'm sure up in the suburbs the parties are more intellectually stimulating."

"What's your problem?"

Cassius stepped between the friends. "Ladies, come on now."

"No one asked you, Cas," said Paola. "I ain't got a fucking problem. I'm nice enough to invite you to a party and you judge how we talk, and complain that it's not as good as your high-class suburban parties."

"Not as good? It's exactly the same! They're fucking lame as hell up there! I was hoping down here would be different, especially on Devil's Night."

"So, what do you want to do? You want to go TP some trees and egg some houses?"

"Yeah, something like that."

Paola's vitriol smoothed out into a puckish stance. "You always been wild, girl. Fuck yeah!"

"I'm in," said Cassius.

"Do you even know what we're doing?" asked Camila.

"We had egging houses back where I used to live. Only we didn't limit it to one night of the year."

"Alright." Camila looked at the two of them. "I'll grab the eggs. Paola, you try to find soap. Cas, toilet paper. Meet in the garage in five minutes."

The three melted into the silent mob that surrounded them, each headed in different directions. Even though she was alone, for the first time that night Camila didn't feel like it. Paola was right, she was a bit of a wild one, and even though the trio had changed, it felt familiar and nice to be *doing*, rather than simply existing.

That idea of being able to start over, leave behind all that you have and are, reinvent yourself as a new person, is a wonderful fantasy. In practice, though, it is wrought with impossibilities. At her new school, Camila tried to be someone different, to suppress her wild side. She succeeded, but in exorcising that demon from her soul, she sidelined herself from her own life, and became a wilted wallflower that only existed to appear, not be.

Eggs in hand, she was being. The attached garage was a mess. Tools piled on top of work benches, ashtrays overflowing with browned cigarette butts, spray paint cans in a heap. Paola and Cassius hadn't returned with their goods yet, and Camila looked out the open garage door.

In the cover of darkness, it took her a moment to realize why the Detroit skyline was so muted and dull. In her memories, and even heading down here, the buildings all shined so bright.

The Loop.

The Loop ran perpendicular between the neighborhood and downtown, and in the night sky the unlit, unfinished construction was a pitch-black band that blocked the glow of whatever progress was happening downtown from shining down on these neighborhoods.

In the suburbs, The Loop was only talked about in reverent tones, the hallowed means of rebirth. Here, it took more than it gave.

She turned away from the lack of skyline, her eyes landing on the pile of spray paint cans.

One by one, Camila rifled through the cans, shaking them until she found a relatively full one. A neon green that matched the piecemealed BMX in the corner. She tucked the can into her bag alongside the eggs.

A minute later, Cassius and Paola came through the door with Renata and her two boy-toy accessories, Mateo and Gael, trailing behind.

Cassius stepped past Camila. "Ready?"

"A lot of us, isn't it?"

"What, you forget we travel in packs down here? Come on suburb-girl."

Over the next hour, the six youths zigzagged across the neighborhood. They took aim at old haunts, settled long-forgotten scores against former junior high crushes, and sought out the corner store they used to stop in on the walk home from school—the one where the crabby old bat behind the counter would rant and rave if there were more than three students in the store at one time—and all the while Camila palmed the spray paint can through the canvas of her bag. Slowly, and unbeknownst to her cohorts, Camila had pushed the group closer and closer to The Loop. Epitaphs swirled in her head. Slogans and statements.

Fuck The Loop.

To Hell With Progress.

I Want My City Back.

They were going to soap the windows of those who offended them, egg the houses of those who wronged them, TP the trees of those who belittled them. And she was going to tag the structure that had destroyed the vision of her youth. And when she stood below The Loop for the second time that evening, she was intimidated by it all over again.

Fuck The Loop.

They walked alongside the chain-link fence that separated the neighborhood from the construction site. Miles of galvanized steel wire rattled in the breeze.

"It's pretty ugly if you ask me," said Renata. The first words of substance Camila had heard from her friend in three years.

"Right?!" Camila fell into step with Renata. "I don't know how you deal with it every day."

"What choice do we have? We couldn't afford to move away." And with that, their conversation was over. Renata fell back even farther and hung her arm around Gael's shoulder.

Ahead, one of the giant cement support pillars loomed, blocking out and blending in with the black sky. Camila stopped and peered up at the column while the rest of the group filed past her.

"Hol' up." Before the others stopped, maybe even before they processed her request, Camila was on the fence. Fingers wrapped awkwardly into the wire diamonds, toes hoisting her upwards.

"What the fuck, girl?" Paola had a cigarette dangling from her lip as she dug through her purse for a lighter.

"Yeah, seriously. You can get in a lot of trouble for that shit," added Cassius.

"It's Devil's Night, isn't it? Aren't we supposed to get into trouble?"

"Camila, come on." Renata glanced over each shoulder, looking for headlights or security patrols. "This isn't funny. Let's go."

"Give me a second." Camila swung one leg over the top of the fence, then the other, and pushed. She fell away from the ten-foot fence and landed on her knees in the hard, packed dirt. Aside from the place where she landed, she left no trace of her trespassing as she crept forward.

A metal skeleton of scaffolding stretched up one side of the pillar. At first, Camila was just going to head around to the other side to make her mark, but the scaffolding offered her message a more prominent exhibition. So again, she climbed.

Paola laughed at the sight, and the boys marveled at her gall. But Renata paced nervously.

The scaffolding swayed as she hoisted herself up, and the wood platforms bowed under her weight. She felt again like she was back exploring those mansions behind the old neighborhood. Diving deeper and deeper inside, hoping to fall through the rotten wood. Camila climbed higher still. Thirty, forty feet up, until a powerful gust of wind rattled the scaffolding and she had to wrap her arms around the metal pole to keep from tumbling off.

With that gust came a whistle. Not of police sirens or a security alarm, but the *hoot* that is produced by blowing over the top of an open glass bottle.

"You crazy," came a shout from the ground when the wind died down. Camila smiled to herself and inspected her surroundings, looking to narrow down the source of the whistle. She found her answer overhead, and a shot of adrenaline zipped through her body and made her palms sweaty.

"Hey!" Camila called down. "There's an open access hatch! We can go inside!"

"Naw! Fuck that!" said Cassius. "Come on down."

Camila shook her head. "You come up!"

"Tag your shit and let's go!"

"Yeah, come on." Renata looked like she was going to vomit. "I don't want to get in trouble."

Paola chimed in before Camila could, "Then why did you come?"

"Seriously?" Renata put a hand on her hip and went off. "Me Dijiste que deberia ir porque iba a estar bien. Que hay de divertido en esto? No puedo permitirme en problemas. No despues de esa mierda con mi papa!"

"Alright, well, I'm going in." Camila couldn't make out the exchange from as high as she was, but their yelling was only going to draw attention before too long. "Don't rat me out if you get caught down there."

"Camila, wait," called Cassius. She heard his call, but was in no position to respond. Her breath was caught in her throat as she hoisted herself up, rung by rung, into the cavernous hatch.

As she climbed, the residual light from the street below fell away. The soft clang of her shoes on the rungs gave more definition to the space than her eyes could. The darkness was complete and full until she reached her hand up for the next rung and found only a flat plateau.

"Hello?" Her voice echoed forever down a long, invisible corridor. She was inside The Loop. Here, the dark wasn't as complete. As she climbed out of the access duct, her eyes adjusted, thanks to the sliver of light coming in from across the open and hallow space.

Once her eyes had acclimated enough to be confident that there were no other open hatches she could fall through, Camila crept to the sliver of light and took a knee. Outside, the glass tube was covered in heavy industrial tarps to protect the surface from any construction accidents and debris. The light that allowed Camila to see was from a place where the tarps didn't quite overlap, and it was through that gap that, at last, Camila saw Detroit from an angle she recognized. The vantage point was higher, but that didn't matter. It was the shape of the skyline that she remembered. The twinkle of a city that, she learned earlier tonight, had been reborn out of flames more times than imaginable.

"Camila?" She turned and saw Cassius peering into the darkness with his unadjusted eyes.

"Hey," she said. He turned his head toward her voice. It was impossible to tell if he could see or not, but he climbed the rest of the way up and headed toward her. There was more movement behind him as Paola and Mateo wormed their way out of the hatch.

"This is crazy," said Cassius, once he was able to take in the room. Glass hung overhead like the inside of a space station against the infinity of the cosmos. A single three-foot-wide rail ran down the center of the tube, flanked by chrome tile and thin grate-like catwalks on either side.

"Where's Renata?"

"Chickened out. Gael took her home," said Paola.

"What's her problem?"

Paola shrugged.

"So where to now?" Cassius asked. They all looked to Camila.

"Which way to Ann Arbor?" she asked as a grander plan formed in her head.

Cassius looked back and forth down the tunnel, pointed. "That way."

Camila held up her cell phone, turned on the flashlight, and walked.

"Then we're going the other way."

Bash had always dreamt of the apocalypse. Burnt cities and napalm skies hanging over roving bands of bandits and survivors, militants and empires, all vying for resources and control over whatever bits of Earth were left. He imagined bombs dropping and zombies pulling themselves from shallow graves and unstoppable viruses sweeping across the landscape.

The visions were always more Studio Ghibli than Cormac McCarthy. Their focus not on the bleak realities of a world without order or life without modern convenience, but instead, he pictured a romantic Armageddon full of the adventure and excitement which order and convenience did not allow for.

His parents thought that these vivid ideas were simply adolescent angst manifesting itself in unique ways. In reality, the infatuation stemmed from an obscure Canadian children's television show called *The Odyssey*. They lived close enough to the border to pick up the CBC, and their after-school programing was far more interesting than anything offered by its American counterpart. *The Odyssey* told the story of a group of friends and a treehouse. When one of the friends falls from the tree, he also falls into a coma-world where there are no adults, and children his own age act out the parts of rebels, fascists, insurrectionists, and victims.

Transposing this concept on his own life, Bash populated that world with cousins and school friends as allies, and the bullies and jerks as the Axis. He pictured no one dead, simply gone. His parents having peacefully drifted away to someplace else, taking with them the realities that trapped him in a world where all the maps had been drawn, all rivers crossed, and all mountains summited.

And without parents and neighbors and teachers, Bash would be left with a world to mold.

History burnt. Science forgotten. Faith and religion left behind.

Then he met Age, and stars stopped falling from the sky, the oceans no longer boiled, and when the rain fell, it didn't promise to drown civilization. The adventure he sought had never lain at the end of the world as he had thought for so long, but in the heart of another. Whenever they kissed or held hands or made love, every apocalyptic vision, dream, and fantasy was wiped from his mind. He no longer wished to see the world end, but to embrace mundanity as an adventure in itself. Because, anymore, the only way the world would end was if he and Age were no longer together.

And Devil's Night was supposed to be their night.

Kids and families had Halloween to dress up and throw parties; the nerds and geeks had to share Comic-Con with every fair-weather fanboy and fangirl jumping on the bandwagon of whatever piece of sci-fi or fantasy media the culture had agreed to embrace that year. But they'd claimed Devil's Night. Because to them, cosplay wasn't a moment, or an event, or even a day where they put on a costume and pretended to be someone they could never be. Nor was it about escaping from a marginalized existence. It was about being who you were, despite the constraints of that marginalization.

Really, it was nothing new, marginalized groups coming together to celebrate their shared experience.

First the women did it, then the blacks, then the LGBTQIA+ community.

Now, it was the Age of Aquarius for furries and crossplayers, for the introverts and e-kids and otherkin, even for the Instagram narcissists and TikTok influencers.

And Age was missing the celebration again.

They'd met at Comic-Con. Bash was dressed as Lando Calrisian, and Age introduced himself as a recovering nerd: "I know Han Solo shot first, but I'm trying really hard not to care," he said, and from then on, they were nearly inseparable.

Yet, this was the third year running that the McGettigan Brothers had hosted the event at their Corktown loft, and it was the third year that Age had missed it. The first year his mother passed away, the next year his sister had a baby, and he'd flown to LA to meet his nephew. Bash obviously hadn't judged him for missing either of those times, but this year was a different story. This year, at the last minute, Age logged on to Uber and began accepting ride requests. And now, Bash's *Antoine de la Mothe Cadillac* was left without its *Nain Rouge* counterpart, and everyone kept mistaking him for a dated, faux pas, and trite Guy Fawkes.

As upset as he was, both at being called Guy Fawkes and that Age wasn't there, it was the idea that one of these other get-ups was going to win the contest after they had spent hundreds of dollars and countless hours crafting what were the best-looking costumes he'd ever seen outside of the big conventions in New York and San Diego.

But it was hard to be mad when it was Age, not him, who was sacrificing fun for the sake of his future. Starting back when he was a teenager, and even still to this day, Bash's parents made him drive his grandfather around for the winter. His cataracts were bad, but otherwise he retained his wits and functions. His grandfather was a coroner for the city of Detroit, and Bash driving that van saved his job, and unquestionably saved his sanity. During those cold months Bash got to know and understand the man in a way that he hadn't before. His grandparents had saved and planned and readied themselves for eventual retirement, but without warning or sickness, Bash's grandmother had passed, and rather than retire alone, the man kept working, and planned to until he was called home to join her.

It wasn't obvious when Bash and Age met, but Age was a kindred spirit of his grandfather. Both had been kids from the proverbial wrong-side-of-the-tracks who worked hard for a menial amount of success, both terminal optimists driven to perfection, destined to walk a thin line between fulfillment and failure, neither allowing themselves the reprieve to celebrate or wallow without a level of guilt reserved for the Catholics.

Bash was glad that Age had that same drive and determination as his grandfather but was equally glad that he himself did not. He didn't want to be a slave to an idea of eventual rest. He wanted amazing moments he could close his eyes and remember, not a lifetime of boredom filled with the fantasy of what could have been.

"Hey, Guy Fawkes! The party's this way!" called a voice from somewhere in the clot of dead superheroes, horror movie villains, and mythological creatures crammed into the loft. Bash had never felt guilt the way Age did. He was, and had always been, content doing what he wanted, when he wanted, without any consideration for his future. Which was why, if someone called him Guy fucking Fawkes again, he was going to knock a motherfucker out.

"Imma fuckin' knock yo ass out!" Bash spun away from the window and threw his scrawny arms up into a faux-thug gesture, and found the source of the taunt strutting through the front door. As if the green hair and brown skin weren't enough to betray the reality of his costume, now he was being goaded into an anachronistic confrontation between his flamboyant Frenchman and Rick's Transfabulous Jon SnoWhite, who stood alongside Stella, dressed in the Undead Princess Charming costume Rick had worn to last year's party.

Bash crossed the room, sidestepping dozens of immaculate and patchwork costumes—all made with love, but not so many with skill—to greet the pair.

He wrapped one lithe arm around Stella and playfully smacked Rick's cheek with the other. Normally Rick had the looks, and problem-solving abilities, of a Greek god, but under the bouncy curls and blue dress of Snow White, and the stark black fur of the Night's Watch, he redefined ridiculous.

"Remember, remember," said Rick as he grabbed Bash's hand and kissed his fingers.

"You know nothing, bitch."

"It's seriously so good to see you, Sebastian," Stella said. "I feel like a bad friend. All I do is work. Is Age here too?"

"Don't even get me started. Adrian decided that he'd rather work than play. So, while we're here looking like fucking gods, he's off shuttling drunken Caucasoids and their Sorortutes from one frat house to the next."

"That's too bad. When Rick told me the party was here I was hoping you'd both be here."

"Don't feel too bad for him, he did it to himself."

"I don't feel bad for him, just miss him."

"Oh, believe me, I'll make him feel guilty as hell for missing you."

"You're the best."

"I know." Bash squeezed Stella again.

"Drinks?"

"*Yas, Queen!*"

He took Stella's hand and pulled her through the crowd. "So when did this," Bash motioned his fingers between the surprise couple, "become a thing?"

"Tonight. I was out with my friend Chris and then, magic, I guess."

Bash nodded, looked back at Rick. "You coming, you confused little man?"

But Rick didn't respond or budge. His attention was glued to the other side of the room, where the gruesomely costumed Toilet-Seat Girl (struck by a loose toilet seat from the de-orbiting Mir Space Station) was perched on the back of a couch drinking some bright pink bullshit. It was Gwen, Rick's ex, who he obviously wasn't over.

Bash swatted at Rick, "Do I need a chorus of forest animals to get your attention, princess?"

"Princess?" Rick smacked Bash's hand away. "I'm the prince that was promised, Azor Ah-Hiiiii!"

Stella laughed. Bash shook his head and frowned. "You'd make the worst gay man."

"What?" Rick looked offended as Bash escorted Gwen away arm-in-arm. "What?"

By ten o'clock the Sanderson Sisters were dancing on the island in the kitchen, Mister Sinister's pancake makeup was smeared off his chin after losing the battle with dry heaves, and Doctor Robotnic was in the corner making out with Avatar Korra. Gwen had left early, claiming she was tired after returning from the bathroom. But later, when Bash opened the wrong door himself when looking for the bathroom and found Jon SnoWhite and the Undead Princess Charming under the covers in the host's bedroom, her early exit became clear. Apparently, she wasn't over him either.

If there were sides to be taken in their breakup, based on guilt, Bash would have taken Gwen's. But regardless of who the real villain in the situation was, he and Rick had known each other years and even though he probably liked Gwen more than Rick (and he definitely liked her more than he liked Stella), the long string of Rick's exes all had one thing in common: the breakups were final. All connection was severed. All feelings and attachments dissolved.

There were no beggars and hangers-on, and if Bash tried to salvage a friendship with Gwen, it would be in exchange for the lifelong one he had with Rick, something that he wasn't willing to do. Not over some girl. Because while Rick had never been a good boyfriend to any of his inamoratas, he never failed to be a selfless friend to those he wasn't interested in sleeping with.

Age had checked in with Bash a few times throughout the night. As expected, he relayed the ludicrous antics of the inebriated college students living it up and nearly puking in his car, and the close call one of his passengers had at an ICE checkpoint. In exchange, Bash appraised him of the drama between Gwen and Rick.

"Are you serious?" said Age over the phone.

Bash nodded. "M'hmm. You should have seen those looks between them."

"I know. And I liked Gw—" *WEE-OO!! WEE-OO!!* The sound of passing sirens drowned out Age for a moment. "Holy Shit," he said when he could finally be heard.

"What? You okay?"

"Yeah. Three fire trucks flew past me. Almost ran me off the road."

"Holy shit! But you're okay?"

"Yeah." Age fell silent for a second. More sirens echoed through the phone. "Oh my God, there's more—"

But the phone went dead.

Bash tried calling him back a few times, but the phone kept going to voice mail. He checked his phone half a dozen more times as he fought his way to the keg, hoping for a call back, but got nothing. Age hadn't sounded hurt, but his tone of voice wasn't sitting right. He'd sounded scared.

"Hey, Bash," said Stella. She stood next to Rick as he pumped the keg furiously.

"Fucking tapped." Rick kicked the keg. "You get a load of this place? I feel like when we were their age, it was us taking the piss out of the geriatrics who were still trying to pass themselves off as hip and cool. Now these fucking pups, they're a generation growing up on second-hand characters."

Bash looked out over the crowd and shrugged. His mind was on Age.

"It's not their fault, but it's still pathetic," Rick continued. "Our generation has become the arbiters of cool. How fucking arrogant is that? We think our childhood was so fucking great, that rather than create new heroes for the next generation, we just recycle and remake."

"Right on, man," said some dude dressed as Will Smith from Disney's *Aladdin*.

"Fuck off," said Rick, and offered the Genie a high-five.

Rick was at once empathetic and aggressive, which made arguing with him nearly as impossible as not hanging onto every word that came from his mouth.

"Holy fuck!" a voice called from somewhere in the loft. "Detroit's on fire!"

The music fell silent, and every person in the loft moved as one toward the windows. They clamored over each other and the furniture, all vying for a better view through the glare of the Christmas and strobe party lights, all chanting: "Detroit! Detroit! Detroit is on fire! We don't need no water let the motherfucker burn!"

Bash and Rick exchanged a look, and without a word, bolted from the crowd. They shot out into the hall and climbed the stairwell toward the roof access six floors above.

The door slammed against the chipped brick wall as they dashed out and across the gravel roof. Winded and sweaty, the cool breeze sweeping in from the west was welcome, even if it carried with it the charred scent of fire and ruin. Every horizon was orange and red and yellow. But unlike the brilliance of a tropical sunset, this one look as though it had been covered in mud. Sirens wailed and helicopters circled.

Bash checked his phone, but still no word back from Age. He was fine. This fire wasn't like those out west that swept through hundreds of acres in an hour. Age was in his car and all he had to do was drive. Just drive, and he'd be fine.

Bzzzt-bzzzt-bzzzt.

Stella's phone lit up.

This was Detroit. Detroit had burnt before. One more notch on the bedpost.

Bzzzt-bzzzt-bzzzt.

Rick's phone too.

Bash turned from the city in time to see the newly minted couple's eyes meet.

"Holy shit!" said Stella.

The breeze hitting their bodies was no longer cool.

Rick smiled, looking to Bash. "Remind you of anything?" He picked up a handful of gravel from the roof and launched it out in the direction of the fire. To no avail, obviously.

It did remind him of something. And before he let that something crawl back out of his subconscious, his phone vibrated again.

Bzzzt-bzzzt-bzzzt.

Bash pulled the phone from his pocket and glanced at the screen. An alert, obscured by a Walmart ad on his lock screen, waited for him:

EMERGENCY

THIS IS NOT A TEST: The fire is fast moving, and while crews are working to contain it, other emergency services may be unavailable. If you are in or near the city of Detroit, please evacuate.

It wasn't immediately apparent that there was any power coursing through the rail below their feet, but after walking for an hour, they'd developed a slight headache which shifted to congestion and sinus pressure. Under the symptoms, the cause, somehow, felt magnetic. It made their bellies queasy, they could feel it in their teeth, and after passing SCHAFFER STATION and the WYOMING JUNCTION they moved off the rail and walked the rest of the way traipsing two-by-two along the catwalk.

"So, you miss it down here?" Camila and Cassius walked together, with Paola and Mateo trailing behind in the gloom.

"Yeah, of course. I grew up here."

"Cool. Yeah. Things seem a little tense with you."

"Natural, isn't it? It's been three years. People change. If Renata ain't as brave as she used to be, so be it."

"Hey, now. I don't really think it's about being brave or not."

"You don't have to defend her. I'm not on the attack or nothing. Only making an observation."

"Me too. You hear about her dad?"

"No. He lose his job or something? Shit has always been hard for them."

"He'd been here illegally for the past seventeen years. They crossed over so that Renata could be born a citizen."

"Shut the fuck up! No, they weren't. She was my best friend. She would have said something."

"Maybe you right. I don't know? Just what I heard."

"Alright. Either way, what's that got to do with anything?"

"We don't have to talk about this." Cassius tried to change the subject. "What's it like up in the suburbs?"

"No. Fuck that. What happened with her dad?"

Cassius took a deep breath. "The line he was working on hit some financial trouble. For weeks they kept saying that paychecks were coming, paychecks were coming. After something like two months, the owners called immigration. Turns out most of the workers were illegals and turning them all in was an easy way to get out of paying them."

"That is sick."

"Oh yeah. My mom cried when she saw ICE coming through the door. Pretty obvious what her boss had done."

"Your mom?"

"She worked there." He paused. "Still works there."

"Naw! I would have been gone. Fuck that shit."

"A lot easier to say when you aren't living paycheck to paycheck, plus still trying to recover from being owed two months of back pay."

"It's funny. The Loop was supposed to help. All I'm seeing is more of the same."

"Maybe the city is getting better. But we wouldn't know, they blocked the view."

Camila stopped in her tracks. That view from the garage burned in her mind. Nothing but the glow visible beyond the glass tube. Tears clung to her eyes as she turned from the void they had been walking into to face Cassius.

"You alright?"

"We're here."

Cassius furrowed his brow. She hadn't turned to face him. He followed her gaze, and etched into the wall, in the same commanding font:

FERDINAND STATION

Like Schaffer Station and Wyoming Junction—both of which they had stopped and peered into, but before they could set off to explore them, Camila chided them to continue on—Ferdinand Station was named after the thing it replaced. Ferdinand Street had been bulldozed to create this local access point to The Loop.

Camila led the way out of the main glass terminal. The steel catwalk gave way to two flights of solid concrete stairs that muted the resounding clang of their steps. At the bottom of the stairwell they found themselves in the commuter portion of the station.

Their flashlight beams showed a nearly finished wall-to-wall facade. Similar to that of a major subway station in décor—tiled walls, benches and maps, turnstiles—but the layout was as otherworldly as the tube itself. At either end of the station was a conveyor belt of some sort, with capsule-like seats that would move in from one side of the room empty, then spiral up through the ceiling and beyond, with or without passengers. It was a circulatory system, with passengers being fed into it heading one direction or the other.

With each unfamiliar sight becoming more spectacular than the last, none of them stood still long enough to understand how the system worked.

As impressed as Camila was, she had a reason for bringing them here. She returned to their place of entry and began to walk. One foot in front of the other, she counted her steps.

One. Two. Three. Four.

It was sixty-three steps from the bus stop to her front porch. Advertisements for Masood Pharmaceuticals lined the walls where the sidewalk she learned to ride her bike on used to be.

Eighteen. Nineteen. Twenty. Twenty-one.

A map detailing the route and each stop between Detroit and Ann Arbor hung on the wall where Mr. Syzlak's house had been.

Thirty-seven. Thirty-eight.

"What the fuck you doin', girl?"

"Do you remember Mr. Syzlak? The way he'd feed that squirrel those spongy circus peanut candies. Or what about Mrs. Adamski, who lived next door?" Fifty. Fifty-one.

"Sure. Why?"

"Cause he used to live there." She pointed back to the map on the wall with her flashlight. "And she lived here." She whipped the light back to herself, plastering her shadow across the wall and up onto the ceiling behind her.

Sixty-one. Sixty-two. Sixty-three.

"And I used to live here." The cellphone flashlight shut off, and Camila disappeared into the black. She dropped the phone into her bag, exchanging it for the can of spray paint. As she pulled the can free, a few spare tampons and some other garbage fell out. Camila shook the can as she bent down to scoop everything up as covertly as possible. The ball bearing rattled in the can, followed by the hiss of paint erupting from the nozzle.

Cassius, Paola, and Mateo all trained their lights onto Camila.

Bright green digits as tall as Camila herself cut across the pristine tile, seeping into the porous grout:

1 0 1 8

And below that, a name:

T O R R E S

Her last name.

She wasn't done. Camila moved twenty feet down and repeated the process:

1 0 1 6
A D A M S K I

Again and again, Camila moved up and down each side of the station, defacing the walls with the names and addresses of the people The Loop had displaced.

"What happened to Mr. and Mrs. Martin? Or Bud and Joni? Paola, do you know where they moved to?"

Paola shook her head. "No. We moved before they did. Haven't really thought about them."

"Right? I mean growing up, I remember running down to their houses and getting ice cream cones, or borrowing a bike pump. Back then, I couldn't picture a life they weren't a part of."

"Every winter my dad would go up and down the block and snow blow everyone's sidewalks and driveways. Now we don't have a garage, and had to get rid of the snow blower," said Mateo. "No one does that shit anymore."

"Shit, or how about Mr. Byron, who ran the corner store? My dad would give me a note so I could go buy smokes for him, and Mr. Byron would always slip a candy bar in the bag for me," said Paola.

Cassius chuckled. "Good luck getting away with that shit now."

"That's just it. Maybe I was lucky and got to move up to the suburbs, and my parents don't worry about shit the way they used to. Or maybe it was you all who got lucky, because you got to stay together. It felt like the whole neighborhood shifted a mile south. Except for me. But thinking about it, even though you got to stay in the same school, you sure aren't on the same block anymore. This fucking tube broke up our community. And it's what they do. Look at Pine Knob or Meadow Brook. Even Stoney Creek. Whatever developer or designer put this all together thought it would be an honor to call this place Ferdinand Station. Like the memory of what it was is better than the place itself." Camila paused. The flashlight beams were still on her and she was suddenly self-conscious. "Paola, you have to tell Renata I didn't know about her dad. If I had, I would have been here. I would have said something. It's obvious that whatever progress is being made, it's not for us. Our home is a fuckin' pass through. Ruin our neighborhood so their life can be more convenient."

"Shit, girl," said Paola. "Glad I don't go to school in the suburbs. You think too Goddamn much."

"Shut up! I'm serious. All I seen tonight is a lot of people who used to care about something, sit down and shut up when that shit was taken away. It's like, if you care about something, care about it."

"Why do you think I'm drinking?!" Paola pulled a can of beer from her purse and cracked the top.

"Here, here!" said Cassius, and Mateo tossed him a beer too.

Camila rolled her eyes at Cassius. "Whatever."

"Whatever? Hey, I didn't grow up here. This ain't my home, ain't my hill to die on."

"And just when I was starting to like you."

"Don't get me wrong, I get it. You spend a night walking on the wild side and you pissed off. They're pissed off too. But they living in it every day. Their options aren't the same as yours. You get to head home and not worry about your future."

"Hey—"

"Naw. You keep throwing that *just when I was starting to like you* shit in my face like you better than us."

"That's not what I meant."

"No? Good. Cause you ain't the only one who cares."

"You said you don't care."

"Who cares if I don't? Am I the only other person here? You ever think Paola and Mateo drink because they care, too? But from in here, shit is so stacked against doing anything, that sometimes you got to do what's easy instead of what's right! Fuck man, you know how exhausting it is to carry that shit around with you 24/7?"

CRASH! At the far end of the station, toward the ground level entry point, glass shattered.

"The fuck was that?" Camila, tears in her eyes, spun toward the noise.

There was silence for a moment. They all waited for a voice. Outside, the sound of helicopter blades chopped through the sky, and somewhere in the distance the wail of police sirens. At the entry point, the slapping pitter-patter of feet racing toward them.

"Security," said Cassius.

"Police," said Paola.

And before they could say the word, they ran.

They shot back up the stairs and into the tube and ran clustered together down the center of the tunnel. Adrenaline flooding their veins, degaussing waves scrambling their heads. And behind them clamored footsteps slapping against the rail.

They were being chased.

The distance that had taken an hour to cover on their casual jaunt to the station, now only took fifteen minutes. The access hatch they'd climbed through still hung open, waiting for them. But before they could begin their descent, they heard the footsteps behind them closing in.

A faint red glow, that grew dim and bright as if it were alive and breathing, bounced down the tunnel toward them as they ran. Not an erratic bounce, like an insect or a bird with a broken wing trying to smash its way through glass to freedom, but a deliberate one like that of a ball directing children to sing specific lyrics at the bottom of a screen.

"What is that?" Cassius stared back at the glowing light.

"A red flashlight?" asked Mateo, but his tone held little conviction. "Don't police use red flashlights?"

Camila gazed down the access hatch at their feet, at the scaffolding ten feet below. It had taken them long enough to finagle up the shaft, and would take them twice that for them all to get back down. The glow was coming faster now. They didn't have time.

"Hide!"

Camila shot away from the hatch and took cover behind the loaded forks of a nearby hi-low. Pallets of the silver tiles rested against the wall and the four of them squeezed behind one.

Backs against the wall, they lined up shoulder to shoulder and listened. The footsteps pattered closer and closer. They lacked the rhythm of a man's gait, but resembled the four-legged canter of a dog, or maybe even a horse. The pattering stopped and the four of them held their breath.

The smoldering light filled this section of the tunnel like a sunrise in hell, illuminating the ceiling and walls around them with that breathy incandescence. It was elemental, not the artificial glow of anything manmade, but of fire, of the coals left after the flames have died. There was no smoke, no smell of burn or crackling of combustion. Instead, the sound was hard. The inhale of lungs. They couldn't see it, but on the other side of their makeshift wall, something not human nor recognizable animal was alive. And it had caught their scent.

The creature silhouetted through the tunnel, and Camila spied it through the gaps between pallets. As it stepped through the narrow bolt of light from outside, she gasped in recognition.

She'd been wrong.

She knew who it was. Not *what*, but who.

"Hey!" Camila called and squeezed through the gap.

Her friends whispered in terrified tones for her to shut up and get back, but she didn't listen. She'd spent her youth waiting for floorboards to give way under her feet, and she'd be damned if a man in a suit was going to stop her now.

It was Age, her Uber driver. He'd told her he wanted to go to some Devil's Night costume party. Their encounter at the checkpoint must have taken a toll on his resolve to work rather than live it up.

Somehow it was him out there in that costume he made. The Red Dwarf of Detroit. Red skin and horns, glowing eyes and rotten teeth.

"Age! It's Camila!" she said as she pulled herself out of hiding.

What had he called it? The Nine Something?

"You said you put a lot of work into your costume, but damn, dude! How did you get those lights to work?"

No, not *Nine*. It was French. The Nain Rouge.

"What are you doing here? You didn't follow me here, did you? That'd be kind of creepy."

The Nain Rouge costume stopped in its tracks, turned to Camila, and opened its mouth.

It was the wail of the sirens that woke the girl. Apparently, the guy could sleep through anything.

Age had picked them up only 10 minutes earlier from the Alpha Kappa Lambda house on campus, and they were the definition of Bash's prejudice. A toga-wearing Caucasoid and his Valley Girl Sorortute. The only thing missing from the pair was the blackface photo that would emerge in 10 years and derail their corporate climbs for thirty seconds.

They'd both passed out before Age pulled away from the curb, which he took advantage of and called Bash to check in on the party. Bash filled him in on Gwen and Rick drama, and the various bullshit happenings at the party.

"I know. And I liked Gwen," he started, when a fleet of firetrucks, six of them, whipped through traffic, cutting around Campus Martius. *WEE-OO!! WEE-OO!!* Their sirens wailed and Age's little Accord rocked in their wake. His foot feathered the brake, his hands strangled the wheel, and every time he let up and inched forward, another emergency vehicle sped past them.

"What the fuck was that?" asked the Sorortute in the back, "Did you get into a car accident? If you did, I swear I'm only giving you one star."

"Holy shit!" Age was barely holding onto the phone and the wheel.

On the other end of the phone Bash was talking to him, but he was only half listening.

"Yeah," he said to Bash as he realized the city had taken on a distinct smell. "Three fire trucks just flew past me." Gone was the musty smell of the city's boiler system billowing up from manhole covers. "Almost ran me off the road." Age smelled ash. He smelled smoke. "Yeah," he said one last time, then fell silent as he looked into the rearview mirror and saw not only a dozen more police cars, fire trucks, and ambulances coming, but down the Northeasterly corridors of Congress and Larned he saw the reflected glow of flames on the glass. "Oh my God, there's more coming. Let me call you back."

Before he could finish his sentence, the signal died and the call dropped.

Be nice if he could blame the carrier instead of himself, but it felt like any time he was alone or depressed or struggling, this happened. Like that old picture that used to hang on his grandparents' wall of two sets of footprints in the sand, and then one vanishing. When you need him most, Jesus carries you. Only time and time again, when Age was cut off from the world like this, it felt like it was Jesus who was asking him for a ride, the weight of the world too much to bear. Even for Jesus.

Age dropped the useless phone and hit the gas before getting stuck in the wake of first responders again. It was now, too, that the shift in the atmosphere became obvious. Driving Uber for months now, the carousel of starts and stops throughout the Metro Area had numbed him to his surroundings. Behind the wheel, with the app running, all he saw was: red light, green light, destination. Every fare was one step closer to his last, and the more he could tune them out the better. Sometimes there was a memorable ride. Like the girl earlier. Sometimes he'd even remember them for reasons not related to the prejudice they suffered in the back of his car. Sometimes they were funny or good people.

"Dude, do you hear me? I'm going to fucking puke if you don't turn the heat down."

These people were neither.

He circled Campus Martius, and as he sped past Cadillac Square, a burst of heat and the blinding light of a wall of flame three blocks away showered his car.

Both Monroe and Woodward were parking lots. Bumper-to-bumper screaming, shouting, and sirens. Men and women basked in light streaming through alleyways and one-way roads. They were all running North along Woodward, or cutting through connecting streets to get there. Vehicles left, abandoned in the road as the fire swept south and west.

It all happened so fast. All within a matter of minutes. One moment the city was going through the motions: parties and patrols, everyone doing Devil's Night in their own way. The next, heat and flames, and everywhere Age looked, the fire was spreading. And the response. It was uncanny. Any other night and the first responders would have either been tucked away in bed for another listless off day, or still gearing up to respond. But tonight, of all nights, they were ready. It's like the fire decided to burn Nakatomi Plaza, but didn't realize John McClane had been invited to the party, pal.

The Accord slipped, screeching and scraping, through the abandoned cars that littered Michigan Avenue, and from somewhere a voice called out, "Dat's my fuckin' ride, bro. You payin' fer the damage! Got yo plate, bitch," as Age knocked the mirror off another car. "I got yo plate!"

Age ignored the threat. At this rate, the fire was likely to consume both the car and the owner before long. It was adrenaline that kept him from puking at that thought. A man burning alive because he's too stubborn to move. Back when he was a kid, and he saw a dead squirrel in the street, Age remembered saying to his mom, "*It's not fair*" that it had to die. It was just living life when a car came along, and squish.

Fight, flight, or freeze. They are all natural reactions to being confronted with fear. And there's not one of them that couldn't get you killed.

"Where are we going?" came the fried little voice in the backseat. "Babe, I don't think he's following the directions you gave him. Babe. Babe!"

Age cut the wheel once, then again. To Griswold, to Lafayette. In the back, the Caucasoid and Sorortute bobbled back and forth. His drunk dead weight crushing her against the one window, sliding back, and bashing his head into the other.

"Hey!" she shouted, and for once it didn't sound like a question.

"I told you to put your seatbelts on when you got into the car," Age shouted, slamming on the breaks as two patrol cars with flashing blue lights pulled into the Shelby intersection.

"STOP!" came the call over the loudspeaker. "ROAD IS NOT SAFE AHEAD!"

An officer hopped out and directed Age the wrong way down Shelby.

Age mouthed, "It's one-way?!" and gave a big and bitchy shoulder shrug, pointing to confirm that the officer was instructing him to violate traffic laws.

The patrol car honk-honk-honked. They didn't have time for Age's shit. The one standing out in the intersection stopped short of ripping his own arm off and using it to motion Age to, "Fucking go, go, go, go, go, go, go!"

Age gunned it. The road was clear, and down every street they passed he saw either blue flashing lights impeding traffic, or the red and white flames of hell engulfing the city.

"Alright, what in the actual fuck is going on?" Her makeup was running and her outfit was malfunctioning, but at least she was calm.

"Fix your shirt," said Age.

She looked down and, too drunk to blush, quietly tucked her breast back into her top. "Is the city on fire?"

If nothing else, at least the fire was going to stop these two from hooking up tonight, because, without a doubt, they weren't the type to use a condom, and the last thing the world needed was this pair to breed.

She asked another question, and all Age could think of was Bash. "Are we going to die?"

He was down here, on the other side of the flames. As fast as the adrenaline hit him, he sobered up from it at the notion of Bash being caught over there, surrounded by flames.

They could get there. They could get to Bash. If Jefferson was clear, if the flames hadn't hit the financial district yet, maybe they could squeeze by. The party was only in Corktown. Could get there easy. For sure. No problem.

Jefferson was a no-go. From Hart Plaza to past Randolph, firetrucks lined the westbound side of the street, wetting down buildings and pavement, creating a barrier to keep the fire from reaching the former Cobo Hall, the Ren Cen, and of course, the main hub for The Loop.

As Age drove the wrong way down Jefferson, they passed the Fist of Joe Lewis, its dark surface quietly reflecting the orange glow sweeping through the city, and then back underneath The Loop. Here, the glass tube was finished, no longer covered in those drab construction tarps. But Age couldn't take the time to marvel at it. As they veered around the entrance ramp to The Lodge, they found themselves surrounded.

Hart Plaza had become an impromptu gathering place for the evacuated. Hundreds, maybe thousands of people filled the Detroit River waterfront. The crowd gasped between stunned silences as the firemen beat back the impossible flames with their hoses, and, without warning, began to whoop and cheer when bricks and stone, brittle with age, cracked and exploded, sending echoes out overhead. Across the city, lights in buildings flickered on and off as the power grid overloaded and went down block by block. There was nowhere to go.

"Damnit!" Age hit the steering wheel and slammed on the breaks.

"Dude, you need to chill, alright?"

"What's going on, babe?" asked her semi-conscious date.

"He's like, driving all over the place cause the city's on fire. And it's been like, really rough. I feel jostled. Can you tell him not to jostle me?"

"Hey brah, no jostlin', cool?"

"Right," said Age, barely holding in his contempt. "So listen, there's nowhere left to go. I can't get you to your destination, I'm going to cancel the ride."

"Brah, you serious? It's only a couple of blocks."

"The city is on fucking fire!"

"Brah, chill. Alls I'm saying is a postman would do it."

Age spun around, incredulity so thick in his brain he couldn't force his tongue and mouth to form words.

"What?" the Caucasoid mumbled. "You know, neither wind, nor rain, nor, you know, fire, will stop the postal worker from getting his packages across the field or whatever? We're your fucking packages, brah. So what's the problem?"

"Babe, he's getting me real mad, and real stressed, and all I want to do is go home now."

"I know, babe. He's going to do it. Don't worry. We're having a meeting of the minds. Now, shh, let Pappi do his thing." He leaned forward like he was going to try to kiss Age. "So, we in this together, brah? Or you gonna do me dirty?"

"Babe, you can't say that to him. He's gay. It's offensive to their culture."

"Oh, brah, I'm sorry. No offense. I'm not a homophone or nothin'. We cool?" He held out his fist and waited for Age to bump it.

"Fine. Whatever. But I still need you to get out. I'm not sitting here watching this shit. My boyfriend was in Corktown tonight. I need to see if—I need to get to him."

"I'm down. Let's go together, brah. It'll be an adventure. You can drop us off after. Word? Cause I don't think you getting past that line without me."

Age looked back down Jefferson where they'd come from. The intersection at Shelby was already cut off by another firetruck working to subdue the flames spreading in from the West Side Industrial area. They'd been corralled, and with the fire now on all sides, they were stuck.

"Looks like there's no way through, huh?"

"Will you shut up?!"

"Don't tell him to shut up. You shut up!"

"I got this, babe." He patted her head and said to Age, "Only trying to help."

"How is stating the fucking obvious helping? Bash is on the other side of the fire and I'm stuck fucking here!" he stopped short of adding *"with the two of you."* But maybe with them in the car he could drive through the fire. Their apparent lack of oxygen would smother the fire, right? Maybe? Fuck it.

"Nah, I only said it looks like there's no way through. It's like play on words, cause there is a way through. I'm an intern at Masood, brah. They got an underground parking structure. Entrances across most of the city. But you got to have a badge to get in." And with that, the Caucasoid held up a white badge clipped to his belt on a retractable tether. "Always free parking down here for me!"

"And there's an entrance close by?"

"Right up there." He pointed to a row of hedges in front of the Ren Cen.

Fuck it. Age shifted the Accord into drive and started toward the underground entrance amidst protests from the crowd.

They said, "Ain't nowhere to go!" as the Accord forced a gap to open up wide enough to pass.

They said, "Asshole! Park it." And looked wide-eyed through the window while Age avoided their stares.

They said, "You ain't goin' nowhere!" while the two in the backseat scrolled through their phones.

They said, "Stop," when the crowd became too thick to traverse safely, but Age kept going anyway. He needed to get to Bash.

How does a city burst into flames in an hour? How does it spread and destroy so quickly? Age wanted to roll down the window and declare: *My boyfriend is black, we're going to save him!* And then what? They would all quiet down, part ways, and bow down in reverence to the white savior heading into the flames to save a brother?

Fuck, the way he'd been driving, they'd be happy to see him speed right into the flames.

They. They. They. They. Age felt sick. The way he was driving, thinking, his privilege was on full display. If he were outside of this car, he'd have been the first to throw a brick through his own windshield for being a piece of shit. But bricks never came. Even as they descended the ramp to the sealed parking garage doors, the only things hurled at them were insults and judgment.

The Caucasoid passed his ID up to Age. He rolled down the window, held it against the sensor. A moment later the door shook and rolled upwards.

Behind the shrubbery and at the top of the ramp, voices called out, seeing the access door open. Before the gap was even large enough for the Accord to slip through, dozens of people were already leaping over the guard rails and running down the ramp to get in. They slapped the car's windows, hood, and side panels as they ran past. The sound of human rain pitter-pattering.

In the backseat, the Caucasoid smiled, waved, and shook his head at the mob. "Uh-uh! No trespassing," he said repeatedly as they ran past.

Once the gate was up far enough, Age laid on the horn and sped into the shaft. The ramp was long, and even those that had slipped in before them and were running downward soon fell behind the car. The ramp plunged another thirty feet. They were below the sewers and power lines, below the original foundation of the city. Up top, the city was going dark, electrical light replaced by the piercing, but dim, flames. But down here the grid remained untouched. The parking structure was not wide, only six rows across, but it seemed to stretch forever.

"That's the West Side exit. It lets out near the Ferdinand Station. But there's a Corktown exit before then."

After the residual rattle of the door rolling shut ceased echoing, the garage was eerily quiet. As Age sped past dozens of cars left parked in their spaces a thought came to him: why didn't Masood open the doors to let the people flee from the fire rather than forcing them to watch their homes and jobs burn in front of their eyes?

"Whoa! Stop!" came a command from the backseat, and Age slammed on the breaks. "Corktown exit is right there."

Age cut the wheel and lost his train of thought.

They ascended another long ramp, and when they got to the top, Age was surprised to see another badge sensor. The Caucasoid handed Age the badge again.

"You need this to get out?"

He nodded.

"What—what about all those people who rushed the gates? Is there another way out?"

"Nope. No other way."

"What are they going to do?"

"I don't know, what do looters do when they get caught? They're not getting trapped down here forever. I'm sure once the fires are out they'll get rounded up, and depending on how much damage they do to the door trying to bust out they'll get fined, go to jail, or whatever."

The fuck? They weren't looters, weren't criminals. They were just tired of watching their city and their homes burn. And now? *Give us your tired, your hungry, your poor*, and we will detain and beat and starve them.

Age tapped the sensor and tossed the badge back over his shoulder. Now he understood the mindset for when truly shitty decisions get made.

They emerged back into the city along Leverette Street, only a few blocks from the McGettigan's place. Inching out onto Michigan Ave, Age looked east toward downtown and his breath caught in his throat so hard it felt like someone had knocked the wind out of him. The fires raged, the tallest buildings vanishing into the web of smoke that hung over every street as miles and miles of neighborhoods and blight and abandoned property disappeared like the rainforest.

In the backseat, the Sorortute spoke up. "Babe, I think I want some champagne. You know, to celebrate." She winked at him. Whatever the fuck that meant.

The roads were clear, and a moment before Age stepped on the gas the Caucasoid spoke. "Hol' up. Gonna run into the liquor store real quick. Come on, babe." The backdoor opened, and the two of them hopped out.

Age turned, looked out the window toward the shop they were heading. It was obviously closed. "They're closed," he shouted out the window.

"It's cool," came the reply as the Caucasoid picked up a chunk of cement from the street and shot-put it into the glass door.

"The fuck are you doing?"

"Getting a drink, brah. Chill. We'll only be a minute."

"You're looting! Don't looters get fined or go to jail?" Age said, throwing the Caucasoid's own words back at him.

"Nah, brah. We're white! This ain't looting; this is mischief." And with that, he scooped up his Sorortute like she was a bride, and carried her over the threshold of broken glass.

Fuck those two. The moment they were out of view, Age stepped on the gas and went west on Michigan. He didn't even bother to look in the rearview mirror as he heard their tiny voices get smaller and smaller behind him.

In high school, Age had come out to only one person. Jon had been his best friend for years at that point, and by the time Age worked up to courage to say the words, Jon said, "I know. Doesn't mean I'm going easier on you in Street Fighter."

It was nothing new for Age to be called *gay, pussy,* or *faggot.* He'd been soft and quiet and easy to cry until he was a teenager, and children in groups, lacking true emotional depth, could be cruel.

Nothing changed. Jon hadn't spilled the beans on Age's secret, hadn't treated his friend any different. But when they were walking down the hall after gym and the supreme asshole jocks of the school shoved Age, saying shit like, "Imma rape your faggot ass, you look at me in the locker room again," Jon said nothing.

He'd never stood up for Age in the past when he was picked on, and nothing had changed, just as he'd promised his friend nothing would. But it wasn't *nothing* the way Age expected. Jon had taken *nothing* to mean their friendship was solid. Age had expected that Jon's gained knowledge of Age's true identity would have brought out some sort of compassion from his friend.

Instead, he remained focused on his own survival of high school. Jon was an ally, but a silent one.

The party had been in a loft behind the old Tiger Stadium, and by the time Age reached it, the building was black. Not burnt, but abandoned.

And he cried.

The tears weren't his emotions catching up with him. They were for the people who he'd let get trapped underground, who'd have to endure whatever punishments the pursuit of solace had to bring. In a moment when it mattered, Age chose himself over those who would suffer. He'd chosen to be silent for the sake of his own survival.

Fuck. He was shaking. He needed Bash, reached under the seat where the phone had fallen earlier. Still no signal.

This happened, his phone losing signal when he was overwhelmed. He needed to calm himself. Look inside and relax.

Picture himself engulfed in a comforting and calming light. Take a deep breath and look inward. He massaged his face with his fingertips. Slow, swirling motions. Positivity in. Always toward the heart.

A moment later, he opened his eyes and found full bars on his phone, along with twenty-eight missed calls from Bash.

He tapped the callback button and there wasn't a single ring before he heard Bash's panicked voice on the other end: "Are you alright?!"

"I'm fine, I'm fine. My phone, it did that thing again. But whatever. I'm good now. I got out."

"Thank god! How? On the news—Where you were—I thought," He couldn't finish any of those sentences.

But he didn't need to. The Loop hung above him as he drove. It ran right alongside Michigan Ave all the way to Ann Arbor. As Age drove west alongside it, putting more distance between himself and the fire, he told Bash what happened and how he escaped.

"You're okay now," Bash reassured him repeatedly on the phone. "You are okay."

Under the traffic light near Ferdinand Station, Age saw something. "What is that?"

"What?" asked Bash.

As the light turned green, a child stumbled out into the street. He was hunched over and naked, stumbling as if injured, and covered in burns from head to toe.

He wiped his eyes and nose, rolled down his foggy window to call to the child.

"Oh my God," he whispered involuntarily as, in the moon-light, he caught sight of the twisted horns rising up from the child's head.

Without the smear of fog, he could see that the figure in the road was not a child. And those were not burns covering his body, but red skin.

It moved like a primate, like a baboon. The creature was injured, holding its side, and leaking flames instead of blood as it raced toward Ferdinand Station.

"Hello?" came the voice from the phone. "Age?"

As the Nain Rouge passed through the headlight beams from Age's car, it stopped, turned its head, and through the windshield, made eye contact with him. Anxiety washed through him, spreading outwards from his heart to every limb, through each finger, and into his cell phone, where he felt the signal blink out before Bash's voice on the other end cut off. But this wasn't anxiety brought on by fear. The creature didn't scare him; he was a believer before, but this was something else.

The whole connection lasted all of five seconds before the creature bolted again. He watched as it ran at Ferdinand Station's glass doors and threw itself at them. The Nain Rouge bounced away as the safety glass warbled, then fell from its frame and shattered on the ground. Then it was gone, rolling back to its feet and fleeing into the dark corridors of The Loop.

Seeing the Nain Rouge was a revelation. The dead cell phone in his hand was no longer just an inconvenience, but a bearing. His whole life he'd never fit in anywhere until he'd met Bash. But that too was only love. The dead signal was a magnetic North to Age's ever lost and spinning compass needle.

And the Nain Rouge, it felt like family.

Crimson skin and horns, smoldering eyes and wicked, barbed teeth. Its mouth fell open, and in its throat were glowing embers and a whisp of flame that curled like a smile.

A trickle of warmth ran down her leg and puddled in her shoe.

The Nain Rouge sniffed the air and crept toward her. It was a baboon, like the legend had said. A red ape with tufts of thick blond hair on top of its head and striped down its back. It stared into her eyes as it approached. Fingernails, claws, hooves, whatever it had. Every step echoed a soft click on the hard floor. Three feet away from her it stood, no longer walking on all fours, but stepping toward her like a man might. It raised its hand as if it were going to caress her face.

Camila closed her eyes and could see the blood in her eyelids as heat and flame glazed her face. Then there was a smash, and her eyes jolted open.

A tile flew at the creature. This one caught it upside the head, and it let out a bellow that echoed as far as their ears could hear.

Camila leaped back. The creature moved, dodging another tile. She fell to the ground and dared to take her eyes off the creature long enough to see where the tiles were coming from.

Cassius.

He'd torn open one of the plastic-wrapped pallets and was now standing on top of it, a tile in each hand, ready to Frisbee another square at the creature.

They were in a holding pattern. Camila on the ground, Cassius up high with the tiles, and the creature somewhere in between. As much as she wanted to, as much as she willed it, she could not bring herself to budge.

The Nain Rouge swayed, bleeding from where the last tile had hit. It was intelligent enough to understand the situation. All creatures have three basic responses to a threat: fight, flight, or freeze. Cassius had chosen his, and so had Camila.

Another roar bellowed out of the creature's mouth, followed by a wad of flame that landed wet and hot near Camila's leg. The Nain

Rouge chose the third response, and fled, leaving a trail of flame behind it.

They all remained still, watching the light from the creature fade into black. They listened until the pitter-pattering footsteps sunk off into the distance and vanished.

"Camila!" Paola ran out from behind the pallet and threw her arms around her friend. "What the fuck?"

"What the fuck was that thing?!" Cassius asked

"I—" The words were there but she couldn't bring herself to answer.

"Holy shit!" said Mateo.

"Yeah," said Paola. "Let's get the fuck out of here."

"No. Look." Mateo crouched at the gap in the tarp that Camila had looked out earlier. His face flickered red and orange and yellow.

The four of them gathered around the tiny gap and looked out at the Detroit skyline, only to find it hidden by black smoke. From one edge of the horizon to the other, Detroit was engulfed in flames.

Camila squeezed Cassius's arm. "I need to get home."

They descended the scaffolding, climbed back over the fence, and turned back toward the party house. Paola and Mateo debated what they had seen, while Cassius stuck close to Camila.

"Where are we?" Camila reached into her bag.

"Um," Cassius looked around, unsure himself.

"I need to give Uber a pickup address." Camila shuffled through her disorganized bag. Tampons and loose change and keys spilled everywhere. "Fuck!" She couldn't find her phone.

"Hey, I'm sorry for attacking you back there."

"It's fine. I just need to get home. My parents are probably freaking out."

"Yeah, yeah, for sure." He peered down the street at the sign up ahead. "Corner of Chase and Ruby."

"Thanks." Camila held her purse up to the dim streetlight above. "Got it!" She pulled the phone out of her bag.

Whoop-Whoop! Blue and red flashers lit up behind them before she could open the app.

"Fuck," said Paola under her breath.

"Naw, it's cool. Everything'll be cool," Cassius said. The police cruiser pulled up alongside them and rolled their windows down. "Evening, officers."

"The fuck you doing on the street?" asked the black officer in the passenger seat. He had zero fucking chill.

"I'm calling us an Uber right now, officer," Camila blurted.

"Oh, you're calling an Uber right now? Too bad you didn't call ten minutes ago," said the giant, hulking white officer in the driver's seat. He shifted the cruiser into park. "Up against the fence. All of you!"

The officers stepped out of the cruiser as the kids backed toward the fence.

"What the fuck is going on?" Paola asked, poised to flee.

"Funny you should ask? I was going to ask you the same Goddamn thing," said the white officer. "The city is fucking burning. Think we need any more of you little shits out here?"

"Shit, chill, man." Paola shot him a look.

"Don't give me shit! I'll take you in, ship you back to Mexico."

"I'm a fucking American!" Her accent never more apparent.

"Let's see some IDs then," said the black officer.

"Do, ah," Cassius stumbled over his words. He was putting on a brave act, but Camila could see his hands trembling. "Do you suspect us of a crime, officer? Could we get your names and badge numbers?"

"Look at this, we got a constitutional scholar here. I'm Officer Jackson," said the black officer. "And that there is Officer Gracie." He rattled off their badge numbers. "And since you asked, we do indeed suspect you of a crime. You see, the city? That's a whole lot of fire to be anything less than a coordinated effort."

"You think we did this?" Paola looked at her friends, "We didn't do shit!"

"Then you got nothing to worry about. IDs." Officer Jackson asked again.

Paola and Mateo produced their IDs under protest, "This is bullshit. Fucking profiling us."

Cassius patted himself down while he watched Camila dig through her purse.

"Young lady, ID, please," asked Officer Jackson a third time.

"I'm looking, I'm looking." There were tears in her voice.

"And you," he asked Cassius.

"I'm looking too, officer."

"Christ, what is this, the retard squad?" said Officer Gracie as he stepped up and grabbed Cassius. He shoved his big meaty fists into every fold of Cassius's clothing until he found the boy's wallet.

Officer Jackson took the ID from Gracie. "I'm going to run these. Be back for hers when she finds it."

"Want me to find it for her? Looks like she could use some help."

Officer Jackson didn't respond as he walked away, but Officer Gracie didn't approach Camila either.

"It's okay, it's okay," Cassius reassured Camila.

"No, it's not. I can't find it. I can't find my wallet. It was in here earlier, and now it's gone." She looked to Cassius, ready to burst into tears. She thought back to Ferdinand Station, when she pulled the spray paint out. It wasn't tampons that fell. "I must have dropped it."

"Don't fucking talk to each other," said Officer Gracie. "Shut up and find your ID."

"Excuse me," said Cassius. "Don't talk to each other? You the fucking Gestapo now, the word police?"

"You think you got a smart mouth? Show me you do and shut it." Officer Gracie stepped forward, pulling out his baton. Cassius was tall, but this white officer was massive.

Cassius didn't shut up. He kept talking, putting himself between Camila and harm yet again tonight.

Then a call came over the radio: *"All units in vicinity of The Loop. Suspect seen entering restricted area. K-9 unit present at Ferdinand Station. Possible evidence located."*

Paola looked to Camila. A tear ran down her cheek. "Fuck," she said, and bolted. Mateo followed behind her.

The thoughts going through her head must have been the same as the ones going through Camila's in that moment: the tags, the spray paint cans, the missing wallet. All at the suspected location of this Devil's Night's prime suspect. Motivation, opportunity, and there were four of them. They had the numbers to be a *coordinated effort*.

Above all that, there was the most damning and irrefutable evidence of their guilt: the color of their skin.

Officer Jackson flung himself out of the cruiser and took off after Paola and Mateo. "Stay on them, I'll get these fuckers."

Cassius didn't budge. He wasn't going to run.

But before he could even think to do so, just to make damn sure he didn't, Officer Gracie smashed Cassius's knee with his baton.

His cry echoed as he fell to the ground.

"What the fuck?!" Camila stepped toward the officer.

"Stay the fuck back," Gracie commanded her.

Cassius flailed on the ground, reaching for his knee, folding into a broken fetal position.

"Stay still! Don't fucking move," Gracie shouted at Camila. He grabbed Cassius by the scruff of his neck and lifted him to his feet.

"He's not doing anything! We didn't do anything."

"Why the fuck you running?"

"We're not!" But the officer had already turned his ears off.

He walked Cassius over to the cruiser and opened the back door.

He said, "Take a seat," and bashed Cassius's face into the door frame. "Oops, gotta duck your head a bit there, little buddy."

He banged his face into the door frame again. "Alright, this is getting stupid. If you keep banging your face into my squad car, I'm gonna have to charge you with resisting an officer and damaging public property."

"I'm not," Cassius choked out. "I can't see." Blood ran into his eyes from the new gash on his forehead.

"Stop! Stop!" Camila cried. "Leave him alone!"

"I can't see—"

"Shut up. Stop resisting." It wasn't a command; it was a laugh.

"Camila."

"Cassius."

"Don't fucking talk to each other." He sounded so bored.

"Let him go, please! Please, officer. I'm sorry. We're sorry. We didn't mean to do it."

She was just saying words now. Saying whatever she could to save Cassius, to put herself between him and harm.

"My stomach hurts. My neck—"

"Stop—stop—please! You're hurting him."

"He shouldn't have resisted!"

"He didn't! He didn't. He didn't—" He didn't. The power behind her voice lessened every time she repeated it until it was only words in her head. He didn't resist. He didn't fight. He didn't flee. He froze. All natural reactions to being met with fear. And not one of them that couldn't get you killed.

Officer Gracie looked to Camila, then to the limp sack of meat she kept calling Cassius.

"Cassius—" Camila whimpered.

The officer spun Cassius around and tossed him toward Camila. He landed in a heap, and Camila wrapped herself around his bleeding face. Cassius opened his eyes and gasped for air. Foreheads touching, eyes together. His breath was hot, was fire.

"There," came the officer's voice from the void outside their cocoon, "Happy?"

There was still a hallway that connected the Sobering Center to the rest of the jail, but at night it all but vanished. First buzzing, then flickering, the ancient fluorescent lights had gone out. One by one the ballasts in the hallway had all gone bad and never been replaced. Just wasn't in the budget. Sitting between these imposing geometric buildings, the hallway disappeared into the night after sunset. The Sobering Center had been converted from an old high school gymnasium when the Tri-County jail went up. Most of the high school had been torn down, but the gym remained. The city dropped a cell into the center of that worn and warped wooden floor, installed half a dozen CCTV cameras, and converted the old Phys. Ed. teacher's office into an observation booth. State-of-the-art facility it was not, but for housing drunks and drug addicts, it would do just fine.

Back in Richard's day, the drunk tank was a place where those who'd had too good of a time were dropped to ensure they didn't hurt themselves or anyone else and then released when they could call for a ride. Then the world turned, politics shifted, and the tank gained the reputation as a gateway to mass incarceration and jail-attributable deaths. With a reputation like that, the financial backer for the city's rebirth and renovation, Masood Pharmaceuticals, demanded that a more humane environment be created for those brought in for public intoxication or they might have to close their pocketbooks.

The city complied, and the drunk tank underwent a facelift along with gaining a new moniker. There wasn't much difference between that antiquated label and this modern iteration; it was still a large, empty room that could hold far too many occupants. The only notable difference is that rather than cement shelves protruding from the walls that served as both bench and bed, they now had a stack of adult-size daycare cots. Four-inch-tall plastic and mesh rectangles that were only a hair nicer than the cement, but did enough to sway public opinion.

The center only had three occupants tonight. In two weeks that would change. In two weeks, swarms of newly-minted drinkers would come home for Thanksgiving and assume that their suburbs were as lenient on inebriation as the Podunk departments that patrolled whatever Liberal Arts college in the middle of nowhere that their parents could afford.

Any night with fewer than ten occupants was easy enough to contend with.

Tonight, these occupants were in rare form.

Occupant One: Black male, mid-forties. Was picked up after midnight on the suburb-side of Eight Mile with the glass neck of a bottle of vodka sticking out of his pants. He was propositioning a passersby to "Drink from my *Vodcock* and live forever." Upon admission, he said he was Bruce Bannister, the black Bugs Bunny.

Occupant Two: Middle Eastern male, thirties. Uber Eats driver. Taken into custody at two AM for yelling at a customer in another language. Arresting officer reported that the man was saying "Allahu Akbar" instead of "Have a good night" when delivering the food. When Jackson asked his name, he smiled and said, "Jesus."

Occupant Three: Caucasian male, seventy-eight. Fit the description of a missing person from the Red Run Retirement Village. He refused to give his name, but Richard recognized him. His name was Roger Green, and the last time Richard had seen him, he'd been wearing a suit of armor and leading a stolen horse to water.

Richard watched the three of them from his desk in the observation booth while Jackson and Dabrowski played cards on the small corner table. Bruce Bannister was sleeping off his inebriation, but the other two, they were chatting it up. After an hour or more of listening to them drone on, Richard killed the speakers in the booth.

"Hey, what you doing, LT?" Jackson looked up from his hand of cards.

Richard rubbed his temples and reclined his chair back. "Christ, I need a break. Guess I'm too old to find the drunk tank humorous anymore."

"Sobering Center," Jackson corrected him.

Richard opened his eyes and rolled his chair forward to shoot Jackson a disapproving look. "Why thank you, Charles, for yet again reminding me how old I am. But I'm sorry, PC or not, there ain't a damn thing sober about any of them."

"Just looking out for you, LT. Belfour is hellbent on knocking you around. Don't want to give him any more ammunition."

"Well, I appreciate the sentiment; however, these two are—Oh, hell no!" Richard looked out the window in time to see Roger and

Jesus sitting cross-legged in front of the stainless-steel toilet, dipping their cupped hands into the bowl, and spooning gulps of water to their lips.

Richard spun around and slammed his fist onto the intercom. "The toilet is not for drinking!" Jackson and Dabrowski threw their cards down and erupted into a fit of laughter. "Please stop."

Before the mic cut out, Roger's voice cut through the static, "He's turned it into wine. You should try so—"

"I can't deal with this shit tonight."

"Need a drink, LT?" Jackson asked. "I know a great after-hours place. Just heard they still serving too."

"You think that shit's funny? They keep that shit up, Imma have to take them to get their stomachs pumped."

"It just me?" Dabrowski chimed in. "Or does the LT seem grumpier than usual?"

"Oh, he sure do," added Jackson. "You good, boss?"

"Got a headache is all."

"Head down to medical. Get yourself an aspirin."

"Doc's gone for the night. Nurse too."

"They got a kiosk down there for third shift," said Dabrowski. "You used one before? I can show you."

"Yes, I have used a kiosk! I'm old, not a Luddite."

"What's a Luddite?" asked Dabrowski.

Richard looked to Jackson. "You can slap him for me, right?"

"Tell you what. I'll slap him silly if you go get your head on straight. Shift only half over and I don't think I can take being stuck in here with two braindead dummies."

"Alright, alright. You keep an eye on the jokers?"

Jackson nodded. Richard nodded back and headed toward the medical wing.

This headache wasn't from being old. Seeing the old man arrive earlier had shaken him more than he was willing to admit to anyone. Almost more than he was willing to admit to himself.

He hadn't always been this grumpy, but the way they had shuffled him around the past year, it was hard not to feel that somewhere along the way he'd taken a wrong path. Or worse, stayed on one. Not that he could see any obvious choice laid out behind him where the road could have split—

Well, except for one: when he called in that there was a Knight and a horse drinking from his birdbath.

As he crossed the dark walkway that connected the Sobering Center to the rest of the jail, he unbuttoned his shirt pocket and pulled out a long gold chain with a pendant attached to the end. It was Roger's, or rather, Roger's wife's. Richard had held onto it for whatever reason, kept it on his person since slipping on it over a year ago. He'd hardly call it a good luck charm given the way the last year had gone, but there was still something comforting about it. Now that the old man was here in front of him again, against his own selfish interest, it was time to return the pendant to its rightful owner.

The medical wing was empty, and the lights flickered on as Richard entered and approached the kiosk. The Michigan/Masood Medical Dispensaries had been popping up all over the Metro area for the last three years. They had been hailed as game changers for the impoverished and have already helped relieve the financial burden of millions of uninsured who would not have otherwise sought medical treatment until it was too late.

With a few simple questions—upwards of three hundred on the first visit, but fewer and fewer the more often the kiosk's services were utilized—a medical analysis could be performed, blood and urine tested, and, if need be, medication dispensed at a pharmacy kiosk which was built into the wall (like an ATM at a bank). The kiosks used an advanced algorithm, AI, and facial recognition software intended to ensure that the system was not taken advantage of by those with less than legitimate needs or intentions.

He'd waited in line for upwards of 30 minutes at the M3 by his house, but here, on this shift, there was never a wait.

"Welcome, RICHARD, please plug in your headphones for your own privacy," said the kiosk as he approached. It followed a script, but punctuated unique words based on visual recognition. Richard didn't have headphones, but this time of night, he wasn't worried about anyone eavesdropping. "How was your recovery from STREP THROAT in OCTOBER?"

"It went fine. Right as rain." Richard peered at his watch. Jackson could hold down the fort fine, but with Roger there, anything was possible. "I'm kind of in a hurry."

"RICHARD, that is great to hear. Did you suffer any ill side effects from MASOOD STREP ANTIBIOTIC 2267?"

"No. It was fine."

"Excellent. Did you know, thanks to the research conducted by the miracle workers at Masood Pharmaceuticals, many common ailments like STREP THROAT will soon be a thing of the past? Trials for custom gene therapy to create a permanent immunity to this and other common ailments are now available. Would you like to join?"

"No. Now, please—"

"Many individuals wish to suffer. This is a psychological condition known as anosognosia, or someone who insists they are well even if they are not. Would you like a referral to a psychiatrist for a formal evaluation?"

"Listen, I need to go, can we hurry this along? I have—"

A small paper cup dropped from the machine, landing on a shelf at waist height. Above Richard, a yellow light attached to the top of the kiosk flashed.

"Please draw the curtain for your own privacy and respect for those around you."

"Say what, now?"

On the floor before each kiosk there was a black rubber mat, and eight feet above this mat, attached to the machine itself, was an exam room style curtain.

"Please draw the curtain for your own privacy, and respect for those around you, then deposit your URINE SAMPLE in the cup."

"You got to be out of your Goddamn mind!" He glanced again over his shoulder; not that anyone was there, but if anyone happened to be passing by, his luck would have dictated it be right then. "The hell you need me to pee in a cup for?"

"A need to GO is common urban vernacular for needing to urinate or pee. Is this need to GO a frequent occurrence?"

"I do not need to urinate! I need to get back to work. Can we please skip ahead to my diagnosis?"

"Of course. I apologize for the delay. The miracle workers at Masood created me to do everything I can for every citizen. We all matter at Masood. You seem stressed. Did you know stress and sleep are the two most crucial factors in determining the health of your immune system? Would you like me to teach you how to meditate to ensure a stress-free day and restful sleep, each and every night?"

"I don't need rest, I need something for anxiety."

"What is causing your ANXIETY?"

The door to medical creaked open. "Hey, sorry to interrupt, LT," said Dabrowski. Richard turned and found Dabrowski loitering in the doorway, pretending he didn't hear the word *anxiety*.

"Christ," Richard muttered to himself, telling the kiosk: "Hang on."

"That sounded like, HANGNAIL. Is that correct? Is a HANGNAIL causing your ANXIETY?"

"What is it now?" he asked Dabrowski.

Then to the kiosk: "No, stop."

Back to Dabrowski, "There a problem?"

"EAR PROBLEM. Is that correct?" the kiosk asked.

"Um, yeah, well, Jackson sent me to tell you, um—"

"Come on, spit it out," said Richard.

"You need to SPIT? Is that correct? Please use the provided cup. Or, if you need a larger vessel, say: LARGER VESSEL."

To the kiosk: "God damnit, I'm not talking to you!"

To Dabrowski: "Just say it."

"The old man, the one who was drinking the toilet water. He's throwing up now. Someone's got to take him to the hospital. You having a rough night? You want me to take him?"

Richard rubbed his temples. Said, "No. I'll take him. I'm good. Let me get my meds here and—"

"I am glad to hear you are GOOD. To continue a healthy lifestyle, please consult the Masood guide to better living. A free copy is available in this office. Thank you, goodbye."

"No, no!" Richard hit the machine as it exited his profile and returned to the default Welcome page. "Hello? Hello? You still there?"

The machine sprung to life again. "Hello, RICHARD. You are only authorized to visit a Masood terminal ONE TIME per day. You have already reached your maximum visits. Please come back tomorrow. Masood cares."

All he'd wanted was a Tylenol. Richard left the medical wing empty-handed.

Masood cares.

Sure they do.

Richard followed Dabrowski back to the drunk tank, or Sobering Center, or whatever the hell Jackson wanted to call it, and found Roger lying on a cot in front of a purple puddle. Even half-conscious and missing his faux suit of armor, the old man still had a singular presence. Not an awareness or a knowledge of anything in particular, but as antithetical as it may be, he had an air of wakefulness that surpassed everyone in the room.

"Can you get up?" Richard asked the old man.

"Of course," he replied.

"Good. Taking you to get your stomach pumped. How does that sound?"

"Wonderful!"

"You want me to take him, boss?" asked Dabrowski, as he and Jackson helped Mr. Green to his feet, and out of the cell.

"You?" Richard chuckled. "No, I got him. I need you two to do cavity searches to see how the wine made it into the cell."

The pair protested, swearing up and down that they'd searched everyone, but Richard wasn't having it. He glanced over at the man named Jesus who was fast asleep on another cot, then to the toilet. The old man had not made it to the toilet to vomit, yet the bowl was full of shimmering red wine.

He shook his head. This place was making them all complacent. Wine didn't get in here on its own.

Beaumont Hospital was only five miles north of Tri-County, and for the first four of those miles the men sat in silence, listening to the radio squelch out dispatch codes. The way nature hated a void, bureaucracy loved its stone tablets. Moses and his commandments had nothing on the resolute sanctity in which Detroit clung to its dispatch codes.

10-28: Driver's license request

10-31: Domestic disturbance

10-40: Dead animal

10-57: Hit and run

10-63: Barricade roadway

10-70: Prowler

Someone, somewhere, had the origin stories of how the codes were assigned to each infringement of the law. Not that it mattered. The codes were the codes, and the city held firm to them, regardless. That's why the Detroit Water Department employed a farrier until 2012, when their last horse died in 1986. Writ in stone and etched into the minds of every officer on the force over their tenure, these codes served to not only inform responding officers of the situation in which they were about to walk into, but also give them the mindset with which to approach it.

A 10-13: Adverse road conditions, was going to garner a decidedly different response than a 10-108: Officer down.

On some shifts, the squelch of the radio was a welcome relief in the monotony of code enforcement and ticket issuing. Others, the constant interruption was just that. An interruption to the plethora of plans and intentions which Richard had had going into that shift. After his shift, Richard would lie in bed and list off his own set of codes. Codes which weren't meant to address the symptoms of the city's problems, but instead were designed to fix the ailment itself.

20-28: Buy a kid a book

20-31: Carry in an old woman's groceries

The Devil's Night fires had not only blackened the city, but, at least for Richard, they had shown that if there was to be any hope in keeping another string of fires from happening again, police officers had to do more than enforce laws. They had to be a beacon for the residents of Detroit, a guiding light for the youth.

20-40: Save a trapped animal

20-57: Start a pickup game with some teens

And for voicing this need to do more, the brass had transferred him again and again and again, from the city to the suburbs to the jail, hoping that with each blow he'd finally learn his lesson and have dinner on the table when dad got home.

And like the stubborn, abused wife he was, he didn't.

20-63: Clean up a neighborhood

20-70: Be an inspiring person of color

The radio squelched, "*We have a 10-70 in the vicinity of Hamilton Road. Palmer Woods. Any available units please respond.*" Richard turned the radio down and looked through the cage into the backseat. The streetlights flickered on Roger's skin as he pressed his face against the cool glass.

The cruiser hit a bump in the road, and Richard heard a faint heave behind him.

"Don't you—" he said. But it was too late.

The old man opened his mouth and more purple slop poured out onto the backseat.

"Sorry about that," said the old man as he wiped his mouth with a sleeve.

"It happens. Feel better, Mr. Green?"

The old man nodded. "Please, you can call me Roger."

Richard chuckled at the familiarity of the request, which gave him the nerve to ask what he'd been rolling around the tip of his tongue all night, "Do you remember me, Roger?"

"Hmmm." Roger lifted his head and craned his body to see around the seat better. "I can't say that I do. Where would I know you from?"

"Nowhere. Forget about it."

"No, no. I can see it in your face. You know me. I apologize for not being able to place you. If we met recently, please let me know. It would bring into question my mental state. However, if we met a year or more ago, I may not have been in a right state of mind, and it is very likely that you slipped it."

"You can say that again. When we met, you were taking advice from a horse."

"Oh, I have been doing that since I was a child. That's hardly a litmus of my mental health. No, a year ago, I stepped off a curb. As it were, that curb was both literal and proverbial."

"You showed up at my doorstep riding that horse, dressed as a knight."

"Ah, so we're getting closer to our nexus. Sadly, that day is but a blur to me. However, my attorney, the DA, and the judge all described it in vivid detail before they relinquished me to the care of the mental health facility. But while they described what I did that day, they all missed what was done to me."

"What was done to you? What do you mean?"

Richard turned the wheel, and the cruiser pulled into the hospital parking lot. The emergency entrance was straight ahead. He made another quick turn onto the service drive that circled the hospital.

"It's not as dramatic as I make it sound; I simply have a penchant for giving my words weight regardless if they deserve it. No, what happened to me was, well, I don't completely know how to say it. An exhaustion washed over me. For seventy some-odd years I'd gone through the motions of life. I'd grown up, gotten married, had a career and children, retired. Each piece fulfilling in its own way. Never once did I ever feel as if I was missing out on anything. And then I realized I was missing the point of everything."

"Of everything? You mean life?"

"Yes. After my wife passed, I mourned and aged. I got a job to help fill my days. And I didn't realize this at the time, or even on the day in which we met, but that day I was acting out the realization that was nesting in my head."

"Come on, spit it out. I'm supposed to be taking you to the ER here, and you got me circling the building."

"And why are you circling the building? Tell me, on your happiest days, are you busy doing what you are supposed to do, or are you off somewhere else?"

They rounded the back of the hospital and headed back to the emergency entrance.

"You think that's the secret of life? Daydreaming, or following through on a daydream? That ain't no secret. That's called hustle and desire and drive. Thing is, life doesn't wait for no man to figure out what's got his goat. Just look at you and look at me. It's not that I don't dream, that I don't stop and wonder what I might do if I took a risk. I do. But I look at you, thinking you can talk to horses. Let me tell you, if we all stepped off the curb like you did, all we'd have is chaos."

"I don't understand your fixation on my talking with horses. It's nothing unique. There are plenty of us in the world with useless powers."

Richard glared at Roger through the rearview mirror as he pulled the cruiser under the emergency awning. "Sure there are."

Roger shrugged.

The cruiser rounded the last corner of the building. Richard pulled up under the awning, shifted into park, and climbed out. It was a quiet night in the ER, which Richard was thankful for. He didn't want anyone to bypass an actual emergency for the old man's antics. Richard swung the backdoor of the cruiser open and helped Roger out.

They walked side by side into the ER.

"Just so you know," said Roger. "You misunderstood me. I was not insinuating that daydreaming was the secret to anything."

"No? Sure sounded like it."

"I insinuated that the way we are existing in the world is a symptom of the problem. Daydreaming only treats those symptoms. No, the solution is to treat the problem."

When Age arrived, the space was empty save for a dozen chairs stacked neatly in a corner and the collapsed folding-table next to them. It felt, and smelled, like an old drunken PI's office, or a rundown depository where someone would shoot at a president as he drove by in a motorcade. In the hours before the meeting began, Age worked to transform the location into a sanctuary where hopes and dreams and fears could be shared without fear of persecution. He unlatched the windows and cranked them open to let in the breeze.

Under the windows he erected the folding table, and after a dozen trips to and from his car he adorned it with corner-store donuts and a full samovar of local coffee. He arranged the dozen chairs in a circle in the middle of the room and poured himself a cup of his coffee. While waiting for it to cool enough to take a sip without burning his tongue, he propped one knee up on the radiator, peered out the window, and waited for the group to arrive.

And one by one, they did.

Carlyle was always first to each meeting, and he lumbered into the room in jeans with a tucked-in flannel shirt that did nothing to disguise the growth of his middle-aged belly.

Following Carlyle was Belinda. Tonight, she wore a shoulderless one-piece summer gown that flowed gracefully with every step. She waved to Age, but as she approached the chatting men, she only had eyes for Carlyle. She was ten years his junior and a beautiful free spirit, and something in her burned for that frumpy man.

Age could see it plain as day, even though the two often played so coy about it that they ended up ignoring each other for the duration of most meetings. Not that he judged, but Age had a tough time pinpointing the origin of the attraction. There were no rules against group members engaging in romantic relationships with one another, but they were an odd match.

Next came Aleksei, a hulking three hundred-pound Russian who worked construction.

As the four of them made small talk and sipped their bitter coffee,

Age checked his watch. The meeting was scheduled to begin at seven AM, and he was getting worried. This was a much smaller turnout than usual.

When he'd first organized these get-togethers nine months ago, they had been meeting after work hours. But rather than discussing the elephants in the room, their gatherings quickly devolved into a therapy session to unwind from whatever kind of day they'd had. Moving the sessions to early in the morning, though, had proven to be quite successful. Each of them arrived not only well rested, but free of the burdens of the day.

This was Age's calling. For years he'd driven Uber to save up for school to work for Masood, but since seeing the Nain Rouge with his own eyes, the idea of devoting his life to something so banal felt like a sideways move in a ridged caste system. He'd originally rented this space to serve as the headquarters for his and Bash's grassroots effort to fund Camila Torres's legal bills, but once Masood took over they all but shut him out, moving the base of operations to their campus downtown. So, with three months left on the original lease, Age decided to finally take the leap forward and explore a thought, a question that had been in his head since Devil's Night. He took out an ad in the Metro Times that read:

Is This You?
We are little fish in a big pond. Though our
abilities may not seem extraordinary, they are
extra ordinary. And though our powers seem
useless, we certainly are not.

Within a week, he received his first phone call from Aleksei. Others followed, and soon the group ballooned to two dozen strong. They had a place in this world, and together they were going to find out what that was.

Not all were as mild-mannered as he and Carlyle and Belinda. Or even Aleksei, who was never quiet, but always jovial. And he soon discovered that just because they all shared these unprecedented traits did not mean they all got along.

Case in point: "Good evening, Adrian. Group," said Ansel as he came through the door.

"Morning, Ansel," said Age, as he walked to the window and

glanced out. "God damnit," said Age under his breath. "Don't come in. Don't come in. Don't come in."

Standing in a shadow having a cigarette: Tyler.

Two things about Tyler. Well, three.

One: Tyler and Ansel hated each other. Every gathering they both attended invariably turned into a verbal sparring match that derailed any potential for discussion.

Two: Tyler and Age, they knew each other. Though, since Tyler never acknowledged their acquaintance status, Age couldn't admit this. The people who came to this group did so because for one reason or another they felt they could not express themselves in the real world, even amongst those they loved and who loved them. Age didn't want to give the impression that the discussions had in this group might in any way continue on privately afterwards.

Three: Tyler was not his actual name.

And four. Shit. Four things about Tyler. And this one is about Ansel, too.

Four: If Age were going to be a stickler for the criteria that allowed one to attend these gatherings, neither Tyler nor Ansel really belonged here. He'd seen with his own eyes; neither of their powers were useless.

The fluorescent lights sung, their discordant hum worming into the atmosphere and turning an already featureless space into a postmodern Norman Rockwell still-life. But Roger here, sitting up on the ER bed between three curtained walls, he was no soda-jerk sniffing the prom date's corsage.

"He's a Goddamn lush is what he is!" Richard said to the physician, a middle-aged Indian woman, as she examined Roger.

"Thank you for the commentary, officer," said the physician. "How are you feeling, Mr. Green?"

"Marvelous. How are you?"

"I'm well, Mr. Green. So, you were picked up intoxicated," she turned to look at Richard, "and then what?"

"I was sober when they brought me in," Roger answered for himself. "I didn't become intoxicated until Jesus turned the toilet water into soma."

"Soma?" she asked.

"Wine," Richard air quoted, smiling at this farce.

The physician kept her focus on Roger. "Do you know what soma is, Mr. Green?"

"Delicious?"

"I'd imagine it would be. Soma is said to be the drink of immortality. The process of making it has been lost to the ages, though. If it ever existed at all." The physician patted Roger's knee. "I'm going to step out into the hall with the officer here for a moment, but when you get back to your friend, make sure you write down that recipe. Alright?"

Roger nodded.

"Be right back," said Richard as he followed the physician into the throughway.

She pulled the curtain behind her and spoke in a hushed tone. "I'm going to recommend that he be admitted tonight for psychiatric observation."

"No," said Richard without hesitation. "Mental health ain't covered on the county dime. We bring 'em here to make sure they going to live, but that's as far as we go. As long as he's not a danger to himself or anybody else, if he's drunk, he can sleep it off in the tank."

"I'm sorry, but does he sound drunk to you, officer? We see a lot of alcohol-related visits here, and most of them, when they come in, you can smell the vodka coming from their pores. Mr. Green is exhibiting none of that. He's lucid and clean, and I believe suffering from some sort of mental break."

"You're not wrong. He was picked up cause he wandered away from Red Run."

"That's it, then. If he's a resident at Red Run, it's on their dime if I admit him."

"It's your call, Doc, but," Richard clucked his tongue against the roof of his mouth and debated giving the doctor Roger's history. "I gotta tell you, he has a history of erratic behavior. You remember a year ago, the old man who stole the police horse and caused all that trouble in Ferndale?"

"I'd almost forgotten about that. This is him?"

Richard nodded. "Easy to forget about considering it happened on Devil's Night. So hey, if you want to hang onto him, he's all yours. I'd recommend some extra security though."

"Absolutely. Can you stick around until they arrive?"

Richard nodded. "Got nowhere else to be."

The doc walked off and made a call on her phone. Richard turned and grabbed the curtain, "Hey, Rog, this is where our night together ends. The doc here is going to—"

But as the curtain zipped along its track, an empty bed came into sight.

Roger was gone.

"God damnit."

There was no lockdown at the hospital. Even with Roger's history of erratic behavior, the security protocol for a drunk running off was more or less a shoulder shrug. Two rent-a-cops, dressed in grey, both as big and slow as walruses, showed up to help Richard search the ER, the hallways, and the parking structure. After nearly two hours canvasing, they agreed that the old man had slipped by them all.

"Sorry, Chief," barked one guard as Richard slid out the door. He waved a *thanks* back without turning around and found his cruiser still parked under the awning where he'd left it hours earlier.

It was 6:30 now, and this time of year, even on the East side of the hospital, the sun would still only be a vague thought on the horizon. The seats had gone cold while he was in the hospital, and even though he couldn't feel his breath, Richard felt a distinct chill settle into his chest. Now that he'd lost a detainee from the drunk tank, there would be no more door open to him. He'd fallen as far as he could in the department: midnight shift at Tri-County. When tonight's report crossed Belfour's desk, the only door he'd have left to be shown was the exit.

"Hello, Richard," said Roger as he popped up from the backseat.

"The hell—" he said, startled.

"Door was unlocked, so I climbed in to wait for you. What took you so long?"

"What took me—Roger, we been looking for *you*."

"Oh, I wouldn't admit that out loud. I've been right here the whole time."

"What'd you take off for?"

"I think you know. I have a purpose. Do you know why Jesus turned water into wine?"

"Because the alcohol in it killed bacteria and germs. But are you listening to me?"

"Are you listening to me? Yes. The wine was a disinfectant. But two-thousand years ago, were we at a point where that knowledge was commonplace? Maybe? I don't know. But what I can imagine is that someone coming along who can clean and heal wounds, it would be easy to believe that they were the Son of God."

"Roger. That man in the tank with you. He is not the Son of God. He's a Middle Eastern man calling himself Jesus."

"Who can turn water into wine." Roger paused. "He needs help."

"So do you, Roger."

"He needs to get home."

"Are you listening to me? They are going to admit you. I need to take you back inside."

"Or, let's say you don't."

"I ain't playing no games with you. You already took off once. And that shit nearly gave me a heart attack. Not in the mood to go through that again."

"I ran. True. But not far. In fact, I came right back. Beat you here, even. That counts for something, right?"

"Roger—"

"I asked you why Jesus turned water into wine. Let me ask you this. Why can I talk to horses?"

Richard rolled his eyes.

"You so readily accept what Jesus can do? Why so incredulous with my claim?"

"Are you the Son of God?"

"Was Jesus? What's more farfetched, that I can talk to horses or that two thousand years ago a man who could turn water into wine claimed to have divine lineage?"

"What are you getting at?"

"Son of God or not, what if the man Jesus simply found a use for his useless superpower?"

"Talking to horses is not a superpower, Roger."

"I appreciate your attempt at normalizing it. However, judging by every doctor's desire to place me under strict observation, I fear that you are in the minority in accepting that we exist."

"We?"

"Yes. We. All of us with useless superpowers. Come now, Richard. You didn't really think it was just me and Jesus, did you?"

Richard turned to face Roger. He wore a face of a man incapable of being anything but earnest.

"Let's make a deal," Roger said. "Let me prove to you that there are more of us. Many of whom are right here in the city. If I give you proof, you'll help me help Jesus. If not, I'll come back here without fight or fuss. Deal?"

"No," said Richard. "My ass is on the line here, and I ain't sticking it out for some nut job, regardless if he's calling himself Jesus."

"Fair enough. How about for me? Give me thirty minutes and let me prove to you I am not crazy, and that there are more of us out there. Once I've done that, regardless of what you believe, I'll let you bring me back here. How does that sound?"

"God damnit, Roger. Enough! You're a nice man, and I'd be lying if I didn't say I felt bad for you. But this has got to stop."

"And it will. Richard, I'm sorry I didn't remember you. But I'm sure now that there is a reason you remembered me. In your line of work you must encounter countless individuals, most of whom make no lasting impression. Yet, it's me who you remember."

"Hard to forget a guy who rides up to my home on horseback."

"Indeed. However, our conversations tonight have not been about me riding a horse. They have been about my belief in the incredible.

The unexplainable. That is where your curiosity truly lies. That is why you remembered me. Had I not been there tonight when Jesus turned that water into wine, would you have still been the one to take the victim to the hospital? Or did you take me in the hopes that I could reveal to you the answer to the question that's been in your head since we first met?"

"And what question is that?"

"Why. Why did I step off that curb! Why did I steal a horse and ride across the city! Those are the questions I believe you want answers to. And that's why you've been holding onto my locket."

"No. I held onto the locket because I'm a sentimental fool, and seeing you and your sons in there, it seemed like something that deserved a little more care than it was being given. As for the rest, sure, I've been curious as to why you'd do what you did. But you seem to think that this curiosity stems from my want to understand something unexplainable. It doesn't. I'm not a religious man, nor a superstitious one. The unexplainable holds no sway over me, Roger. You tell me someone can turn water into wine, that you can talk to horses, I call bullshit. So no, we won't be taking the thirty-minute tour through whatever delusion you've convinced yourself is an explanation for the unexplainable. Not unless it involves medication, or a therapist, or some sort of self-help group."

"Oh," said Roger. "Did I not mention the group?"

The cruiser came to a stop in downtown Ferndale. It was still early enough that there were only a few people out on the streets, most of whom had their heads down, focused on their morning cup of coffee on their way into work.

"Alright, we're here. Now what?"

Roger pointed across the street, toward the record shop, Noir Moon. Richard had driven past dozens of times and never had a desire to enter.

"The record shop? Come on now. If you ain't gonna be serious with me, we just going back right now."

"Not the record store. Above it. The owner rents out the storeroom upstairs."

Richard looked up, and through the old glass windows he saw a silhouette moving about. And there were others too, on the street, converging on the external stairwell on the side of the building. First it was just one person, then another and another. Soon the only person left outside was a thin man in a leather jacket smoking a cigarette in the recessed entry of the record shop.

A moment later the man finished his cigarette, flicked it aside, and cantered out of the recess and up the staircase.

"Are you ready, my friend?" Roger asked.

"Listen, I made no promises," said Richard as he opened his door and stepped out, "Thirty minutes, then we heading back."

"Whatever you say," said Roger.

Richard circled around to the back door where Roger sat and let the old man out. "Lead the way," said Richard. He followed Roger off the sidewalk and into the street as the latter led the way to a covered stairwell on the side of the building.

"Well, I guess it's close enough to the top of the hour. Let's get this meeting started." Age took the seat at the head of the circle of chairs. To his right sat Belinda and Carlyle. Ansel and Aleksei sat opposite them. "Kind of a small turnout tonight, but that's alr—"

The door swung open.

Age stammered and his heart dropped as he expected to see Tyler standing there staring down the group. Relief rippled through him when instead of Tyler, it was a young African American woman with pastel blue hair.

She was wrapped up tight, elbows cradled in opposite hands, and eyes darting cautiously around the room.

"Hi. I'm Age. What's your name?" Age stood to greet her.

"Sauti," she said without looking at any of them.

"Great, Sauti. Thanks for coming. Why don't you take a seat? We were just getting started."

She took the seat next to Carlyle, pulled her knees to her chin, and rested her heels on the front edge of the chair.

"What?" she asked. The question was tinged with hostility, and Age took note of the room's focus on her.

"Alright, everybody. Let's give her some space. You all remember what your first meeting was like. Sauti, you don't have to say anything or whatever until you feel comfortable, okay?"

She nodded.

Aleksei spoke up, "Does Scott know you're here?"

"What?" Sauti said with a furrowed brow. "Do I know you?"

Bzzzt-bzzzt-bzzzt.

She reached into the bag, looked to Aleksei after silencing her phone. "How did you know it was him?"

"It is my, how you say," Aleksei shrugged, "useless superpower."

"Seriously?" Sauti stifled a snort. "So what, you're like Caller-ID Man?"

Ansel let out a boisterous chuckle. Age tilted his head and gave him a look. The instigator rolled his eyes but shut his mouth.

"Since you're new here, you should know we have a few ground rules. One of which is that names, like Caller-ID Man, are a type of labeling. And we try to avoid labels here. At best they can come off as sarcastic, and at worst, purely negative."

"Alright, sorry."

"Another rule. We don't say *sorry* here."

Sauti sighed. But before he could call her on it, the door flew open again, and this time it was Tyler.

God damnit.

"No, no, no, no, no, no, no, no, no, no, no!" said Ansel as he leapt from his seat.

"I know, I know, I know I'm late." Tyler said as he crashed into the seat next to Aleksei, ignoring Ansel's protest. "I'm having a hard time with the world right now, so if it's cool with all of you, can we take care of my shit before we start on anything else?" Tyler's eyes were bloodshot and his skin was pale. He looked thinner than when he'd last attended a meeting.

"This is unacceptable!"

"Ansel, please," said Age.

"NO! He's not welcome here. It's been established! He is not welcome!" Ansel took a deep breath, "It. Has. Been. Established."

From across the circle, Belinda chimed in, "Look at him. He obviously needs help."

"I do! I need help!" said Tyler, "My stocks tanked, my girlfriend broke up with me, and I'm not handling it well. And if I'm being honest, I kind of want to see the world—"

"Surprise, surprise, you fucking loser!" Ansel cut him off.

"You and Stella broke up?" Age blurted out without thinking. "What happened?"

Tyler had never mentioned his girlfriend's name to the group, but thankfully, the new girl spoke up and buried his faux pas before any of the others noticed.

"Whoa, whoa, whoa," said Sauti, "Why isn't he welcome?"

Ansel answered, "Cause he doesn't have a superpower. Useless or otherwise."

"What about Batman or Iron Man, they don't have superpowers." said Tyler.

"You're not Batman!" said Ansel.

"Don't I know it? I'm broke now and stopped taking karate classes in the third grade! Don't get much more useless than that, does it?"

Aleksei chuckled at this. But he was too big to pick a fight with, so Ansel kept on prodding at Tyler. "Well, I don't know karate either, but I do know ka-razy! You gotta go, buddy!"

"Calm down, Ansel," said Carlyle.

"Can it, Boxman!" replied Ansel.

"No labels!" said Age. "We're better than—"

Again, the door swung open, cutting Age off. As calm as the morning had begun, it was quickly devolving, and whoever came through the door was going to either tip the scale into madness or reel the room back to some semblance of order.

Thirty seconds later, it was Roger who walked through the door.

Thank God!

The old man was a welcome addition to meetings, though Age did get the sense (and the text message) that he had to sneak out of his living situation in order to attend. When he did, though, the topics he brought up and the cadence of his speech, they had a calming effect on the group. Today, he had another man with him, too, which was exciting. It had been months since they'd had new faces. Hopefully now, Tyler and Ansel could be controlled enough not to scare them off.

"Good morning," said Roger. "Sorry we're late. Have we missed anything?"

"Roger! Hey! So glad you could make it. No, you haven't missed anything. You care to introduce your friend?" Age said, trying to shift the tone of the room.

"Of course, of course. This, friends, is Richard. He is the man who turned me in to the police on my ride last year."

"Yeah," said Tyler. "Saw you two in that cop car outside. You two steal the car or is he the real deal? Or is there a Village People convention in town? Or no! Don't tell me you're finally coming out of the closet after all these years?"

"That's enough, Ri—" Age stopped himself. "Tyler. We don't talk like that here."

Tyler zipped his fingers across his lips, turned an invisible key, and tossed it over his shoulder. Before he could reprimand him again, Ansel spoke up.

"Good to meet you," said Ansel. He walked over to the pair and gave Richard his hand to shake. "I back the blue. Thanks for all you do."

"Sure," said Richard. "No problem."

"Roger," Age said. "I have to say that I am a bit taken aback here. Group, this is a perfect example of the type of healing and soul searching we are attempting to accomplish here. For those of you who don't know, Roger has gone on more than one tirade since he first joined the group about the way the police stymied his purpose. Now, to see him here with the officer that caused his self-described downward spiral, well, it's a bit of a happy ending, isn't it? A full circle. Welcome, Richard. Would you care to share your USP with the group?"

"Oh, he has no USP," said Roger. "He's not a believer. I invited him here to witness what we can do."

"Well, Roger," Age's body stiffened. "While I appreciate your dedication, we aren't a sideshow to be believed or proven. Something like this, we'd need to get a consensus from the group before—"

"Wait a minute," Tyler cut him off. Age never got to finish a damn thought. "So it's cool if he brings a guest who doesn't have a USP, but me, a member of this group without one, I have to leave? What kind of bullshit is that?"

"See!" said Ansel. "He even admits he doesn't have one."

"That's because I am Iron Man. A socio-economically disadvantaged and physically useless Iron Man."

"Please! You're not Iron Man. Your name isn't even Tyler."

"Come on!" said Belinda, "What do you mean his name isn't Tyler?"

"Ansel," said Age, a bit panicked. "This is feeling like a witch hunt." He knew Ansel was relentless, and if he knew Tyler wasn't Tyler, what else did he know?

"I had a buddy in IT look into him. Turns out his name is Rick Nistal."

"He's not wrong," admitted Not-Tyler. "My name is Rick. I wasn't trying to lie, but I haven't come out to my friends and family that I have a USP. Well, one person knows, but they have been good enough to be coy about it." Rick winked. Not at Age, but he knew the wink was for him.

"BUT YOU DON'T HAVE ONE!" said Ansel.

"Alright, alright. Let's all calm down. We can work this out," said Age, "Last time you were here we had a similar discussion. And we came to the conclusion that maybe it would be best if you find another group to work through your issues."

"Thank you!" said Ansel.

"That being said, you're coming off a little manic today, and I feel I can't just send you away without at least giving you some tools to help yourself. You can stay. But I'm going to need you to not speak. No talking at all. Deal?"

"Oh, for Christ's sake!" Ansel threw his arms up in defeat. "This is bullshit."

"I don't think any of you understand what I'm going through here. I fucking need to be here, otherwise I don't know what I'll do. Have you ever even come close to losing the love of your life?"

"Rick," said Age, as the Devil's Night fire flashed behind his eyes. "I said you are free to stay." An image of Bash, and how close they came to losing each other that night. "You can listen, and gain knowledge and perspective. But, from what I have seen in the past, what you are looking to do here is pick a fight to make yourself feel better. If I'm wrong, I apologize. But if I'm right, let me be the first to tell you, this is not the place. So, what's it going to be, silent compliance or a vocal exit?"

Without retort, Rick fell back into his seat. Without a doubt, Age was now on Rick's shit list. Which meant that Bash was going to hear about this.

"Alright," said Age. "We need to keep things positive. That's what this group is all about, right? We aren't here to knock each other down. We're here to figure out our collective purpose in this world."

"Speaking of that," Richard spoke up. "What are y'all doing here? I mean, Roger refuses to concede that his life is anything less than prophetic. But from what I seen, either he can talk to horses or he's just plain crazy. And which one of them is easier to believe? I don't want to judge any of you. Most of you pass as fine people. But the way Roger made it sound is that all of you got some ability like his. And I ain't seen any of that. In fact, in my near sixty-plus years on this earth, I haven't once encountered anyone with something I'd call a superpower."

"You know Roger," said Carlyle.

"Yeah, okay. I didn't know anyone before meeting him."

"First time for everything, no?" added Aleksei.

"Okay. So what's yours, big guy?" Richard asked Aleksei.

"I know who is calling on phone before it rings." Aleksei had never been ashamed of his USP. And if anyone ever tried to make him feel otherwise, he was big enough to do something about it.

"Of course you can." Richard nodded.

Age could tell Richard wasn't buying it, so he spoke up too. "I create a cloud of electromagnetic disturbance that turns signal into noise. It kills all cell, radio, and Wi-Fi signal when I get anxious."

"So, we got horses and phones." Richard looked around the room. "Well, no offense, y'all weren't joking when you called these things useless, were you?"

"We're more than horses and phones, believe me." Age turned to the group. "Anyone else care to share? Ansel? Carlyle?"

"Pass," said Ansel without hesitation. No surprise there. Especially with a cop in the room.

Carlyle shyly looked away, and Belinda turned her attention to support him.

The new girl, Sauti, put her hand in the air.

"I," she started. "I, well—it's better if I just show you."

She brought her hands together and applauded, and as she did, the sound of gunshots ripped through the room. Loud. Booming. Automatic weapon fire. Round after round, as her hands came together.

Bang-bang-bang-bang!

Age froze. Belinda screamed and fell to the ground. Ansel and Aleksei leaped to their feet, ready to run. Neither Rick nor Roger flinched. Richard drew his sidearm and swept the room, looking for the shooter.

Fight, flight, or freeze.

"Sorry, sorry, sorry," said Sauti, holding her hands out.

Aleksei cried out, "The hell was that?"

"It was me! I'm sorry," said Sauti, her eyes on the floor.

"Are you serious?" said Ansel.

Sauti nodded. And to Belinda's chagrin, she reached out and gently ran her fingers down Carlyle's arm. Over shoulder and bicep, past his elbow. His skin contracted at her delicate touch, causing the hair on his arm to shiver to attention. It would have been sensual if not for the rip-roaring clatter of a chainsaw revving along from the tips of her fingers.

"Um," Richard said, "okay."

"No," said Sauti. "Not okay. Do you have any idea how many schools I've been expelled from, how many concerts I've ruined? I'm fucking Sound Effect Girl! About the only friends I've had are the nerds who need cheap sound effects for their bullshit indie movies."

"At least you found some use for your superpower." Carlyle

climbed back up into his seat as he spoke. "You know what mine is? I can turn into a Goddamn cardboard box. A box."

Belinda touched Carlyle's arm, and he slapped her hand away like she was a mosquito. He realized too late what he'd done, and as their eyes met, it was impossible to tell who was more hurt by the action.

"Fuck!" he said and flung himself out of his seat.

"Carlyle," Age called. But Carlyle did not slow as he reached the door. Instead, he flung it open and ran. Belinda followed him and Age made no attempt to stop either of them.

Each of the group members had confided in Age long before sharing their useless superpowers with each other. In part it was because he was the one who had found, approached, and revealed with the appropriate amount of skepticism, wonder, and fear that he too could perform something so utterly useless that there had to be a purpose for it.

Carlyle, he could turn himself into a box. But it's not as convenient as it sounds. He couldn't just have someone pack his belongings into himself and get shipped to some tropical destination on the cheap. No, when Carlyle turned into a box, all his insides remained inside the box. Organs and fluids alike. And Age had seen him come out of the experience severely dehydrated and constipated for days while his insides reorganized themselves.

Roger, he'd been talking to horses since he was a boy. And like Aleksei, he had no shame in this ability.

Belinda, she calls herself The Werehouse. Once a month, during her cycle, she could turn into a house. Once, when the owner of the record store downstairs received an extremely large delivery of fireworks the fire marshal shut the place down, and until the explosives could be stored safely elsewhere they held their meetings inside her. It was a little awkward. More for her than them, because her house furnished itself based on how she was feeling at the moment. And when they held the meeting, it was empty inside.

There were others, too. Heidi and Samir and Daisy. They'd all trusted Age with their secret. Chester and Annalee and Keaty.

Keaty was a vagabond and busked for a living when Age approached him. His useless superpower was that he remembered his past lives, which he used to his advantage because he, the ultimate hipster, was there, in some form or another, when most songs were written. He'd say, "Why do you think pop songs are so popular? It's not because they're necessarily good, yeah? No, some of them are bloody awful. It's because they're ancient. The sound, the rhythm. They tap into folklore and human nature. Music is in our genome. And when we hear something we like, we are remembering the tribe we belonged to. It's a way to take us back there." He was the first one who was actually able to help Ansel.

Ansel.

As Richard had said, in all his life he'd met no one who had a superpower. Age hadn't either. Even growing up with one, he never put it together that what he did was anything more than a cosmic anomaly. A genetic fluke that he alone had to bear.

On Devil's Night, he encountered the Nain Rouge, which took him on a journey of self-discovery that had begun with Ansel.

Age had done as much factual research on the Red Dwarf of Detroit as he could. But without fail, every path led back to the myth, rather than the truth. Every path, except for that of the Cadillac Family. They were the one piece of the story that was undisputed. He tracked every branch of that family tree, and there, at the end of a wilting branch of bastards, at the bottom of a rabbit hole of Facebook stalking and Google research, Age found Ansel.

It took him nearly two weeks to stop being chicken-shit and approach him in real life. Age had tracked him to the insurance firm where he worked, and to the organic grocery store where he got his lunch every day. It was there that Age approached the man, and over a cup of coffee, he learned that Ansel had a power, too.

Roger had offered to provide proof that there were others in this city that could do what he did. Not just talking to horses, but other, uniquely individual abilities as well. And while the group here self-identified these abilities as useless superpowers, they felt more like delusions of grandeur. Not one of them had demonstrated anything irrefutable. Parlor tricks was a more apt description; coincidence, trickery, or collective delusion a more apt cause than whatever divinity Roger and his group imagined.

"Should we go see if he's okay?" asked Sauti as the door swung closed.

"It's better to just let them be," said Age. "We all deal with our abilities differently. Carlyle can be quite emotional about the uselessness of his. Belinda is there for him."

"I for one am happy to do away with some drama here. Get rid of the dead weight and maybe we can actually accomplish something," added Ansel with a sly nod toward Rick.

"Dude, are you this much of a dick to everyone you meet, or is it just those who don't have a traditionally useless superpower?"

"I actually see myself as a people-person. I just don't take kindly to those who claim to be something they aren't. Life is hard enough as it is. To have someone like you come in, claiming to be one of us, and not having to deal with the true difficulty of navigating this lifestyle. It kind of pisses me off."

"Oh, give me a fucking break!" said Rick. "You aren't a people-person. You were an asshole to me before I ever voiced what my USP was."

"The only ability you have is to give me a fucking headache!" Ansel was getting red again.

"If that's my USP, let me help you out. I got a twelve-gauge aspirin out in my car. Want me to get that for you?"

Age stepped between the men. "Alright, guys! Let's settle down."

About the only thing they had convinced Richard of was that this group did no one in it any favors. Richard checked his watch. The thirty minutes he'd given Roger to convince him were about up, and as Ansel and Rick continued to take digs at each other, Richard turned his attention to the old man as he spoke up.

"Yes, please. Listen to Adrian," said Roger.

Richard watched him sway toward the fight, but never quite step in.

"We all remember what happened last time." The sad old man. His lip quivered as he spoke. For all his talk about stepping off a curb and taking control of his life, here he was, hesitating.

"Yeah, speaking of last time, let's talk about that." Rick turned to Age. "You were right. I came here this morning to pick a fight with him. You know why? Because fuck this place. Fuck this group. Fuck Masood. Fuck this whole Goddamn city. Don't worry, Age, I'm almost done, I got another meeting to get to anyway. Ansel, you burned the city down once, maybe this time you can finish the job!"

It took Richard a full moment to grasp what had been said, and by the time he did, Rick was already on top of Ansel pummeling him.

Aleksei was out of his chair a moment later. He grabbed Rick by the scruff of his neck and ripped him off Ansel.

"What's the matter with you? Don't you—" Age was staring at Rick in total shock.

"Yep," said Rick, and without another word, he bolted out the door and was gone.

"What the fuck!" said Sauti.

"I'll call an ambulance," said Richard, as he pulled out his phone.

"You can't." Roger placed his hand on Richard's.

"The hell I can't. This man needs medical attention! Look at his face!"

Ansel's face was a contorted mess. Bloody and red and broken. But as Richard tried to dial, he found he had no service.

"Fuck," said Age. He was panicked, anxious.

"See," said Roger. "Proof."

"Well, hell," said Richard. "Come on and help me get him out to the car, we can take him to the hospital ourselves."

"No," said Age. "We need to barricade the doors and close the windows. The smaller the space, the better. We need to control the environment. Too much sensory overload and he'll go feral again. Someone turn off the lights. Anyone know how to sing? I'm too anxious, nothing wireless is coming through."

"Sing? What are you talking about?"

"Music has been the only non-violent way we've found to stop him."

"Stop him from what?"

"Richard," said Roger. "I'm sorry you're here. I never meant for you to get hurt."

"Get hurt? What—"

And then it happened.

Ansel's face contorted. It sweltered and distended, as his skin shrink-wrapped around his skeleton, pulling his body into a primatal hunch. Through it all he remained silent, as if his lungs had collapsed. The only sound that came from his body was the screech of joints twisting unnaturally. It was a display so jarring it came across as choreographed. The way sociopaths mimic human behavior only to capture and recreate it too perfectly, so too did Ansel when he dug his fingers into his shirt and ripped it from his chest, sending buttons ricocheting around the room.

"Fuck," said Age again. "For real, can any of you sing? Anything at all. Music calms him down, but it's got to be on key. I got the windows. Aleksei, get the door. Roger, the lights."

Without hesitation, they did as they were told. The deadbolt clacked shut. The windows slammed closed. The lights went out.

Richard remained silent and frozen as, save for the blonde tufts of hair on his chest and head and lip, the transformation tinted Ansel's body fully red. Even his eyes, once a light blue, were now black maws haloed in red.

In the darkness, a noise finally emerged from Ansel's mouth. A guttural scream that shook the room and blew out the windows. As the sound dissipated, a glow replaced it. It was as if a fire had ignited inside Ansel and was fighting to spurt from his pores.

Then it did.

In one moment, the man lay before them, bent and broken. The next, he was engulfed in a raging inferno.

No. He was the inferno.

And within the flames were jagged teeth and twisted horns and burning eyes that stared out at the group. Ansel's useless superpower had manifested. He moved like an injured sparrow, pathetic and hobbled, but as he did so the flames followed him.

Richard drew his sidearm again.

Sometimes pity isn't the right choice, even for those who can't help themselves. Rick had attacked Ansel with full knowledge of what he'd become, but also with the knowledge of how non-violently Age would respond. And if Ansel's fire grew any larger, who knew how much damage it could do.

"Don't," said Age. "He can't help himself. This isn't his—"

BANG! The firearm discharged.

A haze of blue smoke rose from the burning linoleum. The scent of overheated electronics filled the room. Fire leaked from the bullet wound in Ansel's shoulder as he fell.

The concussion from the shot hung in the room. In Richard's ear there was a fly. Not a fly, but a bee. And the buzzing would not stop. It wasn't a bee either.

Before Richard could place a better aim on his next shot, he fell to his knees. Inside his head, the tone swelled to twice, three times its own size, until his own skull could no longer contain it, and the world at large hummed and vibrated.

Ansel lay on the floor before him, no longer pumping fire but straight blood onto the tile. Richard watched the group come together to help Ansel. Aleksei had ripped off his shirt and was pressing it into the wound, Age was stomping out the few residual fires that remained, and the girl was just talking to him, telling him that everything was going to be alright.

But it wasn't.

An auroral gloom enveloped him, blooming from this equinox of failure.

It wasn't how Richard expected his career to end, shooting a civilian while in the midst of a psychotic break. Sure, Roger could speak with horses, but Richard could see demons. Right. Sure. Back at the station, they'd all say they saw it coming. First went the body, limping in on Devil's Night, then the mind followed.

A hand landed on Richard's shoulder. He turned. It was Roger.

"Here," said Roger. "Let me help you." Roger cocked his fist and snapped it forward into Richard's face. His vision glittered white and the membrane in his nose split, letting blood spill down onto his lips.

The blow shattered the haze in his mind, and Richard quickly pinched his nose shut, forcing him to taste copper and sound like Kermit the Frog.

"What the hell, Roger?"

"You saved us. Saving you was the least I could do. I hit you, went for your gun. A single round was discharged."

"Ain't gonna matter. When they pull that slug out of him, they gonna match it to my piece."

"He won't be going to the hospital," Age interjected. "He's been shot before. He heals pretty quickly."

"He's been shot before?" Richard asked.

"Yeah, on Devil's Night. Not sure who shot him. A cop or some random person who saw their city burning, saw the Red Dwarf, and decided to take a shot. Either way, Ansel told me that getting shot was the only thing that kept the rest of the city from going up."

"So, Rick there, he wasn't full of shit? Devil's Night was all on him?"

Age nodded. "Always has been. Him, or his ancestors. They're the Nain Rouge."

"What about that Torres girl? How did she get the blame?"

Age didn't answer. But he didn't need to. Richard knew that one all on his own. Wrong place, wrong time, wrong demographic. If there was anything to be done about it, he couldn't go down that rabbit hole yet. One thing at a time.

"Today, Ansel," Richard fumbled for the right word, but when he couldn't come up with one, he went with the simplest explanation. "He turned or whatever because Rick attacked him. How did it happen last year? Did he get attacked then too?"

Age and Roger shared a quick look before Roger spoke back up.

"Not attacked, but startled without a doubt. I wish he could tell the story. He does it much more justice than I could ever hope to. Last year a man appeared before him. Appeared out of thin air. His first thought was that he'd been hit by a car while crossing the street because the man standing before him, he looked like Jesus. Arab, wearing robes. And here was Ansel, answering for all his sins to the man himself. And in that moment of panic and guilt, he transformed, and well, you know the rest."

"You saying he got hit by a car and went feral?"

"No. He did not get hit by a car."

"You saying you really think the man in the tank is the real Jesus Christ? Like, from the bible?"

Roger didn't answer the question. "Richard, I was not arrested tonight haphazardly. We have been looking for Jesus for some time now. Ansel believed he needed help. The only thing Ansel remembered hearing before he turned was Jesus saying, "Help." It makes sense, doesn't it? The world has gone mad in the absence of its salvation."

"I ain't much of a religious man, Roger. Convincing me that what the world needs is Jesus, that our shallow discontent is because the Son of God went missing, don't know if I quite buy that."

"This isn't about religion or faith, but about a man unstuck in time, displaced and forced to live a life that he did not choose. Tonight, when he and I spoke in that cell, he told me his story the way he remembered it. And it doesn't matter if he is the Son of God, or just another one of us with some useless superpower. He has been used as an effigy against his will."

"What were you planning on doing, breaking him out?"

Roger nodded.

"Christ," said Richard.

"Exactly!" Roger placed his hand on Richard's shoulder. "So, my friend. Our thirty minutes have more than expired. You owe me nothing more. You can take me back to jail and I will corroborate whatever story you wish to tell about the goings-on tonight. Or, you can be honest with yourself and admit that whatever questions you had lingering from the time we first met, that those have now been answered."

An hour earlier, Richard had sat in his cruiser terrified at the prospect of having to head back to Tri-County and explain that the old man had slipped out of a hospital unseen. Sometime between then and now, that fear had shifted and dissipated and morphed into something else: a certain uncertainty that tugged at his insides. There was no suit of armor for him here, no horse to ride, but he could not deny that even before Ansel transformed into the Nain Rouge before his eyes, even before he'd heard all those testimonials, that when he helped Roger out of the cruiser and followed him into the meeting, he'd already stepped off the curb.

Richard pulled the keys from his pocket.

"You know, it's like we had a great first date and everything. We ended up back at her place and, right? We went on another date, and I used this dating technique, and you know, it went great again, but I haven't heard from her since," said Dabrowski as he typed on the keyboard, clicking through various links, mapping his way to the archive.

It had been three months since the Torres defense team had requested the bodycam footage from Devil's Night. Three months that he'd been stuck on this shit detail. Out in the cruiser, Dabrowski wasn't so bad. Most of the time, they were busy enough that he didn't have time to talk about his personal life. But here, stuck between four walls and boredom, Dabrowski was near insufferable.

"So, what do you think?" Dabrowski stopped typing and looked at Jackson.

Kid been droning on long enough now that Jackson forgot what the initial question had been. Didn't matter. Whatever it was, it paled in comparison to the phrase, "Dating technique? What the hell you mean, dating technique?"

"You know, finding out stuff, figuring out what she's thinking. Like reading between the lines stuff."

"Do you mean listening? Is listening a dating technique these days?"

"No, man. You don't get it. Never mind, it's hard to explain."

"No, no, please! I want to get it! I want to understand this crazy ass shit you call dating. But don't let me distract you. Wanna show you some of this shit."

God, the shit that entertained him these days. Dabrowski was good with computers, so to pass the time, Jackson had suggested pulling up old bodycam footage from the archive. Watch some of the departments greatest hits to kill time waiting for the LT and the old man to get back.

"I'm already in. It's all HTML. Can find whatever you want to look at if you know the date. But you want to know about the dating technique? It's a little out there, man. But okay. It's called Social Lube, and this doctor—"

"Nah, man. We'll come back to your love life when this shit gets boring. But that's gonna be awhile. Okay." Jackson rubbed his hands together. "You can look up anything?"

Dabrowski nodded.

"How about June 20th. First day of summer. Look up Paul Gracie's shit. You know that viral clip that got him shit canned. His bodycam shows what really went down."

Dabrowski's fingers went to work, and a few seconds later, a video window popped up on the monitor. He clicked the corner to go full screen and fast forwarded to near the end.

"Don't call me a fucking woman!" The female on camera said as she confronted Gracie, so close to him that her face distorted into a Jay Leno lookalike. "Do you have any idea the struggle we go through because of people like you? Never witnessed actual pain or suffering, never experienced a moment of discrimination unless you were the one doling it out. I don't identify as Ma'am! How dare you assume my pronouns are she/her, you Cis piece of shit!"

She shoved him again, and Gracie didn't budge.

Jackson was actually impressed with his constraint.

The female spit at Gracie.

"Look at that shit," said Jackson. "Fucking assault."

"She spit on him and they fired him anyway?"

"Well, just keep watching. And listen. Listen to this pop. You can actually hear her jaw dislocate. It's fucking gnarly."

The woman hadn't stopped ranting, "—tool of the oppressor. But after meeting you, officer, I am a believer, because it's clear that you have never met an extra chromosome that you didn't like. So, you listen to me now, I am Moonjava of Ferndale and I—"

Gracie's meat wedge of an arm blocked the camera for

a split second.

And then the sound came: POP!

Jackson and Dabrowski reeled back and laughed. Could almost hear her teeth cave in.

"Holy shit!"

"That is disgusting."

When the camera had a clear view again, the woman was nowhere to be seen.

"It's like you can almost see her teeth leaving her mouth, and her soul leave through the gap left behind."

"She didn't die, did she?" asked Dabrowski.

"No. Sued the department. And they wanted Gracie gone anyway. Too much of a social liability regardless of his record. You want to see some more?"

"Oh, I don't know? Feel kind of weird laughing, you know?"

"It's me, man. It's us. No one else is fucking here. You ain't gotta look away to prove you're a good kid. When else are we gonna have the opportunity to see this shit again? There was this one time, fucking Gracie and I got called to a scene where bunch of fucking street kids had two officers trapped in their cars. We rolled up, scared 'em off, and Gracie stopped short of beating the shit out of the officers for being such pussies. God, when the fuck was that? Or shit, how about the dogs? The dogs in the basement! I tell you about that? That was fucking crazy."

"When was that?"

"February. February what? Um, let me think. Oh, hey, how far do the archives go back? Just this year?"

"No. I can pretty much get anything that's in the system."

"Can you pull up Devil's Night? My cam footage?"

"You serious?"

"Yeah, man. Gracie fucked up for sure that night. I don't know if I did or not. Kinda want to see what I did before they make me look at it in court."

"You really think you're going to court? Sounds like the case is getting dismissed."

"That's her case. You think her father gets Masood to pony up for her criminal defense, and is going to stop there? Naw. There's a civil case breathing down my neck."

"You sure you want to look at this? I mean, if you do, I can leave?"

"Nah. Pull it up. And be honest with me. Wanna know how fucked I really am."

Bzzzt-bzzzt-bzzzt. Jackson's phone lit up. Calloway.

"Hold up," he told Dabrowski. "Gotta grab this. You can go ahead and play the clip. Let me know if I want to see it or not."

Bzzzt-bzzzt-bzzzt.

Jackson stood and showed himself out of the office. Neither of the two remaining detainees in the cage paid him any mind as he stepped out into the gymnasium. The one was still asleep, and the other, well, he may as well have been. His legs were crossed, eyes closed, and he was ohm-ing to himself.

Bzzzt-bzzzt.

"Hey, babe."

"Hey, how was the night?"

"Long. Ready to get off this detail."

"You will, babe, you will. But hey, my parents called and want to take us to an early brunch at La Dolce Vita. Think the Lieutenant will let you duck out early?"

"Early brunch? You mean breakfast?"

"Don't be like that. They're trying to be nice."

"Trying on something new, are they?"

"Charles, come on. Please? For me?"

"Babe, I would if I could. But we had an incident here earlier. The Lieutenant had to take one of these assholes up to get his stomach pumped."

"Why? What happened?"

"You don't want to know. But anyway, they ain't back yet, so I gotta hold shit down till they show up."

"Why didn't he send Dabrowski?"

"I don't know, babe. Want me to ask him when he gets back?"

"How long has he been gone?"

Jackson checked his watch. "While now."

Calloway sat silently on the line. He could tell her mind was working.

"What? What is it?"

"Nothing," she replied. *"Just, he's already on thin ice with Belfour as it is. Being gone this long when he could have sent a subordinate, this shit is going to push*

him over the edge."

"Yeah, and?"

"I don't know. I mean, the Lieutenant is on his last leg, Charles. I know he means a lot to you, but if he's being shown the door, you don't want to be riding those coattails. Think maybe you should give Belfour a heads up. Maybe it'll help buy your way out of this detail sooner."

Now it was Jackson's turn to hang on the line in silence and let that thought roll around in his head. He didn't like the idea of being a snitch. Didn't much like the idea of being stuck here either because someone snitched on him. Was the way of things though, put enough dirt on the scale and eventually justice balances itself out. Maybe Calloway was right. For sure, yeah, the Lieutenant was on his last leg, and maybe that euthanasia might be more bearable if some good came out of it. If anything, Jackson had learned that some big percentage of good police work was performing solidarity and managing your superiors the right way, and those are soft skills which he only learned from watching LT perform them so artfully well. Sure, he didn't always wind up where he wanted, but he never once failed to land on his feet.

"Charles," Calloway finally said.

But before she could add to that, Dabrowski bolted from the office. "Jackson! Lieutenant is back. And fuck, he's not looking good."

"What? The hell you talking about?" Then to Calloway, "Hey, I gotta call you back."

He slid his phone back in his pocket while Dabrowski went on. "Caught him stumbling in on the monitors. Bloody nose, limping."

"The fuck? He got the old man with him?"

Dabrowski shook his head.

Looks like Belfour was getting a call after all.

Jackson glanced into the cage, movement catching his eye. The Black Bugs Bunny was still fast asleep on his cot, but the man Jesus had arisen, and was walking toward the door at the far end of the room.

The door to the gym clanked and keys rattled on the other side. They both heard them drop and hit the floor. Dabrowski stepped past Jackson and went to the door. He punched in his code and pulled the now unlocked door open. Richard hobbled into view, looking all the wreck that Dabrowski had described. Dried blood drips saturated the front of his shirt, his hair was sweaty and matted, even his one eye was swollen. And every step he took was labored, only able to support his weight half the time.

"Christ, LT! The hell happened?" asked Dabrowski as he and Jackson took his weight onto their shoulders.

"Don't want to talk about it. Get me down to that Goddamn kiosk."

"Where the old man at?" asked Jackson.

"Said I don't want to talk about it. Let me get an ice pack on my head and some painkillers in my body, then we can talk about how I fucked up."

The Lieutenant winced as the pair had to twist him around awkwardly to fit through the entryway into the hall that connected them to the rest of the facility.

"You sayin' that old man did this? You sayin' he got the drop on you?" He couldn't even get the words out without laughter sputtering past his lips.

"Yeah, yeah. Laugh it up. Gonna remember that when it comes time to write your review."

Jackson and Dabrowski exchanged a look and held in another bout of laughter.

It was eight AM when they limped into Medical. The LT had been gone with the old man for near five hours now, and he wasn't the only one who had to file an incident report for the shift. Jackson could make an excuse for the Lieutenant if he needed to. Or he could tell the truth. Neither was the wrong choice, but only one of them had the potential to buy himself into Pharaoh Belfour's good graces. Which maybe, probably, would absolutely get him out of this detail. Fucking rough though, seeing the LT in this shape and contemplating pushing him under another bus.

There was a pedagogy to police work, and so many believe it comes down to the ensuring that those with proper training are put into the right situation at the right time. For that trifecta to happen, the game of policy and bias and misinformation had to be played, and sacrifices had to be made.

None of them were doing a damn bit of good stuck here.

"Welcome, RICHARD. Welcome, CHARLES. Welcome, HENRY," the kiosk said as they entered. "Please place your thumb on the pad. I will be with the rest of you shortly. Masood cares."

"Anyone else got a visit left today?" Richard asked. "I only have one every twenty-four hours on my plan."

"Yeah, I got you, LT," said Dabrowski.

Jackson and Henry helped the LT over to a chair by the window and approached the machine and place his thumb on the pad.

"Hello, HENRY, please plug in your headphones for your own privacy."

"Hope you got your headphones. The built-in mic on that thing is sensitive as hell," said Richard. Jackson caught Dabrowski holding back a smile.

"Naw, it's cool, LT. You can use the noise canceling toggle in the upper right of the screen. Keeps the machine from picking up background conversations," Dabrowski said with his finger pressed to the screen. "So, what you need? Ibuprofen or something?"

"Strongest shit you can get me without having to wait for the pharmacy to open."

"I got you," said Henry, and took his finger off the screen.

"Welcome back, HENRY. How is your RAGWEED allergy this season? Do you need a refill of MASOOD ANTIHISTAMINE 7007?"

"No, thank you. My allergies are under control."

"Great! How can Masood care for you today?"

"Migraine."

"Ouch. Those are no fun. Did you know, thanks to the research conducted by the miracle workers at Masood Pharmaceuticals, many common ailments like MIGRAINES will soon be a thing of the past? Trials for custom gene therapy to create a permanent immunity to this and other common ailments are now available. Would you like to join?"

"I am listed in another database for this trial."

"Great. Since I am unable to access that database, we will focus on your MIGRAINE at the moment."

Richard snorted a laugh and winced; the bridge of his nose ballooned with each breath. He should have gone to the hospital, not come back here.

"You okay, LT?"

"Yeah. And no. Gonna live, you know, but my time here, it's running short."

"What do you mean?"

"Eh, nothing really. Watching Dabrowski on that kiosk. I always get caught in some infinity loop of questions, where he just says the right thing to bypass the bullshit. I didn't grow up with games like these. Don't know how to play 'em."

"It's an acquired skill. Eventually it becomes the norm."

"Yeah. Not sure that's the type of norm I'm looking for anymore.

Too much nuance in a world full of blind spots. Look at this." Richard reached into his shirt pocket and pulled out a locket. "You know whose this is?"

Jackson looked at the thing dangling there between them. He'd never known the LT to have a lady friend long enough to carry any jewelry. And sure, the man had a mother at some point. Maybe it was hers. But Jackson didn't think so. There was no revelation to be had in carrying a locket that belonged to your mother. No, the LT was bearing his soul. For whatever reason, he trusted Jackson, treated him like the son he never had. Jackson returned the honor by preparing to make mental note of every word that was about to come out of the LT's mouth. He said it himself, he was done being a cop. At least, that's how Jackson took it. Too old for games in a world where games were all that was left.

"Nah. Whose is it?"

"The old man who was here, Roger. It's his. That night I came in limping. It was because of this. The old man had ridden up to my house on that horse and when I saw him, without thinking, I called it in."

"Nothing wrong with that. Old man was having a breakdown."

"Yeah. Anyway, we talked and the cavalry rolled up, and they did what they do."

The LT paused. Only for a moment, only for a look. But in that moment, he was no longer the LT, but Richard, the man behind the rank. And he wasn't looking at Jackson, but into him. Around the force, it was no secret how he and Gracie had handled those kids on Devil's Night. And had the girl's purse not been found at the scene of the last fire with her ID in it, the whole incident would have been buried and forgotten. Simple vandalism and trespassing charges. But instead, shit got real. And with every door that opened for him, it kept getting more and more real, until here he was. Reaping what he'd sewn.

"They drug him off and threw him into the back of a cruiser. And as they drove off, he and I, we made eye contact only for a split second, but I swear he looked into me in a way that, I don't know, felt like he could see my guilt. Anyway, as I was heading into the station later that night, I fell coming off my porch. Slipped, twisted my ankle, but good. Thought it was glass that I'd stepped on, but it wasn't. It was this. His locket." LT turned his focus back to Jackson. "I was going to give it back to him tonight, was actually in the process of doing so when he jumped me. Yeah, I fucked up, let him sit in the front seat with me after the ER."

"That thing's bad luck," said Jackson.

"Eh, if I thought that was the case, I'd submit it with my report to Belfour. Let him walk a mile in our shoes, right? But, no. It ain't bad luck. It ain't nothing. It's just a necklace with a picture of a man and two boys inside. Any meaning beyond that, well, that's up to you."

"Alright, LT," Dabrowski interrupted. "Just about done here. What you want, 800mg? Dozen of 'em? That's the best I can do."

"If that's what you can do, do it."

"Yes, please," Dabrowski said as he removed his finger from the screen. "Twelve count. 800mg."

"Great, HENRY. We hope the Masood NSAID 1645 will help with your HEADACHE. Your medicine will be dispensed below when this session concludes. And remember, Masood carrr-rrrr-rrreeeeee..."

The kiosk's voice faltered from a smooth human facsimile to a sliding digital stutter before falling silent altogether.

"The hell happened?" asked Jackson.

"The hell you do?" accused the LT.

All around them, the lights flickered. Henry tapped the kiosk's screen.

"Hello, USER. This Kiosk is currently offline and cannot access your profile. If you are in need of immediate medical care, please find a phone and dial 911. Otherwise, you can go to MasoodCares.com for a list other available kiosks in your area."

"Internet's down." Dabrowski turned back to Jackson and the Lieutenant.

Jackson pulled out his phone, checked. No Wi-Fi. No signal either. What the fuck? "You got signal on yours?"

Dabrowski checked. Shook his head.

"Security cameras are out too," said Richard, pointing up to the corner of the room. The small dome that hung from the ceiling looked no different than it usually did, save that now it was missing the little red LED that was always visible through the tinted plastic. Didn't matter much. The cameras were just one of a dozen redundancies that kept the facility secure. And of all the measures present, the cameras were foremost a deterrent. Just like out in the real world, they could catch you in the act, but in here, there was no place to run.

One more item to add to his ever-growing report on the night.

"My meds come out?" asked the LT.

Dabrowski shook his head.

"Goddamn it."

"Listen, LT," said Jackson. "Maybe this is a blessing. I ain't gonna lie to you, that shit looks real bad. He popped you good. Think you need more than a few over-the-counter pills."

"I'm fine. Just need to control the pain."

"Naw. You need a trip to the ER."

"The hell I do!"

"Hey!" Jackson raised his voice, took an aggressive pose. "You couldn't even walk down here on your own. Limpin' ass, busted face. We getting you some real help. And before you say shit, with the internet and phones down, ain't got no other choice but to let you suffer."

The LT checked his watch, but didn't put up an argument. "Fine," he said.

They took their time getting back to the Sobering Center; LT refused help this time and limped the whole way back. They crossed the walkway back to their little satellite unit, and the LT patted himself down.

"Where my keys at?"

"What?" asked Dabrowski.

"Said, where my keys at. Was gonna open the door for you fools, but they ain't in my pocket. Either of you pick them up when I dropped them coming in?"

Jackson and Dabrowski looked at each other and shook their heads.

"Well, shit," said the LT. "Best hope they in the gym and not out in the hall."

Dabrowski unlocked the door and immediately heard the screaming.

"Oh, shit! Oh, shit! Oh sheeeeet! Oh, shit! Oh, shit!

Jackson pushed past Dabrowski and the LT, and bombed into the gym. There, he saw Bruce Bannister, the Black Bugs Bunny, wide awake, hopping up and down in the cage, hooting and hollering about superheroes and obscure wrestlers from decades ago.

"Oh, shit! You missed it! Doctor Strange was here, and he cast his magic and turned off the world. And Scarlet Witch, she a noisy bitch. Then fucking Rolof the God-killer came in and tried to bend the bars, but it no use, these things good and strong. Bruce Bannister tells him he already tried, but they don't listen to me, I'm just a bunny."

"Will you shut up? Where the fuck is the other guy?"

"Who? What other guy? Think that's all *their* was. They just came in and were talking to me. Asked me if I wanted to go. But I didn't. I like Earth. Did I use *their* right in that sentence? I feel like I put the emphasis on the people and not the place." He used his finger to spell out T-H-E-I-R in the atmosphere in front of his face. "Yeah, I used the wrong *their*. What I meant to say was: That's all *there* was."

"What the fuck are you talking about? Where is the other guy who was in the tank with you? Long hair, dark skin."

"Oh. You talking about Jesus? He ain't a man, he the Son of God. He dipped."

"He dipped? What the fuck do you mean, *he dipped*?"

"He left. He gone."

Jackson stormed over to the cell door and shook it. It was still locked tight. He looked back to Dabrowski and the LT, who were both standing back out of Jackson's way.

"Was someone here. Did someone let him out?"

"You mean the aliens? Yeah, they were here, but Jesus didn't need them to let him out."

"Please," Jackson slapped the bars. "Stop speaking fucking nonsense!"

Bruce Bannister put both his hands up, squeezed them tightly against his head, and began to hop around the cell like a bunny.

Jackson smacked the bars again. "How the fuck am I supposed to write this shit up?"

"Jesus ascended to heaven?" Richard offered.

"You think this is funny? I know your career is fucked, is over. But my shit ain't. First, I hitch my shit to Gracie and end up here. Now I got your ass dropping his keys and letting someone wander in here."

"I got nothing to say about Gracie. But my keys, they right over there." Jackson followed LT's finger as he pointed across the room. And there they were, lying by the door, out of reach of both the men in the cage and anyone who may have wandered in off the street.

"Well, fuck. Belfour's gonna have us murdered for this shit."

"Don't you mean crucified?" asked Richard with a smile.

Too soon, but he wasn't wrong. Belfour had enough crosses for all of them. Only hope was that he was only interested in one of them.

Jackson shivered.

In the beginning there was God, or some shit. In the end, it didn't fucking matter. There was beer and there was noise and everything and everyone could get fucked.

Gracie sat at the bar nursing his drink. Had to finish it soon though, it was getting to be that time when all those cops he used to know would start showing up and he was in no mood to catch up with any of them, regardless of how many had expressed what a raw fucking deal he'd gotten.

Why he still came to The Bitter Nail, he didn't know. It was more habit than punishment, but still, even after all these months he was beating himself up for the way shit went down. Whether that meant guilt for his actions, or merely that he'd been caught, that answer lay in the depths of some unexplored self-reflective trench in Gracie's mind, never likely to see the light of day.

It used to be that Gracie never stopped at the counter up front. Barreled right into the back room. Now, he never even approached that hallway. It wasn't for him. No longer cop, not quite a criminal. He was the chump he said he'd never become.

"One more," he said to the old woman behind the bar. She took a long drag from her cigarette before grabbing a glass and heading to the tap.

She pulled the handle, and only foam came out.

"Danny!" she cried in her thick accent. "Danny!"

No response.

"God damnit." She slammed the empty glass down in front of Gracie. "Be back."

Gracie chuckled to himself as she vanished down that sacred hallway, entering the void of bass and strobing lights.

Without a beer to occupy his mind, his ears turned to eavesdropping on the only other people in the diner, and what he heard did not disappoint.

"Fuck Masood. This shit is bullshit, the SEC comes in and bails this shit out and we're all left with our dicks in our hands."

Fuck Masood indeed. Gracie spun on his barstool to face the pair. "Fuck Masood!" He raised the empty glass the old lady had left.

"What?" said the one dressed in all black. "I know you?"

"Not yet." Gracie stuck out his hand and slid across the few stools to close the gap in their conversation. "But I can tell from your conversation that we're gonna be fast friends."

"You get fucked on the stock bullshit too?" asked the second man.

At first glance they were an unlikely pair. The man in black had dirty, matted hair and looked like either he hadn't slept in days or he'd been in a brawl earlier that day, while the second man was decked to the nines in that neo-retro look: quasi-hipster beard and mustache, and the half Mad Men/half militaristic slicked hair, a sharp suit with a paisley vest and bolo tie. They were night and day, until the suit moved. His tattoos peaked out from his sleeves and collar. Gracie noticed the symbols on his knuckles. None of the tattoos had been professionally done, but the ones on his hands were the most obviously stick-and-poke—the way transients and meth-heads and clueless idiots tatted each other beneath overpasses—in their shape, size, and quantity. Zodiac symbols and music notes. Arabic, Latin, and moon glyphs. Simple circles, squares, triangles, some with random lines protruding from them.

"Stock?" Gracie laughed. "Nah, that shit is too boujee for me. What happened, the market get fucked and you two lose your asses or some shit?"

"You been living under a rock? You not keeping up on Game Stop, Rocket, all that shit?" asked the second man.

"I had some shit going on. The stock market hasn't exactly been at the top of my mind." Gracie turned to the back hallway to see if the old woman was on her way back. He could tell that his ignorance of whatever the fuck was going on had amped up the fucking suit. Even if Gracie didn't want an explanation, he was going to get one.

"Well shit, brother, let me break this down for you real simple. Basically a few hedge funds bought a bunch of shit stocks at, let's say ten bucks a share. Then they turned around and sold them for ten dollars. But they did this knowing that the stock was shit and the price was going to drop to, say, seven dollars. So they sell for ten, buy back at seven, pocket the three, and the OG investor is in the same place they were to begin with, unaware that their shit got risked for an additional profit."

"What's a hedge fund?" asked Gracie. He didn't care. But it was fun watching this big-brained doofus's head explode.

"It doesn't matter. They are assholes who profit off the misfortune of others. Basically, they deserve to get fucked. And they did. And we fucked 'em good."

"And how did you do that?"

"See, hedge funds, they are obligated to buy those stocks back by a certain date. So, when they turned around and sold those shares, expecting to buy them back before that certain date for a profit, we didn't sell them. We held them. And in holding them, suddenly they had value. And more people started buying and the price shot up and up and up. And now these stocks that they sold for ten dollars, they were worth three hundred, five hundred. And instead of making three bucks per stock when they eventually had to buy them back, they were looking to lose hundreds of dollars per share. And sure, we sold back a little here and there to make a profit for ourselves, but not a lot. Not enough to let the hedge funds bail themselves out."

"And you guys really fucking did this?"

Both men nodded.

It really was the end of the world. First it was Silicon Valley and the nerds who ran it turning innovation into gold, now it was the apathetic hordes of incels living on couches in their parents basements. And even before that, there was the gold rush in California where all these prospectors and backstabbers went West and found gold and founded banks and villas and studios and now it was a liberal haven where big men, strong men, tough men had to play politics in order to hold their own. Everywhere he turned, the days of brute strength and intimidation really were coming to an end.

"How much you make off this shit?"

"Potentially," said the scrawny one in black. "A metric fuck ton."

"Then my pops got wind of what was happening," said the second man. "He made a few calls, and in comes the SEC. They called it market manipulation. I say, what the fuck else would you call it? It's all market manipulation. Masood Pharma has been bankrolling half a dozen hedge funds to maximize profits. Now that the everyman has figured a way to be competitive with the big dogs, the big dogs aren't having any of it. It's one more way they socialize losses and privatize profits. They got pissed that the have-nots were starting to find a way to have, and when you give means to those who are struggling, that noose around their neck loosens and all of a sudden they have choices, and the free market actually becomes free again. So, when the SEC put a stop to trading, which is now deflating the value of the stocks, soon they gonna be worth fuck-all. All so that Masood doesn't end up a billion in the hole."

"So, regardless of the score, the SEC let Masood take the ball home and say they won?"

The pair nodded.

"And who the fuck is your dad? How do you know all this?" Gracie asked.

The second man looked over his shoulder like he was about to tell a racist joke, then whispered, "He's the COO of Masood Pharma."

"No fucking shit?"

"No fucking shit."

Gracie looked to the man in black, "And who are you?"

"I'm just a professional asshole."

"Alright," said a raspy old voice behind them. "Beer!"

The smell of ash and musty sink drain hit his nostrils as the empty glass he was still clutching was ripped from his hands.

"Hey," Gracie called back to the old woman. "Make that three."

"Thanks, brother," said the COO's son.

"Paul." Gracie held out his hand.

"Trip." They shook hands and turned to the man in black.

"Oh, me? Patterson. Patterson Zapruder."

"So, Trip," said Gracie. "I get your beef. What about you, Patterson? Where's your dog in this fight?"

"You pay attention to the shit that happened this last year? This city is a powder keg waiting to blow. Not going to take much for this shit to burn again. I'm trying to get my share before it does."

The bartender brought them their beers. They clanked their glasses and drank.

"Not that we want that to happen," Trip interjected. "We ain't trying to cause the end of the world or nothing, just want our voices heard. Need to put a spotlight on the hypocrisy, you know? On one hand they are funding the defense of that firestarter girl, which is good since she's innocent. On the other, they are funneling billions into these hedge funds, full-well knowing that they are short-selling all these stocks into oblivion. I don't want it to come across like we don't support that girl's freedom, but at the same time I can't think of a better way to get the media to pay attention to us, you know?"

"What are you looking to do? To be heard, you know?"

"We're organizing a huge protest across the metro area. Gonna be blocking access to all the medical kiosks," said Trip. "Like you pointed out, most people don't give a shit about, or even understand the stock market. Why the fuck are they going to care if a bunch of shitheads lost some money? But block their access to free healthcare for a day, they may get pissed at us, but at least they'll be force-fed some truth, whether they know it or not."

"Well, shit," said Gracie. That shit wasn't going to work. "Good fucking luck."

But who the fuck was he to burst their bubble.

Trip raised his glass, and he and Gracie clanked together.

"Thing is, we gotta hit 'em where it hurts." Patterson leaned back and sipped his beer. "Right in the public opinion. And it's gotta be sooner than later cause Masood's got money to burn, and what I heard is that they are planning on sending out gift cards to everybody. Five hundred, a thousand dollars, whatever amount. Just looking to buy public silence by extending an olive branch. If that happens, and people start spending that money, whole city's gonna be in their pocket."

This guy, Patterson Whatever, he saw the writing on the walls.

Jst lk Grc dd.

Trip, he was a well-intentioned idiot. Dime a fucking dozen.

Patterson though, Gracie watched him and felt like a cop again. He hadn't done anything, and had said even less. But that kid got his instinct tingling. And this protest the two of them were organizing? Only one of them wanted it to end peacefully.

The anniversary of the Devil's Night fire had come and gone without incident, and now with Thanksgiving in the rearview mirror something felt off. The weather was the major clue, with temperatures nearing seventy degrees in late November being odd to say the least. It felt less like an Indian Summer than it did the world realizing that a trauma had been inflicted on it and somehow it forgot to respond. The unseasonable warmth was a symptom of this deferred reaction, like the world was backing up, caught in a loop, making up for lost time. Or maybe Nate was just imbuing a psychic frenzy on the atmospheric river of the earth, and he should just enjoy being able to sit on the patio again one last time this year.

After a long, hot summer that never seemed to end, this hoodie-weather, this beer, this relaxation, it was all worth the hype. By all metrics, it had been a fairly mild summer weather-wise, but factoring in Kate's growing belly and aversions to comfort, it was a summer that wanted to stretch on forever.

It felt like blasphemy even lodging that complaint in his mind. A summer that stretched forever. Who the hell had he become that that phrase wasn't steeped in sarcasm or jest? And that's just it, it wasn't who he'd become. It was who he was going to be: a father. Yet another phrase that he never imagined would infect every thought and action and plan. And if he was being honest with himself, Kate wasn't the only one who'd become a bit paranoid. In his younger, more libidinous years, he MacGuyver-ed his parents out of the house to get fifteen minutes alone with Pam Anderson and a whatever tube of non-abrasive lubricant he could get his hands on; now, parenthood on the horizon, he was making the rounds, checking that banisters were secure, electrical sockets were properly covered, nothing smaller than his fist was within the baby's reach, and nothing heavier than a feather could possibly fall on him.

Sitting on the patio was a no brainer, though; that had been the plan all along. Kate had convinced him to be here when it was revealed, to spend the morning anonymously soaking in the opinions of his audience. She sipped her tea, nuzzled inside Nate's stretched out old hoodie from high school, and watched longingly as a cluster of cyclists wove down the sidewalk, winding in, out, and around pedestrians, while Nate worked his way to the bottom of his bottomless Bloody Mary.

"I miss riding my bike, babe" said Kate.

"I know you do. They make those baby seats that attach right to bikes. We can get one after the little guy gets here."

"Yeah, maybe. I don't know. I feel like this paranoia isn't going to go away. Like, honestly, it's taking all I have to not tell you to stop drinking your Bloody Mary."

"My Mary?" Nate feigned a hurt frown and nuzzled the glass close.

Kate rolled her eyes. "Stop. I'm not asking you to not have it. Believe me, I know you deserve it. I haven't exactly been myself this summer."

"Oh, don't say that." Nate reached over and squeezed her foot, a flipflop dangling off one toe. Looking deep into her eyes with a sly grin he added, "You've always been a hormonal basket case."

"Don't patronize me. I know, okay? And I'm sorry. Conception was challenging, and the heat, and work."

"You don't have to explain. Just don't take my drink."

After a week of sleepless nights, this day, this drink, these few hours of relaxation, were exactly what the two of them needed to celebrate the end of one era of their lives, and to welcome in the next. Kate had assumed his insomnia stemmed from the excitement of this impending reveal. And it did, just not exactly from excitement. It had been one thing creating effigies of Charles McGee, Fannie Davis, Tyree Guyton, and Elena & Aubrey Smyth; of the Humpback Whale Mural and The Spirit of Detroit. Even the Beeple-inspired abstracts of the city's litany of corrupt leaders and policies had been riskless creative endeavors. These people, these places, these ideas, they were all images that the city at large could recognize and define, that they could take their own perspective and imbue that on his work.

But this last one was not something or someone that had lingered on in the annals of Detroit's history, but rather, it was the idea that had started this series of monoliths, an idea he'd saved for last.

They'd arrived in time to get the last table on the patio, and while the other groups conversed loudly, Kate put her feet up on the extra chair at their table and Nate gazed upon the new monolith that stood next to the street.

The piece was his tallest yet, and the most abstract as well. In fact, placing it almost anywhere else but here in front of *Trough* would have only caused confusion. As random as the placement of his monoliths appeared, Nate went to painstaking lengths to ensure the environment fit each piece. His whales were at the perfect vantage point to view what was left of the original work, his Robocop was in a notoriously violent neighborhood. The Nain Rouge statue sat outside Ferdinand Station (Nate wasn't above feeding into silly online rumors and theories), Tyree Guyton stood where the Heidelberg Project used to be. A year ago, some old man dressed in armor, riding horseback, ripped an umbrella out of a table from the patio, and in doing so twisted and contorted that table into a cultural lynchpin. The story of this knight, paired with the Devil's Night fire that would engulf the city less than twelve hours later, became a symbol for so many: not just a geriatric old man, but a Phoenix rising from the ashes. No matter how bad things got, every damn one of them could always go Don Quixote. And it didn't require nuance or time, just the willingness to unapologetically strike back at the circumstances that held you back. Eventually, though, as it was with all symbols, the luster of the table and the knight and his revolt wore thin, and then away, and one night as Nate cut through the alley to get to his apartment quicker, he saw the table in the dumpster out back.

Now, here it stood. Placed atop a sixteen-foot pilar devised to resemble the Penobscot Building. And it was already causing a stir again.

Under the cover of darkness, he and a handful of confidants had erected it piece-by-piece and anchored it in place late last night without fanfare or photography. Nate was done with using social media to bastardize art. Maybe he couldn't stop others from using it that way, but he didn't have to join in. His first sale had been an NFT, and no matter how much money it brought him, there was an emptiness accompanied with it. Without something physical, he could never be a passive participant at someone's first glimpse of his work. He was still anonymous, never took credit for his statues. And because of that, he could sit here on the patio and watch as one by one passersby noticed the pilar, and following their eyes up, see the recognition dawning on them that the table had returned. He bore witness to excited phone calls and quick text messages. A quick look at his phone told him that by the time he was two Bloody Marys in, the statue was already trending on social media.

"I'm proud of you, babe," said Kate. "I would lean over and give you a kiss, but you know, I'm kind of stuck here.

She had her feet up on one chair and was leaned back relaxed in another. Her teacup rested on her belly between sips. Nate snapped a quick picture with his phone before she could object.

"Hey," she said.

"What? It's a cute pic." Kate had protested throughout the pregnancy about documenting her progress. She wasn't one of those women to make weekly updates on Facebook with her shirt raised showing off her belly; it was way too easy for photos to migrate from the cloud to social media, she'd say. But Nate wasn't snapping these candid pics for anyone but their baby. He wanted them to be able to see how beautiful their mother was when she was pregnant.

"Let me see."

"No," Nate looked at the pic on his phone. He could see nothing wrong with it, but that wouldn't stop her eviscerating it. "Every time I show you one of these you say you have a double chin or your ankles look fat or your belly looks weird."

"Sounds like a looker, how did you ever keep your hands off her?"

"Will you stop? You'll be glad to have these at some point."

"Will I?"

Nate nodded and turned in time to see another handful of people posing in front of his monolith. Little did they know that the creator was sitting there and would likely end up in the shot. Eventually, if these pieces ever gained cultural clout as a product of the time following the fire, maybe someone would track him down (assuming he'd gained an equal or greater cultural standing as the work he'd anonymously created) and ask if he was the man behind the statues. It was an uncomfortable thought. Not the idea of being found out, being discovered was as much a reward for him as it was for the sleuth who put in the legwork to find him. No, it was uncomfortable because if he was found out, that meant that these pieces were important. At least to some extent. And here he is, unavoidably imagining himself as an important figure in this era of Detroit's history. The fact that he even let his mind wander there colors the possibility of such a thing with a disingenuous shade. No longer could he ever truthfully say, "I never imagined what I was doing would be important," because here he was, imagining just that.

What a fraud he was. An artist, creating these effigies, worshipping his own worth before the world ever had a chance to digest his contributions. If social media created a virus, it was *influencea*. A variant of affluenza, where instead of using wealth to exude power, influence is used to create worth. Instant, raw, and unfiltered worth, curated and cultivated in the thoughtless incubator of the internet.

"Babe, look."

He was far from patient zero of this *influencea* epidemic, but spread it he had, and spread it he would continue to do, because he'd put himself in the position to catch it and need it and yearn for it regardless of how often he told himself he did not want it.

"Nate!"

He was a fraud. But so long as he never said it out loud, no one would ever know.

"Hey, you hear me?"

Nate turned. "Sorry, my mind was elsewhere."

"Look, look," she said, pointing to her belly.

The teacup she'd balanced on her bump was bouncing rhythmically. Bounce. Bounce. Bounce.

"Quick," she said, and reached for Nate's hand. He gave it to her and she ripped him over to her, replacing the teacup with his hand.

Often the baby's movements were so quick or fluttery that Nate hardly had a chance to make it to Kate before the movements had stopped or the baby had moved to some place he could not feel.

Kate lifted her shirt. Skin to skin, he felt the baby's foot or butt or little fist reaching out.

"Hey. Hey there. It's your dad. I don't know what to say, but I'm going to keep talking because I feel like this is the first time you've really paid any attention to me." Her belly bowed, and Nate pressed back against it. "This is amazing."

"Seriously, I wish you could feel the movement inside like I do."

"Yeah?"

"Yeah! It's so weird. It's like my body is an ocean and this thing is living in there."

"Isn't that exactly what's going on?"

"You know what I mean. Don't ruin this."

The baby kicked again and again and again.

Nothing could ruin this. Nate met the first person who would never think he was a fraud.

Nothing could ruin this.

"Oh, hey, did I tell you what we got in the mail yesterday? I reported it already, but wanted to show you." She pulled her purse close, rooted around inside until she found and handed him a five-hundred-dollar Visa Gift Card. *A Gift from Masood* etched in the plastic.

"For real?"

"No, not for real. It's a fake. I mean, there is money on it. I called and checked the balance. But it's not from us."

"Who's it from then?"

"No idea. They have no idea who sent them out, or how many of them there are. Not linked to Masood at all, but I still hope they figure it out before we get raked through the mud over something we have nothing to do with."

Nate raised his glass to that.

They'd all started drinking over twelve hours ago, and while obviously she'd been to The Bitter Nail before, it had never been like this.

#TheseCopsCanDrink

In the past, when closing time hit, and the bartender turned the music down and announced, "Last call!" she and whomever she'd been with would quickly finish their drinks and make for the doors. But invariably, there were always those one or two tables of people who'd sit there like they owned the joint. While the rest of the bar filed out around them, they wouldn't budge. Now, she'd heard rumors that the place stayed open until dawn and beyond, but had never had the nerve to test the waters and stay put after last call.

It had been intimidating enough the first time she'd come here, walking behind the bar up front while the old woman served drinks; walking down that long, dark hallway and, feeling eyes on her back the whole time, finally emerging into a thirty-by-thirty-foot windowless room. A compressor tank where drinks and people built the pressure, filling the room, music crushing conversation, the strobe lights poised to cause a seizure, and the clientele as shady as any dive she'd ever been to.

Even after all that, she still hadn't dared to sit still.

Then Henry asked her on another date.

"Hey," his voice was quiet over the phone. "So, one of my co-workers is retiring and we're all going out for drinks Friday night. Was wondering if you wanted to come?"

"Sure," she said.

And that's when he told her, "I haven't talked about my job. For a lot of people, it's a career or an identity. For me, I want to do good, but it's also not who I see myself as. You know?"

"You mean, you want to do well. Superman does good. You want to do your job well."

#GrammarNazi #CantHelpMyself

"Well, yeah, I want to do well at my job. But no, I want to do good. I," he paused. "I'm a cop, Melody."

#RecordScratch

"Whoa. For real?"

"Yeah. I was trying to give a preface there, but I guess I didn't say it right. Is this going to be an issue? I know we haven't looked great lately, but—"

"No. No, Henry, you're fine. It's not an issue."

#WasThatALie

"I never gave the idea of dating a cop much thought, much less have it sprung on me like this."

"Yeah, I know. I'm just," he stuttered again, "My whole life, I've just wanted to do good, and this felt like the easiest way for me to make a meaningful impact."

Three days later, the only impact Henry was making was with his open hand on the side of his partner's head. Six shots in and the night became toxic masculinity and broken bottles as these off-duty officers took turns slapping each other across the face. Introductions were made as first they, and then others, arrived.

There was Jimmy and Hart and Bell. It could have been any of them retiring, their wrinkly old lead-paint skin dry and peeling and scabby with liver spots, but it was Bell's night and she remembered him by the gold chain around his neck and military tattoos visible under the cuff of his short sleeves.

Jackson and Calloway were next. She was pretty and tall, he was Henry's partner, and when she kissed his cheek and ran off to the bathroom, Jackson introduced himself to Melody.

"You're three loose I've Melody, huh? The brewski wonton slut up about you," said Jackson. Though she was pretty sure she misheard him, cause he didn't come across as drunk, she hadn't understood a thing he said over the music.

"Yeah," she replied, gave him a thumbs up.

He nodded, fist-bumping her thumb. "He's a gold nun. Tree Tim light."

After that, the names blurred together as Friday flattened out into its last hours and slid under Saturday's door without notice. Before long, there were forty-plus people in their party all clotted together in the back corner of the back room. Then, a late arrival barreled into the party, and brought the gathering to a halt. Either he wasn't invited or hadn't been expected to show, but now that he was here, he was being greeted like a prodigal son returned. Between the back-slaps and handshakes, fist bumps and shoulder jabs and headlocks, it took a few minutes for Melody to get a good look at him, and when she did, a name for the man formed on the tip of her tongue, but it was a name she didn't know. She only knew him as a time: Eleven O'clock. Yannis had double-booked the two of them the afternoon of her first date with Henry, and she'd almost taken a baseball bat to the head that was meant for him. Instead, she'd made it to the date with Henry and later witnessed the doctor strangle and leave him for dead. Now here he was, shaking her hand, introducing himself as Gracie, and either pretending he didn't recognize her or still filtering through that oxygen-starved grey matter to place why she's so damn familiar.

"Last call," came the bartender's voice as the music dipped, and the lights came up halfway. It was already two in the morning, and as Melody grabbed her coat from the back of her chair, she saw her party hadn't budged. Jackson and Henry laughed as Eleven O'clock became the center of attention with his jokes and stories, while around them the rest of the room was standing, stretching, and settling their tabs at the bar.

Oh, shit. This was happening. She slowly, casually slung her coat back over her chair and hunkered back down.

#GuitarRiff #Sunglasses #CSI #DealWithIt

Little by little the room emptied and with the music lower she could now hear all the various conversations happening in their corner of the room, even though her eyes darted elsewhere. She felt like a bird watching ants ready themselves for an incoming storm. They scurried about, snatching up cellphones and keys from the table and making for their little homes while she stayed put, already nuzzled into her nest, listening to stories to keep her mind from the inevitable deluge that threatened to dislodge her from her safe little haven.

It was the most exhilarated she'd ever felt sitting still. Growing up, Melody had never been popular, had never been invited to sit at the cool table at lunch. Now here she was, and even though it wasn't the table she felt she belonged at, they weren't handing her her hat and asking that she move along.

"Alright, everybody," said Jackson as he climbed up and stood on top of his seat. "I know the night is still young, even though it is so very very early in the morning, but some of us don't have to work tomorrow, so fuck it, right?!"

Glasses clinked and a drunken cheer filled the room.

"We're all here to celebrate Dan Bell, right? I feel like we'd be remiss if we didn't talk about this fucker at least once tonight. What can I say about Dan Bell and his long and illustrious career? For starters, he's put in thirty-five years with this department."

They applauded, raising their drinks again.

"So, after that long, to say he's overstayed his welcome would be an understatement!"

"Fuck you, motherfucker!" Bell's grouchy voice sounded from the crowd, and a roar of laughter followed.

"Look at him, the smart man just repeats the things his wife has said to him." Another laugh from the gallery. "And there is proof positive that behind every successful cop, there is a lady there to keep him in line."

Melody's eyes followed Jackson's as he looked down at his girl Calloway and raised his glass. Henry's lips were on hers and she closed her eyes. Defenseless and exposed, she was caught in a moment that wasn't hers, call-and-response theater. Henry's kisses were always sweet, and this one was no different, and it's not like he was put up to it this time, but it almost was.

#HeyBrain #ShutUp

"And that, of course," said Jackson, short-circuiting her train of thought and giving her something else to focus on, "brings us to LT. Richard, you here?"

Jackson peered out over the crowd, eyes squinting through the sparkling pulse of the dancehall light.

"He ain't coming," called Bell again. "The shit over at Hollings' place scared him off. Why do you think he retired so quick!"

"The fuck happened over at Hollings' place?"

Bell and the handful of his ancient contemporaries burst into laughter and brushed off the question, pointedly ignoring him and continuing to drink.

"Imma get at you later so you can fill me in."

"What happened?" Melody whispered to Henry.

"I don't know. I know Belfour and some of the brass put together a thing for these older guys, but that's all I heard."

"And who's Richard?"

"Well," Jackson started again as if responding directly to her, "I was hoping he'd show his ugly mug, because, for what it's worth, and regardless of whatever shortcomings he had, he was probably the wisest motherfucker in the department. It ain't no surprise to any of you that I saw that man as a father of sorts, and while fathers and sons don't always see eye-to-eye, that don't stop knowledge from being passed on. All of you know that while the LT never had a wife, that didn't mean he wasn't married. He was married to this job, to the city itself. And while that made him a wise man and a good cop, that didn't mean he was without fault. I guess I shouldn't be surprised he's not here, seeing as he took that quick retirement a few weeks back, but his absence makes my point all the more. Bell, no one ever said you were a wise man or a good cop, but at the end of the day, at the end of your career, look at you. You weren't married to this job, you're married to your wife. You didn't come in to do a good job, you came in to make friends and have a good time. And here you are, surrounded by all us motherfuckers wishing you well."

Once again applause, hoots, and hollers resound in the space, and Jackson hopped down from the chair, headed over to the cluster of old timers crowded around Bell.

By the time *Last Call* had been announced the night was already half over, and as the hours passed and more light from the new day's rising sun seeped in through the cracks of the emergency exit door, the room became smaller. At night, in the dark with only club lighting and alcohol to give the room depth, the walls blended into the atmosphere. Now the sticky residue of spilled beer was unavoidable, and everywhere she looked the room was shrinking.

"I gotta run to the bathroom," Melody said into Henry's ear.

She had to get out of there. She was starting to panic but couldn't say why.

In the bathroom, the faucets *wooshed* on, air sputtering out of the line as if the sinks hadn't been used in a while. She splashed water on her face as behind her a toilet flushed and a stall door opened up.

"Oh, this place has got great bagua, doesn't it?" said Calloway, fixing her outfit.

#WasThatAGunUnderHerDress

Melody shrugged, nodded.

#Sure #IGuess

"You alright?"

"Yeah," Melody nervously laughed. "Think I'm a little overwhelmed being surrounded by so many cops."

#What #IDontGetNervous #ImNotNervousYoureNervous

"Hey, I get it. And to top it off you're seeing most of them, shall we say, showing fewer inhibitions than they normally would."

"Hell of a time to meet everyone, right?"

"Trial by fire. Make it through the night, and I'd say you're an honorary member of this derelict fraternal order."

Calloway patted her on the back and made her way to the door. Before she could leave, Melody stopped her. "Did Jackson ever find out what happened at Hollings' place with the older guys? That reaction in there's living rent free in my mind. Gotta know, you know?"

"I do. He did," said Calloway. "But we'll save that one for next time. If you're having a hard time being surrounded by all these guys now, what happened over at Hollings' place will only make it worse. And I don't want to do that to Henry, or you. But I'm getting gone. Work tomorrow night. Good to meet you."

Melody waved and waited just long enough to catch her breath, compose herself, and silently scream.

#WhatTheFuck #ImNotYourChild #ImABigGirl #ICanHandleMyself #TryMeBitch

For a second, she debated chasing after Calloway and telling her about the last time she'd seen Gracie.

#Choking #Purple #LeftForDead

Show her what she can fucking handle.

But she didn't. Not tonight. She would, though. One of these days she'd put Calloway in her place.

With that out of her system she left the bathroom and made her way back over to Henry, only to find Gracie sitting in her spot.

"I don't want to talk about it, man," said Gracie as Melody slid over to Henry and took his stool.

The room was light now, not misted but bathed in sun. Melody checked her phone and was shocked to find that it was already ten in the morning. Twenty-six hours awake. She hadn't pulled an all-nighter like this since she was in her early twenties.

She wasn't feeling it yet. That woozy, over-tired haze would hit once she stopped drinking for sure, so to stave off that crash, she stole Henry's beer and kept drinking.

"Well, Gracie," said Jackson. If there's anything you need. Place to stay, a loan, anything. Let me know."

"I appreciate it, Charles, but I got a third shift security position down at the Kingsland. Four nights a week. Premium pay for overnights. I'm good."

"Alright. I'm here if you need it though."

"Where's Calloway?" Gracie glanced around. "She be good with her man flirting with me? How about you, Dabrowski? I seen your woman looking at me all night."

"Hey," Henry spoke up. "Leave her be, man, she had a rough week at work."

"A rough week?" Gracie exaggerated a gasp. "Well, this I gotta hear. What did you say her name was again?"

"I'm right here, and my name is Melody," Melody answered for herself. Gracie was teetering on a line. If he patted her on the head or called her little lady, she was going to slap him. Not really. But she was going to tell herself that's what she was going to do. Psyching herself up to be a badass and actually being one were two very different things, and as much as she'd had the urge to hit people in the past for running their mouths, she never did.

"Melody, alright. So, what constitutes a rough week for someone in your field?"

Henry grabbed her hand, looking her in the eye to reassure her that she didn't have to answer if she didn't want to.

She wanted to tell everyone that she saw him cry, saw him choked out and on the edge of death over the summer. That she was there when Yannis got the drop on him, and she watched him squirm and fight and lose.

The room was near empty now, the music even lower. All eyes were on her.

"You probably saw it on the news," she said. "My boss killed a lion."

#NoFilter #GlovesOff #TryThatOnForSizeCalloway

Gracie looked to Henry, "Motherfucker, you holding out on me? She works for Masood?"

Henry shrugged, and Melody spoke up again. "Yeah, I work for Masood."

"Fuck Masood. But it is pretty badass that he took down Simba."

"Is Disney your only reference point for world culture?" asked Jackson.

"Just Disney and you." Gracie finished his beer. "I'm an American, our culture is world culture."

Jackson shook his head. "Fair enough."

"It's pretty funny if you ask me," Gracie continued. "Masood fucking invests all this money into the infrastructure of Detroit. Gets us all universal healthcare and affordable transportation, then flies halfway around the world to shoot a Goddamn lion for sport."

"Not for sport exactly," said Melody.

"The fuck you mean not for sport? He eat the thing after? Did it taste like chicken? You don't have to defend him you know, he pays people to do that. It's his MO, paying to defend people who don't deserve it."

Melody let the jab at Camila Torres go for the moment, and focused on his attack on her. "Yeah, he pays people to defend him. People like me."

"You a lawyer?"

"PR." Melody squeezed Henry's arm, and asked, "Hey, can you grab me another beer?"

"Sure. But you got this? Gonna be okay?"

How fucking fragile did they think she was? Melody nodded, and Henry stepped away.

"So, listen," said Gracie. "I know the old man tries to be a good person. It's obvious he's got his heart in the right place, but if he wasn't starving, if he didn't make a hell of a fur coat to keep from freezing to death, then shooting a defenseless fucking creature is sport."

"Hey man," Jackson chimed in. "Detroit Lions been getting murdered for sixty years and no one's complaining."

She ignored Jackson's quip and kept at Gracie, "Didn't expect the high and mighty route from you."

"Do you know me?" Gracie's voice was semi-rhetorical.

Henry came back with Melody's beer, and she grabbed it, chugging it down instead of answering.

"I'm not getting high and mighty." Gracie snapped his fingers, made eye contact with the bartender, and gestured another round for the group. "I'd love to shoot a lion. Just saying."

"It's not quite as simple as you make it out to be. A lot of these big game hunters, really all of them, are bloody fucking rich. And it costs a small fortune to shoot a lion."

"Gotta bribe those game wardens!"

"Actually, the wardens are the preservationists themselves. They run the sanctuaries."

"So it's a scam? They get the moral high ground by protecting these endangered species, all the while profiting off their deaths? Fucking typical."

"Yes and no. They profit off the death of the animal, but they also choose the animal that the hunters go after. A sick one or dying one, one that's picking off too many of some other species. So maybe one animal dies, but the species as a whole wins. The conservationists use that large sum of money to buy more protection, or food, or whatever they may need to preserve the herd."

"That's fucked up."

"If the conservationists didn't do it, the sanctuary would run out of money, or poachers would rise up and offer the same service at twice the price, but with no return benefit for the surviving animals. They would let the highest bidder shoot whatever they wanted."

Gracie nodded his head as he finished his beer. "Makes sense. Shame we can't get away with that shit in the fucking ghetto."

#HelloJimCrow #WhereAmI #WhatYearIsThis

"Excuse me?" said Melody, and even the others were taken aback.

"Yeah, man," said Jackson. "Are you suggesting we start hunting elderly black people as a way to make money?"

Gracie burst into laughter. "Oh, Charles! Bless your bleeding fucking liberal heart. No, I'm not suggesting an ol' fashion coon hunt. I'm saying that it would be nice if someone figured out a way to profit off all the Goddamn misery and give it back to the citizens. Everyone's making money off the shit that happens down there except the people who living in it. Dealers, lawyers, whores, cops, politicians, non-profits. They aren't all corrupt, just part of a dirty system. There's this river of money flowing through that city and the residents can't even get a sip. None of us are geniuses, that's why we became cops. But that don't mean that we aren't trying to do right by as many people as we can. We can't be superman, but be nice if we could do some good."

The room never went quiet, but after that, Melody stopped listening. Whatever side conversations were happening while she chatted with Gracie rose to take the floor while she fell backward into that web of self-diagnosing her issues, second guessing the choices in her life that wound her up here. With these people.

And who was Henry? She was fucked up and broken, barely held together by the hard and jaded cynicism she'd distilled from too much alcohol and internet. But Henry, he'd come across as the genuine article. Not untainted, but not broken either. She'd been in enough co-dependent relationships to know that without any real stability, instead of fixing each other they'd pick up each other's broken pieces and make them their own.

#Fuck

He'd said he became a cop because he wanted to do good, and while there was no way his version of good came anywhere close to the dystopian vision Gracie had described, what if it did? She didn't know

Henry. Not really. Dating a few months is not enough time to locate all the skeletons in all the closets. Hell, couples married for years still have dark recesses in their minds that they refuse to share.

"Hey." Henry rubbed her shoulder. "You okay?"

They'd had the talk about fucked up shit from their childhoods, about past sexual partners, about shitty financial decisions. But never had they talked about equity and social status. Being two straight white people, it wasn't something that just came up. But maybe it should.

"Melody?"

"Hey, yeah, sorry. Just in my head. Everything's good."

"Here they are!" Gracie's voice bellowed out.

The bartender had arrived with a dozen pint glasses, and Gracie was passing them around. He walked two glasses over to Henry and Melody.

"Cheers," he said, and clinked his glass against hers.

"What do I owe you?"

"Owe me? Shit, even if you weren't making Dabrowski a happy man I'd still cover this round."

"Well, thanks."

"It's nothing. I'm a lucky motherfucker, you know that? Yesterday I got this in the mail." Gracie shoved his fist into his back pocket and pulled out his wallet. He opened it and produced a credit card. "Gift card from Masood. Five hundred bucks. This round's on me."

"Seriously, from Masood? What the fuck?" asked Henry.

"Crazy, right? Let me learn you something here. These cards, they are buying our silence for the sake of their stock!"

"What the hell are you talking about?" Henry asked, snatching the card away from him.

"It's all about them controlling public opinion."

"I think you're drunk."

"Maybe, but tonight, the only control Masood will have over us is as patron saint to all us lost causes. Now come on, let's go get some bagels."

"Bagels?" asked Melody.

"Yeah, there's a great little shop around the corner. We can walk. I got a story to tell you on the way." Gracie put his arm around Melody's shoulder and escorted her to the door. He was surprisingly gentle. It wasn't the arm of someone who'd realized where he knew her from, but that of a new friend and protector. A big brother or good neighbor. Only one that she'd never asked for.

"Um," she looked back at Henry. "A little help here?"

"Gracie," Henry called as he ran over and stepped into Gracie's path. "What are you doing?"

"We're going for a walk. Gonna tell her about the cat."

"The cat? What cat?" asked Henry.

"Ask Jackson, he'll tell you."

"Jackson, Gracie wants to tell her a story about a cat?"

"Oh, hell no!" Jackson was at the bar settling up the tab that Gracie said he'd get. "Paul, don't put her through that."

"Fuck that. She can handle it. You can handle it, right?"

#FuckYesICan #NotALittleGirl

Melody nodded.

"Well, alright. Boys, let's roll out. Bagels are on me."

And like the Pied Piper of police officers, Gracie led the retirement party's exodus from The Bitter Nail into the streets.

Franny & Bert's smelled of yeast and sesame seed and cinnamon and garlic and more. Established in 1947, a few years after the bakery's patriarch returned from the second World War with his French wife in tow, the bakery, still family owned and operated to this day, first by their children and now by their grandchildren, was known across the region for serving the finest pastries in the tri-state area. Awarded "Best Bagel" by the Metro Times for the last thirteen years, bestowed the same honor by the major television network's local affiliates for a decade now, and this year named "Best bagel outside of New York" by Food Network.

Even given all the accolades, the line to get into the bakery was outrageous. Bash had placed his order the night before to avoid the long wait and still, it took more than thirty minutes before he even made it within an arm's length of the front door. The warm morning breeze and the smell of coffee and baked goods, mixed with the line that inched forward like molasses, mixed with the diesel fumes of mid-morning deliveries still hanging in the atmosphere made Bash regret volunteering to come pick up breakfast for the group. The bagels would be worth the wait, but what he wouldn't give to be cozied up in bed, snuggling Age, inching a Netflix binge into a chill.

Not that Age would have been having any of that on the mornings that the group met, but a boy could dream.

In all honesty, putting a little distance between himself and Age was what he needed now. Since Rick's disruption of their meeting a few weeks ago, the hours and days leading up to each subsequent meeting had been near unbearable. Age paced and pondered, created scenarios and timetables reasoning why this week would be the week Rick would return. Bash tried to help Age prep and ready the space as much as he could to take a little off his plate. He volunteered to sit in at the meetings, not as general security, not as some doorman or bouncer, but as a singular deterrent should Rick dare show his face there again.

It wasn't how he wanted to spend his Saturday mornings, but neither did he want to believe that Rick would throw out their friendship fucking around with whatever bullshit he was fucking around with this time. So, what do you do when you're stuck between the potential appearance of a sociopathic friend and a neurotic crumbling of your boyfriend? You volunteer to go get bagels.

Once through the front doors, the reason for the longer than normal line became apparent. The café area was filled with protestors and their discordant sounds and conversations. Wallet chains clinked and boots stomped, posterboard signs warbled like deflated thunder. It had broken on Reddit weeks ago, the connection between Masood and the hedge funds, but had yet to gain any traction in the mainstream media. So here they were to change that. Black, brown, yellow, red, white. Combat boots and hoodies, blazers and khakis, piercings and tattoos and dreadlocks and buzzcuts, camo gear and polos. All shapes and sizes, races and ages gathered, attempting to build up enough weight in one place to break the manufactured brake pads of society's wheel that kept the powerful on top and left the rest to fight for the scraps they dropped. Their signs, stapled to long wooden sticks, read:

We got 99 PROBLEMS but the RICH got none!
Stop Hedge Fund Greed! Pay taxes like the rest of us!
Close The Tax Loophole!
Journalists hold the powerful accountable! Why isn't this on the news?!

The smell of cigarettes and pot clung to their clothes. God, their hearts were in the right place, but these people hadn't met an exclamation point they didn't love.

These people weren't helping Age's mental state either.

"Hey, Bash," came a small voice from the mass of activists.

He turned, but there were too many faces smudged together for him to pick out the one that knew his name.

A *Free Camila Torres!* sign bobbed through the crowd toward him. Raven hair slicked to one side of her head, and half shaven.

Stella.

"Hey," she said again, stopping in front of him.

He nodded without hiding his indifference in seeing her. "Hey. Wrong protest today?"

She looked up at her sign and giggled, spun it around. "Repurposed. You know, for the trees and the planet." The other side read: *Carried Interest = Rip-off!*

"So, what? You taking up that crisis actor mantel too, now?"

"Crisis actor? What?"

"Nothing. Never mind."

"Oh, okay. No, didn't you hear about all the hedge fund bullshit with Masood? We're doing this grassroots thing some guy put together. Showing up at all the kiosk locations, not letting anyone in."

"To protest carried interest?"

"Yeah, carried interest, tax loopholes," she read off all the signs her comrades were holding.

Stella was proof that the heart's connection to the brain was purely coincidental.

"So, what brings you out?" she asked, not getting the hint. "Never pictured you one to suffer a line like this."

"Yeah, well, Age is having a day and didn't have time to grab refreshments before the group met. So, I volunteered."

"That's awesome. You really are a good guy, Bash. How's that group going? What's it for again? He probably told me. I don't remember."

"No. He doesn't talk about it. It's just a support group. But you know that, Rick had been going for a while there."

"Wait, what? I didn't know he was going to some support group. For real, what's it for?"

"It doesn't matter. He didn't belong there."

"No, seriously. Tell me. What was he going for if he wasn't supposed to be going?"

"I don't know, Stella. Alls I know is that last time he was there he started shit and hurt Age. Not physically, alright? But this group is super important to him, and Rick fucking with that pisses me off."

"Are you okay, Bash? Did I do something to you?"

"Stella," Bash paused. Rick had gotten under his skin, and he'd left the stinger in there to remind himself to be pissed at him and everyone and everything associated with him. This included Stella. It took all his energy not to go off on her, and instead just dismiss her. "I don't want to talk about it, okay? So why don't you run off to Rick, tell him I said hi, tell him I was rude to you, or whatever you want, okay? I'm just, it's been a morning. And Rick, you, this protest, none of this is helping."

"Rick and I broke up."

"What?"

"Yeah, a few weeks ago. His whole professional asshole thing got to be too much, you know? Well, yeah you know, you said he was fucking with Age. I'm sorry about that. Guess it's who he is. Can't help himself."

"God damnit," Bash said under his breath. That stinger was just twisting itself in his wound now. Stella was annoying but ultimately innocent, or worse, as much a victim as he and Age had been.

"What? What is it?"

"Nothing," he said instead of apologizing for his embittered tirade. Against his better judgment and screaming morals, that wasn't going to happen. At least not right here, right now. Not in front of all her protest people. "What finally did it for you? Calling it quits with him."

"I don't know if it was one thing, or maybe it was the whole experience. An experience is about the closest thing you can call a relationship with Rick, isn't it? I mean, he told me how long you two have known each other, I can't imagine this is the first time he's gotten under your skin."

Bash arched his eyebrows, every instance of his and Rick's childhood antics congested on the tip of his tongue, and all he could do to respond was shake his head. No. No, that was not the first time. And if he were being honest, this wasn't likely to be the last time. Eventually, Rick would reach out with some gesture of apology and Age's better nature would seep into a conversation, and he'd tell Bash that he's forgiven Rick and that Bash should as well since they have been friends for so long. And Bash would reach out and forgive him, and in another year or two this would all happen again. Yeah, life with Rick was an experience.

"Actually, you know what. Now that I'm thinking about it, I think the last straw was the name thing."

"Name thing?"

"Yeah, I thought it was," she paused, trying to find justification within herself for tolerating him for so long, "I don't know? Cute or funny at first. The way he used these stupid fake names all the time. Dan German, Skip Intro, Pierre Delecto. But it got to be too much when he started actually talking about legally changing his name."

"Changing it to what?"

"It was something ridiculous. I don't even know if he went through with it, but it was Masood something. *Masood Cares, Greeting from Masood.* It wasn't even a name. It was just bullshit. And that was it, I just couldn't—"

"Hey, Stel! We're rolling out."

Stella turned away from Bash to find the voice. Standing amongst the other sign holders was a tall man who smirked at them with his hands at his sides. The toothy grin stood out because the man's eyes, nose, and ears, while there, may as well have not been. They were miniscule, could have easily faded from his face and it would be hard to account for what was different once they were gone. Bash quickly looked away from him as if he were the reason his mother told him it was impolite to stare.

"Be right there, Indrid."

"Cold out there," said the man. "Don't forget your coat."

She held up her hand, coat clenched in it. "Hey, so yeah, guess we're heading out."

"Yeah," said Bash, coming back around.

"Well, it was good seeing you. Tell Age I said hi. And I guess, I don't know, sorry about Rick?"

Bash nodded as if to say, *You have nothing to be sorry for.* This was no doubt lost on Stella, who left the bakery without another word, falling into step with the dozen or so other protestors.

Maybe she would cry. Maybe she'd scream. Maybe she'd channel all of that churn into her cause and really effect some sort of change in the public's perception of Masood. Age came to mind, and it was obvious how pointless protests were in changing people's minds. They felt great to those participating in them; the opportunity to be loud and proud and heard. From the Tea Party in Boston to Dr. King's March on Washington to the 99% to the Capital Insurrection. Not one of these events changed minds, only served to gauge the public's opinion on the topics at hand.

Rick and Bash had met in middle school and even back then Rick had his eye on people. "For the most part, we don't trust each other. We ignore each other until we no longer can. And even then," Rick trailed off. But it was the *even then* that stuck with Bash all these years. How old was he—eleven, maybe twelve—and here he was recognizing what collectively we, for so long, ignored. We are a people with our hackles up, so afraid to listen, to have our minds changed, all out of fear of being wrong.

"We need to be wrong more, fail more. Because we don't learn if we don't fail. And we all want to be right." Him and his platitudes. One of three white kids in an all-black school, he spoke like Kurtz, like he was a God-emperor to the natives of Farwell Junior High. In middle school, none of them knew what White Savior Complex was, but they all knew he had it. It was only after high school that Bash, who'd always found his rants amusing, came to realize that his savior complex had nothing to do with race. Rick was convinced he could save the world, even if he had to destroy it to do so.

The line moved forward, and Bash stepped up to the counter.

"What can I get you?" asked the kid behind the glass partition.

"Um," wrapped up in his ruminations, the question caught him off guard. "Yeah, got a pick-up for Sebastian. Or maybe it's under Adrian. Not sure which name he used."

"Sebastian or Adrian. Got it. Let me go check."

"Word."

While the barista rifled over the pre-orders stapled into paper bags behind the counter, Bash's insides hollowed. Stella had managed to do what he'd never been able to do: set Rick solidly in her rearview mirror and walk away. Anytime Bash had attempted this, he'd found that even the slightest glimpse into the mirror would bring Rick racing back. And try as hard as he could, he could not keep himself from looking into that mirror.

Even now, waiting for bagels and donuts, an image, a moment, was swirling up from his subconscious. It hadn't been the first time they'd snuck out of Bash's room—at thirteen they'd become experts in dislodging the screen from his window silently and traversing the rocks and thorny weeds and broken glass outside the apartment quickly—but they'd spent the hours of dusk making what Rick called *Buddy Burners* for the express purpose of turning that night's excursion into something of an adventure akin to *Goonies* or *Stand By Me*.

Buddy Burners were the poor man's Streno. Cardboard coiled inside a tuna fish can, with wax poured into the corrugated spiral.

They weren't looking for a body, nor were they searching for pirate treasure to save the homes. Sneaking out, their destination was the same each time: school. And once there, they'd play out their end-of-the-world scenarios together in real-time. During the Cold War, the building served as a bomb shelter for the community, and the roof still held a gigantic thirty-foot satellite dish and an emergency cruise missile launcher that were installed by the US Government. These two objects alone gave their imaginations enough backdrop to release every whim from their mind and place it firmly in reality. Over one hundred years old, the building's ornate brick façade gave the boys more than enough foot and finger holds for them to first climb up to the awning above the main entrance, and from there to the roof itself where they discovered the evidence of years of remodeling and additions. They could tell from the ground that the roof wasn't flat, but once atop it, they got the impression of how true that was. It was a maze of roofs, with steep cliffs and sudden valleys. Steel ladder rungs sunk into the brick led to every section that would have been unreachable otherwise.

That night beneath the satellite dish, Rick lit a half dozen Buddy Burners and the two got to work repelling the ancient descendants of the dinosaurs who'd crawled out of their caves and tunnels to take back their earth from the apes. The gravel and tar covering the roof served as munitions for the missile launcher, and during one particularly violent volley with the enemy, Rick kicked up the offensive a bit too high.

"Gonna nuke 'em!" he shouted.

Before Bash could even hope to ask what that meant, Rick grabbed one of the Buddy Burners and launched it across the roof. The fireball arched through the sky, tearing through the air like a jet engine. For a moment, the two stood silent, waiting for the burner to blip off their radar and ignite the enemy in hellfire.

The flame fell and fell and fell through the night sky, and before vanishing, it fell short. Instead of dipping over the edge, it crash-landed on the gym roof. In his mind the impact matched the desolation he saw in his future. The school would burn to the ground, he and Rick would be charged with arson, and they'd never see their parents or each other again. In reality, the crater created by the impact was far less extravagant, and it took them less than a minute to snuff out the smattering splash of flaming wax and cardboard and tin.

Afterwards, out of breath and heart still racing, Rick looked at Bash and laughed. "Can you imagine if we burned down the school? I mean, how do you even come back from that?"

Bash could imagine. He'd imagined a million ways their lives would have been irrevocably destroyed. After that night, Bash didn't speak to Rick for a few weeks, until one day at lunch he happened to glance over his shoulder and saw Rick sitting alone at a table. He turned away, and as he contemplated picking up his tray, joining his friend, and letting go of that fear and anger he still harbored in his heart, Rick slid onto the bench across from him and said, "You know I wouldn't have let you get hurt or anything. If we'd burned down the school." He paused, tapped his chest, "I would have said I was there alone."

"Whatever, bro," said Bash.

"Hey, at least next time the world comes crashing down, you'll recognize the feeling and be able to get out before shit gets bad."

He had that feeling again now.

The card reader at the cash register let out a harsh error noise that placed the woman in front of Bash and the little blonde girl behind the counter at odds with each other.

"I'm sorry, Ma'am. That card was declined. Do you have another way to pay?"

"Excuse me?" the woman replied, already clenching her donuts and poised to race for the door. "I just got that card. It's a gift card. It's never been used, how was it declined?"

"I don't know? Our system says it's declined though."

"This is ridiculous. Maybe you should learn how to use that thing. But fine, you know what, I'm in a rush, so here." While she reached into her purse for another card, the man behind Bash accidentally knocked into him.

"Oh, sorry, man."

"It's cool," said Bash. The man was holding the same gift card as the woman yelling at the cashier.

Again, the card reader spat the sound of rejection into the air, and the woman lost her mind.

"What the fuck?!"

"Hey," a voice from farther back in the line called. "I got a kid here?"

"What's wrong with your machine? Is it connected to the internet? Wouldn't be surprised if you forgot to pay your bill!"

"That's enough!" Another voice from the line. "Just cause you ain't got money don't give you the right to harass the employees."

"I have money! Maybe you need to mind your own beeswax!"

Cashiers whispered questions to each other as the line of customers grew restless.

Bash craned his neck, trying to casually steal a better look at the card itself. And as soon as he saw the name on the card, Bash dipped out without his bagels or donuts.

Glitches happen. Mistakes too. And every once in a while, the infrastructure behind our financial system hiccups and throws our sense of security and comfort into question. These are all temporary, fixable situations and are no reason to panic.

This wasn't that.

Bash knew what to look for if the world was ever going to come crashing down. It's why they got out of the McGettigan's loft on Devil's Night before the fire even got close, and it was why he was leaving his bagels and donuts behind now.

Outside, the same anthropomorphic emotions on display in the bakery were pouring out from behind every closed door in the vicinity.

When Bash was young, he loved the monkey bars and jungle gyms in the school yard. Just bars and poles arranged in simple geometric shapes, but it was exhilarating to climb up and up until his feet rested above where his head sat when he was on the ground. And then to keep going. To wrap his fingers around the bars, to twist upside down and swing from the crux of his knees and watch the world hang upside down. He could never pinpoint the moment the world flipped. One second he was upright, and so was everything else. Then he'd slink down below the monkey bars slowly, tilting his head to carefully observe the world turn. But it never did. No matter how far off-kilter he went, his brain made sense of it all. Until, a blink later, it didn't.

Stella was wrong. Rick hadn't changed his name to *Masood Cares*, or *Greetings from Masood*.

Etched on the gift cards was the phrase: *A Gift from Masood*.

Henry's lady friend barely had time to let one foot touch the ground before she had to take another step as they marched out of the bar and into the glaring daylight. It was like those old cartoons he'd watched as a kid. The big bruiser dog quietly looming while the little yapper bit at his ankles, looking for approval. And even if she wasn't looking for his approval, he was going to give it to her anyway.

He owed that to her. He didn't know how, but he recognized her. The simple properties of mathematics told him that if these statements were true, chances are he'd wronged or offended or crossed paths with her somewhere. And it's not like he was going to give her an apology for some shit he didn't remember—hell, maybe she owed him one—but his approval, sure, he could give her that.

"So alright." Gracie still had his arm around the girl's shoulder and even he could hear his voice booming in the streets. At this hour, traffic, both foot and vehicle, had picked up and the twilight ghost town here was beginning to resemble a downtown again. Now it was a battle of internal combustion, one ignition for another, and Gracie wasn't about to let Goddamn machines and fucking explosions best him in a battle for volume. "Alright, here's the thing about fucking global warming or climate change or whatever the fuck it is."

Jackson was the first to laugh, but it was as contagious as a yawn, and as he said, "Thought you were going to tell the cat story?" the rest of their throng was snorting and wheezing drunkenly at Gracie's tangent.

"I'm getting there, but looking at all these cars fucking with the ozone, I'm thinking maybe they are on to something."

"The cars are on to something?" said Henry's lady friend. More giggles from the peanut gallery. Fuck, he'd already forgotten her name. Maybe he didn't owe her anything after all.

"So, this shit, fucking heat waves and shit, what if it's all a conspiracy to avoid global catastrophe? Like, we're all floating on magma, waiting around for Yellowstone and San Andreas to fucking rumble us to oblivion, right? What if we were heading that way, and like, the science people figured out that if the polar ice caps got too big, got to weighing too much, that they would cause the Earth's crust to shift. You know, what if global warming is keeping Detroit from ending up on the equator."

"Science people?" laughed Henry.

"You mean scientists?" Jackson added, leading to a new iteration of cackles.

"Fuck you guys," said Gracie, and without warning, Henry's lady friend still in tow, he stepped into oncoming traffic. Horns blared and brakes locked up, but at twenty-five miles per hour there was little riposte outside of the eruption of alarm from Henry and company.

"What the fuck? Melody, you alright?"

"I'm fine." she turned her head to look back at Henry.

Melody! That's it. Gracie gave the bird to his former coworkers, then to the drivers laying on their horns, and continued across the street.

"Okay, so fuck those guys. You know what I'm saying, right?"

"Sure. Why not?"

"Fuck yeah. I can see what Henry sees in you. But, now that I'm thinking about it, what do you see in him?" said Gracie, unsure if he was flirting with this chick, or just cock-blocking Henry for the hell of it.

"Nope. Not going there. You gonna tell me this cat story, or we just getting bagels?"

Gracie laughed now. "Oh shit, almost forgot. Okay, so one night me and Jackson, we were out over by Jefferson and Van Dyke, and wait, you know I was Jackson's partner before your boytoy came along, right?"

"I'd heard."

Traffic was backed up four or five cars deep by the time the clot of cops finished crossing Nine Mile. He could feel both Henry and Jackson hanging close, hanging onto his every word.

"Cool, so yeah, we were just chilling there, having a midnight snack when all of a sudden: ZOOOOM!" Gracie zipped his hand in front of Melody's face. "This car shoots through a stop sign. Not even a slow-and-roll, just right through."

"Oh, Christ," Jackson said under his breath. "Here we go."

"So I figure," Gracie continued, "it's some suburban kid buying into that 'In Detroit, you don't stop at stop signs bullshit. We start pursuit. No lights on, just keeping pace. Kind of want to see where he's going, you know. All of a sudden: Break lights! Tires squeal! Car skids to a stop."

"He hit someone!"

Gracie holds up a finger, tries to hold back a smirk. "So at that point, you know we got no choice. I toss on the lights and roll up on him. We get out. Jackson's telling him to stay put and I'm rounding the passenger side. And I see the body."

"Fucking knew it! How bad was the guy?"

"Not a guy. Not even a person. He hit a Goddamn cat."

"No! Not a cat!"

"Right? And, in case you didn't know how I am with animals, I'd have shot the kid before Harambe. Needless to say, I'm tearing up just thinking about it."

"So, you're an animal person is what you're saying?"

"The biggest."

"Except for lions, right? You said you'd shoot a lion," said Melody. More snickers from behind his back.

"Did I? I don't know, maybe I was making a point?"

"You weren't." Henry patted Gracie on the shoulder.

"Don't touch me, Dabrowski! You're distracting me. Anyway, kid's in the car crying and I'm starting to feel bad for the fucker. We weren't smelling any booze on him. He was just a dumb kid who hit a cat. We could have given him a ticket for distracted driving or running a stop sign. But, being the generous types, we checked the cat for tags and told the kid that if he fessed up to the owner, apologized for killing the cat, we'd let him off with a warning."

"Cops, man." Melody shook her head. "Y'all cruel bastards."

"Hey, the punishment fits the crime, right? So, we take him over there. The house is right around the corner. He's all nervous and shaking, standing on some stranger's porch in Detroit in the middle of the night holding a dead fucking cat. This is a white kid, mind you. So, depending on who answers the door, he could be in for a whole new world of hurt. And who answers the door? This ancient-ass black lady. Easily two hundred years old. Cane. Coke-bottle glasses. Jackson and I are standing back a ways, watching this whole thing unfold."

"Laughing your asses off, I bet?"

Gracie shrugged. "Maybe." He grinned.

They passed the parking lot for Kingsland, and usually Franny and Bert's would have been within sight from here. But not this morning. This morning, the view was blocked by a glob of hoodies and scarves, signs and chants loitering in front of the local medical kiosk branch. From this distance, their call and response chants were dim echoes hovering above the sound of the passing cars, but he could clearly see that a handful of them were wearing disguises to conceal their identity. Some wore *Guy Fawkes* and *Mr. Moneybags* masks to sell their originality and free thought. Idiots. Others wore these green leathery reptilian masks from the latest Jurassic film. These had hinged jaws that moved when the wearer spoke. Gave Gracie the fucking creeps.

He cracked his knuckles as Melody asked, "Did the kid actually apologize?"

"Like a fucking champ. We were both shocked. There were tears and hugs. He came back and asked if we could take him to an ATM."

"What?"

"Obviously, the lady was upset. She just lost her cat. The kid tells us that she asked him for money to get another one."

"Fuck, for real? I mean, I guess it makes sense in like a street-justice type way, but still. Damn."

"Are you fucking kidding me? We fucking marched up there, grabbed that old bitch by her cheap-ass weave, and dragged her down to the cruiser!"

"Dude!" Melody swung her head around, looked to Jackson as if to ask him to confirm this series of events. Jackson shrugged sheepishly.

They were no longer partners, but that didn't stop Jackson from having his back.

Only ten yards away now, Gracie could make out the signs held by the protestors.

We got 99 PROBLEMS but the RICH got none!

And with each step closer—

Stop Hedge Fund Greed! Pay taxes like the rest of us!

Reading sign after sign—

Close The Tax Loophole!

He remembered meeting these guys back in the bar a few weeks ago.

Journalists hold the powerful accountable! Why isn't this on the news?!

And as if their cause wasn't stupid enough to begin with—

Free Camila Torres!

They had to go and double down on the stupidity—

Free Camila Torres!

Had to go and double dip on causes.

Free Camila Torres!

He read that sign again and again.

Free Camila Torres!

It was virtue signaling at its worst.

"So, what happened?" Melody asked. "Did you really fucking arrest the old lady, even after the kid killed her cat?"

"Goddamn right we did! The law is the law, and in the state of Michigan, it is illegal to buy and sell pussy!"

Gracie let the punchline hang for a moment before bursting into full-blown roaring laughter.

Melody's face shifted from utter engagement and concern to dumbfounded bewilderment. Again she looked back, this time to Henry, to confirm the betrayal.

"Sorry," said Henry. "He loves that joke."

"Sorry?" she asked.

"I do! I really do!" He gave Melody a pat on the back for being a good sport. "You ever hear the one about Hitler and the clown?"

"No! And I don't think I want to."

The group laughed, but Gracie didn't hear them.

As they drew closer to the few dozen men and women marching in front of the kiosk station, all he could hear was the vowelless and guttural call of malcontent societal leaches. Their voices, sandwiched into this narrow sidewalk real estate, seemed to have no unity, just separate discordant words lumped together by tone and purpose.

"Masood got bailed out! We got sold out! Masood got bailed out! We got sold out!"

The closer he got, the more these political buskers and their guttural drum circles of rhetoric transformed from incongruous piss to ear worms that hooked into his soul.

"Hey-hey, ho-ho! Akbar Masood has got to go! Hey-hey, ho-ho! Akbar Masood has got to go!"

And no matter what he heard—

"Tell me what democracy looks like? This is what democracy looks like! Tell me what democracy looks like? This is what democracy looks like!"

All he saw was:

Free Camila Torres! Free Camila Torres! Free Camila Torres! Free Camila Torres! Free Camila Torres!

That fucking bitch.

Without slowing or attempting to avoid the protest, Gracie led his tribe into the throng of combat boots and hoodies, blazers and khakis, piercings and tattoos and dreadlocks and buzzcuts, camo gear and polos. The smell of cigarettes and pot clung to the breeze and jointed their voices.

He kept his eyes locked, fixed to a single point on the horizon.

Free Camila Torres!

He read the sign over and over again, while in his peripherals, he could see he was alone. Melody had slipped away from him, and Jackson and Henry and the others, they were dispersed amongst the protest. They were all alone too.

Free Camila Torres!

It was a woman holding the sign. Tiny. A breeze could knock her over. H cld smsh hr skll btwn hs fsts.

"Masood got bailed out! We got sold out!"

He watched her mouth say nothing.

"Hey-hey, ho-ho! Akbar Masood has got to go!"

She wasn't engaging in her right to protest.

"Tell me what democracy looks like? This is what democracy looks like!"

She was here to rouse rabbles. She was an actor to give the cause another body.

Fuck her. If she believed in the bullshit, fine, whatever. But being here, taking up space without her heart being in this. She deserved what she got.

Three steps away. Gracie waited for her to engage.

Two steps. She held that sign high and proud.

One.

Free Camila Torres!

Gracie's elbow jabbed into her back. She howled in pain, fell forward. Her face plastered into the brick wall outside the Three M and slid. Before she hit the ground, a fist struck Gracie's face and his mouth filled with blood.

When Aleksei arrived at the meeting, he pulled Age aside, and told him that Carlyle was in the bathroom downstairs. "He have date last night with Belinda. Now she not here, and he overreacting."

Age found Carlyle in the bathroom, slowly dripping down through the stainless-steel rack onto unopened bottles of bleach. Or at least, he'd assumed it was Carlyle. It was a lone unmarked box, moist amongst the dry cello-wrapped toilet paper rolls and spare lightbulbs.

"Hey, Carlyle. Heard you had a date last night," said Age as he lifted the box from the shelf. The viscous red fluid seeped through the cardboard, the viscera smearing across his button-down shirt and running down to his waist as he carried it toward a dry spot on the floor. Last night he laid out an outfit for today: blood orange shirt and boot cut white denim pants. Good thing Bash talked him out of those pants.

Careful not to spill, Age supported the saturated bottom of the box and slowly got to his knees. He placed Carlyle on the tile floor and put his hands on top of the box. His fingers found their way into the complicated folds of the cardboard box the way a lover might hook a finger into their partner's waistband while they slept. Nothing sexual, just the comfort of a reassuring touch.

"Listen, I know Belinda's not here yet, but she is on her way. I talked to her a few minutes ago. She's having some car troubles, but I swear, she will be here as soon as she can get a ride."

If the cardboard box had eyes, it would have stared back at Age blankly.

"I know, I know. Had a date last night, now it feels like she's ghosting you. But I swear to you, she's not."

Again, the box said nothing. Made no movement. Age was starting to second guess if this was Carlyle, or if it was just a random box with poorly packed cleaning materials inside.

"Carlyle, this is you right? I'm not just sitting here talking to an inanimate object for nothing, am I?"

God damnit. There was only one way to know for sure, but he

wasn't ready to go there yet. He wasn't afraid to look inside. He knew who Carlyle was and what his abilities entailed, but he was hesitant to violate him in such a way if he didn't have to.

"Listen, Belinda has worn her heart on her sleeve from day one. From the moment you two met, she never shied away from professing her feelings for you. And I know it's difficult to feel special with some of the others here. But you," Age paused, doubling down on his assumption that this was indeed Carlyle, "It takes a lot of courage to expose yourself and share your feelings the way you do. Let them have their loud and showy superpowers. There's a reason Belinda always sits next to you. To her, you're the beautiful one. You're the special one. The others, they all call you Boxman, because they assume that that is your superpower. Turning yourself into a box. But Belinda and I know different, like you do. The box, that's a side effect. Your real power is the way you show the world the truth about what lies beneath the skin. You expose yourself in such a way that when others are around they can't help but lash out because the world has conditioned them to fear that type of honesty and truth and warmth. You aren't a box. You are what's inside the box."

It was time.

Age caressed the sides of the ribbed cardboard. Ran his nails across saturated corrugation slowly, feeling the pulse within.

Now he knew for certain that this was Carlyle.

He breathed in, scooched closer, and unfolded the top of the box.

Inside, he saw Carlyle for the first time. Stomach and intestines churning, liver and lungs lapping up what little fluid remained in the box. Nerve endings wriggled away from the sudden burst of light the way worms inch across scorching pavement in the summer sun. And the smell. He'd never be able to cook pork ribs again.

Nestled in the entrails, held sacred and safe, was Carlyle's heart. Age reached in with both hands and the muscle beat faster. His fingers fished through the smooth innards and he cradled Carlyle's heart gently. The organs began to roll and shift, as if coming to a boil. The pink wrinkles of his frontal lobe broke through the guttural surface, dragging with it the twin dangling ocular anchors. His brain bobbed there next to his heart, shimmering, shivering pointedly. The vibrations pulled taut those optical nerves, and Carlyle's gaze revolved unblinkingly toward Age.

"Hi." He smiled.

Age blinked, and when he opened his eyes, Carlyle was no longer his feelings manifest, but contained within a human body again. He was both pale and frail, but those eyes that met his were still as bright and full as ever.

"Water," he managed to choke out. "I've lost a lot of fluid."

"I know. It's all over me."

"I'm sorry."

"We don't say sorry here." The men embraced. "Think you're ready to join the group, now?

Carlyle nodded.

"Great. Now wait here. I have a change of clothes in my car that should fit you."

Fifteen minutes later, the two climbed the stairs back up to the loft space above the record store. Upon entering, Age couldn't help but glance at the refreshments table. The samovars of coffee looked lonely without the normal accompaniment of bagels and donuts. Bash had already been gone thirty minutes, and at this rate the meeting was likely to be over by the time he got back.

Richard nodded *hello* to the pair and turned back to his book. Even though he did not have a USP, Age agreed that since Richard already knew about them, he'd be allowed to stay for the meetings for Christ's sake. Not to mention he was a good deterrent to keep Ansel, or anyone else for that matter, from letting the meetings continue to turn into a farse.

Through the open windows, the chants from the protestors in front of the building next-door could be heard.

"Hey-hey, ho-ho! Akbar Masood has got to go! Hey-hey, ho-ho! Akbar Masood has got to go!"

"Masood got bailed out! We got sold out! Masood got bailed out! We got sold out!"

"Sorry we're a bit late everybody, Carlyle needed a lift. But we're here now, so who's ready for affirmations?"

In addition to Richard's role as a deterrent, Age had created an affirmation that the group recited together at the beginning of meetings to remind them that they are all in this together.

"I'm ready for bagel," said Aleksei, pointing to the half-bare table by the windows.

"I know, Aleksei." Age took his seat in the circle between Sauti and Daisy. "I'm sure Bash will be back soon. He's going to Franny & Bert's, so at least the wait will be worth it, right?"

"I guess." Ansel placed a hand on his belly and gazed at his shoes.

Carlyle took a seat next to Aleksei, making sure to leave an empty chair on the other side of him for Belinda. Whenever she got there.

A moment later, after the small talk faded away and the chair legs ceased jittering back and forth as they each got comfortable, Roger stood from his seat between Jesus and Heidi.

"Morning. We are little fish in a big pond." He recited the affirmation, and the group joined with him. "Though our abilities may not seem extraordinary, they are extra ordinary. And though our powers seem useless, we certainly are not."

Roger nodded and took his seat again as a short round of applause echoed briefly.

"Great. Thank you so much, Roger. And thank you all for being here," said Age. "I don't know about everyone else, but it's been a trying week for me. Between school and, Jesus, you'll be able to relate to this, you used to drive for Uber Eats, right?"

Jesus nodded.

"I thought I remembered that. But, between school and my fares, I was about at wit's end with people."

"Not to mention no bagels!" added Aleksei. Everyone laughed.

"Not to mention that, thank you, Aleksei," said Age before veering the conversation back to his point. "What I was saying, though, is that I don't like feeling that way. You all know I'm working on my pre-reqs at WC3, and between group projects and so many interruptions in class, it's easy to get fed up. But I don't want to be a person who finds faults in everyone I encounter. Even if their faults are what define them to me. Let me tell you, on more than a few occasions, my mood, my outlook and feelings, they exacerbated the situation. Cause I get upset, and frustrated. And my USP kicks in, and next thing you know, the internet in the room goes down. And then the professor can't get ahold of IT, and neither can any of my classmates, because unbeknownst to them, I killed the signal."

"We make the world we live in," said Jesus, and Age, followed by the rest of the group, all turned their heads to him. In the handful of meetings Jesus had attended, he had yet to share anything outside cordial greetings and earnest support of those who chose to share their own journeys.

"Exactly. That's it in a nutshell." Age took a sip of his coffee. "We may not be able to change the world, but we can affect the cognitive attitude around us."

"Yes, but so can others," added Jesus. "Age, may I share?"

"Please. By all means, the floor is yours."

When a toddler hands you a plastic teacup, it doesn't matter who you are, you sit down and have that tea party.

"I hope this is okay to share, because it's not anything that happened this week, but rather back when I was still driving for Uber."

"Not all our journeys are linear. Please, go on," said Age.

"Ok, so when I first arrived, I didn't realize at the time, but I was an illegal immigrant. Technically, I guess I still am, but that's neither here nor there. I was without papers, without a home, without friends or family. And it took time to adjust and adapt. But I did, and I did what was necessary to survive and blend in. Easiest way to sustain myself was driving for Uber."

"But how did you afford the vehicle?" asked Aleksei.

"Have you heard of the Dead Sea Scrolls, Aleksei?"

He shrugged, nodded.

"Well, let me tell you. There is a reason they were left out of the bible. Do you follow me?"

"Not really, no."

"How I got my vehicle is a story that has no bearing on the journey we're on now. So regardless of how interesting it may be, overall it does not matter. No, what I am sharing with you today is not about the remarkable things I did to survive, but rather about the utter boredom I and all of us experience being stuck alone in a vehicle all day long. I didn't pick up fares the way Age does, so the only time I ever got to speak with people was usually in those fleeting moments picking up food from the restaurants and dropping it off to the customers. Between those moments, which always ran the risk of turning hostile or bitter over missing food or wrong orders, I had to grapple with the silence. But rather than turn inward and reflect on my life and my choices, the silence became deafening and made me complacent. Then the ladies at the animal shelter downtown, whom I delivered food to on nearly a daily basis, they gifted me this."

Jesus reached into his pocket and pulled out an iPhone. Earbuds and cords wrapped carelessly around it.

"And they told me about podcasts. It was life-changing."

"Have you listened to *Serial* yet?" asked Carlyle.

"Or how about *Science Vs*? That one is good," Ansel suggested.

"*Hello from the Magic Tavern*! Is very funny," said Aleksei.

"I like *Ghost Gal*. But I'm into the paranormal stuff," said Sauti. "So, if you're not into that it might not be for you."

Say what you will about religion, but Jesus knew how to engage an audience.

"Thank you all. I'm sure I'll get to all of those eventually. Now let me suggest one to you. Off the top of my head I cannot remember the name of it, but it was an interview with some American soldier who, at 23 years old, became the first living Marine to receive the Medal of Honor since the Vietnam War."

"I listened to that," said Ansel. "It was fascinating."

"What did he do to get the medal?" Age asked.

"He was in Afghanistan on a security patrol outside of a village when out of nowhere they were ambushed by more than fifty Taliban fighters. They were getting bombarded by mortars and rockets, being shot at by machine guns on horseback."

"And you condone this? War and horses being forced into combat?" said Roger with gruff indignation.

"Will you stop?" Ansel rolled his eyes. "Let him talk." He just can't help himself.

"Is this not a place for discourse? If you could have dinner with three people, living or dead, would one of them not be Jesus? And if he told a parable of war, is it out of line to ask for his—"

Jesus cut him off. "Please, Roger. My friend. Just because I do not condone war and violence doesn't mean that we cannot learn from them, from the acts of valor that come from deplorable situations."

"Yes, please," Age stepped in. "Everyone, let's give Jesus the floor here. We can discuss semantics afterwards."

"Thank you, Age. So this Marine, over the course of six hours, tried five times to breach the borders of the village and retrieve his fellow Marines who were inside. And every time he went he was able to aid and rescue handful after handful of Afghan soldiers from the assault, but the Marines they were embedded with were too far into the village for him to reach. Until, by the sixth attempt, this Marine finally made it to the location where they'd hunkered down. And when he got there, he found that they were," he paused. "All of his friends were dead. Killed by enemy fire."

"That's awful," said Sauti, while both Heidi and Carlyle pretended they weren't drying their eyes.

"And that's just the start of it. When he came home and was told that he'd be receiving the Medal of Honor for going beyond the call of duty for his actions that day in Afghanistan, he personally told the president not to give it to him."

"Why? He deserved it. He's a hero," said Sauti.

"Because he felt like a fraud. Imagine coming home alone, all of your friends are dead, and they want to award you for it. They dress you up, send you on a press tour where everyone is calling you a hero, and all that's in your head is that image of your friends all hunkered down and dead. Their faces and voices slowly fading from memory until all that's left is just your own impression of them. Who they were is gone, that died with them. Now, he is their storyteller. Now, since he couldn't save them, he has to keep their memory alive. He turned to the bottle. Understandably. And learned to cope by telling himself that this Medal of Honor is not an honor, but a punishment. It was his cross to bear for not saving everyone. And now he's being celebrated for what he feels is his greatest failure. The same way I am."

The room had been filled with the silent murmur of everyone waiting for Jesus to finish so they could speak. Now that anticipation was gone, and all they could do was wait for what he'd say next.

"I died. And the story is that I died for you. And now, some two thousand years later here I am living in a world where I am worshipped, where my image is on walls and necklaces and buildings. All because I died for you, to save you all. But did I? There is the justification given that I died for your sins, for your eternal soul. And that this temporary, physical life is a fleeting detour to your everlasting life in the Kingdom of Heaven with my father. And maybe it is, I don't know, I have only been to Hell. And this is it. Enduring the legacy of my greatest failure. I didn't save anyone. My death gave the world an excuse to forego kindness and compassion and love in exchange for the promise of everlasting life. I heard a Pope say that *those who do not tremble because, fearing God who is good, they are not afraid of the world or the future.* It's a beautiful statement from someone whose heart is in the right place, but whose mind is too occupied to realize that he'd given his followers permission to turn away from both. The world and the future. And to instead concentrate on their own soul's place in the Kingdom of Heaven. This existence, these eighty to a hundred years you all get, is it not enough? And if not, why? What do you expect from an afterlife that life itself cannot provide?"

"Hey-hey, ho-ho! Akbar Masood has got to go! Hey-hey, ho-ho! Akbar Masood has got to go!"

"Masood got bailed out! We got sold out! Masood got bailed out! We got sold out!"

The group in the room remained silent while the protest songs from outside poured through the windows. Age didn't want to be the first one to break the silence after that.

Even Richard, who never said much at these meeting, but also never looked up from his book in order to respect privacy and the process taking place, put his book down and was contemplating what Jesus had said.

Age had only attended church occasionally when he was younger, and hadn't gone back once since becoming an adult, but if this was what church was like, he could see himself finding a home here. Not for the religion, nor the people, but the analytics of it. Take God and devotion out of church and what you have left is a critical dissection of what makes us human. And with a useless superpower that hung on the razor's edge of his anxiety, he'd be lying if he said he didn't question what exactly made him human at times.

Age opened his mouth, and his wish was granted. He didn't have to be the one to break the silence. A loud thunk, followed by gasps and screams and curses disrupted the protest chants, and Roger leaped from his chair.

"Do you hear that?" he asked. He stood rigid, ears focused, legs poised to spring him into action.

"Yeah, Rog," Ansel said. "The natives are getting restless. What are you going to do, go ask them to be quiet?"

"Not going to ask them anything. Going to tell them to stop."

"Yeah," Ansel laughed. "Okay."

"God damnit, Ansel!" said Sauti.

"Ansel." Age buried his face in his hands as he said it. "We've had this conversation. So. Many. Times. Why is it so difficult for you to be supportive of your fellow USPs?"

"Listen, okay. I'm one hundred percent on the side of us sticking together and being there for each other, but when one of us wants to run off and do something stupid, I'm not going to sit by and let them do something stupid. I'm going to stop them."

"But you're not stopping Roger from doing anything. You're mocking him," said Heidi.

"He's still here, isn't he? I've learned my lesson. I know that if I actually stood up and tried to stop Roger from rushing down into some fray that there's a good chance I'm getting triggered. Either from you all trying to stop me, or by them when I have to go down there and rescue Methuselah. So, it's better that I'm just a dick. Take one for the team, change the subject to me for a little while until you all get your panties untwisted."

"Ansel." Age was at the same time legitimately impressed and at a loss for a response.

"What? You've said it yourself a million times, we can't always get involved. The world is not ours to save."

For the longest time the arguments and rivalries, egos and powers, they were all too much for a single group to contain. But if Ansel could contain himself, could think rather than act, maybe this group was accomplishing what Age had intended it to all along.

"God damnit!" Richard's voice bellowed through the room.

"What?" Age jumped to his feet. "What's wrong?"

Richard, now standing, his book splayed open on the floor, pointed to each of the people in the circle. Again, he said, "God damnit!"

"What, Richard? What is it?" Age asked.

"Where the hell did Jesus go?"

In the stroller, Trinie entertained herself by passing a wooden block back and forth between her hands. She held the block in one hand and spread her arms apart, winding up for the pitch, while the fingers on her other hand unfurled like a Venus Fly Trap waiting for its prey. She slammed her hands together. The fingers on one hand let go while the ones on the other curled around the toy and took hold.

A year ago, this would not have held his attention. Six months ago, it wouldn't have. For that matter, a month ago he would have only pretended to be interested for Erica's sake.

Now, he got it.

He still had flashbacks of all those other lives that he'd never lived, and he still remembered who he actually had been in this life for the first five months of Trinie's. Neither scared him, nor carried enough weight to pull him back, pull him down. They were glimpses of moments that bled through randomly when the particles of reality overlapped and a scene played out in near perfect unison across every iteration of his lives. Sometimes it was as quick as a reflection in a window. He'd be walking hand-in-hand with Erica, and in the storefront window he'd see himself with Stella instead. Other times they were longer than moments, a word or a full conversation or even a kiss where their voices and lips fell into sync, and he was speaking with both Erica and Stella. A single thought, an identical set of words pouring out of two overlapping mouths. These exchanges and actions, they were the glue of his existence, moments of inconsequence that happened regardless of whom he was with or where he was at. He had to teach himself to ignore those.

This sync started after selling his records but had become less and less frequent as he veered further from his routines, which is how these walks through downtown became a daily activity for them. At first they happened as a whim to get out of the apartment. But a walk was something he and Stella never would have done. Never did do. And without her ghost haunting their chats, Chris found his way back to Erica and Trinie in a tangible way, and these moments of altered déjà vu began to serve as road cones and danger signs, as cautionary realities to keep him on the right path and remind him that all that mattered was here with him now.

For a Groundhog Day's year, his life had been dictated by an unknown invisible impossibility. And even now, even having experienced and endured the lasting paraphernalia of being strained through various pores of reality, the mind-fucking enormity of it all made it easier to flat-out accept as fact than to fight back against how insane it all sounds. In the end, it didn't matter if anyone else believed his experience. All that mattered was where it had gotten him, where he was now.

And now? Now he was free.

If there was a subtle destiny left weighing on his life, it was his alone to manipulate.

Well, his and Trinie's.

He was in baby jail and doing the time of his life.

Probably every minute or so, the block fell from her hands. She went from silent contentment to five-alarm wail as Chris and Erica failed to notice the falling block as fast as Trinie expected them to.

"Testing your resolve today, isn't she?"

"You ain't kidding," said Chris as he bent and scooped up the block. He handed it back to her. No sooner had her little hands touched the wooden cube than her scream fell utterly silent, and the truth was revealed.

"You little faker." Chris pointed his finger at Trinie and smiled. "Now, don't drop it again."

Aside from Trinie's block dropping game, the walk from their apartment had been uneventful. A perfect fall day where the leaves crushed underfoot with every step and the wind was crisp enough to require a hoodie. On their morning walks, they sipped their coffee and talked about anything but work while Trinie babbled along, interjecting her own opinions into her parents' discussion. As nice as these morning walks were, Chris relished the times—few and far between as they were thanks to opposing schedules—that they could go for a walk in the evenings. Not only did the exercise before bed help him sleep better, and decompress after a long day, but the atmosphere in the evenings was nothing short of magical for Trinie. Without the distant rush of roads packed with vehicles, the ambient noise was instead the wind rustling dead leaves and the soft hum of thousands of fireflies flickering in the trees and grass, around streetlights and city benches.

They looked more like faeries than insects, and transfixed Trinie so, and Chris saw where the old-world lore that the fairy folk had the ability to enchant children came from.

This morning, beyond the edges of their blissful suburban enclave, downtown Ferndale was alive with the echoing chants of reform. Chris had been hearing about this for a few weeks. Aleksei on the clean-up crew told him about it first, said that he'd heard some group was going to protest in front of the medical kiosks in the metro area. Later, at his DJ gigs—he'd only sold enough records to make ends meet, not shoot himself in the foot—the talk escalated quickly to include a coordinated attack against The Loop. That fifty-thousand people were going to descend on every station along its route and bring the hyperloop to a screeching halt. To what ends were they going to essentially clog the main artery of the city and induce a heart attack? That's where the rumors spiraled. Drunk or high, rolling or tripping, the people at his gigs spouted on about Masood's animal rights violations and stock market manipulation and connections to child sex trafficking. Any and all of which was as likely to be true as it was not. People grabbed onto the rumor that made most sense in their world view, rallied around that idea, and given the right state of mind, actually believed it.

Whatever the truth was, the reaction was more opposite than it was equal. At least here in Ferndale it was. They heard the chants before their route led them to Nine Mile, but once on that main strip, the actual sight did not match the intensity and conviction of the noise being created.

There were maybe two dozen people clustered together on the sidewalk a few blocks ahead. The old brick and new high-rises worked in congress to give their collective voices a more intimidating presence than their numbers could.

"You want to cross the street?" Erica asked.

"We will," he said. "I wanna see their signs first."

"Why?"

"Curious, I guess? I don't know, I like that shit. Sometimes they put funny shit up there, you know?"

"Sure."

"What?"

"Nothing. You're just a weirdo." She smiled and squeezed his hand as they continued to push Trinie toward the crowd.

"I'm a weirdo? How am I a weirdo?"

"How are you not? Even when we put gas in the car, you always go to that same gas station off of Eight Mile. At first I thought the gas was cheaper there, but it's not. And it's so trashy, and there are always people there hanging out. I think you," she chose her words, "seek *that* out." She pointed to the crowd ahead.

"*That*? What is *that*?"

"I don't know, you tell me. That Rick guy we used to work with, you hated him, I know it. But still, the shifts where you two were on together you always had a smile going into work. To some degree, I think you wanted the confrontation."

"What? Come on."

"Not saying you do now. But for sure you did before. Look at all those times you got those spam calls and you asked me if you should answer just to abuse them."

"Yeah," Chris smirked. Answering those calls was cathartic. But what did that say about him? "Maybe you're part right. But I don't think it was ever that I was looking for confrontation. I don't want to throw down with nobody, nothing like that. But, shit, why am I telling you? You know this. I was angry. Just low-key mad all the time. No money, no voice. And, one on one, I can hang with the best of 'em. Find what I want to say and say it. But around a bunch of people, I clam up."

"I know you do. So why do you put yourself through that every chance you get?"

"I don't know," Chris lied. He couldn't bring himself to say it yet, but he knew why he sought out confrontation. He was envious of those that had no fear to use their voices in such a way. Whether it was howling to bum a smoke from motorists as they fueled up, or chanting about the inequality of our society. Admitting that to himself was proof enough for now that he had come a long way. Just as the fact that he couldn't express this to Erica was the reason he still gassed up at that gas station, the reason he still answered those calls, the reason they still walked toward the crowd.

"That thing is ugly," Erica said, pointing to the statue in front of *Trough*.

"Yeah, no shit. When did that even go up, yesterday? We walked down here yesterday morning, and it wasn't here, right? Or am I losing my mind?"

"No, it wasn't. What's it even supposed to be? Just looks like, I don't know, bent up metal."

"Modern art, babe. It's what you make of," he stopped mid-sentence as his gaze finally reached the top of the statue. "Holy shit. That's the fucking table."

"What?"

"You remember back, I don't know, what was it, was that Devil's Night? Ran down here that morning to grab bagels for us and I saw that old man dressed like fucking King Arthur an' shit? That's the table he wrecked. One hundred percent it is. Ripped that umbrella out, and the cheap-ass thing just twisted and shattered."

"Oh yeah!" said Erica. "I remember that."

Chris's eyes darted to the street as a large group of men crossed, heading towards them. He took Trinie and her stroller and scooched it over closer to the building—he wasn't about to fight through both crowds with her unwieldy stroller—and as he did, he was no longer standing next to Erica, but Stella. The wide consignment shop windows reflected the crowd and Chris and Trinie and, there she was, Stella too. Some buried pit inside of him opened back up again. He hadn't had a hallucination in weeks, let alone one this vivid.

He blinked to clear the specter from his reality, but when he opened his eyes, she was still there.

"Chris!" her voice pierced him like a gaze, and he could smell her body on the breeze.

"Chris," said Erica next to him. Somehow their voices hadn't overlapped.

"Hey!" Stella said again and waved.

"Earth to Chris!" Erica smacked his chest. "Do you hear Stella saying *hi*?"

"Oh," he glanced from the reflection of Stella to that of Erica and saw that, regardless of what his mind had told him, one had not replaced the other. "Hey. Sorry, lost in thought, I guess. What's going on?"

Stella stepped away from her throng of compatriots, her posterboard sign falling lazily onto her shoulder, and gave Erica a quick one-arm hug. "Hey, mama. How have you been?"

"Busy, you know? How about you? Just doing this?"

Stella shrugged. "Just trying to give back what I can where I can, you know?"

"Heard," said Chris.

She looked down at Trinie. "OMG. She's just perfect, isn't she? Can I hold her?"

Chris had no problem letting her hold Trinie, but he still looked to

Erica for confirmation of this.

"Yeah," Erica confirmed. "Of course."

Stella squealed and handed Erica her sign.

Chris held the stroller still with one hand and unbuckled Trinie with the other so Stella wouldn't have to fumble with the latch.

"Look how chunky she is!"

"I know, right?" Erica smiled. "Be nice if being chunky like that as an adult didn't make you feel so self-conscious."

"You kidding me? You look great."

"Thanks. Still got this pouch though," Erica put her free hand on her belly. "No matter what I do it's just not going away."

Chris watched Stella. The way she held Trinie gently, cooed and raspberried her lips in a way that brought on a fit of laughter. He thought of what Yannis had said: *You could be real happy, brother.*

"You want to trade?" Stella asked Erica.

"What, your body for mine?"

"No, Trinie for the sign. It fits you. You've got this effortless thing going on. Can tell you care."

"Oh," Erica forced a laugh as she looked up at the sign. One side read: *Carried Interest = Rip-off!* The other: *Free Camila Torres.* "Thanks. Not sure I have the time to spread that care around."

A murmur rippled through the protestors, and a moment later the crowd parted, giving way to a boisterous voice that Chris recognized. Chris made eye contact with Gracie, who had his arm wrapped around some drunk redhead. They hadn't worked a shift together in a few weeks. Maybe even a few months. Rumor was he'd been attacked or something. But here he was, looking as big and blustery as ever.

Chris opened his mouth to call out, but before the words formed on his tongue he watched, frozen, as Gracie buried an elbow into Erica's back. If only it had happened in slow motion, he'd have had the time to react, to catch her before her face smacked against the brick between the panes of glass.

But there she was flailing, falling. Stella's sign tumbling to the ground, red tatters of her skin promising to bleed once her body caught up to the trauma it experienced.

Gracie. Whatever familiarity there had been with the man vanished in an instant.

There were no words, there was no time. Chris balled his fist and stepped out of his body. In the million different realities he'd been a part of, he'd never had so much ripped away from him in so little time.

He couldn't speak, couldn't think. The pieces of his brain that still functioned were now firing at half capacity. Maybe less. Erica fell out of view, or maybe even out of reality. If he had ever been a rational person, he could no longer say.

A blink, a blink, a blink. Every blink of his eyes was another pull of the trigger on his reality roulette gun. He was walking a dog he never owned, or he was looking at his reflection in the store window, standing alone on the street. Panicked, he spun, looking for Erica and Trinie but found Stella next to him instead. Erica and Trinie were gone in every way but his mind. He rifled through memories and moments and dreams for her name.

Trinie.

Trinie.

Trinie.

But here, with Stella, Trinie was gone. Replaced by Aimee. Same face and smile and giggle. The only change, the only thing different, the only thing she was missing, was him

"Oh my god, look how big she's getting!" said Stella, staring at Chris's phone as photos of Aimee, being sent by Erica, started popping up on the screen.

Chris stared at his phone, tears welling up. Before the tears could fall, he looked up and without a blink it was only he and Gracie on the street.

He was all muscle and instinct as his fist crashed into Gracie's mouth. And as the return blow barreled into his belly, he was sure that neither of them would ever speak with vowels again.

Jackson inserted himself between Gracie and the black man before the looming assault charge turned into a murder investigation.

What the fuck? The last thing in the world you could call Gracie was harmless, but that didn't mean Henry expected him to clock some random man on the street. And now the natives were restless. Bell and Travers and Hollings were all running interference with the combat boot crew, shoving them back away from Gracie, while Jackson consoled Gracie.

"Calm the fuck down, calm the fuck down!" Jackson told him over and over and over again.

And Melody, she's the type of girl you don't bring home to meet the parents, because leave it to your parents to point out how out of your league she is. Melody threw herself into the mix without thinking, crawling on her hands and knees toward the injured woman while her man and Gracie exchanged blows. After a handful of concussive hits, Jackson and the other cops stepped in and separated the two, and Henry got stuck trying to talk the man down.

"Naw! Fuck that! Gracie, you motherfucker!"

"Hey, hey," Henry remained calm, matching his movements to keep him from getting around him and making it worse. "I get it. I get it. But you see all these guys here? They're all cops. You want to get into a brawl with this?"

"He hit my wife! He hit my fucking wife!" said the black man.

The chanting from the crowd hadn't stopped, only shifted from one focus to another. They went from *"Hey-hey, Ho-ho, Akbar Masood has got to go,"* to, *"Fuck you, fascist pig,"* with Pavlovian efficiency.

"Bro," a voice from the crowd shouted. "You African, bro! Don't take that shit, go to work! Knock his ass out!"

"Oh, fuck off! Maybe if she weren't parading around like a social justice whore, fucking loser bitch, maybe I wouldn't have hit her," Gracie shouted back to no one in particular in the crowd.

"Gracie." Jackson's voice tried to edge into his diatribe. "Shut the fuck up!"

"Represent for Wakanda, bro," the protestor shouted again. "Come on, Black Panther! Hit that white motherfucker again. Wakanda forever!"

"We just standing here! We just standing here! This ain't our shit! This ain't our shit. Our friend's holding our baby! We just standing here, and you come up and fucking check her into a wall!"

In his periphery, Henry could see Melody's shock of hair kneeling over the woman. He did not give a shit about the bravado bullshit her husband and Gracie had going on, but if he left him to his own devices, Gracie would kill him.

Oh, Gracie. The politically incorrect idiot savant. He had no idea how to use his mind for his own gain or salvation, but deep within the confines of that meathead's skull lay an amazing capacity for insight.

All night and all morning he'd been spouting off stories, ideas, and thoughts like a coin-operated fortune teller trying to get laid. Henry wasn't worried about Melody falling under that spell, she was far too intelligent for his bullshit. Himself though, he was smitten. Not with Gracie himself per se, but with his ability to see the truth behind the façade of reality. Masood, the media, the police, the city, even Gracie, and Henry himself, they were all feigning a fight to save the city from its own self-destructive nature. When, in reality, all they were doing was profiting off that nature. Buying up that misery and blood, and turning it green. They were, none of them, any better than the game wardens selling off lions to the highest bidder. Maybe they were worse, because at least they invested that money back into their fake empires for the benefit of those who still lived there.

It was a narcoleptic brilliance that would lay dormant for ages only to stir at the oddest moments, only then to be overshadowed by some fucking act of physical dominance that forced the world and anyone in it who may care to immediately disregard anything and everything that came out of his mouth.

His whole life, all Henry ever strived for was to do good, to be on the right side of history. And being a cop was the easiest way to make a meaningful impact.

Gracie was still pressing his chest against Jackson, trying to get at the man who'd punched him. "Shut the fuck up, you whiney little—" Then he exhaled a word.

Some words you forgive people for saying wrong, like when it's obvious they've only ever read the words and are now trying to use out loud for the first time. Henry constantly fucked up hyperbole, crudites, and tirade. It happens.

It didn't happen to Gracie, not with that word. It was a yawn, a heartbeat, a reflexive truth so honest that there was no way he was saying it out of unhinged rage or anger, or in spite to goad the other man into a frenzy. It wasn't a word he read. It was a word he used. A lot.

Fuck.

Good cop. Good boyfriend. Good person.

Anymore, he couldn't be all of them.

He hadn't brought his service weapon with him to the bar, because why would he.

Apparently, he was the only one, because one second Jackson was holding Gracie back and the next his hand was brandishing his weapon and giving orders to "Stop," to "Freeze," to "Keep your hands where I can see them." And even Gracie and Bell and all the other wild west motherfuckers backed away as, from the crowd, a man emerged.

Someone put a pair of handcuffs in his hand, and he looked to Melody, who didn't understand what was happening any better that he did.

"Jackson! What the fuck are—" Henry's voice trailed off as his brain calibrated, caught up, and finally recognized the figure amongst the crowd. "Jesus Christ."

"God damnit!" Richard's voice bellowed through the room.

"What, what is it?" Age asked.

The squabbling and bickering that comprised most of their meetings was as much a detriment as it was an inevitability of this group Age had put together. They were, all of them, misfits and outcasts. Blessed and burdened in equal measure with the capability, want, and desire to change the world, not to mention each of their own unique and extraordinary abilities. And gathering them together week after week in a loft space above some record store, with what potential they had, what room they had to grow could only emerge from the chaos such close quarters imposed on them.

"Where the hell did Jesus go?"

While Ansel had been doing his best impersonation of himself, Roger had been the only one who noticed Jesus get to his feet and make for the door.

Oh, the chaos.

Having two children of his own, Roger had embraced chaos long ago.

"He walked out the door," Roger said, getting to his feet.

"God damnit." Richard cursed under his breath again.

"I know you're not a religious man, Richard, but what did you expect? Jesus isn't a genie. You can't expect to keep him bottled up and hidden away the way you have, to turn a blind eye when turmoil erupts in the streets."

"Roger," Richard cut him off. "Now is not the time."

"Regardless of my timing, it's in his nature to intervene."

"His nature? Roger, you telling me you still believe that he's Jesus? The real Jesus?"

"He did turn water to wine."

"Toilet water. He turned toilet water into prison hooch."

"Tomato, tomato," said Roger.

"No. This ain't a tomato, tomato thing. He been staying with me, making breakfast, cleaning and what not for the better part of a month now and I ain't seen nothing that tells me this man is, without a doubt, the Son of God. The night you first brought me here, you convinced me otherwise. After meeting all of you, I thought maybe this is the real deal. Maybe his name is Jesus, maybe not. But if he's the Son of God, he's got a lot of work to do to convince me of that."

"Maybe that's why he walked out the door. He's not here to preach to the choir, he's already got them. He's here for you, Richard. Maybe he's here to save you."

"Well, then he picked about the worst way to do so. Whatever's going on down there, police gonna show up. And what do you think they gonna do if they find him?"

"I don't know, but I can't imagine it would be worse than crucifixion."

Behind them Ansel snorted a laugh.

"Go ahead, laugh it up. Cause let me tell you, they find him, they find you too, Ansel. And you, Roger. You burn down the city. You steal a horse, assault a police officer, escape from both your nursing home and police custody." Richard pointed to each of them. "And here I am with all three of you. This ain't ending well for any of us if he gets caught up in whatever's going on down there."

A murmur shuddered through the room, and their faces betrayed their thoughts. They were all contemplating the way they'd describe their role in all this to the police. Were they simply attending a self-help group that so happened to be harboring three fugitives, one of whom is guilty of causing the largest fire in Detroit's history, or were they complicit in an organized terrorist attack against the city?

For not being a father, Richard painted a vivid picture without having to explicitly spell out the ending he wanted them all to see. It was a parenting technique Roger himself had used on his children when they were still children, and apparently, he was the only one who saw the manipulation for what it was. Even Aleksei and Sauti, both normally as gung-ho as Age when it came to supporting and standing up for each other, remained silent.

"So, what do you think we do?" Age asked.

Embrace the chaos, Roger wanted to say. They were all refugees, and if a voice of authority told them what they needed to do to survive was to run and hide, they'd listen. For so long, that's what this group had been about: mutually assured survival.

Just as Roger's life had been. For so long after his wife passed, after the kids moved away, he focused on survival, not living.

"What do we do? We shut it down. Right now. We turn off the lights, walk out that door."

"Are you saying we abandon Jesus?" Roger got to his feet.

"Not going to be the first time he made a bed and laid in it, is it?"

Maybe they tried to stop him from leaving, maybe they didn't. But before Richard had finished speaking, Roger was already out the door and clamoring down the stairs. Stepping down and down and down and down this endless succession of curbs until there was no way for him to turn back. Richard was likely correct that intervening in this squabble would lead them down a path where their survival was put into question. Not in a life-or-death way, but more of an incarceration and police record way. But it also meant living. And if Age and Richard were going to plead survival, he would have to show them what life looked like.

The stairwell let out into the little walkway between the record store and the patio of the restaurant next door. Under green and white umbrellas, couples and groups sat eating their eggs benedict and sipping their mimosas, their brunch interrupted first by the protestors and their chants—though, they were easy enough to ignore—and then by the curse words and shouts brought on by whomever they were now clashing with.

"Pardon me, pardon me," said Roger as he slithered his frail frame through the swarming hive of ideals. It was body versus mind. Broad brick shoulders contrasted against gangly appendages holding their signs like pitch forks. "What seems to be the problem?"

"You too? Motherfucker!" said the black police officer Roger recognized from his time at the Tri-County jail, "The fuck is going on?"

He was part of a wall of men that had formed around the handcuffed Jesus to keep the raging protestors at bay.

"Profiling!" they shouted. "He didn't do shit!"

They swarmed and popcorned around the officer and his gun and all his friends. There was a woman kneeling on the ground in front of another, holding a jacket to the latter's bleeding head. Somewhere a baby screamed inconsolably.

"I'll tell you what's going on," Roger couldn't help but respond to the rhetorical question. "You are apprehending your lord and savior, Jesus Christ. I respectfully plead to you to take a mind of compassion towards—"

"Oh, shut the fuck up," came a voice from beside Roger, followed immediately by a blow to the side of his head. The world didn't spin, but sprung up all around him like fungi and flowers in a nature film. Spores and pollen spiraling in the sunlight and he was surrounded by giants. One giant cracked his knuckles while standing over Roger. "Nd sty fckng dwn," he said, speaking in the vowelless tongue of angels and witches.

The sky was the color of his children the day they were born, bright and shining and too perfect to even imagine. From one horizon to the other, stretched forever and poised to become anything.

"Roger! Oh my God, Roger! Look at me. Look at me." Belinda knelt over him. She pressed her hands to his face and neck, and when she wiped the tears from her eyes, blood smeared across her cheek, as if she belonged to some cannibalistic hunting party.

"Belinda," Roger smiled. "Better late than never. Carlyle will be happy to see you."

She'd emerged from the crowd as he fell. And though she'd come alone, she was not alone at Roger's side.

"Back!" Aleksei's voice boomed out. "Get back, all of you!"

Roger titled his head back and saw Aleksei standing over top of him, flanked by Age and Daisy and Sauti, Carlyle and Belinda, Heidi and Ansel.

They'd come. They'd all come. They'd stepped off that curb and chosen to live.

"Wh th fck re yu?" asked the vowelless man.

"Who are we? We are little fish in a big pond," Age spoke, and the others joined. "Though our abilities may not seem extraordinary, they are extra ordinary. And though our powers seem useless, we certainly are not." As they recited their mantra, the shouts and calls, the rumblings and fronting subsided, until, as they finished, they were surrounded by silence.

The vowelless man was the first to laugh, but others joined in, and soon this ragtag group of superheroes with useless powers was surrounded by an unending barrage of chortles.

"Now," said Aleksei. "Let the Jesus go. I will not ask again."

Roger squeezed Belinda's hand. She looked down at him and began to weep as if she knew something he didn't.

It had been seven thousand miles since he'd met her. Ten thousand miles since he'd escaped from the nursing home the first time. Five thousand since he'd brought Richard into the fold. Less than a thousand miles since speaking with each of his boys, though it felt like a million more since he'd seen them face-to-face. And a lifetime since his horseback flight through the city.

He could hear the sirens again. Their long droning calls whooping and hollering closer and closer.

He couldn't feel his legs. There was no running from them this time.

He opened his mouth to speak, and another quarter mile passed silently as his breath became air.

A pinprick of light ripped across his field of vision, and where Belinda once knelt, he found a house. He was up, floating up. The house was a home with the door open, welcoming him. Nothing held him any longer. Not gravity, nor fear. He was free. And waiting for him inside the door, he saw

Are you ready to be wowed?

This stunning Ferndale bungalow appeared on the market out of nowhere. Inside, look for the meticulously updated kitchen with all new cabinets and fingerprint-resistant stainless-steel appliances, beautiful hardwood throughout, and the completely updated master suite with built-in dressers and jaw-dropping vaulted ceilings with hardwood beams. Outside, the landscaping is all local foliage designed to attract and harbor bees, butterflies, and wildlife. See how the clover and moss ground coverings splay out into Nine Mile and beyond. Seconds from downtown. You'll want to see this one before it's gone, because it will move fast.

It was like something out of Wizard of Oz. Only the house hadn't fallen from the sky; there was no high-pitch whistle of this incoming domestic mortar. One moment the street was packed elbow-to-elbow, while stupid men fist bumped each other's faces, and the next a house sat half on the sidewalk and half in the road. Cars screeched to a halt as the house's sudden expansion from nowhere flung bodies in every direction.

Erica pressed herself against some yellow brick road which wasn't yellow, but red. And was redder still from the smeared streak of her own blood and peppered with ripped chunks of her skin. It felt like a mass grave, only maybe no one was dead. All around her people were piled and mixed. The house hadn't discriminated in its trajectory, and protestor and aggressor alike had been lumped into piles like snow being cleared from a sidewalk. They'd been pushed and shoved and launched and were now sandwiched between the new house and the mint green exterior of Noir Moon.

Sirens wailed. Police and paramedics and fire department all coming this way. A strident choir of screams and cries disharmonized into wailing echoes that poured down the street like a wave, and accompanied the forever tone of broken car horns. Together, the tones created the blare of a discordant dial tone. So loud and massive that it could only be the direct line to God.

"Erica! Erica!" she heard Chris's voice finally.

"Over here!" said the woman who'd been helping her. "She's under all these people!"

Erica couldn't see. Her vision was the black and red gleam of sunlight through closed eye lids. Only her eyes were open.

The people pile moaned and writhed, and through their heat and steamy, tangled coughs a hand wriggled into hers. Fingers intertwined with fingers and suddenly she could see again, emerging from the dark.

"Hey," Chris said, his voice rasp. "Erica, you alright? You okay?"

Chris and the woman helped her up, pulling her free from the pile. Once on her feet, Erica could finally see maybe not what had transpired, but the devastating effects of the sudden appearance of a house in the middle of downtown. And the chaos was stranger than she ever could have imagined.

"Oh, fuck! Kate?" said the woman, gazing off toward the patio in front of *Trough*. "You got her? I see my friend. I gotta go!"

And then she was gone, leaving Erica and Chris to make sense of the sudden house all on their own.

One corner of the house was wedged at a forty-five degree angle against the aging brick and mortar strip of storefronts, while the opposite corner was battered and beaten, having been slammed into by three or four cars that had happened to be driving down Nine Mile at the exact moment the building manifested.

It wasn't just a house, but a yard, too. Long swatches of grass spread out over the street and sidewalks and up the sides of buildings, slid under every foot like the reverse of a magician pulling a tablecloth away without disturbing plates and silverware and champagne flutes. Trees and shrubbery sprouted from cracks in the cement. Flowers bloomed.

A minivan had collided with and upended one of the tall Cypress shrubs that lined the side of the house. The roots hung limp in the air, red, with blue shocks of electricity jolting between them like something in a biology class used to demonstrate how nerve endings communicated with the brain.

And on the breeze, it wasn't gasoline and burning and wreckage she smelled, but instead Franny and Bert's Bakery. Wafting upstream against the flow of the stochastic tones, garlic and sesame, blueberry and asiago, cinnamon and lavender.

"Chris," she found her voice again as cinnamon filled her head. "Chris."

She looked at him but couldn't find the words. He was already standing, looking down at her, offering his hand to help her up. Offering both hands. He reached out to her with both hands. Both empty hands.

"Chris," her voice vibrated. "Where is Trinie?"

Their eyes shifted to the last place Stella had been standing before the house appeared. She was gone. The house split them apart.

"Fuck!" Chris left her on the ground and ran. He shoved past those stumbling and disoriented in the street, leaped over those still on the ground and struggling, and crossed over the yellow line, rounding the corner of the house. And he was gone too.

Alone, all she could smell was the cinnamon.

Lavender for his protection, cinnamon for hers. She'd gone head-to-head with the universe. Told the wind and the earth and her soul that she'd take the risk. That he was worth it. That she didn't need protection.

And the universe answered with the only way to hurt a mother.

Trinie was gone. She knew it. Maybe Stella, too, by proxy.

Gone.

Gone in the arms of another woman. Trinie's object permanence was starting to develop. To her, being handed to Stella did not carry the same benign feeling it did them. To Trinie, she was given away. It was sadistic in the way playing peek-a-boo was the blackest of magic, ripping love and sight and warmth away from those infantile senses, only to materialize again when her hands were removed from her eyes.

Only this time, no hands were removed.

Trinie was handed off and spirited away.

And now Chris went after her, and there was no way of knowing if he'd ever return.

The universe, in its cruel ambivalence, had taken Erica's object permanence.

Her sigil had failed her. The book said sigils never failed, and she had followed and acted upon every instance that she'd seen it. She'd sung along with the bouncing ball teaching her the lyrics to the song of the soul of the world, but rather than chasing the fade into infinity, the song had abruptly ended in this feedback loop of anarchy.

In the street men argued and gunfire erupted, and a man burst into flames.

And they were gone, tumbling out of her periphery, past the veiled edge of the house. Out of sight and out of mind. Gone.

"I'm sorry." She cried into her hands. Whatever intrinsic negative force had lived in Chris felt like it now rooted in her. A dark spot, a disassociation. "I'm sorry. I'm sorry. I'm sorry."

Lost and shaking and alone.

"It'll be alright," said a voice that seemed to come from inside and outside of her at the same time. It was enough to give her sobs pause, to allow her to catch her breath, to realign.

Erica imagined a comforting and calming light surrounding her, but found only darkness. Her hair was down and disheveled and if she could have shaved herself bald in that moment she would have nicked her scalp deep and long and bled on the street to prove that she too hadn't vanished into nothing. Her breaths weren't deep or inwards no matter how hard she tried, but labored and functioning only to expel.

She crossed her legs and massaged her arms and body and face with her fingertips. Slow, swirling motions. Like clouds.

The first step to using magick was to practice every day. The final step was, inevitably, to destroy all that you love. The universe had brought this house through the veil of reality to shake her self-assured hubris. It had taken Trinie as payment, and left her Chris as a reminder.

Or it hadn't. The book had cautioned not to get overzealous with applied magicks and assume that the greater the experience the greater the understanding of the magick. But, by its very nature magick is not a science, and no matter how much we follow our own nature and equate capability to knowledge, magick cannot be understood.

"I'm sorry. I'm sorry," she said to the universe. She moved her hands so that her fingers flowed toward her heart. Positivity in. She pleaded for forgiveness over and over. Until finally, she heard Trinie cry out for her.

And when her eyes opened, she saw her sigil again for the first time.

Trinie and Chris together. They were her sigil.

Cradled in Chris's arms, Trinie was curled up into a ball. She wasn't weeping, but was stalwart in a way that brought Erica to tears. Her daughter was strong, strong and defiant, and she looked at the world with an impossibly resilient fragility.

Trinie's eyes shimmered like glass, ready to shatter. But they never broke.

Erica's grandmother had died when she was six. This was before her parents made a steady enough income to support themselves on their own, and they'd been living with her grandma. Looking back at it, she now understood her dad's shame in arriving at both adulthood and parenthood without the means or ability to successfully manage either. But at the time, Erica was only ever ecstatic to be living under the same roof as her grandmother. When she died, her parents sat her down on her grandmother's couch and gave her the talk.

"Your grandmother, she was old, and very sick."

"She's in a better place now."

"I hope you know she loved you very much."

And Erica, she sat there, not emotionless—a stage play of emotions unfolded in her eyes, in the quivering downturn of her lips, in the sharp inhales—but not crying, either.

This was over thirty years ago, and whatever had been on her mind in that moment had long been forgotten. But she liked to think that she was trying to be strong, to be an anchor for her dad who had lost his mother.

That was the look Trinie gave Erica now.

As Chris got closer, Trinie raised her arms, and silhouetted by the rising sun behind them, she became the sigil Erica had seen in the light of her dreams all those months ago. The circle with the outstretched lines branching off.

The universe wasn't punishing her. It was teaching her to trust it by saying exactly what the book had told her.

Sigils.

Always.

Work.

"What do you mean it's been declined?" The waitress stood by their table, check and gift card in hand. "It's a gift card. Got it in the mail yesterday."

"Did you activate it?" Nate asked.

"Yes. I activated it." Kate didn't need his two cents at the moment. "Can you try running it again?"

"Ma'am, I don't think it's just your card. The readers are acting weird like, everything is getting declined. My manager just told me that for the time being we can't accept any type of card."

"We don't have any cash. There an ATM nearby?"

The waitress pointed toward the kiosk storefront, the entrance of which was currently being blocked by two dozen men and women marching and chanting and protesting whatever.

"Cool. Thanks." Nate stood. "Hey, I'll be right back, okay."

"Wait. Is it safe? I mean, you hear them. They have some grievance with Masood?" she said, feigning ignorance. They had a grievance, alright. And if the rumblings around the office were accurate, maybe they were even justified.

"It's cool. I'll just tell them I'm using the ATM. And if they still want to give me shit, maybe I'll tell them I created those." Nate pointed to his monolith. "Show 'em how woke I really am."

"Babe." Nate's bad idea aside, she wasn't concerned that they wouldn't let him in, but that once he put their card in the ATM one of the protestors would glance over and see the screen. Not their balance or even their PIN. But the Masood logo. Being a Masood employee, she'd opted into the Masood account to get discounts on banking and waived fees at all ATMs. "Isn't there another ATM around the block?"

Artist or not, Nate lacked any real grit when it came to confrontation. And if he outed himself as a Masood employee-by-proxy, woking and taking credit for anonymous street art while trapped in a twelve-by-twelve glass room surrounded by the tolerant left wouldn't help him the way he pictured it would.

In that moment, the tone of the protestors shifted from the defiant drawl to harrowing cry.

"Oh my God," said the waitress, mouth agape, staring down the barrel of her finger at the crowd in front of the Three M. "Did someone just hit that woman?"

Kate turned toward the crowd. She hadn't seen nor heard the hit, but the mass of protestors was now swelling, spilling down the sidewalk and, beyond that, threatening to spill over onto the patio where they sat.

"Oh fuck," said Nate. "What do I do?"

"What do you mean? Nothing! Call the police!"

"But shit, that guy just hit her, like, I don't know. I feel like I need to do something."

"Nate," Kate slid her feet from the chair and reached for his shirt. "Call the police. Getting involved is only going to make things more confusing."

"You don't think I should step in?" Nate turned away from the scene and back to Erica. He was looking to her to see if the expression on her face matched her words.

"No. We should probably pay and get the hell out of here before we get stuck in the middle of whatever's going on." Kate stood and grabbed Nate's hand. "Come on. Let's go talk to the manager and see what we need to do about the bill. I'm not having you go into that to get cash out of an ATM."

Nate glanced back to the crowd again and Kate saw the tension in his body release.

"You okay? We good?"

"Yeah, look. That old timer there, he's giving them all a talking to," Nate laughed.

"Don't get any ideas."

"What do you mean?"

"Look, babe. Some people are cut out for heroics and stepping into situations like that. Others aren't."

"And you're saying I'm in the latter category?"

"Don't get upset. I'm not saying that you're incapable of protecting me or," she put her hand on her belly, "or him. But—"

She stopped herself, covering her mouth with both hands.

"Him?" Nate said. "It's a boy? You found out? I thought we were going to be surprised!"

"I'm sorry. I'm so sorry. At the last check-up, the nurse was showing me a growth chart on her tablet and there was a note on there about the gender. I'm so sorry. I've been trying so hard to not slip. I wanted it to be a surprise for you."

"It's a boy though? For real? You're sure?"

Kate nodded. "I asked after I saw it. Are you mad?"

"God no! I," he stumbled over his words as he rounded the table, got down on his knees, and put his hands on top of Kate's. "I just— I— I love you Kate."

"You want to know what I think about? I never mentioned it because, because whatever, I didn't want other people to get into your head. But I get it from a lot of people. They ask me why I'm having a baby."

"What? Are you serious?"

"Yeah, they look at me and my role at Masood, my education and whatever, and wonder why I'd have a baby with the world going to shit the way it is, you know? Like, what kind of life is that going to be for them?"

"Like, they ask you that? To your face? What the fuck?"

"I don't think they mean anything by it, it's just that a lot of progressives see it as morally irresponsible to bring another life into the world both because of the state of things and how many babies there already are out there that need mothers and fathers, families."

"And you work with these people?"

"Yes, but listen. You're not listening. What I think about is how sentiments like that only make the world worse."

"For real. It's ignorant as shit."

"No, but it's not just the ignorance. Look, I mean, I'm not saying anything, but the reason they feel that way is because the people having babies all the time, they either aren't thinking things through or see it as doing God's will. Or, I don't know, that sounds bad. I'm not trying to say anything bad about anyone here, only that us having a baby that we can pass down our morals and ideals to, it feels like we're tipping the scale back in the right direction rather than letting the future belong to the children of people not interested in seeing the world become a better place."

"You are an amazing woman."

"And you're an—" Her eyes bolted open. She grabbed both his hands and shifted them to lay directly on her belly. "Do you feel that? He's kicking!"

Before he could answer, the sound of an atom ripping in two hit her ears, followed by a handful of bodies. Their table shattered and twisted, the legs of her chair buckled. She was crushed between the ground and the sky, and whichever way she looked was a twisted blur of double-vision as twin worlds spun away from each other and crashed together and fell still.

She opened her eyes and found a sea of grass lapping at her toes. Green waves rolled toward her as if someone were grabbing the landscaping by one end and shaking it out like a dirty rug. For a moment Nate was lost to her, but from beneath the waves, he emerged, punching his way through the dermal layer of sod, blood-red roots and dirt covering his face and hands.

He called her name.

"Kate! Kate!"

"Over here."

Beyond the grass, she saw the impossible. A house had appeared in the road. It was a cute little starter home, and looking at it made her feel better. She was lightheaded and daydreaming, which was better than trying to figure out if she could feel the baby move.

"Kate," Nate was at her side now. "Are you okay? Look at me."

"I am," she said. But she wasn't. She was saying what he wanted to hear. "I can see you."

"Shit. Shit. Help! Someone help!"

"Did you climb out of the ground?"

"What? Kate, oh my God, you're going to be okay."

"I know I am! Melody is here!"

"What? Who?"

Kate pointed at the woman rushing toward them, her mess of hair tangled in the wind. It was suddenly a very pretty day. The sun was shining, the birds were chirping, a man was on fire, and even though it was because they had crashed into the new house, the traffic had come to a halt and fallen silent.

"Kate! Are you okay?" said the redhead as she fell to her knees beside her and Nate.

"Who are you?" asked Nate.

"We work together. She's my boss. Sorry we never met. I got a lot of stuff going on."

"Whatever, yeah, hi. I'm Nate. Her husband. What the fuck happened? Could you see from wherever you were?"

"Heard a lot about you. Hi? And what happened? I— I— look, what do you want me to say, a house fucking materialized out of thin air. Your guess is as good as mine." She never even looked at him.

"Kate, can you hear me? Can you feel the baby?"

"Melody! I'm so happy you're here. What are you doing here?"

"Was on a date. Ended up taking a turn."

"Oh, with Henry? How's that going? Did you meet Nate yet?"

"Hey, hey. Focus. Kate, can you feel the baby?" she asked again, and placed her hand on Kate's belly.

"I can't," Kate said with a smile.

Nate leaped to his feet and squeezed his stomach before ripping his fingers though his thinning hair. "Fuck. Oh fuck, oh fuck, oh fuck."

"Babe," Kate said. "Did you hear what Mel asked me? Can you feel the baby? Maybe you can get a better angle than I can."

Melody looked over to Nate. "Did you call an ambulance?"

"What?"

"Call a fucking ambulance."

"Hey, hey, guys. Calm down. It's okay. Everything is going to be fine."

"Listen to me," Melody said. "You're in shock, okay. I'm glad you're calm, at least one of us fucking needs to be. I'm trying to be there with you, okay? You want me to calm down, right?"

"Mel, I love you! Of course I do! Nate, isn't she the best?" But Nate was on the phone, ignoring them. "Nate, get off the phone! I want you to meet Melody. We work together."

Bang-bang-bang-bang!

Automatic weapon fire erupted somewhere in the crowd.

Bang-bang-bang-bang!

Nate dropped to the ground. He screamed into the phone for help.

Bang-bang-bang-bang!

Bang-bang-bang-bang!

Bang-bang-bang-bang!

Melody pulled her hands over her head and threw her body on top of Kate's.

"Melody, everything is going to be fine." Kate placed her hand on Melody's cheek. "Look, Jesus is here. And oh, he's a good climber!"

Worst-Case Scenario Number Six: Gracie. Fucking Gracie and his fists that gravitate toward trouble. One second, he's walking down the street, the next, he's force feeding his fingers through the back of someone's skull.

Why he brought his service weapon, Jackson couldn't say. But he'd chalk it up to instinct to keep his brain from short-circuiting. Too much had happened too quickly, and questioning his own internal logic would tip the sensory overload into something far more dangerous.

Worst-Case Scenario Number Five: The man in the robes, the one who looks like Jesus, the one in handcuffs. Yeah, him. Worst-case scenario, he really is the Son of God. And if he was, did that make Jackson Pontius Pilate?

There was this old stand-up bit that Jackson had never seen. He didn't know who'd performed it, only that back in middle school a friend of a friend had repeated this line, and it had wormed itself in Jackson's head and now, in this deluge, had emerged, butchered and paraphrased: What if that homeless man who's always talking to himself, what if he's talking to God? Always screaming to stop, that he didn't want to hear it, to, please, not choose him.

Jackson, his gun leveled at Jesus's head, said, "Stop!"

"Or what?" The man Jesus, his hands cuffed, struggled against Henry's grasp. "You going to shoot the Son of God?"

"Shut up! Get on your knees!"

Worst-Case Scenario Number Four: God damn, Gracie. Punching a protestor was one thing. That they could spin. There wasn't one person in their group who'd throw Gracie under the bus if push came to shove over knocking the teeth out of an activist. And even when her husband or boyfriend or whatever got involved, he was easy enough to sweep under the rug. But the old man. Fuck. Now it looked like the Titanic sinking and he was watching someone punching out the women and children and elderly as they climbed into the lifeboats.

After years of friendship and passively putting up with Gracie's entertainment value, now that he'd taken it too far, Jackson needed a win. A trump card. Something, anything, to keep him from being stuck at Tri-County for good.

"Dasbrowski!" Jackson yelled.

"What?" he answered, standing between Jesus and the rest of the officers. "What do you want me to do?"

"For fuck's sake, Dabrowski," said Jackson. The kid was shook. Can't blame him, but fuck. "Here, catch." Jackson fished the keys from his pocket and tossed them to his partner. "Put him in my car. We taking him in."

The keys sailed right at Dabrowski, but he didn't reach out, just let them fly past, clink, and slide across the pavement.

"What the fuck?" said Jackson. Now was not the time for Dabrowski to lose his shit. "Get him in the fucking car!"

Worst-Case Scenario Number Three: Big Foot and Mothman and Loch Ness Monster. They are all real. They stalk our back roads and night skies, our lakes and rivers. Not hunting us, but rather hunting for a home. First the deer moved to the city, then the coyotes followed. Up in Canada and Alaska and The UP there were wolves and moose and bears that showed themselves in urban centers as much as squirrels and rabbits did here. It was only a matter of time before urban sprawl brought the rest of them out of the woodwork. But still, if he hadn't seen it with his own eyes, he never would have believed in the Nain Rouge. But watching a man combust into flame and transform into some hideous red dwarf, that was not something the mind mistakes. He'd heard the legend from when he was young, even read about the creature in the Cadillac biography LT had given him a couple months back.

It was stupid. A man on fire. But there he was. Calling it a man, though, was that even right? Jackson had seen the man, near albino-white with platinum blonde hair and wide-set eyes. He'd watched that glowing skin braise over, plump, and contort into the red dwarf he'd always been warned about.

What's that saying: Never meet your heroes?

Same goes for your nightmares. Because the Nain Rouge gave Jackson more sleepless nights than he'd ever care to admit, and now this red devil was here in the flesh, being chased around by those fucking well-meaning activists, always shifting from one worthy cause to another.

They were yelling, "Stop! Drop! Roll!" at the creature as they stripped off their shirts and squeezed their water bottles and tossed their cold brew coffees at the thing. "Let us help you!"

If Yakety Sax and reality had a baby, it might look something like this. It was the height of all imaginable absurdity until the fires started. Then it was just another worst-case scenario. First there were only little drips of molten flame falling from the red dwarf. Globules of flaming mucus that looked like demonic road apples. But as the creature fled from those well-intentioned shits, scampering over cars, brushing up against storefronts and trees to squeeze out of their pursuing grasp, the fire began to spread.

Worst-Case Scenario Number Two: A Goddamn house sat in the middle of Nine Mile Road, and rather than bulldoze or relocate, or at very least put up caution tape, the city turns it into a tourist trap. Come see Michigan's newest mystery spot, where the laws of physics and nature need not apply!

And that's when the radios went out.

The music blaring from those wrecked cars embedded in the house, the muzak the city pumped through the hidden speakers throughout downtown were casually ignored until, instead of regurgitating Top 40 hits from the past thirty years, a static bomb of dead signal bled out into the air. Like an EMP or something went off, and all that remained was the electromagnetic atmospheric noises of the ambient world.

Dabrowski held his hands over his ears. "What the hell is happening?"

Worst-Case Scenario Number One: The world was ending. Reality and all of its constructs and laws and rules that we'd come to take for granted were unraveling, and now they were all hanging by a thread that slowly unraveled into oblivion.

"I don't fucking know, man. Just get him in the car, and fucking fly to Tri-County." Dabrowski held the man Jesus firmly, though it was apparent he wasn't going to put up a fight.

"Hello, Charles." Richard's voice cut through the milieu effortlessly and shook Jackson in a way that he couldn't hide and definitely didn't need right now.

When Jackson turned, he half expected to find Richard there, book in hand saying, "It's situations like this, I've found comfort in this book." And it wouldn't be the Bible or some Tony Robbins self-help bullshit. It would be Erik Larson or Mike Davis or Theodore Roszak. Academics who didn't seek to solve the world's problems, only examine them in such a way that gave those capable of solving them broader context with which to find the solution.

Whether Richard intended, or even realized, he'd groomed Jackson to examine the world through the eyes of a police officer, the heart of a noble fugitive, and the mind of a rogue academic. If he lived up to any of those, he wasn't the one to say. But with his gun on Jesus, and Richard's eyes softly burrowing into Jackson's soul, he had an inkling of his mentor's thoughts on the subject.

Christ, first Jesus, then the old man, and now Richard was here.

"Hello there, Henry," said Richard.

"LT, what are you doing here?" Dabrowski asked over the static.

Jackson didn't like the answer his instincts gave him. "Don't fucking talk to him. He ain't LT no more. This ain't none of his business."

"Unfortunately, Charles, this is my business. And Henry, I'm going to need you to step away from Jesus."

"Yeah, I don't think so. I don't know what the hell is going on here, but that man ain't going nowhere with you."

"Oh, I think you have a pretty good grasp on what's happening."

"Fucking house appears out of nowhere. Goddamn man on fire running around. Radio taking a shit. Hate to disappoint you, but nothing could be farther from the truth."

"Well, when you say it like that." Richard smiled. His calm in the face of danger was infuriating.

Jackson held his gun on Jesus, but as Richard edged closer his aim began to drift. "Richard! Stay put. Imma put this on you."

Training said to never point your gun at something you weren't going to shoot, never shoot something you weren't willing to kill. But it wasn't as simple as that. In a purely mechanical way, sure, fine, whatever. But in his experience, only those looking to shoot someone took that shit to heart. Guns don't kill people, people kill people, and the use of deadly force is just one more symptom of a failing system. The gun in Jackson's hand wasn't a weapon to him, it was a shield. He wasn't going to shoot anybody, but he'd seen it a million times; if he got scared enough there was no telling how his body might react.

Jackson stepped toward Richard. Under his feet, the grass from the house was disconcerting. It felt like the opposite of finding a twenty-dollar bill on the sidewalk. Below the roots and rocks and trees, the sidewalk and road were still there, fire hydrants and garbage cans poking through the layers, flattening the moors of this new property to match the rest of the city's landscape.

"Charles." Richard had his hands raised in front of his chest. "You need you to relax. I'm gonna tell you something, and it ain't gonna be easy to hear. That man in the cuff's—"

"LT, if you call him Jesus, Imma shoot you both."

"No, no. Don't be silly. You know I'm not a religious man. Naw, that ain't Jesus. But he thinks he is. And Jesus or not, he's special. And so is Roger, and Adrian, and the others too. They are all special in ways that you and I may never fully understand. I don't know why or what they're going to do, but they are going to do something."

"Not if I can help it."

"See, that's what I'd thought too. That it was my job to make sense out of the world so that we could preserve the status quo, keep the established order functioning. I started thinking about mosquitos. Annoying as hell, ain't they? Real easy to imagine a world without them. Billions of mosquitos in the world and imagine an evening under the stars without getting eaten alive. Get rid of them and give order to that chaos. Sounds nice until you ask yourself what the bats are going to eat. The frogs and fish. Mosquitos are about the lowest of the low, with nothing but natural predators. Nature abhors a void, and wouldn't put something here for no reason. It's not our job to upset that balance, even if it feels like we're doing so to uphold the order that's most convenient for us."

"So, you calling this man Jesus and all your friends insects?"

"Now you're being purposely obtuse, Charles. You know damn well what I'm saying."

"Yeah, maybe I do. But it doesn't change a thing. It's not up to us to make that judgement. Police, and you gonna love this, it's not our job to contemplate the mysteries of the universe and the human condition while on duty. It's our job to keep the peace, to allow for law and order to serve the public. Me, you, Dabrowski, we ain't ever been anything other than glorified taxi drivers. We aren't judge and jury. We move people. We move them into the system. We move them where we are told to move them. The order that we uphold wasn't put in place by one man. And it can't be dismantled by one either. That's why Jesus, or whoever the fuck he is, he's going back. And it ain't up to you to change my mind."

"I'm not trying to change your mind, I'm trying to open it. Expand it. I see potential in you, Charles."

"And you want to know what I see in you? One more failed

fucking father. You know, my dad, when he found out I was going to be a cop, he was not happy about it. Irate, even. To the point that to this day we still hardly talk. Then I met you. And you were everything he wasn't. You were everything I wanted to be in a police officer. Now look at you. The fuck happened?"

"Ain't it obvious? I stopped trying to preserve what we had, and started working towards what we wanted."

"We? You mean you!"

"No. I mean us."

Bang-bang-bang-bang!

Automatic weapon fire erupted somewhere in the crowd and Jackson spun toward the sound.

Worst-Case Scenario Number WTF.

Bang-bang-bang-bang!

Bang-bang-bang-bang!

Bang-bang-bang-bang!

The sun shone down on this hive of writhing hornets. Shattered glass and blood on the streets, waves of flame dashing against trees and telephone poles and parked vehicles. Downtown Ferndale had been torn from its foundation. And where the fuck was the gunfire coming from? He looked for hands on weapons, but everywhere his eyes darted and stopped he saw only fire. It was a living organism.

"Shit!" Dabrowski bellowed. Jackson spun again and saw Henry ducking on the grass, shielding himself from the gunfire.

"What the fuck?" said Jackson as the strobe of Richard and Jesus escaping toward the house flickered along the edge of his field of vision.

"Richard, stop!"

Their feet battered up the steps of the front porch.

"Richard!"

Hand on the doorknob.

"God damnit!"

His heart throbbed in his chest. That moment of honesty with Richard had dulled his senses, and his legs no longer felt real. Or if they were real, they weren't attached to his body. Richard and Jesus vanished into the house, and with thoughtless execution Jackson went after the closest thing that he'd had to a father in years. Across the front lawn and up the step, Jackson kicked through the front door.

Whatever he'd expected from an incorporeal event turned physical structure, it wasn't this.

The door clattered against the wall and a nearby picture frame fell and shattered. It was a photograph of a tiny Indian woman and a chunky white man engaged in an embrace. In fact, all around the living room there were photos of the two together. On walls and in frames on end tables.

"Richard," he called, letting go of the existential. "Let's not make this worse. Come on out."

He moved through the living room, eying the Hawaiian Gothic décor. It was like two clashing personalities came together and formed something that shouldn't work, but somehow did. The dark walls and furniture intersecting with the warm pinks and purples and oranges of the throw pillows and tropical flowers. The creeping greens of hanging leafy vines.

Room to room he went, gun in hand, praying in equal measure that he both found Richard and Jesus, and that they'd gotten away. Why was it that the love children had for their fathers was matched only by their disappointment in them?

"Richard. Come on now, let's talk." But again, he got no answer.

The bagua in here the was off the charts. Each room encapsulated the balance of elements. Wood, fire, earth, metal, water. Talk about clashing personalities; he didn't give a shit about bagua the way Calloway never shut up about it. She'd tried to feng shui their home to create harmony and balance, and it felt like she had until he stepped in here.

Here, the themes Calloway had to explain to him in his own home were on clear display. The house plants in wooden vases in the southwest corner to promote wealth and prosperity. Along the south wall, a display of candles representing fire and fame. In one of the bedrooms, along the northwest wall, sat crystals and photographs on an alter surrounded by blue and beige and taupe pillows and blankets.

It was a New Age game of clue. The murderer: asymmetrical shapes, on the north wall, with a career and a life path in mind.

So much for escaping the existential.

Jackson opened the basement door and descended. One step at a time. Breath hushed and controlled. Any normal basement there were what, twelve, fourteen steps? This house, despite materializing out of nothing, had so many that he stopped counting at thirty and it still took him another ten seconds to reach the cold floor. He could no longer hear the car horns and dead radios blasting. In here, all he heard at first was the furnace cycling on and off. Only it wasn't cycling. It was breathing. At his ankles was an air duct, and what should normally have been forced air was instead breath. In and out. In and out. The house was breathing. But there was something else too. An ambient hum, an electric thump that reminded him of being in a womb. And for a moment he feared that if he pounded on the walls hard enough his mother would feel him inside her.

Any other day it would have been a ridiculous thought. Today it was insipid. Almost obvious, even.

At the far end of the basement, there was a vault door. Sealed and free of rust, despite the sudden humidity of the room. Between him and the vault, cardboard boxes overflowed with childhood memorabilia. Trophies and yearbooks and stuffed animals. Old furniture that could have belonged in Jackson's parents' home when he was growing up littered the room. The ceilings above him were jagged and malleable, and contorted around what had been placed below. A small stack of boxes, and the ceiling was only four feet high. A tall vanity with a frosty and faded mirror, the ceiling skyrocketed to fifteen feet. Enough room for an ego to see itself. He found himself breathing in rhythm with the house itself.

He approached the vault and found that it had a sliding peephole on it. The steel door was warm despite itself, and Jackson moved the slider, took out his phone, and with the flashlight app, he peered inside.

It was black as pitch. Empty.

No, wait! He swept the beam of light from side to side. "Richard, I see you in there. Listen, man, I don't want to take you in. But I gotta take your buddy. Just send him out and we can talk. Alright?"

He'd gotten a glimpse of something. The whites of eyes, maybe.

Slowly, he scanned the room.

There!

Crouched in the corner down by the door. There she was. She. It wasn't Richard, wasn't Jesus. It was a child. A naked toddler. Featureless, and looking past the pigtails that he'd assumed belonged to a girl, he now saw that the toddler was genderless. Dark hair, olive skin, big eyes that found the light and looked beyond it to stare into Jackson.

"The fuck?"

More eyes appeared in the dark. Eyes on top of eyes on top of eyes on top of eyes. Far more than could conceivably be held in a room that size. Or maybe not. The blackness Jackson had taken for walls was actually space. The room appeared to spill out past the self-contained boundaries of the vault itself.

These thousand eyes, they swarmed slowly. Their featureless faces shimmered in the dark, golden halos flaring up around them from the flashlight. And one by one, in irregular tones and pitches and volumes, they began to speak in no unison whatsoever: "get out!" **"Get out."** "GET OUT?" "Get out!" "Get Out?" "Get out!" "gET oUT?" "Get out!" "Get out!" "Get out!" "gET oUT!" "Get out." **"GET OUT."** "Get out!" *"Get out*!" "Get out!" "Get out!" ***"Get out."*** "Get out." "Get out." *"Get out!"* "Get out!" "Get out?" "Get out!" "GET OUT!" "Get out!"

Jackson listened. He listened like a motherfucker. One foot in front of the other, it ain't called walking, it's called fucking running. Back up the stairs, the bellowing-ing-ing-ing-ing voices yapping-ing-ing-ing-ing at his heels.

Back through the bagua bullshit. Love and marriage, health and ancestors, knowledge and self-cultivation. All those perfect, positive reverberations could fuck off in so many ways.

Who was it who was tempted by the sirens? Theseus?

Fuck it.

Jackson barreled out the back door and found himself face-to-face with the woman Gracie had shoved into the wall. She was leaning against the wall of the record store, holding a baby in her arms. Her face had stopped bleeding, but the deep scrape stretching from forehead to chin, that was going to leave a scar.

"Well, fuck," Jackson whispered to himself.

"Say what?" said the woman's husband, boyfriend, whatever. He'd punched Gracie, and now with those same hands, he was caressing faces gently.

"Nothing. Sorry. You all alright?"

The boyfriend looked at Jackson like he was a fucking idiot, but the woman, she smiled.

Jackson tucked his gun away and got to one knee, "You all need anything?"

Above them, the sun was now high in the sky and Richard could fuck himself. They sat in the shadow of the house and listened to the baby babble to herself. He reached his finger out and wiggled it against the little girl's cheek. She giggled.

"You okay?" Jackson asked the woman. "Can you walk?"

She shook her head.

"Alright, well, we should get her moved." Jackson looked up at the husband. "That fire's spreading."

Say what you want about Jesus, but he sure as shit knew how to make trouble for himself. And who the needed Jesus anyway? Jackson sure as hell didn't. At least, not right now. Thoughts and prayers fell on deaf ears when all they wanted and needed was compassion and time.

Jcksn cld gv thm tht.

Bang-bang-bang-bang!
 Bang-bang-bang-bang!
 Bang-bang-bang-bang!

The thunder of Sauti's faux gunfire was all Richard needed to get to Jesus. As soon as the gunfire resounded, Henry fell to the ground, letting go of Jesus's shackles, and Jackson turned to confront the more pressing threat. It wasn't the distraction he would have asked Sauti for; throwing however many people happened to be on the streets into a panic was not his idea of being a responsible citizen. But he'd take what he could get.

"I'm sorry, Henry," he said as he rushed the kid, bulldozed over him, and grabbed Jesus. "Come on."

With Jackson's back turned, Richard bolted for the only cover immediately available to them: Belinda.

He did not like the idea of entering her without her permission, especially knowing from the meetings that the only reason she ever lost control of her USP was in moments of extreme stress or sorrow. She'd told them all that the first time it happened was before they'd immigrated to the States. Her sister had been swimming and went under, and when her father returned from rescuing her, he found a house sitting on the shore rather than his other daughter.

Richard and Jesus raced across the lawn toward the house.

"Richard, stop!" Jackson's voice clung to his ears.

They climbed the steps of the front porch.

"Richard!"

Richard shoved the door open, peeking back in time to see Jackson starting after them. And beyond him: fire. And it was spreading thanks to the well-intentioned idiots chasing after Ansel, trying to extinguish him. They covered him in shirt after shirt to smother the flames, only for them all end up ash and smoke, and threw cup after cup of coffee or kombucha or sparkling water on him, only to see sheets of flame wash away and spread like a grease fire.

"God damnit, Ansel." He'd have to take care of him later. If there was a later.

He pulled Jesus into the house and stopped.

During one of their meetings, Belinda had told the group that the outside of the home always reflected some ideal version of a life she wanted. Inside, though, that was her reality.

And hidden in that reality was the trauma that had forced her to become a werehouse today.

He slammed the door behind them and found there was no lock to keep Jackson out. Oh, Belinda, she wore her heart on her sleeve through and through. Though it did make him wonder, had there been a lock that Jackson would have had to bust through, what physical effect would that have on Belinda when she returned to her normal form? And for that matter, what effect would he and Jesus have if they lingered inside her too long?

"Richard," said Jesus.

"Save it." Richard held his index finger in the air. It was shaking. "Let's get you out of here. Then we gonna have a discussion. What the hell is wrong with you, running out of there like that?"

"I'm not like you, my friend. It's in my nature to act."

"I said save it, come on." He pulled Jesus along. "And nature? Please! Suicide by cop ain't nobody's nature."

"Do you know who Thich Quang Duc is, Richard?."

"Just stop."

Wall-to-wall, the room was covered in effigies of Belinda and Carlyle as a couple. Photographs and paintings, pint glasses and coffee mugs, napkins and menus of places they'd gone on dates. It was embarrassing to see. Not that their love and relationship was wrong in any way, but knowing them as little more than acquaintances, this felt like walking through someone's diary. But before Richard could lead Jesus on, the TV caught his attention.

"Before he self-immolated, he said: *Before closing my eyes and moving towards the vision of the Buddha, I respectfully plead—*"

"I said stop! Respectfully pleaded? You didn't respectfully plead nothing. You just left. After weeks of keeping you fed, giving you a home, keeping you safe. And you just left without so much as a word."

Richard watched the television, trying to figure out which overly dramatic supernatural cop drama was playing on loop in Belinda's mind.

Then he saw Belinda on the screen, on her knees bawling over somebody. This wasn't a TV show. It was a memory. Richard almost turned away, expecting the body to be her sister. He didn't want to learn that Belinda had lied about her sister's fate. If she hadn't wanted to share, this was no way to glean that information from her. But the camera angle switched to her POV, and he saw that the body belonged to Roger. On TV, Belinda's transformation happened slowly and dramatically, so that the viewing audience at home could make sense of the confusion. She ballooned and shifted, veins becoming pipes, nerve endings wires and roots.

And Roger. His soul rotoscoped up to heaven, his body shoved aside.

"What is this?" Richard asked.

"He was trying to help."

His heartbeat thrummed in every limb, and he was acutely aware of the fists his fingers were becoming.

Whatever part of the brain dealt with trauma, the television set was it. The way there was no lock on the door, there was no power button on the TV. This loop played over again as Belinda, and now Richard, worked through Roger's death, searching for the one in a million different decisions that either of them could have made to prevent it. But there was no way, and if he had to watch Roger's CGI soul, on horseback, of course, climb out of his corpse and gallop to the heavens one more time, he was either going to slam his fist through the TV or Jesus. Neither of which felt ideal.

Footsteps on the front porch.

Richard grabbed Jesus by the arm and pulled him on. They turned through the kitchen as he heard Jackson kick through the front door. The house creaked in pain. Richard opened the back door as Jackson bellowed, dangerously close.

"Richard! Let's not make this worse. Come on out."

But they'd quietly slipped out before he finished calling for Richard.

Behind the house, sandwiched between the back door and the record store, they found a red-headed woman crying. Curled up in a ball, her knees to her chest, hands rubbing the sides of her head, she said over and over again, "I'm sorry. I'm sorry. I'm sorry."

"It'll be alright," Jesus said, and started toward the woman. Before he could take a knee at her side, Richard ripped him back.

Through the back door, Richard could hear the clatter and clamor of Jackson searching the house for them. It sounded like he weas heading into the basement, but it'd only be a matter of time before he checked out back. All around them, sirens whooped and hollered. Which direction they were truly coming from, he couldn't tell.

"God damnit." There was no clear getaway. He grabbed the record shop door's handle. Inside was dark. They were obviously closed. It wasn't even a real option; he needed the knob to stop staring at him, begging him to try it.

The knob turned and the door swung inward, ringing a tiny bell above.

"You gotta be kidding me."

He shoved the door the rest of the way open and pulled Jesus into the record shop with him, slamming and locking the door behind him.

They sped down the mausoleum-like aisles. Bins containing thousands of records lined each row. Concert posters and decades of memorabilia hung on the walls and sat on shelves. Richard didn't pay attention to any of it. He moved Jesus far enough away from the door to look him in the eye and demand answers.

Richard grabbed Jesus by the collar, tears brimming. "You tell me what happened to Roger. Tell me right now, God damnit!"

"Help, Richard. He was only trying to—"

"No! I don't want to hear it!" Anything Jesus could say at this point would only be an excuse. "You happened! I keep saying to you, to all of you, that you can't be heroes. That's not the world this is. Sure, y'all got superpowers, but, by your own admission, they useless. Got sound effects and dead radio signals. And I ain't seen you do nothing but turn water into wine."

"When I talk, people listen," said Jesus calmly.

"Do I sound like I'm listening?"

"No, you're too busy talking."

"Hell, no. You not turning this around. My friend is dead because you couldn't leave well enough alone and let them figure it out on their own, could you? No, you had to put yourself in the middle of it. Only this time, it wasn't you who died for anybody's sins. It was him!"

"You know the story of the frog and the scorpion?"

"Damnit, Jesus," Richard was shaking. "I don't want to hear about what's in your nature, alright? Your nature has gotten you arrested, crucified, and now trapped in a record store waiting to be arrested again. Maybe it's time you rethink your nature."

"I did rethink my nature. Before we met, when I was making my way in your world delivering food, I had a moment of doubt where I entertained the idea that the only reason I was put on Earth was to die.

I mean, it was everywhere. Everyone seemed to know that I died for their sins, and that was a good thing. But what about the rest of my life? Was that nothing? Am I only defined by my death because it benefits everyone? What about my sermons of love and acceptance? Sure, they're talked about, but how many who praise my sacrifice, my death, follow my lifestyle? Not many. And then I met Roger, and then you, and then the rest of the group. And you all exemplified the acceptance and work that goes into making the world a better place."

"Even Ansel?"

"Well, there is always the exception that proves the rule. But you all showed me that somehow, despite those that worship me, my philosophy survived. And it did so in my absence. I'm sorry for running out of the meeting. I'm sorry that Roger had to follow me. But I had to see if you were right."

"If I was right? Right about what?"

"About not getting involved. And you were right. There are far too many people looking to me to justify behaviors, when they should be looking to each other to change the world. I thought I was needed. That I could help. That by sticking around I could be a guiding light in the darkness. But I think maybe there is enough supernatural influence in the world as it is."

"What are you saying?"

"I'm saying I think it's time for me to go."

"Well, well, well," a voice cackled from the darkness, interrupting their conversation. "What have we here?"

The twilit darkness of the shop receded from the blue glow of a flatscreen monitor situated behind the counter, surrounded by other random items being offered for sale. Some guitar signed by some musician, first pressings of albums, framed set lists. Along with even odder items, long samurai swords, a massive unsold stock of industrial fireworks from this year's ban, along with fresh herbs and pendants and crystals that looked like they were likely used for witchcraft or alchemy, hammers and screwdrivers and duct tape, and picture frames covered in hot-glued seashells.

On screen was a man dressed in a mismatched suit, his face and head covered in wild tufts of hair which gave the impression that his morning routine was sticking forks in electrical sockets rather than a subtle dose of caffeine from a cup of coffee.

"Thieves, eh? Well, here at Noir Moon, we have our own way of dealing with thieves," said the man on the monitor. Richard glanced around the room. No cameras in sight, but there were motion detectors.

"This is a misunderstanding," said Jesus. "We aren't thieves, we—"

"Stop." Richard cut him off. "It's a recording. He can't see us."

"Oh, this isn't FaceTime?"

"No, this isn't FaceTime. There's a silent alarm. I'm sure more police are—"

"The police have not been called," continued the man on the camera. "There is no silent alarm. Hell, if we're talking right now, it's because I left the front door unlocked for you."

"Are you sure he can't see us?"

Richard did another sweep of the area, no longer sure.

"Not for *you*, you," said the screen. "The proverbial you. The you that wanders through the unlocked doors of people and places they do not know. The you who exhibits free will. You know who else walked through unlocked doors? Richard Chase, the Vampire of Sacramento. Once he'd been caught by the police, he told them that he took locked doors as a sign that he was not welcome, but unlocked doors, they were an invitation to come on in. So, I leave my door unlocked as an invitation for those who dare. See, this location is special to me. Not just to me, but it is special in and of itself. A place not dictated by the laws of nature. This is a safe space. And all are welcome, just as all are welcome to whatever is here that they may need. I'm a man of science, and the only nature this building has been unable to repel is that of my own curiosity. So please, make yourself at home. Find shelter from whatever storm you're caught in. This building is your sanctuary. Use it as you will. Indulge me. Stay as long as you'd like, take anything you need. I'm as curious to see how this turns out as you are."

The man faded from the screen, replaced by an American flag waving in the wind.

Jesus looked from the screen to his hands. He ran his fingertips up his arms toward his heart and smiled. "He's right. Can you feel it?"

"Nothing about that man is right." Richard stepped away from Jesus and began to pace. "He crazy. Dealt with him down at the station on more than one occasion."

"I think I know what I'm going to take."

"What?" Richard's gait slowed to a halt. "Nah, we aren't taking anything. What we need to do is find a back door and get you out of here before Jackson comes through that door."

"No, Richard. Don't you get it? I can't feel anything."

"Good for you. It's called depression. Welcome to the human race."

"No, Richard, listen to me. I was serious about it being time for me to go. And this, now I feel it. You know what that is? It's Age killing the signals, clearing the path. It's not the place that's special, it's us. It's all of you. It's time for me to go."

"Go? Go where?"

"Home, maybe? I don't know. We'll see what happens."

"Home? Where is home?"

Jesus smiled at Richard and pointed up.

"Oh, hell no. Can we stop this for a minute? I mean, I seen Roger talk to horses, Age is killing signals right now, and Aleksei has told me who's calling me on the phone more times than I can remember. But you, all I ever seen you do is turn water into wine. Is that enough? Do you really believe that you're Jesus? Like *the* Jesus?"

"Honestly, I don't know."

"Let me help you. Do you remember being crucified? Do you remember being betrayed by Judas? Do you remember your mother, Mary? Did you grow up being told stories about how you were born in a manger, and when passing through Bethlehem, did your parents point it out and say, look how far we've come?"

"No." Jesus took Richard's hands. They were shaking now. "I have no memories of anything before Devil's Night, before seeing Ansel transform into his red dwarf."

"And why Detroit? Two thousand years ago, Detroit wasn't even a place. This land here, it has zero connection to you. Maybe you were hypnotized, and someone just made you believe you're Jesus at some point and you just never been snapped out of it."

"I'm here because of you, Richard. I needed to meet you, to learn from you."

"Me, what did I do?"

"You know. And now I need your help one last time."

Jesus reached across the counter and grabbed a roll of duct tape.

"With what?"

Jesus looked behind the counter again and pointed.

"What? No. Hell no. Ain't gonna happen."

"If you can think of another way, I'd be happy to try."

Richard had never married, never had kids. His city burned down, and when it was rebuilt it looked nothing like the one he'd dedicated his life to protect. With the city gone, all he had left was his friends.

And now Roger was gone, and soon Jesus, too.

"I know," said Jesus. "I'm going to miss you too. But, look at the bright side. If I am the son of God, we'll see each other again!"

"Don't think my kind make it up there."

"Please. My father is a lot of things, but racist is not one of them."

"Racist? Jesus Christ, I didn't mean black people! I mean people who don't believe in God."

"Oh! That makes more sense. I was like, where did that come from! Don't worry about that, we take everyone. We'll put you in the back. You can polish our halos."

Richard cocked his head, unamused.

"I'm kidding! Geez. Everyone is always surprised that Jesus has a sense of humor. But no, seriously, Richard. You have nothing to worry about."

The back door opened quietly, and Jesus ran. In his robes and his Nikes and a belt of red, white, and blue fireworks duct taped around his body like a patriotic suicide bomber, he ran.

He ran, and Richard followed him. If they'd left footprints behind them, there'd be only one set.

Red and blue lights flickered and sirens whirred as more police officers arrived, guns drawn and shouting, "Freeze!"

All around, the city was engulfed in ever-spreading flames; men and women and children, all scared, all needing help and aid and guidance, and instead of offering any, the police pursued Jesus.

Jesus dodged the officers as they tried to tackle him, jumped the railing that surrounded *Trough's* patio as they clamored to grab hold. From one tabletop to the next, he hopped out of their grasp until he reached the monolith, and started to climb. He fit his fingers into the windows, his feet pressing him farther and farther up as he found leverage on every ledge and sill.

At the top of the Penobscot monolith sat an abstract twist of metal that looked like little more than an artistic flair added by the artist to signify something or other. But then Richard recognized it for what it was: a table. A broken table. Roger's broken table. The table he'd ripped the umbrella out of. The table he destroyed his entire past with. This is where it all began, and now, with Jesus using it to hitch a ride home, this is where it would end.

Roger had told Richard that the way we exist in the world is a symptom of the problem, not the problem itself. To Richard, that was a call to action, a call to find the problem and snuff it out. An easy mistake to make when wisdom comes from the man who'd stolen a police horse and ridden it across the city.

Now he saw what Roger meant: Everything needed to change.

Action, inaction, both are still only symptoms.

The world was coming, had come, apart at the seams, and the only ones struggling to return it to the way it once was, they all had guns in their hands. That used to be who Richard was. A prisoner of quiescence. A soldier for the status quo. And the cycle continues.

Ferndale burned. And inside that inferno there was nothing to do but wait for the end, for the fire to engulf them and those whose last minutes they were sharing.

At Richard's feet sat a man and his pregnant wife, crying, their hands pressed to her belly, praying for their baby to kick again. Not for things to remain the same, but for change, for a different outcome. And from this angle, Richard could see the baby moving inside her.

Henry passed Richard without a word, and went to his lady friend, wrapped his arms around her.

The house that had been in the road, it was gone, too. In its place were Belinda and Carlyle, holding each other. Aleksei and Sauti, out of fight, out of breath, stood there as well, looking on. And Age. Age lay on the ground, his panic attack subsiding, the muzak in the streets returning as Bash held and kissed and caressed him.

And there was Jackson, on his knees, cooing and smiling at a little infant.

Those with something to lose hunkered down. Only those with something to gain held their ground, and let panic dictate their final minutes.

The world wasn't a violent and ugly place, but it was easy to see it that way when change and progress are swept under the rug by those who want nothing more than to hold onto whatever little, make-believe power they think they have.

It was then that Richard saw Roger. His body lying in the road, on that yellow line that stretched on forever in either direction. Gracie sat next to him. Not weeping, nor laying his hands on the body in remembrance or regret. That wasn't Gracie's way, and that would likely never change.

In this aftermath, there was only calm, and those who sought to disrupt that calm.

Jesus reached the top of the statue. This wasn't an end, but a beginning. And Jesus lit the fuse.

It had been Richard who'd tied all those fuses together to ensure that once lit, they'd all ignite at once.

The warning label on the fireworks cautioned that each one of these was strong enough to lift a car from the ground. Jesus had strapped a dozen of them to himself. The label also called these mortars, not fireworks. And they were not for personal use.

"Stop!" the officers called out. "Freeze!"

But it was too late. Change was coming.

The world couldn't stop. It wasn't going to freeze.

Sparks zipped up the fuse along Jesus's leg toward the mortars. The smell of gunpowder mixed with the lingering cinnamon on the breeze.

It'd be nice to say that there was no evil in men. But that wasn't true.

The fuse hit the first mortar and lit. Flame shot down, and Jesus's robes began to burn. The other eleven followed, and in a flash, Jesus was engulfed in flames.

Against all odds and reason and sense, the world needed evil.

The flames hit the second stage of the mortar and Jesus stepped off the monolith, off his curb, and rocketed up and up and up and up. Spires of yellow and orange and red and purple smoke trailed behind him.

It's evil that reveals the poison in the world that keeps change at bay. Without it, we'd never recognize the need to change.

Up and up and up. His body withered and shriveled, turning black and charred.

It's hard to recognize, though; the face of evil changes all the time.

But the good, the good is constant. Not easy, not fair, not without sacrifice. But constant in a way that nothing else in the world is. The good of caring for each other, of looking to ease suffering, and helping each other find our place and purpose.

Life is short, nothing lasts forever, and our bodies are nothing more than flesh.

Humans burn surprisingly quick, and the air changed from cinnamon and gunpowder to human flesh and hair. And here was Richard, hoping for something to change, wanting nothing more than to see his friend again, alive and somber rather than burnt to a crisp. Thirty minutes ago, Jesus had said that this was hell. If that was true, then maybe he wasn't gone. Maybe once his body and soul burnt away, maybe he'd awaken two thousand years ago in a cave. Come back. Resurrected with the knowledge to empower men to change rather than hold onto ancient ideals and sacred nostalgia and the misremembered past. In the end, though, if Jesus was more than just a man, Richard would never know.

The third stage of the mortar burst against the blue sky, shooting red and green and gold sparks everywhere. He never moved a muscle as he burned into the sky, never cried out as his body was sacrificed. And now he was gone. But only in spirit. His body, scourged and eviscerated, splattered to the ground. The city sizzled as his blood rained down onto the fires of the Nain Rouge. The communion the city never asked for.

Alone, Richard looked from the embers of the extinguished city to the trails of colored smoke that spun in every direction in the sky.

The sky, glimmering like the drink Richard needed right about now, was no longer an unrecognizable horizon. A swirl of blue and pink. A twist of orange and purple. He'd seen this sky before.

AK WG
3/31/2018 - 10/30/2021

Acknowledgments

To those who read, critiqued, complained, and made us better writers over the years: Andy Hill, Cody Stasiak, Sarah Liekweg, Shiu Lee, Jeff McHale, Christy Kelly, Matt Welch, Matt Dewitt, Rich Ferrando, Jamie Fuller, Dick Rockwell, Bob Fox, Jason Arsenault, Kris Lee, Jeanette Harris, Greg Goers, Sara Scott, Russell Stahl, Lacy Southgate.

To the one who had no reason to believe in us but did so anyway: Art Held.

To our editor, Bailey Sims, who helped make this book better than it deserves to be.

Thank you all.

If we forgot anyone, let us know. We'll get you next time.

Adam thanks:

Mom and Dad and Matt, for being the right family for me, no matter what.

Uncle Joe for showing me Detroit before I cared to know anything about it.

Adam Rozak, your friendship means more to me than you know.

Billy Good, you're my *Adam Savage,* who keeps me on my toes in every possible way.

Aidan, Logan, Xander, and Zelda, really, I'm doing all this for you. Love you all.

And Liz, the most understanding and supportive partner I could hope for. You're my cheerleader when I'm down, put in my place when I'm being stupid, challenge me when my head gets too big, but most of all, you're there for me no matter what. Love you, always.

William thanks:

My parents... Who always supported me no matter how crazy my ideas were. I am truly blessed to be your child.

Shira who saw the potential I didn't. Who loved me when I didn't deserve it. A true partner and the architect of our amazing life together.

Adam, the right side of the right side of my brain. Who kept this train rolling even when we didn't have any track.

Beba, Ellie, and Teddy, for showing me what love actually is and constantly reminding me of what is really important.

And the Detroit Lions, who taught me how to go on and find meaning in the face of constant suffering.

Adam Kowal is a recovering nerd. He knows that Han Solo shot first but is trying very hard not to care. Currently, he resides in the middle of nowhere where he is renovating and restoring a nearly two-hundred-year-old Second Empire home. He lives with five cats, four kids, two dogs, two guinea pigs, and one very understanding wife.

William Good is married to his very understanding wife Shira. They have three kids and reside in Denver, Colorado. He is a veteran of the US Army, and most of all, despite the pretentious appearance and unrelenting mockery, he loves writing about himself in the third person.

Find us…

Online:
www.soottown.com
Facebook: **@soottown**
Twitter: **@soottown**
Instagram: **pattersonzapruder**
Spotify: **SOOTTOWN: a playlist**

Podcasts:
Apophenia (coming 2022)
Ghost Gal Podcast

Editing Services:
www.lenacreativesolutions.com
bailey@lenacreativesolutions.com